Stay With Me Forever

Starry Hills
Book 2

Kayla Chase

Mythical Lake Press, LLC

This book is a work of fiction. Names, characters, places, and incidents are either the product of the writer's imagination or are used fictitiously, and any resemblance to actual persons, living or dead, business establishments, events, or locales is entirely coincidental.

Stay With Me Forever

Mythical Lake Press, LLC

Print Edition

Cover Art by Laura Hoak-Kagey of Mythical Lake Design

ISBN: 979-8891560048

Also by Kayla Chase

Starry Hills

Want Me Forever

Stay With Me Forever

***Marry Me Forever* (March 2024)**

Reader Note

This book contains thoughts, memories, and discussions about a family member who struggled with addiction, a car crash, and the death of several family members. I hope I have treated these items with the care and consideration they deserve.

Chapter One

Weston

My children were missing again.

Since it happened almost every day now that they were out of school for the summer, I didn't panic. Well, not too much.

But as I left my brother Zach's office and headed down the hall, in search of my aunt, I resisted taking out my phone and texting *her*. I'd even tried sending messages to my sister, Abby, but had yet to hear back, which meant I might have to bite the bullet and contact the woman I tried to avoid at all costs.

My gut said Avery and Wyatt were over at Emilia Mendoza's place again.

Ever since my daughter had helped take care of the kittens Emilia had found in her barn weeks ago, she'd talked nonstop about Millie. Millie this and Millie that. As if the woman was some sort of hero and could do no wrong.

I still didn't understand why she went by Millie instead of Emilia—or Emmy—like when she'd been younger. However, I'd left Starry Hills sixteen years ago with my new wife when Emilia had been almost nine and I'd been twenty. I'd returned home only twice since I married, and I didn't really know who Emilia had become.

The first time I'd seen her again since she was a child, my brain had stopped working as I took in how fucking beautiful she was—dark hair, deep brown eyes, light-brown skin, and curves I never would've guessed she'd end up with as a grown woman.

Not that I had stood staring at her for long. Because Emilia had immediately opened her mouth, told me to go fuck myself, and we'd barely spoken to each other since.

If only my children would stop finding excuses to run over to her place—which bordered my family's vineyards and winery—to play. Because whenever I saw Emilia, I invariably had dreams that night of her—under me, her wrists pinned above her head, as I fucked her hard.

She'd arch under me, tightly grip my dick with her pussy, before she'd moan as she came hard, taking me with her.

Even now, just remembering last night's dream had me growing hard.

Stop it. She was most definitely off-limits. And not

just because the rest of my family viewed her as a little sister. No, I'd learned my lesson about casual sex when I was younger. One night of fun had changed my life forever, and I wasn't going to risk it again any time soon.

Find your kids and stop thinking about that woman.

As I approached the stairs, I spotted below my next youngest brother, Beck, smiling at his girlfriend.

Fuck. The pair were lovey-dovey as hell, and I had no desire to see it. I wanted to believe Sabrina O'Connor was different from my late wife and wouldn't end up cheating on Beck or stomping on his heart. But my experience made me a cynical motherfucker.

As cowardly as it was, I went into the nearest room—the one my kids shared inside the big house at Wolfe Family Farm and Winery—and slipped out the glass door to the veranda that encircled the second story.

Leaning against the railing, I surveyed the land below, doing one last search to see if my twins were playing in the fields. Rows upon rows of leafy grapevines, still months away from us cutting the fruit that we turned into wine, were my current future. I'd spent the morning doing canopy management—cutting and trimming the leaves just right—but it looked different from up here. With the rolling hills in the distance, it looked like something you'd put on a postcard.

While being back in Starry Hills after so many years away was nostalgic, it didn't inspire me as much as it did my brothers Beck and Zach. It was good to be home, but I didn't feel like this was where I belonged.

Just like I hadn't belonged at my in-laws' place, back in the California Central Valley.

Pushing away thoughts of the past, I stood and crossed the veranda until I found the stairs to the ground below and descended.

As I turned the corner, I nearly bumped into the short form of my aunt Lori. She was barely five feet, her black hair mixed with silver, and her eyes a dark brown. She might have been in her sixties, but she was a force of nature—one that had kept my family mostly together after the death of first my father and later my mother.

Not wanting to think about how I'd missed my mother's funeral thanks to my late wife, Andrea, I grunted at my aunt. "Have you seen Wyatt and Avery?"

Aunt Lori raised a dark eyebrow. "Hello to you too. How was your day? Isn't the weather nice?"

I rolled my eyes. "I don't do small talk."

My aunt sighed but then smiled. Taking hold of my forearm, she pulled me along to walk with her. I basically took baby steps to keep pace with her short legs.

She squeezed my arm before releasing it. "I'm just glad you're back, West. I say it every day, but I'm going to keep saying it—we missed you."

The thing about my aunt was that she ignored cues that you didn't want to talk about something. When it came to family, she believed we should be forthright and honest and never hold back.

I shrugged. "I'm here now."

"An understatement as always." She glanced up at me, but I kept my gaze trained straight ahead. She'd been

Chapter Two

Emilia

Abby: The bride needs your magical pep talk. <fairy emoji>
Me: <sighing emoji>
Abby: <laughing emoji> You could give it in your sleep. Now, stop complaining and go so the wedding can start.
Me: You know exactly what I say. Why don't you try it this time?
Abby: I don't have the feeling and delivery you do. So unless you want them to cancel, get your ass to the bride's prep room.
Me: Fine. I'll remember this, though, for the next time a kid throws up at the reception. You're on vomit duty for the rest of the summer.

Abby: We'll negotiate terms later. Just go.
Me: <tongue out emoji> <runner emoji>

I took a deep breath, pasted a smile on my face, and knocked on the door of the small room where the bride was freaking out.

No response. I knocked again and said, "It's Millie."

The lock on the door clicked, and it opened a crack. The dark-brown eyes of Vivian Tran looked out at me. "I can't do it."

There was no fear, just nervousness. My gut said she had cold feet, not well-founded doubts. Gentling my voice, I said, "Vivian, I just want to talk. I promise no one else is with me, and if at the end of it you still want to call off the wedding, I'll march out there and tell everyone myself. But at least let me talk to you first. Okay?"

After a second, Vivian nodded and stepped back. As soon as I entered the room, I shut the door behind me. "So, tell me what's bothering you?"

Vivian started pacing the small room, the skirts of her white wedding dress billowing as she did so. "What if this is a mistake? I mean, marriage is a huge step. Not to mention, if things don't work out, divorce is messy. Maybe I shouldn't have dropped hints that I wanted to marry him. Maybe it only made him feel like he had to do it. And that's not the way to go about it, right?"

I'd heard a similar speech too many times to count. I wouldn't push or manipulate her, but I needed to try and see if I could save this wedding. "Travis loves you, Vivian. He hates crowds and yet he agreed to a big wedding for you."

She paused, her gaze softening. "That's true."

I took one of her hands and really looked at the woman in front of me. After watching Vivian and Travis over the past six months, I knew they belonged together. The groom's mother had been a right pain in the ass, and yet Travis had always stood up for Vivian, ensuring she got what she wanted. And judging from all the times Vivian had also stood up to his mother, defending him, she loved him too.

This was a case of nerves, nothing more.

I took her other hand and gently squeezed. "Plus, don't forget that Travis hadn't ruled out arriving to the ceremony on horseback, even though horses terrify him."

Vivian's muscles relaxed a fraction. "It's why I couldn't make him do it."

"Then what's really bothering you, Vivian? Because anyone with eyes would notice how much that man loves you."

She paused, looking down and then back up. "I keep thinking that we haven't dated long enough. Or maybe we need to live together for more than a few months. What if I'm wrong about him?"

"Well, I've seen firsthand how every journey is different. Some people need decades together before they want to make it official. Others only need a few weeks before they know they've found the one. This is your story, Vivian Tran, and how it unfolds is up to you. So, what is the next chapter going to be about?"

She bit her bottom lip for a second before saying, "Me being married to Travis."

"Good." I released her hands and patted her upper arm. "He's out there waiting for you. Shall I help you freshen up and get this party started?"

Vivian smiled. "Yes." She nodded to herself. "Yes, I'm ready."

"Just let me fix your veil and then you can start writing the next chapter of your story."

In less than five minutes, I had Vivian ready, and she walked down the aisle on her stepdad's arm. One thing I never grew tired of was watching the groom or bride when he or she saw their partner walk down the aisle—with such love and hope and happiness.

Once the ceremony was over and it moved on to the celebration, I breathed a sigh of relief. I had another wedding tomorrow, and it was always better when the one before went well. I wasn't sure if I believed in karma, exactly. However, fate could be a cruel bitch, as I'd learned at a young age. It was part of the reason I worked so hard to make my weddings a success. It'd never fully make up for what I'd done, but it was at least a start.

It was over an hour later when my sister in all but blood—Abigail "Abby" Wolfe—slipped into the barn and whispered in my ear, "Tag, I'll take over from here."

"Thank goodness. I'm exhausted, and it's only four in the afternoon. Tomorrow is going to require lots and lots of caffeine to make it through."

"Why you book them back-to-back, I'll never understand. Yes, I get it's summertime and the busy wedding season. However, you're doing just fine and could turn down a job or two without blinking an eye, or at least hire some more help so you're not running yourself into the ground."

No, I couldn't hire more people. As much as I loved Abby and her friendship, I'd never shared the full reason for why I crammed as many weddings into the summer as I could. Well, only to a number where I could for sure put on the best show ever, without cutting corners.

So I merely shrugged. "You never know what the future brings. Besides, seeing them happy makes me happy. I love weddings."

Abby remained silent at my words. I was probably the only person in Starry Hills who knew why working for my wedding and event business was beyond difficult for her.

Changing the subject, I asked, "Are the twins still here?"

She motioned to the outside of the barn. "They're playing with Miss Fluffypants and Flynn."

"Of course they are." After sharing a few details to help Abby with the winding down of the reception, I exited out the small side door for staff only.

I wasn't more than a few steps outside before I spotted Avery crouched down, petting Miss Fluffypants's belly as the black cat rolled around in the dirt.

Once I was close enough, Avery looked up at me and grinned. "She let me pet her belly again, Millie."

"Why wouldn't she? After all, you helped with her babies and found good homes for them."

I'd found the cat in my barn months ago, with five kittens. When the little girl had learned about it, she'd begged to help care for them. At first, I'd said no because she was West's daughter, and I didn't want to see him.

But Avery was hard to resist and probably the most opposite of her father as a person could get, and we'd bonded a little.

I looked over and saw Wyatt playing with the boy kitten I'd adopted, Flynn. Avery had named him after the hero in the Disney movie, saying the cat was just as adventurous and a tad mischievous.

I asked Wyatt, "Did you have to get him out of the tree again?"

Wyatt shook his head. "Not today."

He went back to playing with the cat. In some ways, Wyatt very much resembled his father. And not just because they both shared the same dark hair and blue eyes either.

Avery bounded up to me, the fluffy black cat in her arms. "We've been too busy teaching Flynn to fetch. He's actually getting pretty good at it."

"You do know he's not a dog, right?"

Avery stood taller. "You can train cats. It just takes more work."

Before I could ask *why* she was determined to train my cats, I saw the tall form of Weston Wolfe striding up the path—the one that connected between my land and his—with a scowl on his face.

Of course he'd arrive after Abby had switched out

with me. It was going to take every bit of patience I had to be nice to him in front of his kids. I may not like what he'd done to his family, but I couldn't deny how much he loved his children.

When West met my gaze, I kept my reaction to his strong jaw, delicious scruff, and broad shoulders to myself. Yes, he was handsome, and I'd dreamed a few times of running my hands over his chest and strong arms.

Okay, maybe touching even more than that. But he'd still been an asshole to his family, and that fueled my anger, erasing any attraction. "West."

"Emilia."

I gritted my teeth. I didn't like being called by my full name any longer. He knew that. And still, he ignored my wishes to probably irritate the crap out of me on purpose.

I decided to focus on his kids instead. "Your dad's here, which means it's time for you two to go home."

Avery frowned. "Are you coming to dinner at the big house tonight?"

"No, sweetie. I have another wedding tomorrow, and I need to get ready for it."

Wyatt stood, crossed his arms, and kicked a rock away. "Everyone's always too busy for us."

I blinked. The boy had rarely said anything, and now he dropped something like that?

I couldn't resist glancing over to West. For the briefest moment, pain flashed in his eyes, but it was gone before I could blink. A very small part of me wondered why.

But then I remembered how he'd turned his back on his family, and I pushed my curiosity aside. After going over to Wyatt, I placed a hand on his shoulder. "It's not because I don't want to see you, Wyatt. But people hired me a long time ago to help with their wedding, to make their day special, and I can't let them down." He said nothing. I crouched a little until we were eye to eye. "Besides, don't you want to help out your dad this summer? He could teach you the family business, like his dad probably taught him at your age."

Even if West had never told me that, I'd moved in with the Wolfe family after my parents died when I was ten and had heard plenty of stories about their childhood.

Wyatt kicked another rock. "No, I don't want to help Dad." He hesitated and then asked, "Can we come back tomorrow? We won't be any trouble and we'll stay out of the way, I promise."

The boy's words made my heart hurt because I had a feeling he'd had to use them with his mom. I didn't know much about his late mother, but the bits and pieces I'd heard from the Wolfe family hinted at addiction problems and not wanting anything to do with her children.

As much as I wanted to say yes, they could come over, it wasn't my call. I looked up at West. "If you give them your permission, they know the rules and can play here anytime they want. Even when there's a wedding on, they can stay in the kids' play area I have for my clients' children. Or they can explore the old pastureland that's basically an overgrown meadow these days."

West frowned. "When did you get rid of the cattle?"

"Years ago." Hadn't he heard of it? Everyone in Starry Hills knew I'd sold them shortly after my eighteenth birthday, when I'd inherited the place. The only thing I'd kept was the name, as I couldn't bring myself to change it.

Avery went to her father and took his hand. "Please, Daddy. There's not as much room to play at home with all the tours and construction and stuff now. Here we can play with the kitties or visit the little creek and the meadow. Not to mention the little swing set Millie has. Please, Daddy. It's so boring at home."

West's frown deepened. "She's too busy to watch over you."

I should keep my mouth shut. After all, they weren't my kids. West, despite his faults, was protective of them, one of the few things I admired about the bastard.

And yet I blurted, "Were you constantly watched when you were ten going on eleven? Because I wasn't—Abby and I roamed around wild during the summers. Plus, my neighbors are the Evans and the King families, both of which are friends and they'd let us know if anything happened."

West crossed his arms over his chest and studied me. I never looked away. He could intimidate a lot of people, but I wasn't one of them.

Wyatt walked up to his dad. "Please, Dad. Just listen. You never ask what we want."

Pain flashed across West's gaze again before he squatted down to his son's level. "That's not true, Wyatt."

"It is. You made us come to Starry Hills."

"You stayed here before and said you liked it."

"For one summer. Now I have no friends. I hate it here."

Wyatt walked away, toward the fence beyond my lavender fields. Avery blurted, "I'll follow him," and dashed after her brother.

West remained crouched down, his hands on his knees, and for a split second, I felt sorry for him. Being a parent wasn't easy, and a single one doubly difficult.

But then he stood, glared at me, and any nice feelings I had for the man vanished. He growled, "My kids aren't your business, Emilia. Stay out of it."

With that, he walked away, and I saw him catch up to the twins in the distance.

As much as it grated to agree with him on anything, Weston Wolfe was right—they weren't my concern.

So even though every part of me wanted to help the twins, to make them happy in a way I would never deserve, I ignored it and stomped off toward my house and my office. All that mattered was running my business, helping people make happy memories year after year, and maybe one day I'd finally forgive myself for killing my parents.

Chapter Three

Weston

Aunt Lori: <hourglass emoji>
West: ???
Aunt Lori: Time's ticking. Don't be late.
West: Okay.
Aunt Lori: <sighing emoji> You're no fun.

Maybe I shouldn't have snapped at Emilia. However, I'd been trying my fucking hardest to do right for my kids, even if it meant they hated me. They didn't know what their maternal grandparents had wanted to do with them. Not only had they wanted to send them to a fancy boarding school where I'd rarely get to see them, but they'd also talked about filing for joint or maybe even sole custody.

It was bullshit, of course. They had no reason or grounds to take my kids away from me. I'd been the one busting my ass to improve the quality of their cattle, the one to try to get their daughter the help she needed, the one who'd moved heaven and earth to try to keep my family together.

At first, I'd tried to brush off their scheming as some sort of way to deal with their grief. Even if I hadn't loved Andrea in many, many years, I'd never wished for her death and had tried to respect how hard it must have been for her parents.

But my hard work and attempts to help my in-laws had backfired. The Grenvilles used it to say I was neglecting my children. Another email from them earlier hadn't helped my mood either.

Then I was in front of the woman I'd dreamed about the night before, looking all sexy as the sun shone down on her while my kids smiled up at her, as if tempting me with a dream that would never become reality.

So, yeah, the combined forces of my former in-laws' threats and lusting after a woman who hated me didn't make for a good mood. I might have to actually apologize to Emilia later.

But as I caught up with my kids on the path leading home, I wedged myself between them and placed a hand around each of their shoulders. It was still hard to believe they were getting so tall, but the years had flown by before I'd known it.

I squeezed each of them gently against me before saying, "Summer is busy and crowded at the Wolfe Family Farm and Winery, and I don't want you to be bored during summer vacation by staying inside all the time. So tell me—what do you want to do? Play on Emilia's property, checking in with Aunt Abby and Emilia at regular intervals? Or should I find someone to watch you and maybe some other children during the day, when I have to work?"

Avery spoke first. "Did you already make the decision? Or do we really get to have a say?"

Her words only made me feel guiltier—I hadn't given them a choice about moving here.

But then I remembered how I'd done what was best for us all. "I want to hear about what you want, Avery. I can't always say yes to everything, but I'll always listen. So, what do you want to do for the summer?"

Avery bounced a little before answering, "I like Millie's place. It reminds me of Grandpa and Grandma's ranch. Well, except she has tons of lavender and no animals. Maybe she needs to get some cows. Me and Wyatt can help take care of them."

I nearly smiled. "They're a lot of work, love. And Emilia's busy with her wedding stuff and probably couldn't handle running a ranch on top of everything else."

"But you could help her run a ranch, Daddy. I know you miss working with the cows."

I did, but I tried my best not to let my daughter see it. "I have to help Uncle Beck and Uncle Zach with the grapes, remember?"

"But your hands are too big, I think. You'll squish all the grapes when you try to pick them."

"I can be careful, just like how I was careful when you were a baby and really tiny."

Avery paused to tap a few stakes at the edge of the grapevine rows before she asked, "Will I ever get a baby sister or brother? I'd be the best big sister ever."

For a second, my brain scrambled on how to respond. Avery had never asked me this before, and I wasn't about to scream, "No fucking way."

Not because I didn't like kids—I did. But there was no way I'd get involved with another woman long enough to make a baby. It'd been years since I'd even had sex, and I didn't know if I'd risk having it again until my kids were grown. A one-night stand had changed my life sixteen years ago, and I'd learned that fucking lesson.

However, I quickly gathered my wits and replied, "I know you'd be the best big sister. But you and me and Wyatt are a family. We need to stick together."

"Don't forget about Anna and Elsa."

Those were the names Avery and Wyatt had picked out for the two kittens we'd adopted from Emilia. "And of course them too. Plus, you have all your aunts and uncles who love you."

"I guess I do have lots of family." She paused to kick a small rock in front of her. "But maybe one day we can have a mom too."

Shit. I'd known this would come up at some point but had hoped it wouldn't be for a long time yet.

Before I could reply, my brother Zach's voice

boomed out, "Here comes the prince and princess of the manor!"

I spotted him on the outside veranda and rolled my eyes.

Avery giggled. "Uncle Zach said he'd get me a crown soon. Then I really can be the Wolfe family princess. Although I'm not sure about Wyatt being a prince. He's not very prince-like."

"I don't want to be a prince. I want to race horses."

"But princes can do whatever they want, even race horses."

Wyatt wrinkled his nose. "But then I'd have to wear fancy clothes. No thanks."

I smiled as the two continued to bicker about the merits of being royalty.

Since they'd slowed to a crawl, I pushed gently against their backs. "Come on, you two. It doesn't matter if you're royalty or not. If you're late to dinner, Aunt Lori won't be happy."

Avery shrugged. "I can bake her some more cookies tomorrow. Then she'll forgive me."

My daughter had recently discovered that she loved to bake. At the rate she practiced, we'd all be rolling down the hallways soon from eating too many cookies.

Still, I loved how she'd found a new hobby and ruffled her hair. "My little Star Baker."

She moved away. "Da-ad, don't do that. I'm not a baby."

"But you'll always be my baby girl."

Wyatt sniggered. I pulled him close and kissed the

top of his head. He made a gagging sound before he wiggled away.

I couldn't stop smiling.

Zach appeared in front of us and raised his eyebrows. "Stop it. You're scaring me."

Avery looked up at me and back at her uncle. "Why?"

Zach smirked. "Your dad is smiling. The world must be about to end."

I gently shoved him and, he shoved me back.

Avery rushed between us. "Be nice, Daddy."

I saluted her and she turned toward Zach. He tossed her up into the air a second—he wouldn't be able to do that much longer—and set her down on the ground.

I grunted. "Is your leg even strong enough for that?"

Zach had broken his leg a few months ago and had only recently started walking on his own again.

My brother waved a hand in dismissal. "I'm fine, West. I'm not a little kid anymore."

He was right, although it was still hard for me to accept it. Zach and his twin brother Zane hadn't been much older than my own kids when I'd left Starry Hills.

Not wanting to go down that train of thought, I grunted. Grunting was always a good way to avoid saying too much. "Avery, Wyatt, go wash your hands before dinner."

Begrudgingly they went, leaving me alone with my little brother. Zach stared at me and then grinned. "You're being an ass because you had to see Millie, aren't you?"

Rolling my eyes, I pushed past him. "Grow the fuck up, Zach."

"Never. It's too fun to tease you about this shit." Zach easily kept up with my long strides. He added, "Are you still looking for someone to watch the twins? I need to go into town tomorrow, and I can ask around."

I should say yes. It would be easier to find someone to watch the kids, someone who didn't both stare at me with anger and turn my dick hard at the same time.

And yet, I couldn't completely ignore what my kids wanted. So I asked Zach, "Do you trust Amber King and her family?"

Zach blinked. "Um, of course. Why?"

"Her property is on the other side of Emilia's. If—and that's a big if—I let them go over there to play during the day, I want to make sure I can trust everyone nearby."

"Millie's third neighbor is the Evans family, and of course you can trust them. Kyle is best friends with Beck, and one of the girls—Katie—is best friends with Abby and Millie. I'm sure even you remember the BFF Circle."

"Is that thing still around?"

Zach snorted. "Yes, and going strong. I sometimes think they're planning to take over Starry Hills, maybe even all of Sonoma, whenever they meet. Not that I know for sure. No matter how often I asked Amber to let me attend one of their meetings at the bakery, she says no." Then he cleared his throat and added, "I asked Millie and Abby too. Katie is the only one open to it, but only because she likes to stir up shit, I think."

I glanced over at Zach. He'd teased me, so payback was a bitch. "You still hanging out with Amber like when you were kids?"

He looked away. "No. We're both too busy these days."

Pretty much every sibling still in Sonoma—which was everyone but Zane and Nolan—had joked about how Amber had loved Zach since middle school. I wondered if he'd ever noticed.

However, Aunt Lori appeared out of nowhere before I could ask anything else.

She clicked her tongue. "Cutting it close, weren't you? Now, come on. You can help set the table."

Zach grinned. "Well, you didn't text, so I know we still had some time."

Aunt Lori lightly swatted his arm. "Don't tempt me to use the most embarrassing emojis, promise or no promise. Now, get a move on before the food gets cold."

Not long after we reached the dining room, my kids soon raced in, and we all helped set the table.

With both Emilia and Abby absent, the table was a little calmer than normal. Although I did my best to avoid watching Sabrina and Beck. I knew they weren't deliberately trying to make anyone uncomfortable, but each little touch, smile, and whisper made me wish I'd had that at some point. Early in my marriage to Andrea, I'd believed I was in love with her. But in retrospect, I think it'd been more wish and lust than truth.

Especially given her actions over the years.

Thankfully, my children distracted me, and we went through the bedtime routine. After they showered—both were proud of the fact they didn't have to take baths any longer, like "little babies," as they put it—I tucked them in and asked, "Do you want me to read a book or make a story tonight?"

Avery bounced in place, scaring the kittens from her bed. The black-and-white cats glared from their new perch on Wyatt's blanket but soon purred from Wyatt's chin scratches.

She said, "Let's make one together, Daddy."

I glanced at Wyatt, who shrugged. Avery said, "He says yes."

Studying my son, I looked for the happier boy he'd been before his mother's death. While Wyatt had never been chatty like his sister, he was way too quiet and reserved, especially for his age. I'd suggested therapy, but he'd refused. And then we'd been uprooted here, and I hadn't asked again. I might have to.

Regardless, now wasn't the time. I wouldn't spoil what had become my favorite part of the day. I nodded toward my daughter. "It's your turn to start this time, love."

She sat, tapping her chin in thought, and I smiled. Avery took the make-a-story ritual more seriously than anyone else. Although I knew it'd be some sort of fairy tale, as she always wanted something with a little fantasy to it.

With a nod, she finally said, "There was a fairy queen who had lots of magic. With a wave of her hand, she could..."

Avery tossed a stuffed rabbit at her brother, who'd been focused on the kittens, and Wyatt sighed. "Fine.

With a wave of her hand she could make anyone happy. One day..."

His words went straight to my heart. I wanted to ask what I could do but knew that some of it was beyond my control.

Except for what they'd asked of me earlier in the day —to spend the summer days over at Emilia's.

Since I sat on Wyatt's bed, he poked my arm. "Your turn, Dad."

I cleared my throat. "One day, a hairy, grumpy orc appeared. He was mean and rude and liked to destroy things. However..."

Avery moved until she kneeled on her bed, clearly excited with the story tonight. "However, the orc had a big secret—he loved his kids and he wanted to find them a new mother."

I eyed my daughter. It was going to be another single-dad-finds-love-again story tonight.

My son added, "The orc's kids had met the fairy queen once before and liked her, and thought she'd be a good mother. Their dad was strong and smart, even if he was hairy, and so they told him about a quest she'd advertised so their dad could meet her."

Fuck, if they were hinting, they weren't being subtle about it.

Well, time to dust off my creativity. "But the orc knew he could never find the lost cat and bring it to the queen for a reward. So instead he..."

Avery scowled at me, and I bit back a smile. I didn't mind making the story romantic, as long as it didn't hit so close to home. Because I wouldn't give them hope, even through the veil of a story, that I was going to marry again.

Then triumph flashed in Avery's eyes, and I held back a groan, knowing she'd thought of a way to steer the story back. "So instead of the lost cat, he brought the fairy queen a pair of kittens, the cutest kittens ever, with shiny golden fur—like real gold—that was still soft and eyes that changed color depending on if they were happy or sad or mad. She saw them and..."

A little of the old Wyatt returned as excitement filled his eyes. "She loved the golden kittens, but she knew taking them away from the orc's kids would make them sad. So she invited all of them to live close by..."

Oh, for fuck's sake. They really were determined to put the orc and fairy queen together, weren't they? "So she invited them to live close by and since the orc was good with animals, he became in charge of her horses. The kids played with the kittens every day, and the fairy queen went away to..."

Avery glared at me, but I didn't bat an eyelash. Sometimes I liked messing with my kids a little.

But the determined glint in my daughter's eye said game on. "The fairy queen went away to learn some more magic. She could tell the orc was unhappy. But no matter how much magic she used, she could never make him happy. But then she found out he was cursed. And so when she returned..."

Wyatt jumped in. "And so when she returned, she had enough magic to take away his curse, and he finally became happy. He spent a lot of time with the fairy queen and his kids, until one day..."

Avery growled. "Don't stop it there. You know Daddy's going to ruin it."

I waggled my eyebrows. "But that's part of the fun. Predictable can be boring."

"No, because every journey is different."

As I stared at my daughter, I wondered where the little girl who went around pretending to be a pirate princess, out on the seas, waving her plastic sword around and making her stuffed animals sail her ship and fight her battles had gone.

People always said kids grew up fast, but it was only starting to really hit me how true that was.

"Dad?" Wyatt asked. I looked at my son, and he added, "Let's finish the story. I'm tired."

Even though I shouldn't, I really fucking shouldn't, I decided to make the story end how they wanted tonight. "Until one day the orc and fairy queen got married, joined forces to make the kingdom the strongest and kindest in the world for their children, and they lived happily ever after. The end."

Avery jumped from her bed and tackled me with a hug, scaring the kittens again.

She whispered, "You didn't ruin the story, Daddy. Thank you."

As I hugged her little body and took comfort from her familiar warmth and scent, I wished I wouldn't keep ruining the story of our actual lives.

But what they wanted and what I could give were two different things. I would do nearly anything for my kids, but I wouldn't find some woman I could never love to be their mother and marry her for their sake alone. That wasn't fucking fair to anyone.

However, I could find other ways to make them happy, ways that didn't involve risking my heart, let alone my kids' hearts.

So once I kissed them goodnight and went to my room, I sat in the overstuffed chair and decided I couldn't let fear of my own weakness—my attraction to Emilia—stand in the way of giving them a small piece of happiness. I'd take them over to her place tomorrow, do my own check to ensure the area was safe, and then probably say they could spend their summer days there.

Maybe, if I was lucky, Emilia would constantly be busy with weddings, meetings, or other business-related stuff. Summer was the high season for her, just like it was for my family's winery.

Yes, I'd probably never see her. Abby could keep me updated on what was going on. And in the end, it shouldn't be that bad.

Chapter Four

Emilia

Me: Do you know where West and his kids are now?
Abby: Maybe. Are you going to spy on them?
Me: <eye roll emoji> I just want to know if the kids will spend their days here or not.
Abby: You could text him.
Me: It could be days before he replies.
Abby: Only with you. Hmm. <thinking emoji>
Me: Focus, Abby. Where is he? The wedding starts soon.
Abby: He mentioned the rear pastureland. The one on the King side.
Me: See, was that hard?

Abby: <tongue out emoji> I still think spying would be more fun. Who knows, maybe he belts out show tunes when no one is around but his kids. <laughing emoji> x 3

Me: Have you been eating those special gummies again?

The next day, when Abby had told me that West was with his kids in the rear pasture, I hadn't expected to find him without a shirt, fixing one of the fence posts, with a light sheen of sweat coating his chest, back, and face.

I'd always had a thing for broad shoulders, and West's were even more drool-worthy without clothes on. Combined with his lean muscles and the patch of dark hair on his chest, I almost forgot why I disliked him so much.

Avery spotted me first and ran toward me as she waved. It gave me time to close my jaw and erase any sign of desire from my face. Because lusting after Weston Wolfe was something I needed to avoid.

When Avery was close enough, the little girl said, "Daddy's fixing the fence today. He said we couldn't let any stray or lost animals get inside."

I finally looked back at West, and he'd stopped working for a second to take a drink of water. I most definitely didn't watch his throat work as he swallowed. Nope.

He said, "You should've repaired this a long time ago, Emilia."

I straightened my shoulders, unwilling to bend at his firm tone. However, I didn't want to fight in front of his kids, so I said to Avery, "How about you go play over there with your brother for a little while, sweetie? I need to talk with your dad." She glanced between us and then ran to her brother. Still, I kept my voice low once she was out of earshot. "I didn't even know it was damaged, so how could I have gotten it fixed? In case you haven't noticed, I have a thriving business to run and don't have time to frolic in pastures."

"Maybe not every day, but surely you come out this way sometimes? Even for just a walk? You never liked to be inside all the time as a kid."

I was surprised he remembered that. But things had changed since he'd left, and just walking out to the former pasture today had taken every bit of strength I possessed. Especially since all I wanted to do was run in the opposite direction and avoid memories of my childhood. "I'm super busy, if you hadn't noticed, and I don't have a lot of time to hike around. I only came to check on the twins."

His eyes looked me over, and I resisted crossing my arms. I was wearing one of my work outfits—black skirt, bright-pink flowing top, and a simple necklace with an opal pendant.

He took his time taking me in, and it almost felt like he was caressing me with his hands, which made my nipples hard.

Stop it. It wasn't as if anything would ever happen. Not only were relationships not for me, but the Wolfe family were my family now. I should think of him as my brother.

Except West hasn't been around the last sixteen years, and you most definitely don't think of him as a brother.

Pushing that thought aside, I strode toward the fence. "You don't have to do this, you know. I can hire someone to repair it."

"Why didn't Rafe fix it before you inherited the property from him? The rusted wire tells me it's been like this a long time. And your brother could've more than afforded it since he's a world-famous soccer player, for fuck's sake."

I had reached the fence and froze. I didn't talk about my older brother. Ever.

Comfortable with anger instead of regret and guilt, I narrowed my eyes at West. The man who had, many years ago, been close friends with my brother before Rafe left town. Maybe he still was. "I appreciate you fixing the fence, but I didn't ask for your opinion. And if you're merely here to report back to Rafe, then you can fucking leave right now."

"There's the girl I remember."

Not letting my cheeks heat, I barked, "What the hell are you talking about now?"

"When you were younger, you were always strong and determined and unafraid to stand up to anyone. But since I've returned to Starry Hills, you've been more reserved, unless you're with Abby. I prefer the younger version of you."

Maybe if he hadn't delivered it as a backhanded compliment, I might've acknowledged how I missed that version of myself too. The one that had died the day I'd woken up in a crumpled car, screaming for my parents but never getting a response.

Mindful of the kids, I growled softly, "Fuck you, West. Just fuck you."

I turned and stalked off. I made some half-assed excuse to the twins about needing to get back to work, even if I had another two hours before the wedding party would arrive.

Taking deep breaths as I went, I carefully packed away the memories, storing them inside the mental box I'd learned to make. I rarely suffered PTSD or nightmares any longer, but I wasn't going to risk them returning if I could help it.

By the time I reached my office, I was mostly back in control of myself. But instead of finding some much-needed solitude, Abby sat at my desk, looking over something. However, as soon as she noticed me, she stood. "What happened?"

Abby, the friend who'd never, ever given up on me. Not even when I'd tried to push her away, not wanting her to also get hurt because of me.

My eyes heated with tears, but I cleared my throat and took a second to steady myself. I hadn't broken down in front of someone in years, and I wasn't about to do it again. I'd caused the pain in my life, and I had to live with it. End of story.

I replied, "Just West being West."

Abby searched my gaze. Since she towered over me—she was nearly as tall as her brothers—she had to crane her head down. Eventually, she sat on the edge of the desk, putting us nearly at eye level, and raised an eyebrow. "If you think I'm going to let you stop there, you're crazy."

With a sigh, I grabbed the water bottle on my desk and took a long drink before I could reply. "He mentioned Rafe. Hearing his name shouldn't still bother me, but apparently, it does."

Abby reached out and took one of my hands. "I know it hurt when he declined custody of you all those years ago. But that is your brother's loss and my gain because I finally got a sister when you moved in with my family."

I did my best to smile. While it was true that Rafe had been nineteen when my parents had died and had been first in line to get custody of me, only to turn it down, it was more than that. I knew, just knew, he'd kept his distance all these years because he blamed me for what happened that day.

However, that was the one revelation I'd never shared with anyone—not only did I blame myself for the car crash, but my brother did as well.

Since we had another wedding to deal with in a little over an hour, I decided to distract and pivot. "You *are* my sister, Abby." I quickly hugged her and then went to the folio on the desk. "Now, let's discuss the last-minute changes so we can ensure this wedding goes as smoothly as the last one."

Abby wasn't fooled but also knew me well enough to know pushing wouldn't accomplish anything right now. So we went over the event details, got lost in the work, and I soon forgot about West, Rafe, and my memories for a while.

Chapter Five

Weston

After I finished fixing the fence post, I asked Avery and Wyatt to show me around. It'd been decades since I'd last been here, getting into trouble with Rafe. Then he'd gone to England to play soccer, and I'd barely heard from him since.

To be honest, I hadn't thought about him in a long while. Andrea had taken so much of my time and energy, and then my kids took even more. But I still had trouble believing Rafe would abandon his sister and never talk to her. And yet, my family said that was exactly what he'd done.

Avery tugged me along, and I listened to her chatter about what we saw. The three of us walked and walked, and I had forgotten just how big the Mendoza ranch was. It was eerie to see so much overgrown pastureland, with no animals in sight.

It didn't make sense to me why Emilia had sold all the cattle and stopped her father's legacy. Beef from the Mendoza place had been some of the best, sought after by top chefs and restaurants, and had provided a nice income. To throw all those years and generations of breeding, care, and knowledge away seemed like such a waste.

But seeing as I'd already pissed off Emilia once today, I wasn't about to ask about it and risk another heated encounter.

And yes, it'd been heated in more ways than one.

Fuck, seeing her all worked up and putting me in my place shouldn't have turned me on. And yet, I'd wanted to argue with her until I pulled her close, kissed the living shit out of her, and watched all that fire transfer to another kind of heat.

Namely, having her legs wrapped around my waist as I fucked her against the fence until she came around my dick.

I was so lost in the fantasy that I actually jumped when Avery touched my arm. "Daddy, are you even listening?"

Quickly wiping away my thoughts, I cleared my throat. "Sorry, I was too busy thinking."

"Thinking about?"

I took the safest route. "How it's weird to see this place empty. When I was your age, cattle roamed this land as far as the eye could see."

"More than at Grandma and Grandpa's place?"

"Yes, way more." I gestured beyond the fence—we were now on the opposite end of the property from earlier—and replied, "The land actually goes past the barrier. They used to rotate the grazing fields, to give the land a rest."

Well, if Emilia hadn't sold the land beyond the fence, which was entirely possible.

Avery slipped her hand in mine, and I smiled. Soon she'd be too old for that, so I clung to every little-girl moment I still had with her.

She swung our hands and pointed ahead of us. "The creek is just over there. Auntie Abby said she and Millie would go searching for frogs near it when they were kids. They're loud in the summer, she said. But even louder at the lake where they used to camp as children. Can we go camping at the lake? I want to hear the frogs."

She probably meant Lake Sonoma, the biggest one in the area. Even if man-made, it was still beautiful. "Would you want to camp there even though it's so close to home?"

Wyatt muttered, "It's not close to home."

Because he thought Ridgefield—where we'd lived in the California Central Valley—was home.

Since I knew arguing with him would get us nowhere, I ignored the comment, and thankfully, Avery answered, "Yes! I miss camping, like we did that one time. Will the whole family go with us?"

I ignored the regret swirling in my chest. "Maybe. When I was little, we'd all camp with some of the neighboring families, in a giant group, and have these huge bonfires and barbecues. Although it might be harder to do that now, since everyone is busy, and there's the Summer Star Festival next month."

Avery stopped just short of the creek and released my hand. "Uncle Beck said I could help with his booth at the festival and give out pamphlets. But I'd rather help Millie. Her job is way more interesting."

For a little girl who loved happy endings and longed for me to marry again, a wedding planner would be the best job ever. "We'll see, Avery. We'll see."

Avery squealed and pointed toward the creek. "Come on, Wyatt. I saw a salamander, I think. Or maybe it's a newt? You like that stuff more than me, so come help me find it, and we can show Daddy."

Smiling, I watched them and started to think how spending their days here might not be so bad.

It wasn't long before I said we had to go home. Wyatt asked me, "So we can come back here every day for summer vacation?"

There wasn't any real reason for me to say no. It was safe enough for them to walk between the properties—the only danger had been some asshole out to destroy Beck's girlfriend, but he was now in prison—and I'd laid out that they had to stay within the fences.

So I nodded. "Yes, as long as you check in frequently and take the emergency cell phone with you, in case you need it."

Avery hugged me. "We will do both, Daddy! I promise!"

Wyatt nodded. "Yes, I promise too."

Uncaring if he was embarrassed, I brought my son close, and we had a long overdue group hug. Once

Wyatt finally wiggled away, I released Avery and gestured toward the house and barn in the distance. "We'll say goodbye first and then head home. Make sure to thank Emilia for letting you play on her land during your summer vacation."

We started walking back, and Avery asked, "Why do you call her Emilia?"

"That's her name."

"But everyone calls her Millie."

Which, to me, didn't suit her, not one bit.

Although, I didn't know why she'd started going by that nickname. Maybe I should ask her.

No. The last thing I needed was to get to know Emilia better and maybe start to like her. Well, more than I already did.

I replied, "That's true. If she ever asks me again to use Millie instead of Emilia, I'll do it."

Avery sighed. "I can't really have a nickname for Avery. I mean, what? Ave? Ri-ri? Both sound stupid. But at least it's the same for Wyatt. I mean, Wy sounds like Why, and it would only get super confusing."

"But your Uncle Beck and Aunt Lori call you Tater Tot."

"I didn't mind it when I was little, but I'm older now."

She'd earned the name during the one summer my kids had stayed with my family in Starry Hills, when I'd tried—but failed—to help my wife at her lowest.

Thankfully, we were nearly to Emilia's house, and my kids raced toward it, so I didn't have time to go down memory lane. Abby greeted us at the door, dressed in black pants and a light-blue button-up top, probably an outfit left over from her teaching days.

She hugged my kids and then pulled my grumbling ass into a hug as well. I gently patted her shoulder, and then she released me. It was still weird to meet her gaze, since she was only a couple inches shorter than me.

About the only good thing about being away so long was that I'd been instantly able to see just how much she looked like our mother, with the same brown hair and green eyes and slightly too long nose. She probably had fought off the boys in high school, and I wish I could've been there to protect her.

But I hadn't.

Like with the rest of my family, my cowardly ass had let her down too.

Abby lightly swatted my arm. "Do you ever stop scowling? I swear, sometimes I think you're a grumpy old man in a younger skin."

Avery giggled. "He's not like that with me and Wyatt, though. He pretends to be mean and rude, but he's not. Not really. Just not always happy."

Abby raised an eyebrow, and I raised one back. I knew about how she'd left her dream teaching job in San Jose and had returned to Starry Hills rather abruptly. She never talked about it—at least to my family—and we both knew it. If she was going to pry, I'd do the same.

My sister rolled her eyes. "Whatever." She looked at my kids. "Did you have fun today?"

"Yes! We found some salamanders near the creek. Maybe next time, we'll have the emergency phone Daddy is going to give us, and Wyatt can take some pictures. That's allowed, right? I know we can't use it unless it's an emergency, though."

I hadn't wanted to give them cell phones for a couple years yet, but if they were to be roaming Emilia's land, they needed one. "Pictures are fine. There won't be any internet or games on it, though. So just phone calls, text messages, and pictures. Okay?"

She nodded. "If it means we can play over here all summer, I promise to follow the rules."

I glanced at Wyatt, and he nodded. Nothing else.

Abby gently bumped her shoulder against mine. "Well, we won't be at dinner again tonight. Maybe tomorrow, but I can't guarantee it. Millie has a big wedding expo event thing to go to soon, one Beck is probably going to as well, so she's been planning for it in her free time."

"Well, Beck always makes enough food to feed an army, so whenever you can drop by would be great. Avery and Wyatt will miss you." I couldn't quite bring myself to say I missed getting to know my sister a little better too.

"I'll text you."

I groaned. "I've never texted so much in my life as I have in the last few months."

"Well, get used to it. I guarantee one day you'll get addicted to our family group chats."

"I doubt it."

Abby merely shook her head and turned to my kids, hugging each of them again. "I have to get back to work, kiddos. Remember to check in when you get here in the morning, okay?" Avery and

Wyatt nodded. "Love you both, and I'll see you tomorrow!"

Abby waved and rushed off. I could hear noises coming from the barn, and I assumed it was the reception after the ceremony.

Not wanting to see anything related to a wedding, I herded my kids toward the path home. As they chatted about what they'd found today near the creek and what else they hoped to find tomorrow, I went through everything that still needed fixing on Emilia's land. I'd noticed how anything beyond her home and renovated barn was somewhat neglected. It shouldn't be because of funds, unless her brother had truly abandoned her.

Not like I'd ask if she had the money to do it. Besides, me repairing things was far better than the winery shit my brother often had me do. I wouldn't shirk work again, but maybe on my days off I could fix things up for Emilia.

Only because it made things safer for my kids. Yes, for that reason only and none other.

Chapter Six

Emilia

Aunt Lori: We miss you! <heart emoji> Come to dinner tonight. Sabrina and I need more women to even out the numbers. <flexing arm emoji>
Emilia: lol. You can handle all the Wolfe brothers, no problem.
Aunt Lori: Just because I can doesn't mean I want to. <pleading emoji> I'll bring out the '16. <wine glass emoji>
Emilia: Not fair! That's my weakness.
Aunt Lori: <smiling demon emoji> I know.

The days flew by in a blur. I had so many bookings this year, it was insane, and when I added preparing for the upcoming wedding expo event and the Summer Star Festival, I pretty much didn't do anything but sleep, eat, and work.

I'd started to miss the Wolfe family dinners, though. So much so, I was determined to walk back with Avery and Wyatt today and force myself to take a break.

So when they swung by the house around four o'clock, I gave them each a hug—like I did every day—and then said, "I'm going back with you two today. Hopefully, Beck will have enough food for me at dinner."

Avery rolled her eyes. "Of course he will. Uncle Beck makes so much, it's crazy. Daddy alone eats enough for two people. But then he's been really busy and needs all the food so he can keep going."

I hadn't seen much of West since the day I'd stormed off nearly three weeks ago, when he'd brought up Rafe. Once or twice he'd been with the kids when they came to say goodbye to me. But apart from small talk, we'd kept our distance. "Is he busy with rebuilding the bottling facility?"

A few months ago, a crazy man named Justin Whitmore had been out to destroy Beck's girlfriend and had hired someone to set the place on fire. The town had come together to try and get it rebuilt as soon as possible, although it was still a work in progress.

Avery shook her head. "No. Daddy's been fixing things for you when he's not working for Uncle Beck, like today." Her eyes widened as she slapped a hand over her mouth. "I wasn't supposed to tell you that."

"What's he fixing?" She hesitated, and I shrugged. "You've already told me some, so you may as well tell me the full truth."

She shifted her feet before finally saying, "He's fixing fences, the outbuildings, and a bunch of things. Just in case you want to use them or maybe bring the cows back someday. I told him me and Wyatt could help with a cow mama and her baby. But he said it's too much work, and we have our kitties to take care of anyway."

"How long has your dad been fixing things?"

Avery didn't even hesitate, clearly happy to no longer have to keep a secret. "Three weeks or so? Not every day, but when he can. Mostly on his days off but some evenings too."

I blinked. Why in the world would Weston Wolfe spend his days off repairing things around my ranch and not tell me? Did he believe it a danger to his kids? Or more unlikely, was it a sort of apology for bringing up my brother?

I had no damn idea, but I was going to find out. Keeping my voice calm, I asked, "Can you take me to him? I want to surprise him."

"Sure!" Avery looked at her brother, who was staring at the pictures he'd taken today on the phone. "Come on, Wyatt."

With a sigh, he got up and put his hands in his pockets. "He's just going to tell me I can't help again."

I had been about to walk to the door, but something made me stop and go over to the little boy. "Did you ask to help him?" Wyatt nodded but remained silent. So I continued. "Why did he say no?"

He shrugged. "It's too dangerous, or something."

The twins would be eleven in the fall, and I'd seen Zach and Zane helping Beck and Nolan when they'd been that age, learning how to repair things around their property. "Are you interested in learning how to fix stuff?"

"Yeah." He looked to the side. "Dad doesn't like soccer, but I thought maybe he could teach me how to repair fences, or lights, or something."

Wyatt loved soccer—I'd found that out early on when he'd asked about my brother, who was a famous striker in England—but the boy didn't really have anyone to share his passion for it. To have found something he liked and wanted to share with his dad but couldn't, well, it probably made him sad and feel a little rejected.

It's not your place, Millie. Leave it.

And yet, seeing Wyatt's little dejected face, I couldn't leave it alone.

I placed a hand on Wyatt's shoulder and gently pushed him toward the door. Avery followed us. "All right, well, let's go find your dad and see what he says."

The twins chatted a bit—mostly Avery, although Wyatt liked animals in general, horses specifically—and I tried to keep track of what they said, replying when necessary.

But in truth, my heart rate kicked up as we headed toward the farthest edges of my land, where the calving barn was located.

Memories of helping to soothe the breeding cows when their labor went long, or running to fetch supplies to help my parents, or waiting to see if the lucky cow had twins again came rushing back. My mother had never balked at helping my dad at that time of year, and seeing my parents together, helping to save a struggling cow and calf, had always brought tears to my eyes.

And now I'd be going back there for the first time since they'd died, and I wasn't sure if I could handle it.

But then Avery slipped her hand into mine and said, "Why are you sad, Millie?"

I blinked, doing my best to compose myself. "When I was little, I used to come out here with my mom and dad. But they're gone now, so it brings up memories. Good ones, but it can still hurt."

Avery fell quiet, which was unusual for her, and I wondered if she was thinking about her own mother.

However, I most definitely didn't feel comfortable opening that wound for her—who knew what kind of damage I'd do?—and I wanted to make her smile again. "Did you know we had a lucky cow when I was growing up?"

Avery's head popped up. "Why was it lucky?"

"Well, she always had twins—which isn't the norm. And if that wasn't special enough, she had a knack for finding lost cows or calves. I used to tease she was part bloodhound."

Avery shook her head. "We never had lucky cows back at my grandparents' place. But maybe one day I can one too. Then she can always find the lost ones and make sure they come back home."

Wyatt scoffed. "Why would you want any cows when you can have horses? They're so much smarter."

"Every animal has its place and role, Wyatt."

He looked at me like I was crazy, but while chatting to the kids, I hadn't noticed the calving barn in the distance. I stopped and sucked in a breath as I took it in.

Just like when I was a kid, it was painted a bright red with white trim, but the paint was definitely new. And since I couldn't see any sign of neglect or disrepair, it meant West had repaired it before painting it, which must've taken hours and hours.

Why? echoed repeatedly inside my head.

Avery tugged my hand. "Come on. The inside isn't finished yet, but Daddy's been working on it."

We went inside, and the smell of wet paint hit me as I looked around. While a working calving barn had lots of indoor fences set up for stalls, hay on the floor, and a few other things, it was currently empty. Posts were situated just off-center to support the structure. The walls were white, the floor swept, and a lone work light shone on West, who was standing on a ladder, doing something with the overhead light fixtures.

He wore jeans and a T-shirt, covered in dirt and dust, and yet he still looked sexy as hell with his broad shoulders and long legs. His arm muscles flexed as he finished attaching the light fixture and put it into place. His back was mostly toward us, and his jeans highlighted his curved, taut ass.

One I wondered what might feel like in my hands.

Oh, hell no. Not going to happen.

I cleared my throat, and West stopped working. He glanced over and frowned. "What are you doing here?"

"I might say the same of you."

"Just a second." He did something to finish securing the light and then descended the ladder. He went to the breaker box, switched something on, and then flicked on the lights.

In the dark I'd thought it was big, but now? With the lights and white walls, it was huge, nearly as big as the barn I used for my weddings. In fact, if I put in some flooring and a few things—such as a bathroom and kitchen space—it could be another event space.

And yet, the thought of converting the calving barn squeezed my heart. Did I really want strangers constantly coming and going, slowly erasing the memories I had of this place? Of my parents?

Part of me thought maybe I deserved that anyway. My parents would be alive if not for me, so I didn't deserve the memories.

I hadn't noticed West approach, so when he spoke, even softly, I jumped. "Do you hate it?"

Looking into his blue eyes, it was strange to see concern there. I was used to the grumpy asshole who mostly grunted and glared at me.

I could say yes, I hated it. He needed to stay off my land, away from me, and then I could go back to fuming at him. After all, he'd abandoned his family. In my books, that was one of the worst things you could do.

And yet, in the moment, I couldn't hate him, and so I wouldn't lie to him. "It's amazing, West. But why did you restore it?"

He shrugged. “I had to do stuff like this back at my old job, and I'm good at it. That's all.”

I searched his gaze, not quite believing him. Although I found it odd he called previously working for his in-laws as his “old job.”

Regardless, I wasn't going to ask about it. I may not hate him, but we weren't even friends. Instead, I focused on something that had slipped my mind at first. “This place was locked, so how did you get in?”

He grunted, and the concern in his eyes vanished. “Abby gave me a key.”

“Abby knew about all this and didn't tell me?”

“I told her to wait before telling you. I wasn't sure if I'd have time to do anything, and I don't like to make promises I can't keep.”

I'd be having words with Abby later, that was for sure.

From the corner of my eye, I saw the twins near the ladder. Wyatt and Avery were both looking at the tools lying inside the toolbox. Remembering the earlier conversation with Wyatt, I said, “You should teach them and let them help you.”

“They're too young.”

“Most of the kids their age around here have probably helped out on the farms, vineyards, and dairies for years already.”

He set his jaw, and I thought he was going to shout at me again. Instead, he grunted, turned, and walked over to his kids. I was tempted to follow but reminded myself that they weren't mine, and he should handle it as he saw fit.

Still, I listened as West crouched next to the toolbox and said, "If you two want to help me, you need to learn the name of some of the tools. And most importantly—you never touch these unless I'm here, until you know what you're doing. Understand?"

Avery nodded. "Of course, Daddy. I'm not sure I want to get super dirty, but I want to learn how to paint walls and put up shelves and pictures. That way, whenever I get my own room someday, I can decorate it by myself!"

The twins currently shared a room. They wanted to, from what Avery said, because they didn't have any good friends yet.

I inched forward to better hear them as Wyatt pointed toward an electric drill next to the toolbox. "I want to use that."

West chuckled, and I blinked. I was pretty sure it was the first time I'd heard him laugh since his return to Starry Hills.

"We'll cover the basics first, and then we'll get to the power tools." West packed up his stuff and stood, carrying his toolbox and a bag that contained all the power tools. "Let's head home tonight, though. It's too late to teach you anything, especially as my stomach is already rumbling."

As if on cue, West's stomach did exactly that. Before I could think better of it, I blurted, "I can bring you snacks on the days you do repair work. I always have plenty left over from events, and I do my best to give them away and not waste food. So it's no trouble."

Damn, why was I offering to willingly come and see the grump? And alone, to boot?

The corner of West's mouth kicked up, and I nearly sucked in a breath. When the man smiled, he became dangerously handsome. A full-blown grin might give me a heart attack.

Realizing that was ridiculous, I decided to brush it off. "If you want. If not, that's fine. I can give it away to others instead."

"Oh, I won't turn down free food. If you know my family at all, then you know meals and snacks are a serious business."

I did know that—of his siblings.

But maybe West was more like them than I'd realized before.

And of course Avery piped in. "Millie's coming to dinner tonight! So maybe we can plan how to take all the best stuff first, as a team."

I laughed at her words. The Wolfe family had a rule —whatever ended up on your plate stayed there, no questions asked. It really could be borderline chaos at times, which I'd always loved growing up.

However, it was hard to imagine Weston Wolfe engaging in such silliness.

I spoke up. "We'll need to include Abby, though, as we're usually partners in crime."

The smile lingered on West's lips as he said, "Well, five against four will make the odds better for us."

"Then let's hurry and grab Abby so we can make a plan. Zach is the hardest to distract, usually," I said. Avery took my hand, and I smiled down at her. "Maybe you can help your aunt Abby too. You're Zach's favorite niece, after all."

"I'm his only niece."

"I'm sure you'll always be his favorite." I glanced at Wyatt. "Just as you're the favorite nephew."

Wyatt grunted, too busy staring at the bag of power tools, so I asked, "Did you want to help your dad carry stuff back?"

The boy nodded, and West looked down at his son for a moment, as if seeing him in a new light. Maybe he was finally realizing that his little boy was growing up, and not just because he was already tall for his age.

After clearing his throat, West handed Wyatt a bag of miscellaneous stuff. "These are some of the delicate supplies, like light bulbs and special fixtures, so keep it safe and be careful, okay?"

Wyatt's face lit up. "I will, Dad."

West put down the toolbox and patted him on the shoulder. "I know, son. And I'll give you both your first lesson soon." After squeezing Wyatt's shoulder, West picked up his tools again and then gestured toward the door. "Come on. If we don't get a move on, then Aunt Lori will raise hell."

Avery giggled, and I rolled my eyes as I said, "Surely you're not afraid of her. I mean, what will she do—send you some crazy text messages?"

West shuddered. "No, thank you. She's mostly spared me, but I've seen some of what she's sent to Beck and Zach, and let's just say I could do without her raunchy emojis."

Wyatt asked, "What's raunchy?"

I bit my lip to keep from laughing. "Yes, West, do explain it."

He gave me a half-hearted glare before saying, "We'll look it up later, in a dictionary together."

Wyatt and Avery both groaned, but Avery spoke first. "Always the dictionary."

"Yes. Nothing wrong with figuring things out by yourself. You remember it better that way."

As West's stomach growled again, I clapped my hands. "All right, let's go. Hearing your dad's stomach makes me hungry too." I lowered my voice to a fake whisper. "Maybe we can grab some leftover rolls from my place to munch on the way."

Avery brightened. "With your homemade strawberry jam?"

"Probably, if your dad says it's okay."

West grunted, any trace of his smile gone. "Fine. Anything to keep me from dying of hunger."

As we made our way out of the calving barn—Avery took pride in switching off the lights—and headed toward the main house, the kids filled the silence. I stole a few glances at West, but he never took his gaze from his kids or the path ahead of him.

Which was for the best, really. I wasn't sure what had just happened inside the calving barn. But given how I kept remembering his smile and wondering how firm or soft his lips might be, I most definitely needed to stay away from him.

So why had I offered to bring him snacks?

Chapter Seven

Emilia

Abby: We're totally going to pull this off.
Me: I hope so. Zach deserves to go down a peg.
Abby: You only say that because he took the biggest slice of cake last time, even knowing it was your favorite.
Me: He did it precisely because he knew it was my favorite.
Abby: Well, there were leftovers.
Me: That's not the point. I want bragging rights.
Abby: West? Are you there? We want bragging rights, so do your part.
West: I will.
Abby: That's it? Really? We could do with some pumping up.

West: Woo.
Abby: Okay, that just plain sucks for encouraging us. Negative two for effort.
Me: Hey, be nice. We need his help.
West: Yes, be nice to me, Abby. Maybe even grovel a little.
Abby: Well, they do say to listen to your elders. And you do have gray hairs. <laughing emoji>
West: <middle finger emoji>

We made it to the house, washed, and finished setting the table before Abby sidled up to me and whispered, "Ready?"

Even though I was twenty-five years old, at times like this, I felt all of twelve again, back when I'd finally joined in with one of Abby's crazy dinner games. "Yes, although it's going to depend a lot on West and his kids."

"Don't worry about him. He promised. Besides, he loved driving us siblings crazy as a kid."

"But didn't you say that Beck and West often teamed up against the rest of you?"

"Maybe. But West promised his kids he'd help, and he always follows through with the twins."

"That's true."

Zach entered the dining room, spotted us together, and grinned. "Now what kind of trouble are you two coming up with?"

Abby and I both looked as innocent as possible. "We never get into trouble."

Zach snorted. "Right, tell yourself that." His eyes turned calculating. "Try your best, ladies. I won't fall for any of your tricks."

Abby stuck out her tongue. "Stop being so cocky. It's annoying."

"I can't help it if you're just a sore loser."

Squaring my shoulders, I said, "We'll see how you feel later tonight. I think it's safe to say it'll be the pot calling the kettle black."

Zach winked. "I won't lose, so we won't have to find out."

"Ugh, you're so annoying," Abby muttered.

After blowing a kiss, he replied, "I love you too."

We all sat down, and I waited for West to arrive. Maybe to some, our dinner games were silly—because of course Beck made enough food to feed us all to the point where we had to unbutton our pants—but the prize tonight was getting the best cuts of steak and watching the irritated expression of the person who got the smallest.

Because Beck always, *always* made them different sizes.

West entered the room with his kids, his usually grumpy expression in place. I glanced at him, and he gave an imperceptible nod. *Game on.*

Aunt Lori entered from the kitchen, carrying the open wine bottles, and handed them to Abby. "Your turn, dear."

"Yes, Aunt Lori." She took them and started to fill

the wine glasses around the table. Even if Beck and Sabrina were still in the kitchen, Abby knew their preferences. So when she poured chardonnay into Beck's glass—he viewed white wine with steak as a sacrilege—I bit my lip to keep from laughing.

Aunt Lori merely raised an eyebrow, but humor danced in her eyes. I sometimes wondered what she'd been like when she was younger and married to her "Navy SEAL stud muffin," as she called her late husband. Probably trouble personified.

Beck entered, carrying the plate of steaks, and Sabrina followed him into the room before placing the respective potatoes and broccoli bowls on the table.

Beck raised his brows. "Remember the rule."

We all said, "No breaking the dishes."

He grinned—a sight that had been rare before he'd met Sabrina—and then nodded. "Okay, ready?"

Just as Beck set the plate down, the twins raced to Zach and tickled his sides. He laughed—more like squealed—and West went over, clamping his hands on Zach's shoulders to keep him in place.

"Stop it!" Zach said while laughing.

Abby and I wasted no time grabbing the plate of steaks. I took one, she another, and then we put the biggest one on West's plate, a decent one for Aunt Lori, and then dished out for the twins. By the time we were done, three tiny steaks remained.

Sabrina laughed. "Well done, ladies. Well done."

Beck grumbled as he dished out for him and Sabrina, leaving the tiniest, saddest looking steak ever on the plate.

West murmured something, and his kids stopped tickling Zach.

Avery said, "We love you!" And she threw her arms around her uncle's neck.

Zach shook his head. "How can I stay mad at that?" He hugged her and then Wyatt before giving them puppy dog eyes and clasping his hands under his chin. "Will you share with me?"

Avery crossed her arms. "Maybe if you trade your dessert."

We all laughed at that, and Zach ruffled her hair. "We'll see, Tater Tot. Now, let's eat before it gets cold."

As the kids and West sat down, I caught West's eye. He smiled a second before dishing out potatoes and broccoli for his twins and himself. I must've been staring because Abby whispered, "Close your mouth."

Aware that I was sitting in a room full of people who knew me well, I did and sipped my cabernet sauvignon and moaned a little—Aunt Lori had pulled through on giving me my favorite vintage.

I felt West's eyes on me but refused to look at him. Instead, I met Aunt Lori's gaze and raised my glass at her. "The best bribe ever."

"Maybe you should take a few bottles home to help relax."

Zach jumped in before I could reply. "You've definitely been working hard this year. Even though it's the end of June and fucking madness for you, you usually find time to come to dinner on Sundays."

They were right—we all tried to eat together on

Sundays. It didn't always happen, but missing three Sundays in a row like I had, well, it was noteworthy.

Yes, I'd been busy with work. However, it was getting closer to my mom's birthday, and whenever that happened, my guilt at still being here and my mom not became nearly unbearable. Even as a kid, I'd always tried to hide my sadness at this time of year from the Wolfe family. And I'd been successful, except for when it came to Abby.

Which was why Abby quickly jumped in to save me from replying. "Well, this year *is* different. She was invited to a new wedding expo show next month in Reno, and it's taking a lot of extra time for us to prepare for it."

Beck nodded. "Yeah, they invited our winery as well. There's going to be a whole booze section."

Sabrina rolled her eyes. "They most definitely don't call it the 'booze section.'" She looked over at Aunt Lori. "It's really exciting, to be honest. There's a wine alley, a scotch alley, and a beer garden, and a few other specialized areas. Getting the permits for it all was no joke, so I'm impressed."

Sabrina ran her own business—Starry PR and Marketing—and even if it was new and had only opened about a month ago, she'd been working in the field for years and had taken the invite to the new expo rather seriously.

After swallowing my latest bite of steak, I spoke up. "I'm nearly ready for the expo. I just need to get a little ahead so I can attend the Fourth of July parade in town and the Evans's annual barbecue and baseball game afterward."

Beck raised his eyebrows. "Miss the latter at your own peril. Katie will find you, tie you up, and force you to attend."

True, Katie was known as the town wild child, but she was part of the BFF Circle and one of my best friends. "I'll be there. But who are you sending to the wedding expo? You and Sabrina?"

Beck made a face, and Sabrina placed a hand on his arm as she laughed. "No. Beck is good at a lot of things, but being charming with strangers isn't one of them."

As Sabrina shared a glance with Beck, one of love and some hidden story they both knew but no one else did, a stab of jealousy pierced my heart.

However, I brushed it off. Relationships had never gone well for me, and I always felt guiltier the longer they lasted. My parents had loved each other to distraction, and I'd cut that short. So I shouldn't get what I'd denied them.

Thankfully, Zach spoke up, pulling me out of my head. "I wanted to go, but yesterday one of our biggest potential clients scheduled a meeting for the same time."

Abby asked, "Then who's going?"

Zach replied, "West will go in my place."

West's gaze snapped to Zach's. "What the fuck?"

Avery said, "That's a bad word, Daddy."

West grunted in apology and said, "Explain. If Beck's not friendly enough, then I sure as hel—er, heck, am not."

Aunt Lori jumped in. "Abby is going to help you

during the daytime and stay with a friend from college at night. But she'll need help with everything, and I'm sure you can cart heavy boxes and pour wine. Maybe even answer some questions without barking at someone. From what I've heard, you dealt with sellers back at the Grenville place, so you do have some experience."

I frowned at Abby, but she didn't look at me. She'd known about this and hadn't said anything?

West grunted. "But Beck could do that."

Beck sighed. "This is me giving you some more responsibility, brother. Don't you want it?"

My eyes darted between Beck and West, waiting to see what happened. The entire time I'd lived with the Wolfe family, Beck had acted the part of oldest brother in West's absence. He'd taken on a lot of burdens I hadn't noticed as a child but later did as an adult, namely trying to do as much as possible without asking anyone for help. Only after he'd met Sabrina had Beck finally been able to hand off more duties to his brothers. It was a big deal, and West knew it. Hell, we all did.

West finally sighed. "Fine, I'll go. But in the future, it'd be nice for you to ask me rather than order me to do it."

The corner of Beck's mouth kicked up. "But it's way too much fun ordering my big brother to do shit."

"I can still dump your ass in a horse trough, Beckie."

"Don't call me that."

"Beckie."

The two men growled at each other, and I tried not to laugh. Even as adults, brothers could act like children.

Aunt Lori clapped until she had our attention. "And

since Beckie is taking Abby away from you, Millie, West will help set things up for your booth too."

Being alone with West without his kids, even in a room with other vendors, was something I wouldn't risk. "There's no need. I can do it all myself. I have before."

Abby snorted. "Just accept his help. This event is bigger, and I'd wager everything I own that you'd struggle to get everything put up by yourself in time."

I could hire someone from Starry Hills to do the setup, but that seemed extreme. After all, West helping for an hour or two a day wasn't going to be a big deal. I'd be too busy getting things decorated to care, let alone notice his muscles flexing as he worked.

No. I was definitely not going to think about his muscles. "Fine." I looked at Abby. "But you owe me, big time."

Abby shrugged. "I'm sure by now we've both racked up favors and are pretty even. Besides, you know I can't talk about weddings like you do. You're the magic behind your business, Millie. Not me."

And just like that, I couldn't stay mad at her.

I bumped my shoulder against hers. "Just pack a few extra bottles of wine for us to enjoy, and we'll call it good."

"I'd do that anyway, so deal."

Talk turned to Sabrina's latest clients, the twins' recent salamander discovery, and Zach's suggestions for the Fourth of July barbecue, which always included crazy competitions and games. Since it usually had like forty or fifty people attending, it was no joke.

All the while, I snuck a few glances at West, but he

merely scowled and avoided my eye. The only time his expression softened was when one of his kids started talking to him and asked questions.

Well, if he was pissed off because he'd been ordered to help me, then he could take it up with Beck and Aunt Lori. I wouldn't ask him to do much, only the bare minimum. And with any luck, our booths would be on opposite sides of the room.

The only downside was that we'd be staying in the same hotel. I'd have to do my best not to bump into him, if possible. Because if we were alone, and he continued doing nice things for me like fixing up the calving barn, then I might want to do something stupid, like kiss him.

And that would be a disaster, no question. The Wolfe family was my family, but if it ever came to them choosing between me and West, they'd side with West. And since I'd lost most of my family already, I'd be damned if I did anything to jeopardize what I had with the Wolfes.

So I'd be polite with him—he'd earned that much from me, after doing the repairs—but nothing more.

Chapter Eight

Weston

Zach: My offer to give you charm lessons still stands.
Me: <middle finger emoji>
Zach: See, you definitely need my help. And you probably think you can't teach an old dog new tricks, but I think that's bullshit. I believe in you, brother.
Me: <middle finger emoji>
Zach: Even Avery could give you some lessons. If she didn't look so much like you, I'd wonder if she was yours.
Me: <middle finger emoji>
Zach: Sigh. And I was just trying to help.
Me: Fuck off.
Zach: He speaks!
Me: Fuck. Off.

Zach: I have a lot of work to do. But don't worry, I'll definitely find you later and impart my wisdom.
Me: <middle finger emoji>

Helping my kids tickle my brother—and ensuring he got the tiny steak—had been the most fun I'd had in a long time. Things had never been that relaxed back at my in-laws place, even when Andrea had been alive. Dinners had been full of tension, with the twins expected to be quiet and have good manners. Some bullshit about children being seen and not heard. I'd tried to argue about it with both Andrea and her parents to let them be kids, but they always said it was their house and their rules.

So many times I'd wanted to leave and take the twins with me. But then Andrea would threaten me with a custody battle, knowing she had my balls in a vise. Her parents were powerful people in the Central Valley. Judges, cops, politicians, you named it, her mother's family had a connection with them all.

Only Andrea's death had given me a chance to escape.

And to finally see Avery and Wyatt laughing and acting like children should with my family? It warmed my heart. Despite all the shit and trouble and pain I'd caused by bringing them to Starry Hills, it had definitely been the right decision.

However, then my brother ruined my mood by telling me I had to work at a wedding expo in Reno. If there was a better version of hell for me, I couldn't think of it.

Only because Beck was giving me something he probably would've done himself six months ago made me begrudgingly agree to it. Still didn't mean I had to like it.

Somehow I made it through dessert and the bedtime routine with my kids. The next day, however, after I finished checking the construction progress of our bottling facility, I went in search of a new project on Emilia's land.

Not because her expression at seeing the calving barn restored, with her lovely brown eyes wide and her lips parted in surprise, had poked at my frozen heart. Definitely not. Rather, it was more how the experience and talking about repairs had helped bring me and my kids together.

To hear Wyatt ask about tools and tell me what he wanted to make eventually—a bookshelf for his sister, since she loved books—still made me smile.

But first, I needed a project where I could take my time teaching my son and daughter. There were too many people visiting the winery in the summer to find something there. Emilia's place was perfect for it.

Since I vaguely remembered an old storage building from when I was younger, where Mateo Mendoza—Emilia and Rafe's dad—had kept a small office, I headed in that direction. The building was a little away from the barn and main house, hidden behind some trees. It was a faded red—they had loved red buildings here—and had seen better days. Some of the paint was chipped, and the huge doors on the front of it, where machines and trucks could enter, hung lopsided.

Apart from the big doors, there was a smaller one off to the side. I went to it and tested the handle, but to my surprise, it turned. If Emilia locked it normally, then maybe someone had broken in. At the thought of danger being so close to her house, worry churned my stomach.

Opening the door inch by inch, relieved to find it didn't squeak, I tried to let my eyes adjust to the dimmer light. The space was mostly empty, apart from what looked like stacked chairs and tables, probably something Emilia used for her weddings. I didn't hear anything to suggest someone was inside, so I crept carefully, keeping my eyes and ears out for the slightest movements or noise.

It was only as I approached the small office in the corner that I noticed light coming from under the door. I didn't have any tools with me, but I picked up a stray piece of wood on the ground. With one hand holding the wood and the other on the door, I waited for a noise.

Then I heard it—someone was crying.

Confused, I slowly opened the door and found Emilia sitting in a chair, her face in her hands, sobbing as if the world was about to end.

Tossing the wood away, I crept up to her. Crying women weren't my strong suit, but I had to do something. Because each sob was a stab to my heart.

I crouched down next to her and asked softly, "Emilia, what's wrong?"

She jumped in her seat, and her head shot up. The sight of her puffy eyes, tears rolling down her cheeks, squeezed my heart. She blurted, "What are you doing here?"

"I was looking for a new project. But don't change the subject—what's wrong?" When she hesitated, I growled. "Did someone hurt you?"

Her gaze left mine and rested on something to the side. It was only then that I noticed the room was set up exactly as it had been when I was a kid, as if time had stood still, and there was a picture of the Mendoza family on the desk. Rafe had to be about eighteen, Emilia eight or nine, and their parents stood behind them. Everyone smiled as Rafe held up his jersey, the one for the first soccer team he'd ever signed with.

Silence lingered, and I tried to think of what I could do. I'd become an expert in dealing with my late wife's temper, lies, and dramatic actions. But this? Tears and sadness and silence? I was way out of my fucking depth.

Eventually, Emilia whispered, "It's my mom's birthday today."

Ah, fuck. My first instinct was to hug her and try to reassure her like when my kids were upset. But would that be crossing a line?

Emilia then added, "My mom should be here, not me."

I frowned. "We don't get to decide that shit, Emilia, no matter how much we might want to control our own fate."

Her voice broke as she said, "Don't call me that."

"Why?"

"Because my parents did. A-and it hurts. So much." Her gaze met mine. "Because it's all my fault."

She started sobbing again.

I pulled her close, stroking her hair and making soothing noises as she cried in my arms, the sounds like some dying animal. My hardened heart softened a fraction, and I wondered what she wasn't telling me.

I let her cry herself out until, eventually, she pushed against me, and I released her. Still, she avoided my eyes, and I sensed she didn't want to talk about it.

My curiosity screamed to ask for more, but she was too fucking fragile right now. Later, I'd try. Because something was fucking hurting her, and I didn't like it.

"What should I call you, then? Millie doesn't seem quite right."

She frowned as she wiped away the last of her tears. "Why would you say that?"

"Honestly? It makes me think of some old aunt, with gray hair and a collection of dog statues, knitting an ugly scarf in a room full of plastic-covered furniture."

Her lips twitched, and I suddenly felt like a fucking hero. "What kind of books are you reading to make you think that?"

"You remember that I like to read?"

She nodded, still not meeting my gaze. "As kids, my brother complained about how..."

Her words died, and I couldn't help but blurt, "What happened between you two, Aunt Million-Collector-Plates-on-the-Wall?"

Her eyes finally met mine. "What the hell are you talking about?"

I shrugged. "If you insist on being called Millie, I'll keep up my Aunt Million something or other teases."

Her lips twitched again. "You're ridiculous."

"I can't say anyone's ever called me that before, Aunt Million-Clipped-Coupons-in-a-Drawer."

Emilia—fuck, it was what I still thought of her as—laughed, and I wanted to take a picture. She was too fucking beautiful when she laughed.

"I may have clipped a few coupons in my time."

As she smiled at me, I itched to reach over and wipe away the last of her tears.

Instead, I clenched my fingers into fists against my thighs and asked, "Do you really prefer Millie? Or is it something you adopted to distance yourself from the past? Like it made you feel reborn or something?"

She glanced back at the picture. "At first, it was just because I missed my parents so much. I wanted to remember their voices for as long as possible and didn't want to muddle how they said Emilia with everyone else's voice."

Plucking at her jeans, she remained silent.

I gently touched her arm. "And then?"

Sighing, she raised her hands and rubbed her face. "And then, well, it helped organize my life neatly into before and after." She shook her head. "Maybe it sounds stupid, I don't know."

I sensed there was more to it, more that she wasn't telling me, but I wasn't about to push. After all, I had zero right to demand anything from her. "Then if you want me to use Millie, I will."

She dropped her hands and frowned at me. "You say it weird."

I adopted a fake, horrible British accent. "Millie."

She smiled again, and my stupid heart wanted to thaw a little more.

So I quickly sealed up that bastard and focused on her words as she said, "Emmy. Try Emmy."

"Emmy. How's that?"

Pretending to ponder, she tapped her chin. "Try again."

"Emmy. Emmy. Emmy. There. I said it three times. Does that mean you'll grant me a wish? Three, if you're being really nice?"

She snorted. "Who are you and what have you done with Weston Wolfe?"

This was who I'd been when I was in my late teens, charming the ladies, and doing my best to be less of a grumpy asshole. It'd been so long since I'd been anything but the latter that it was weird to show it to someone again.

Except, remembering Emmy's smiles and laughter, I thought maybe it was okay for her to know. Just her.

I put on a scowl and grunted louder than was necessary. "Is that better?"

She shook her head. "Silly man."

No one had ever called me silly before. But I wasn't insulted. No, I was rather...charmed.

Fucking hell. I needed to be careful.

I stood quickly and retreated a few steps as I cleared my throat. "If Emmy's fine to use, then I should probably get on with inspecting the place. Well, if that's okay? I wanted to fix up this building too."

She stood and crossed her arms over her chest. Not in anger, but more like she was hugging herself.

The urge to pull her close and wrap my arms around her was strong. But there was no way that would ever fucking happen again.

She replied, "Emmy from you is better, I think. Just not Emilia."

"Emmy it is. And the repairs?"

After glancing around the room, she replied, "As long as you don't touch my father's office, go for it."

"I won't. I promise."

She bobbed her head. "Although make sure to charge me for the supplies. I use this building for storage, so I can write it off as a business expense."

The thought of charging her didn't sit right with me. But if I did, then it would be a job and make it all the more formal. And formal was good. "Okay. I do plan to teach Wyatt and Avery some basics in the process, though. Hopefully that's okay?"

"Of course." She eyed the door behind me. "I really need to clean up and get ready for a meeting."

I opened the door for her and stepped back. "Then I won't keep you."

We stood and stared at each other, neither of us moving, and time stilled.

Her eyes were sad, filled with a mixture of loneliness and longing, and all I wanted to do was to make her laugh and smile again. To brush away her tears, hold her close, and be the rock I thought she needed.

Because I could still hear her soul-wrenching sobs, and everything in me screamed to make things better. To finally be the partner and protector I'd so desperately tried to be with my late wife.

Not that any of that could happen. Hell, Emilia wasn't my anything, and I had no claim on her.

But right here, right now, it was nice to pretend otherwise.

Before I could do something stupid, like pull her close again, Emilia looked away and walked out the door.

Free of her presence, I realized how dangerous it was to be alone with Emilia Mendoza. Which meant I couldn't let it happen again.

Chapter Nine

Emilia

Katie: Who's ready to kick some ass today? <baseball emoji>
Amber: Me! <flexing arm emoji>
Me: I'm bringing my A game, for sure. <heart emoji>
Katie: Good because I won't let my brother win again this year. He's too fucking cocky and it's getting on my nerves.
Me: <laughing emoji> I thought you were going to hide his lucky outfit today?
Katie: The bastard hid it first. <angry emoji> I know he's up to something.
Amber: To be fair, you tried to trip him before the game last year.

Katie: Whose side are you on?
Amber: <zipped mouth emoji>
Katie: Traitor! <crying emoji>
Me: Maybe this year is our year. <fingers crossed emoji>
Katie: I hope so. Otherwise, my sisters will bitch and complain for the next twelve months. Seriously. <swearing emoji>
Amber: We'll try our best. I have a secret new pitch this year! <dancing emoji>
Katie: That's the spirit! Abby? Where are you? We need your batting skills, missy.

I managed to avoid West for nearly two days. I'd secluded myself in my office the next day, and the day after was the Fourth of July, and I hadn't seen him at the Starry Hills parade.

But as I walked up to the Evans house, the sounds of laughter and talking and music filled the air, and I knew I couldn't hide any longer. He would be at the barbecue, along with his kids.

For West, of all people, to find me bawling my eyes out had been beyond embarrassing. And I still couldn't believe I'd shared as much as I had about my parents.

Yet, when he'd held me in his strong arms as I sobbed, his touch gentle and voice soothing, I had felt safe. Almost as if I could be myself, reveal some of my burdens, and he wouldn't run the other way screaming.

If that hadn't been ridiculous enough, him making me laugh had made things even weirder.

And the stare down right before I'd left my dad's old office? His gaze had flashed with heat and yearning, which had confused the hell out of me.

It was hard to believe West desired me.

But if he would've leaned down and kissed me, I wouldn't have put up a fight.

Warning bells rung inside my head. I definitely couldn't be alone with him like that again. I may not hate him, and I was a lot less angry about him leaving his family than before, but I needed to start thinking of him as my brother. And fast.

Because if he kept being so nice to me, I could see myself "like" liking him, in a way that had us ripping off our clothes and moaning as we came, all sweaty, hot, and delicious.

Stop it, Emmy.

Wait, what? I hadn't scolded myself silently as Emmy since I was a kid. No, Millie was the person I'd become after the car crash. Millie. Not Emilia, and most definitely not Emmy.

Except for West.

As I rubbed my eyes, a familiar voice called out, "Millie! You need to hurry up! Otherwise we won't stand a chance in hell at beating their asses this year."

I glanced up, and the dark auburn-haired, blue-eyed form of Katie Evans dashed toward me. She might be short with curves I wished I could have, but she was fast as hell and was right in front of me in a second, if breathing a little heavily. "Kyle is a cheating bastard and moved the start time for the baseball game. And I know he's only doing that because most of my team hasn't shown up yet."

As she pushed me from behind until I started moving, I laughed. "It's just a game, Katie. Who cares?"

"Who cares? Are you serious? You don't have to live with Cassie, Sam, and Kyle like I do. My sisters are pissed, and I'll never hear the end of it if Kyle wins because he cheated."

The baseball teams were always led on one side by Kyle Evans and the other by the three Evans sisters. On the surface, having the sisters—Cassandra, Samantha, and Katherine—on one team against their only brother, Kyle, might seem unfair. The three sisters had a whole secret language they used for the game, one I'd never really figured out.

However, Kyle had played ball all through middle and high school, as had some of the other guys. Including...

I mentally cursed. "He has West on his team this year, doesn't he?"

"Kyle kicked Zach off his team to get him too. Which means we're stuck with Zach."

I bit my lip to keep from laughing. Zach Wolfe was charming and hilarious but quite possibly the worst baseball player I'd ever seen.

We entered the backyard and headed toward the open space just beyond, which served as the field for the Evans games. "Did you get Amber for our team, at least?"

Amber King had played softball in high school and

was one of the best players on the local adult team. "Yeah. And, well, I felt bad for Sabrina, since this is her first year, and so I picked her too, before Zach, so she wouldn't be last. And I don't even know if she can play."

"She at least knows the rules. Her best friend is married to Ben Adams, and Sabrina has gone to quite a few games with them and Beck recently."

Kate squeaked in surprise. "As in the famous-baseball-player-turned-coach Ben Adams?"

"Yep. Maybe next year we can secretly invite him to play on our team. It might give Kyle a heart attack."

Katie laughed. "That's evil, which means I love it!" She waved. "Come on. I said you were on my team if you arrived on time, so let's hurry before my cheating-ass brother comes up with some other reason as to why you can't play."

I patted the bag slung over my shoulder. "Let him try and stop me. I brought my lucky glove with me."

"Woot. I'll take it. I hid Kyle's favorite, so maybe he'll suck today."

All I could do was laugh. The Evans family took this annual game way too seriously.

And yet, it was familiar and gave me something to focus on. Especially once I spotted West in a pair of baseball pants and a jersey. The pants weren't overly tight, but enough, and they highlighted his large muscled thighs.

Damn, the man was strong. Probably from wrestling cattle back at his in-laws' place.

I wondered what it'd be like to run my hands over those legs, up, up, until I reached...

Nope. Not going there.

Katie shouted, "She's here, Kyle! So Millie's on my team!"

Kyle rolled his eyes. "Fine. Can we start now?"

Katie stuck out her tongue. "If you hadn't changed the start time at the last minute, with no warning, we wouldn't have to hurry."

Kyle shrugged. "I'm helping the volunteer firefighter association with the fireworks later. It's my first year, and I'm not going to be late."

The local volunteer firefighters put on the sole big fireworks display in our area.

As I took out my glove and changed my shoes, I heard Katie reply, "You had plenty of warning to tell us. But that's fine. We'll beat your cheating ass anyway. Just wait and see."

Kyle put a hand on his face, full of mock horror. "Oh no. I'm shaking in my shoes."

Cassie Evans jumped in. "You should be, brother. You're going down this year. Maybe even face-first, if you happen to trip. By accident."

I could hear a few familiar people laughing—Beck was on my team too, it seemed—and then West growled, "Can we fucking start now and stop this shit?"

Avery shouted, "Two bad words, Daddy!"

I spotted Wyatt and Avery sitting with Aunt Lori and Abby. Weird, as Abby usually played. I'd have to ask her about it later.

Ready, I took my position on third base and punched my glove a few times.

For the next two hours, I forgot about anything but

catching, throwing, and swinging the bat. Even when West was up to the plate, or caught one of my balls as shortstop, I only viewed him as an opponent.

But in the end, my team lost. West was just too good, and when combined with Kyle—who'd been all set to go pro when he injured his knee and ended that career—we didn't stand a chance.

As Kyle and his team celebrated, Katie gathered ours together and whispered, "Next year is our year, all. If Sabrina can get her friend here, he'll be our secret weapon. Can you do it, Sabrina?"

Sabrina blinked. "Who are you talking about?"

I clarified, "She's talking about Taylor's husband."

Sabrina cleared her throat. "Oh, well, we'll see. He's kind of a busy guy."

Katie shook her head. "We'll think of a way to get him here. I can't pay him millions or anything, but maybe if we bribe him with cheese, wine, and whatever else we've got, it could be enough."

Sabrina chuckled, and I sighed before saying, "That's next year, Katie. For now, just shake hands with Kyle so we can end this and get some food. I'm starving."

The parents of the Evans family had a rule—no one ate until the two teams congratulated each other on a job well done. Something about not wanting the hostility to ruin the rest of the day or something. All I knew was that it was tradition.

Once Kyle and Katie did that—Kyle looking smug as all else, and Katie scowling—the Evans dad, Henry, shouted, "Food's ready!"

Everyone gathered their crap and headed toward the

large barbecue and tables set up with burgers, hot dogs, and a lot of other food. I was about to find Abby and talk to her when Avery took my hand. "You were amazing, Millie! You can throw so much farther than I can. Can you teach me how to do it?"

I smiled. "I could, but your dad is a lot better than me."

Glancing over, I noticed West and Wyatt together. West must've heard us because he grunted and said, "I had more practice growing up. If we had a swim contest, I'd lose."

It'd been so long since I'd been on the swim team that it took me a second to comprehend his meaning. "That was years ago, West."

"But you have a pool in your backyard."

"Yes. But I rarely use it."

I never had the time.

Avery jumped a little. "I didn't know you had a pool! Can we use it? Please, Millie?"

West frowned. "You can't just invite yourself over, Avery."

Wyatt spoke up. "Can we come over, pretty please?"

I bit back a smile at his overly polite tone. The little guy was laying it on thick. "It's up to your dad. If he says it's okay and can watch you, then sure."

As soon as I said it, I regretted it. The last thing I needed was West bare-chested in swimming shorts, showing off those arms, shoulders, and chest. So I added, "Or if someone can watch you. An adult has to be there."

Wyatt looked over at West. "Dad? Can you take us?"

West grunted. "We'll talk about it later. For now, let's get some food before it's all gone."

As he herded his kids away, part of me itched to follow.

But then I reminded myself I needed to keep my distance from Weston Wolfe. His hidden charm and kindness were something I didn't think I could keep resisting.

So I headed over to Abby, who was with Katie and Amber—the four members of the BFF Circle in one place.

Amber smiled at me. "So you are alive. I haven't seen you in the bakery, apart from wedding cake tastings or orders, in weeks."

The four of us usually had tea or hot chocolate and scones once a week, when Katie often smuggled in some Baileys to add to the hot chocolate. "I know. But it's turning out to be an amazing summer for me and my business, and I just have so much to do."

Amber looked at me in that way she had, the one that I swore could read my mind and knew I was hiding something, and then she said, "Next week, you're coming, no matter what. Even if I have to send Katie to kidnap you."

Katie rubbed her hands together. "I've always wanted to try that. Well, in a non-creepy and completely legal way, of course. But we're besties, so kidnapping is allowed. You'll never see me coming."

And knowing Katie, she wasn't lying.

"Fine, I'll come." I switched my gaze to Katie again. "But no sneaking alcohol into my drink. I need a clear head, since I have the big expo coming up, not to mention the Summer Star Festival."

"Fine," Katie grumbled, and we all laughed.

I forgot about everything but hanging out with my friends, teasing and chatting about nothing, and time flew by. To the point when Avery took my hand again, I jumped.

The little girl said, "Sorry! I didn't mean to scare you. But we need to leave to see the fireworks soon, and I wanted to sit next to you. Will you come with us?"

I should say no. After all, Avery was becoming more and more attached me, even if I only saw her and Wyatt at lunch sometimes or when they said goodbye in the late afternoon.

However, as she gave me big puppy dog eyes and said, "Please? I haven't made any good friends yet since I was only at my new school for such a short time before summer vacation. But you're my friend, right, Millie?"

And just like that, my heart melted. "Of course I am." I looked at Katie, Amber, and Abby. "I'll see you all at tea next week. I promise."

After saying my goodbyes, Avery tugged me along. "Daddy said it should be an amazing show. Uncle Beck and Kyle are good friends, and he hinted at what's to come. I can't wait! I almost never saw the big fireworks near Grandma and Grandpa's place, so this is special."

"You didn't go to see the fireworks back in Ridgefield?"

"No. Grandma said too many criminals went to the events, and they would try to hurt us or kidnap us. So we had to stay home."

Given what I knew of where West had lived with his kids, it was a fairly safe place. There had to be more to it. "Your dad agreed?"

Avery looked at the ground and kicked a small rock. "Well, most years, he had to go looking for Mom. So he wasn't there."

"What?"

"Mom disappeared sometimes. She had a lot of guy friends and liked to see them. Sometimes she stayed too long, and Daddy had to bring her back." Her voice was barely a whisper when she added, "I think she liked her friends better than me."

My heart squeezed at her words. I stopped and knelt until I was eye level with her. "I don't think that's possible, Avery. You're kind and funny and creative. Not to mention smart and caring. If I had a daughter, I'd love for her to be just like you."

Avery threw her arms around my neck. "I'm glad you're my friend, Millie."

As I hugged her back, I wished I could do more for her. To think Avery's mother had made her feel unwanted or not precious stirred anger in my belly.

But all too soon, Wyatt called our names and told us to hurry up. And so we piled into West's truck and headed to where we could see the fireworks display. Sitting in the front with him, I stole a few glances at his profile. It was on the tip of my tongue to ask about why he'd had to go looking for his wife so often.

However, he never took his eyes from the road. And even once he parked and we headed toward the area where we could lay out our blanket, he focused on talking with his son and daughter.

I should've been relieved. And yet, now I was curious at what West had been up to during the years he'd been away.

Chapter Ten

Weston

Me: Can't you take them swimming?
Aunt Lori: You used to love swimming as a boy. <swimmer emoji> You take them.
Me: You have weekly water aerobics. And you always say you want more time with my kids.
Aunt Lori: I'm tired this week. These old bones need some rest. <sad face emoji>
Me: You walked two miles yesterday to visit a friend, and then walked back before pruning flowers in the garden. And you still had enough energy to play a board game.
Aunt Lori: Exactly. I need a nap. <sleeping emoji>
Me: ...

Aunt Lori: What?
Me: It won't work.
Aunt Lori: What? I'm not a mind reader.
Me: Whatever. I'll remember your old bones when I eventually take my kids camping. I won't trouble you by asking.
Aunt Lori: But I love camping! You'd better invite me. <angry demon emoji>
Me: Then just admit what you're doing.
Aunt Lori: I have no idea. <angel emoji>
Me: Fine. Whatever. I'm leaving now.

Three days later, my kids wore me down, and I agreed to take them swimming. Abby had said there weren't any events that day, and I had it off. When given the choice between helping me fix up the storage space or going swimming, the pool had won hands down.

I didn't know where Emmy was, though, and rather hoped she'd be in town or away visiting with a client. Watching her during the baseball game on the Fourth of July, grinning and unafraid to dive for a ball at one point, had stayed with me. Add in how hard it'd been to ignore her during the fireworks display when all I wanted to do was pull her close and kiss her, and, well, the damn woman had ended up visiting me in my dreams over the last few nights.

Dreams that had resulted in me waking up hard and

aching and having to take myself in hand to release some tension. Several times.

Fuck. When had I started to think of Emmy that way? And if she showed up in a bathing suit, even an old granny-style one, I would be doomed to stay in the pool and hope the cold water would tame my dick.

We reached the wooden gate leading to Emmy's backyard. I reached over, lifted the latch, and walked inside.

The area was different and yet the same from when I'd been over here as a kid, back when Rafael "Rafe" Mendoza and I had been best friends. The rectangular pool hadn't changed, ranging from three to eight feet with a diving board at one end, but there was now a hot tub situated a few feet from the pool. I could easily imagine Emmy and Abby sitting in it, laughing and drinking wine, relaxing after dealing with some difficult bride or groom. Not to mention the plants that surrounded the yard, hiding most of the fence, made it feel isolated and special, like a private retreat.

Avery tossed her bag down, kicked off her flip-flops, and tugged off the little swimsuit cover dress she wore. We'd all put on sunscreen right before we left—it was an ordeal—so I didn't have to worry about it until later.

Avery grabbed my hand and pulled. "Hurry up, Daddy. You promised to teach me to swim in the deep end today."

Wyatt was stripped to only his swimming trunks and sat on the steps in the shallow end. He splashed water over to hit his sister, and Avery shrieked. "Stop it, Wyatt! I don't want to have a water fight."

So, of course, my son splashed her again.

I bit back a grin—I'd done the same to my brothers when I'd been their age—and tugged off my T-shirt and removed my sandals. "Come on, Avery. Time to learn how to swim." I glanced at Wyatt. "Stay only where you can stand, like you promised, okay?"

Wyatt nodded and eyed the deep end before shivering. "I don't want to go over there."

"You don't have to if you don't want to. Once I'm done with Avery's lesson, I can blow up the ring for you."

Before Wyatt could answer, a familiar female voice came from over my shoulder. "I can do it, if you want."

Slowly, I turned around and did my best not to stare. Emmy wore a black bikini, the top fully covering her small breasts, and the bottoms highlighting her curvy hips. Unlike my family—where everyone was tall, broad, and almost too much—Emmy looked almost delicate. Fuck, if she was under me, I'd worry about crushing her.

Just no. Clearing my throat, I said, "We don't want to bother you."

She rolled her eyes. "If I didn't want to do it, I wouldn't offer."

Avery spoke up. "Daddy's going to teach me to swim in the deep end today!"

Emmy smiled warmly at my daughter, and the ice around my heart cracked a fraction.

"That's amazing, Avery. It might be hard at first, but once you get the hang of it, it's like riding a bike—you never forget it."

Avery walked over to Emmy. "When did you learn to swim?"

Emmy laughed, and fuck, it was hard not to stare at her tits as they wobbled. Which they'd also do if I pressed her legs up and thrust hard into her.

Damn it, what was wrong with me?

After setting down her towel, Emmy gathered her hair up into a ponytail, revealing a neck that didn't help my imagination at all.

Unaware of my dirty mind, Emmy answered, "My mom took me to a Mommy and Me swim class at six months. So, I guess forever? I had lessons from a young age, and it wasn't long before I loved jumping from the high diving boards. Maybe once you learn to swim, you can try them out at the community center pool." She gestured toward her own tiny diving board. "I can give you a quick glimpse of what you can do eventually, if you want?"

"Yes, please! I almost never went swimming before, and only with Daddy. But I want to learn. Then maybe I can swim at Lake Sonoma later this summer, when we go camping."

I mentally sighed. "We haven't made any final plans to go camping yet, Avery."

"But we might." She smiled up at Emmy. "Maybe you can teach me too? With two teachers, I'm sure to learn super fast."

Emmy glanced at me, a question in her eyes. She didn't want to interrupt my father-daughter bonding time. I shrugged. "If Emmy's okay with it, then why not?

Just let me blow up Wyatt's ring while you two get into the water."

Avery frowned. "Emmy?"

"My full name is Emilia, but your dad calls me Emmy." She bit her lip a second—and bastard that I was, I couldn't stop staring at it—and added, "You can call me Emmy, too, if you want. I'll answer to either."

Avery nodded. "Emmy is much better. I like it." She reached for Emmy's hand. "Now come on! It's hot today, and I want to get into the pool."

Emmy walked toward the deep end and released Avery's hand when they were nearly to the diving board. "Stay right here, okay? I'll show you a quick dive, and then we can start your lesson."

My daughter nodded, and I couldn't tear my gaze from Emmy as she walked onto the diving board, perched on the edge, and bounced a few times—again, I couldn't stop staring at her breasts—and then she jumped and dived in gracefully.

Avery clapped. "Yes, I want to be able to do that too!"

Emmy surfaced, and the ring in my hands was forgotten as the water ran down her face and shoulders. It made me want to go over, pull her out of the water, and give her a nice, long rubdown. One that ended with both of us breathing hard and desperate.

Scowling and scolding myself—my kids were here, for fuck's sake—I put the ring to my mouth and blew it up, watching as Avery sat at the edge and slowly eased in, never letting go of the side. Emmy swam just beside her, treading water as if it were nothing, and murmuring something to Avery I couldn't hear.

Soon Avery's look turned determined, and she nodded then moved to hold on with only one hand. Watching Emmy encourage my daughter and then seeing Avery grin at Emmy, well, damn, it did something to my heart.

Because in a fair world, that sort of ease should've existed between Avery and her mother. Except Andrea had never wanted to watch the kids on her own. In fact, she had usually disappeared right after Avery or Wyatt had asked to do something with her.

Even something as mundane as eating dinner together, or making cookies, had sent Andrea scrambling.

Emmy glanced at me and frowned. Not wanting her to ask shit—because I might actually spill some of the truth—I turned away and headed toward my son. I handed him the ring and walked into the water, turning to face him. "You sure you don't want to come over near us? The ring will keep you afloat."

He shook his head and merely floated in the shallow end, his feet up near the surface. "Nope. Avery really wants to learn to swim. I don't." He hesitated and then added, "Do you think Uncle Beck will let us ride his horses again soon?"

I'd taught my kids to ride early. And while they weren't old enough to go out on their own, riding with Wyatt had been one of our special things, back at his grandparents' place. We'd only managed it a few times before the vineyards and winery had become too crowded. “I’m sure he will. It just has to be a quiet day.” Wyatt glanced away, and I added, “I’m not trying to do that adult thing where I say we’ll do it later and then never follow through.” Something my wife had done plenty. “Once the summer is over and the grapes are harvested, it’ll be a lot quieter, and we can ride all the time.”

Wyatt twirled in the ring. “If you say so.”

I stopped the ring and made him face me. “I promise, Wyatt.” I put my pinky up. “And you know how seriously I take pinky promises.”

Long ago I’d come up with a way to convince my kids that I’d follow through when their mother wouldn’t. And so the deadly serious pinky promises had been born.

I was sure my brothers would laugh their asses off at their growly brother doing such a thing, but when it came to my kids, I didn’t fucking care what other people thought.

Wyatt smiled and hooked his pinky finger with my much bigger one. “Pinky promise.”

Once he released my finger, I splashed him. And for the next few minutes, we laughed and tried to soak the other. Until eventually, Avery shouted, “Daddy! Come look what I can do!”

With one last splash at my son, I turned and swam to the deep end. I made the mistake of looking at Emmy’s face. She smiled, her eyes warm, and something about it just felt...right. The warmth and happiness were what she deserved, not the tears and fears of whatever she hadn’t yet shared with me about the past.

It was fucking difficult to tear my gaze away, but I somehow managed it. "Show me what you've learned, Avery."

As I watched my daughter tread in place for five seconds before gripping the wall again, I smiled at her and then went to give her a hug.

And I felt Emmy's eyes on me the whole time.

Chapter Eleven

Emilia

Avery: We're coming over this afternoon to swim!
Me: Good! Have fun!
Avery: Will you be home? You should come too.
Me: Should you even be texting me right now?
Avery: Um, no. Please don't tell Daddy.
Me: <thinking emoji> I should. But if you promise to save it only for emergencies or check-ins, I won't say anything.
Avery: I promise! See you at the pool! <splashing emoji>
Me: Er, sweetie, maybe talk to your dad about that emoji and don't use it.

Avery: Why? We're going to the pool and I want to splash around.
Me: I know. Do that! But ask your dad or Uncle Zach about it. Promise me.
Avery: Okay. If you come to the pool.
Me: We'll see. <heart emoji>

After getting Avery's text messages, I had planned to hide out and keep my distance. And yet, the thought of staying inside on such a nice day and avoiding Avery and Wyatt didn't really appeal. Avery had a way of making me smile and forgetting about my past for a little while.

And if I was honest with myself, I wanted to see West bare-chested again, up close and personal. I really shouldn't. Especially since I'd dreamed of him last night, pinning my hands above my head as he took me rough and hard, and I'd woken swollen and aching. When I'd finished myself off, I'd come harder than I ever had in my life.

Definitely a huge warning sign for me to keep my distance.

But when I'd heard them entering the backyard and spotted them from my upstairs bedroom, I forgot about all the reasons why I should stay away. I put on my bathing suit and headed downstairs.

Of course Avery had charmed me, and I was soon helping her learn how to tread water. Once West started playing with his son at the far end, my heart warmed at the sight of the tall, burly man splashing water with his little boy.

The more time I spent with West and his kids, the harder it was for me to believe his late wife had wanted so little to do with them. I might never have kids, but if I did, I'd want them to be just like the twins.

As I finally helped Avery tread water for a few seconds before she gripped the wall again, she grinned at me and said, "I did it! I can't believe I did it!"

"Amazing job! Look at how fast you picked that up. At this rate, you'll be swimming in no time." I moved close enough to grip the wall and gave Avery a hug. "I'm proud of you."

When I pulled back, Avery looked at me with tears in her eyes. "You are?"

The disbelief in her voice went straight to my heart. "Of course I am. Anyone would be."

She looked down at the water and whispered, "Not my mom."

I knew it was bad to think ill of the dead, but I was starting to hate the woman who'd obviously neglected her daughter.

Still, I kept those thoughts to myself and placed a finger under Avery's chin, making her meet my gaze again. "Well, I am really proud of you. Now, let's try it one more time, and then maybe we can show your dad."

The sadness vanished, replaced with determination, and she nodded. "I'll try to do it a little bit longer."

It wasn't long before West came, watched his daughter, and then hugged her. The tender look West gave

Avery as he brushed some of the wet strands off her face did strange things to my heart.

I'd hated him for abandoning his family, for taking things for granted, but now I started to wonder about the reasons why he'd stayed away. Because he clearly loved his kids, and I couldn't imagine why he'd keep them from his family.

As soon as we finished with Avery's lesson and she went to play with her brother in the shallow end, West and I remained in the deep end. I treaded water, and he held the side, and we both stared at each other. Almost as if we both wanted to ask something but knew we probably shouldn't.

Screw it. Who knew when I'd be alone with him again like this so I blurted, "Did you really have to go searching for your wife a lot?" His brow furrowed, and I quickly added, "Avery told me about it."

At the mention of his daughter, his gaze moved to where the twins were trying to do handstands in the water and sighed. "I thought I'd done a better job of hiding that."

I moved closer so I could also grip the side of the wall. "You can tell me to fuck off, if you want. But I just want to know how to better handle your kids, West. I don't want to trigger them or hurt them unintentionally."

His gaze moved back to mine, and I held my breath. My reasoning was pseudo-bullshit, and he could probably tell. True, I didn't want to bring up painful memories unintentionally. But I also wanted to know more about what had shaped West into the man he was now. Because while I hadn't known him well as a kid, he'd often played with his brothers and smiled more. In general, he'd seemed happy.

His kids made him happy, but I sensed he wasn't in the other areas of his life.

And since my life goal was to spread happiness to make up for what I'd done, this was just doing that.

Liar. Ignoring my inner voice, I focused on West as he finally replied, "After the twins were born, I soon realized Andrea had zero interest in wanting to be a parent. I thought maybe it was just postpartum depression at first, or her being overwhelmed with having twins. But over time, it became clear she wanted to pretend they didn't exist and to go back to living her life as if she were still nineteen, hell-bent on getting into trouble, uncaring of the consequences."

His gaze moved beyond me, fixed on something, and I could tell he was debating if he should say more. I'd learned from years of helping brides and grooms through jitters that sometimes people needed a push, whereas others needed silence to gather their thoughts.

With West, I suspected the latter.

I was rewarded when he finally spoke again. "Andrea and I had our troubles, for sure. I only married her because she got pregnant from a one-night stand. But not long after we married, she lost the baby."

He paused, pain flashing across his eyes, and my heart ached for him.

Just how many times had life turned to shit for him in his thirty-six years?

West's eyes moved back to his kids. "I did everything I could to try and be a good husband. For a short while, I even thought I loved her. But then she started hanging out again with people she knew from high school, and eventually, she started taking pills. After that, her focus became doing whatever it took to get her next fix, and I struggled to get her the help she needed. When she finally came to me, crying and asking me to forgive her for cheating on me, begging for me to help her, I said I'd get her into rehab, and then we'd talk once she was sober."

His gaze moved from his kids to the sky, to watch the bird flying overhead. "For a while after she got clean, it was almost nice. She tried to get to know me, and I did the same, as if we were truly dating for the first time. It even got to the point where she suggested we try for a baby again. Discovering we were having twins was a big fucking surprise, and yet I was a goner as soon as I held them that first day. Andrea, however, soon realized that being a parent was a lot of work, and she fell back into her old ways. And unlike the time before, she never came to me for help. In fact, she rejected any offer I made." His gaze met mine. "I fucking tried, Emmy. I swear I did. But no matter what I did, or how many times I brought her home, Andrea didn't want my help. I don't know if she felt trapped—her parents would've cut her off completely if she'd divorced me—or that she didn't like how the twins took so much of my attention and was jealous. Either way, she started drinking in addition to the pills, and slept with so many guys I lost count. The last straw was when she came home wasted one night and I woke up to find her holding our screaming three-year-old son out a second-story window, laughing as she was about to drop him. After that, I was done."

He paused a second, as if reliving that terrifying moment, and I wanted to cry. Wyatt wasn't even my kid, but the thought of someone try to hurt him made me want to kill that person.

Oh god, and what if Wyatt still remembered it?

West cleared his throat and continued, "I told her parents I wanted out. I'd done what I could, but clearly, Andrea wasn't going to change unless she wanted to. Not to mention she was a danger to my son and daughter. But instead of admitting their daughter needed support and help with her addiction problems, they threatened to take my kids away from me if I tried to leave."

"What? How could they do that?"

He shrugged. "They have powerful friends in the area—both judges and law enforcement—and I knew it wasn't just an idle threat. No, they could probably make it a reality. So I stayed on the condition Andrea lived in one of her parents' rental places and away from the kids, only seeing them under supervised visits. Once Andrea got herself killed by going home with a drunk driver, I still stayed for my kids' sake, afraid the Grenvilles would pull strings and get full custody." Anger flashed in his eyes as he spit out, "But once they threatened to send them away to some boarding school, I said fuck it. Let them try to get custody, but I wasn't putting up with their shit any longer. My aunt had reached out to me by that point anyway, and I took the lifeline. I didn't care if I had to grovel to my family. I wanted my kids out of that toxic place. And so we came here."

He fell silent and kept his gaze averted. Probably a good thing because I wasn't sure if I wanted to cry or cuss out his in-laws. But I knew one thing for sure and said softly, "You're a good man, Weston Wolfe."

His blue eyes found mine, full of surprise.

"It's true."

"But you hate me."

"I hated how you abandoned your family. They're wonderful, and loving, and still alive..."

My voice died as I did my best not to cry. Damn it, why had I said that to him?

West moved toward me, but then Avery shouted, "Daddy, will you blow up the other ring? Wyatt won't share his!"

I dared a glance over at West, and he looked torn between pressing me on my comment and going to his kids. Doing my best to smile and put on a strong face, I nodded toward the twins. "Go. I have some things I need to do anyway."

Before he could say a word, I hefted myself up and out of the pool, grabbed my towel, and dashed into the house.

I knew it was cowardly, especially after West had shared so much with me.

But I'd be damned if I broke down in front of him again, let alone his kids. After all, it sounded like the twins had suffered enough in their past and didn't need any of my baggage added to their lives.

Not that I had a long-term future with them or West.

Because as much as I might dream of sharing West's bed, laughing with him and his kids, and maybe hoping for more, I wouldn't let it happen.

Love and laughter and family were for other people, not for me.

So after I showered and changed clothes, I went back to what mattered most to me—work and the ability to bring other people's dreams to life.

Chapter Twelve

Weston

Me: Thanks for letting us use your pool.
Emmy: You're welcome.
Me: Avery wants to bake cookies as a thank you.
Emmy: Okay.
Me: Is it all right for us to come over again soon?
Emmy: Any time.
Me: Will you help Avery again?
Emmy: I wish, but I'm really busy. Sorry.
Me: Okay. I'll make sure they don't leave a mess.
Emmy: Sounds good.
Me (typed but deleted): Are you okay, Emmy? I didn't mean to unload on you. I won't do it again.

. . .

Later that night, as I finished getting my kids ready for bed, my thoughts drifted back to Emmy and what I shared with her in the pool.

Who the fuck knew why I'd blabbered on, telling her about Andrea. I'd thought to leave all that behind in Ridgefield and hopefully move on.

But there was something about the woman that made me want to spill everything. I didn't know if it was because she was so kind to my kids or that she had a way about her that said she could keep secrets.

Regardless of the reason, I'd shared and now strangely felt lighter. As if sharing with her had made the past a little less painful.

More than ever, I wanted to ask about her parents or her brother and return the favor.

As I tried to convince myself it was a bad idea, Avery poked my side, garnering my attention. "You should take Emmy on a date."

I blinked, not sure how to answer that. "How do you know about dating?"

She rolled her eyes. "I'm not a baby. Half my friends back in Ridgefield had girlfriends and boyfriends. Jenna's mom told her all about how her dad had taken her to dinners and the movies and even to see pretty views in the car before he asked her to marry him. You should try that. Then Emmy will fall in love with you and marry you and stay with us."

Fuck, now I was in for it.

Clearing my throat, I did my best to keep my voice

calm. "I know you like Emmy, but she's just a friend. Well, more like family. I'm not going to date her, let alone marry her."

"But she makes you smile sometimes, Daddy. And I know she likes us. She even said she was proud of me today."

"She did?"

She nodded. "Yep. She's also nice and smart and always has the best snacks."

"Snacks are not a reason to date someone, no matter how good they are."

Wyatt spoke up. "No. But she's sad a lot. I think she's lonely and needs us."

I peered over at my son, trying to figure out how a ten-year-old would notice such things.

But then, Wyatt had always been the quiet, more observant one.

Still, the perceptiveness of my kids was terrifying. Because now I wondered just how much they'd noticed about their mother and me, despite my best attempts to hide the worst of it.

Avery added, "She's pretty too. Don't you want to kiss her?"

"What the hell do you know about kissing?"

"Bad word, Daddy. But I'm not a baby, remember? One boy kissed me last year, when I asked him to."

Part of me wanted to go back to Ridgefield to find the boy who'd kissed my daughter and tell him to stop kissing girls until after his voice changed.

But I tamped down my anger since it wouldn't help anything. And after a deep breath, I replied, "You shouldn't kiss anyone that's not family until you're older."

"But even Disney characters kiss, Daddy. If I can watch it, I can do it."

Holy hell, Avery was getting better at arguing with me. I didn't look forward to her teenage years.

I stood. "By that logic, that means we should all go and toss lions off cliffs because it was in a Disney movie."

"Daddy, no! Don't mention that. That scene always makes me cry."

I kissed Avery's forehead. "Sorry, love. But I just wanted to make a point that we shouldn't do something just because it's in a movie. Do you see that now?"

She sighed and tugged the blankets up closer to under her chin. "I suppose."

"Good." I ruffled her head and she squealed.

Smiling, I turned toward Wyatt and kissed his forehead too. "Goodnight, Wyatt."

"G'night, Dad. And don't worry, I won't toss lions off cliffs."

I snorted. "Good to know."

After flicking off the lights, I closed the door.

I was just about to head to my room when Beck came down the hall. He took one look at me and snorted. "What happened?"

"Apparently, my daughter is already kissing boys, and both of my children are giving me dating advice."

Beck's lips twitched. "It was bound to happen eventually." I growled, and he smacked me on the shoulder. "You look like you could use a drink. Sabrina's away tonight for a business trip, so how about we head to The Watering Hole?"

The Watering Hole was the bar for locals in Starry Hills, on the outskirts of town. Even in high-tourist season, it remained mostly free of out-of-towners.

Since Aunt Lori would keep an ear out for my kids, I nodded. "Let me talk to Aunt Lori about watching the twins, and we can go."

"If you text her, it'll make her day."

"Why? She went on and on about not seeing me, and now she wants me to use my phone instead?"

Rolling his eyes, Beck shrugged. "It's fun for her. And besides, maybe she'll leave me the fuck alone if you amuse her for a little while."

I glared at my little brother, and he took out his phone. "I could always start a group text with you, me, her, and Millie."

There was a devious glint in Beck's eye I didn't like.

"Fine. I'll fucking do it."

I took out my phone and decided to make it as boring as possible:

Me: I'm going to the bar with Beck. Can you watch my kids?

Aunt Lori: <smiling face with hearts emoji> <heart emoji> <party popper emoji>

Me: ???

Aunt Lori: I'm so happy you're joining the 21st

century! Time to celebrate! <wine glass emoji> <fireworks emoji>
Me: I've texted you before.
Aunt Lori: Oh, that's right. When you were afraid to swim at Millie's place. <smirking emoji>
Me: I wasn't afraid. So will you watch them?
Aunt Lori: <sighing emoji> I've work to do with you yet. But yes, I'll watch the twins. Have fun. <beer mug emoji>

Lowering my phone, I sighed. "How the fuck is that fun?"

Beck laughed and pushed me toward the stairs. "Hey, it's not for me to say. But it makes our aunt happy, so why not?" He narrowed his eyes. "But if you ever fucking tell her I said that, I'll take you outside and dump your butt in the horse trough."

"I was the one who did that to your stubborn ass. You couldn't lift me if you tried."

Beck raised an eyebrow. "Why? Getting fat, old man?"

"It's all muscle, brother. And you're not strong enough to handle it."

Beck rolled his eyes. "Let's go before this turns into a childhood tussle and Aunt Lori takes us by the ears again."

We made our way out the door and into Beck's truck. Even if he wasn't as chatty as Zach, Beck more than filled the silence, letting me stew in my own thoughts.

While I rarely did so, getting a little drunk sounded like a great plan for the night. My daughter wasn't the little girl I still thought her to be. Soon she'd be dating and doing more than kissing, and before I knew it, she'd be moving in with a partner and maybe even having kids of her own.

At the thought of being a grandfather, I decided a little oblivion for the night sounded fucking wonderful.

A short time later, we walked into The Watering Hole and headed toward the bar. The familiar weathered wood and collection of road signs and pictures on the wall reminded me of home for some reason. Even though I'd been too young to drink when I'd left Starry Hills, I'd been spending more time here with my brothers since returning, shooting the shit and beating them at pool.

Once we each had a beer and ordered a plate of nachos to share, we sat down and Beck asked, "So what kind of dating advice did your kids give you?"

I scowled. After Beck not bringing it up in the truck, I thought he'd dropped it. "You're annoying, you know."

Beck shrugged. "And yet, Sabrina loves me. Sometimes I wonder why, but she does all the same."

He got that goofy look on his face, that of a guy in love, and I grumbled, "Do you have to be so damned happy all the time?"

"Yep," Beck said before taking a swig from his beer bottle.

"Then maybe we should play pool so I can destroy and humiliate you."

Just as Beck was about to reply, he stopped, and his gaze fixated on something near the door. I glanced over and mentally cursed.

What the fuck were Emmy, Abby, Katie, and Amber doing here? "I thought they met for tea at the bakery or some such shit."

Beck shrugged. "They're twenty-five, West, not fifteen. I'm sure they get cocktails and laugh over stuff from time to time."

Hearing their ages should've reminded me of yet another reason not to stare at Emmy and lust after her—she was more than a decade younger than me.

And yet, my eyes still latched on to her. She wore tight-fitting dark-blue jeans and a black tank top, and her hair was pulled back into a ponytail. The clothing revealed every curve and valley of her body, and the final piece of torture? Black cowboy boots.

Fuck, she was like my fantasy come to life.

"You might want to wipe that drool from your chin, brother."

I tore my gaze from Emmy and glared at Beck. "You're annoying as fuck, asshole."

"And you love me anyway." He stood. "Come on. I'm feeling lucky tonight and plan to beat your butt at pool."

Needing the distraction, I stood, and we headed over

to the empty pool table. Maybe I'd catch a break and Emmy and the BFF Circle wouldn't notice I was here.

I ordered another beer and concentrated on the game. Yes, beating my brother was the most important thing right now. Because then I wouldn't stare at Emmy, walk over, and make a fool of myself.

Chapter Thirteen

Emilia

Katie: Let's celebrate Amber's news at The Watering Hole tonight! <martini emoji>
Amber: Hey! I haven't shared that yet with Millie and Abby.
Katie: Oops. <sweat drop emoji>
Amber: <sighing emoji>
Me: What news? I'm hurt Katie knows but I don't. <crying emoji>
Amber: She came into the bakery, and you know how she is.
Katie: <grinning emoji> Sorry not sorry.
Abby: Well? I might have to friendly-kidnap you if you don't spill.

Katie: Hey! I want to friendly-kidnap first. <pouting emoji>
Me: What is friendly-kidnapping?
Amber: Stop with the friendly-kidnapping! My stepmom is finally giving me the bakery.
Me: Congrats! <party popper emoji> <martini emoji>
Katie: The Watering Hole then? I promise not to try and friendly-kidnap any of you tonight too.
Me, Amber, and Abby: <sighing emoji>

I noticed West as soon as we entered The Watering Hole but did my best to avoid his eye.

A few months ago, it would've been easy to ignore him and pretend he didn't exist. And yet, it took everything I had not to stare at him as he bent over a pool table, his jeans highlighting a very firm, round butt. A butt I itched to dig my fingers into to keep him close as he fucked me.

Stop it right now.

While Amber would never have brought it up—after all, she hated being teased about Zach Wolfe—Katie had no problem whistling and then saying, "That's the finest ass I've seen in a while. Don't you agree, Millie?"

It was on the tip of my tongue to both deny it and ask her to call me Emmy, but I resisted. Instead, I sipped my margarita before saying, "You said the same thing about that tourist you flirted with last week, when you were giving a tour of your family's place. The one who bent over to pick up something and who you shamelessly checked out."

The Evans family had award-winning cheeses and not only had samplings but also had tours of their dairy farm. Katie usually gave the latter since she had a natural talent for putting on a show.

Katie finally forced her gaze from West's behind and looked at me, grinning. "Well, he was hot and I couldn't resist. But a week ago seems like forever."

"What, do you count how fast or slow a day goes by how many sexy guys you see during it?"

Katie tapped her chin. "That'd be an amazing way to judge how good my week is. Maybe I'll start taking a tally."

She waggled her eyebrows, clearly joking, and we all burst out laughing.

Amber finally spoke up. "That wouldn't work for me, though. I suck at flirting. Not to mention I'd die before I'd ever ask a guy to bend over for me."

Katie clicked her tongue. "Drop something and casually ask him to pick it up. I do it all the time."

After a few more sips of my drink, my tongue was a little looser, and I jumped in. "It wouldn't work for me either. Even if some of the groomsmen are pretty hot, they're usually in coats, and it covers everything."

Abby snorted. "Except for that one wedding, where everyone wore Star Trek uniforms. After seeing just about *everything* during the ceremony, I suddenly became a huge fan of sci-fi weddings."

I laughed, remembering the black pants and black-

and-colored tops. Some of them had been on the tighter side, for sure. "I was mostly a sucker for the shoulders."

Katie leaned in. "Like broad shoulders, do you?" She glanced back over at West, bit her bottom lip, and all of the sudden, I wanted to tell her to stop checking him out.

As soon as I was about to say something, I held my tongue. *Shit.* West wasn't mine, would never be, and I shouldn't care if Katie eyed him like a piece of meat from now until eternity.

So I drained my drink and ordered another.

Katie studied me, and a sense of unease fell over me. I asked, "What are you planning now?"

"Who said I was planning anything?" Amber, Abby, and I all shook our heads, and Katie asked, "What?"

I replied, "You get this glint in your eye right before you do something that will probably be outrageous, embarrassing, or both."

Katie shrugged. "Life's too short to care what people think of you."

The words might seem lighthearted to most, but I knew there was more to it. Once upon a time, Katie had been more reserved and determined not to stick out. She'd always been curvy, had developed big boobs early, and had been endlessly teased for it. That was around the time she'd started acting out, and I thought she did it to distract people and take control of what they said about her.

I decided to steer the conversation back on track. "Anyway, I thought we came out tonight to celebrate Amber taking over the bakery." I raised my glass to her.

"Well deserved and about time. You're a way better baker than your stepmom."

The others followed suit with their glasses and cheered.

Amber's cheeks turned bright pink. "I don't know about that. My brothers are already taking bets about how long I'll last."

Katie growled, "Your brothers are assholes."

Amber shrugged. "They're still young. I'm sure they'll grow up eventually."

Katie looked about ready to argue, so I jumped in. "Ladies, we need to celebrate with more than just drinks. How about some dancing?"

Amber shook her head while Katie and Abby nodded.

I said, "Oh, come on, Amber. You know you want to. Let me just pick some songs from the jukebox, and we can all dance together as a group. If we're lucky, some guys will come join us."

I drained the last of my second margarita and headed toward the jukebox. I was definitely buzzed. Otherwise, I never would've suggested this. Not many people danced at The Watering Hole. But I wanted to not only forget about West and his fine ass and shoulders in the corner, but also help Amber let go a little.

After selecting three songs, I ordered a round of shots at the bar and brought them back to my table. I set the tequila and lime wedges in front of each of us. "For courage."

Once we each finished the salt-tequila-lime process,

Abby snorted. "You'd better slow down, or you're going to pass out soon, Millie."

It had to be the alcohol that made me blurt, "Emmy."

Abby frowned. "What?"

"Call me Emmy, like when we were kids."

The three ladies all shared glances, but it was Amber who spoke first. "Of course, if that's what you want. But why the change?"

The tequila shot had made me cross over into tipsy, and I shrugged. "I don't want to sound like an old auntie, knitting bad scarves, and surrounded by dog statues."

Well, that wasn't the real reason, but it was the only one I'd give.

Amber moved to my side and laid a hand on my shoulder. "Are you all right, Millie? I mean, Emmy? Maybe we should take you home."

I shook my head. The former song finished, and the first from my queue came up. I grabbed Amber's hand. "Come on, let's dance."

I tugged her with me, knowing the other two would follow.

It took some coaxing, but soon I had Amber attempting to dance—more like sidestepping in place and swinging her arms—along with Katie and Abby. Moving my hips and swaying my body, as if I didn't have a care in the world, I felt powerful and free.

I'd always loved dancing but usually didn't let myself do it. Because I wasn't supposed to be happy and enjoying life, only helping others do so. It was my penance.

But the drinks had made me forget about what I'd done, who I'd hurt, and all that mattered in the moment was the music and letting go of everything for a little while.

Chapter Fourteen

Weston

I lost the pool game to Beck. Not because he was suddenly a better player, but because I couldn't concentrate on anything but stealing glances at Emmy on the other side of the room.

By the time she walked to the jukebox—a little unsteady—and then dragged her friends to the floor to dance, I'd given up any pretext of not watching her.

Because, fuck, her moving to the music and swaying her hips was so goddamn erotic, it almost hurt.

And as I noticed other men staring at her, it took everything I had not to go around and tell them to look away.

As I clenched my hands into fists, Beck spoke, and I

nearly jumped. "She's been stealing glances at you too. What's going on with you two?"

I somehow tore my gaze away from Emmy's tempting hips and ass. "Nothing."

Beck raised his eyebrows. "Bullshit."

"It's true. Besides, I'm done with women. I won't risk putting my kids through hell again."

Beck studied me a second before replying, "I've watched Millie grow up over the last fifteen years, once Mom was made her guardian. From what little I knew of your wife, Millie is about as opposite from that woman as you can get."

I grunted, not wanting to answer. I already knew that, of course, but I wouldn't admit it. Because that might feel like giving myself permission.

Beck said, "Fine, close off and scowl until your face freezes that way." His gaze turned deadly serious. "But if you fucking hurt her West, I don't care if you're my brother. I'll cut off your balls and stuff them down your throat."

I raised one eyebrow. "Really? You couldn't come up with something more original?"

"You know what I mean." Beck's expression softened a little. "I won't meddle like Aunt Lori, but I will say this—it's okay to take time for yourself sometimes, West. I may not have kids, but I struggled to do anything but work until recently. And thank fuck I made room for Sabrina, or I might never have found the happiness I have now. So, tell me—what would Weston Wolfe the man do right now if he wasn't burdened by his past?"

I'd ask Emmy to dance and make sure she got home

safe. Maybe even steal a kiss, depending on how sober she was—I'd never take advantage of her like that.

I sure as hell wouldn't be standing here, eye-fucking her and wishing every guy in the bar to hell for looking at her.

There was a squeal, and I turned, only to see Emmy crash to the floor. Without thinking, I rushed over and squatted down near her, next to Abby.

"Are you okay, Emmy?" my sister asked Emmy.

For a second, I frowned, wondering when Abby had started calling her by her old nickname. However, as soon as Emmy spoke, I focused solely on her.

"Fine. I'm fine. Help me up. I want to dance."

Her words were a little slurred, and for a second, I was transported back to memory after memory of my late wife being in the same state, often in the lap of another guy when I found her, and telling me to fuck off when I tried to take her home.

Amber's no-nonsense voice snapped me back to the present. "I think it's time for you to go home. Give me your keys, Emmy."

"They're in my purse."

I knew Amber would see her home safe. The woman was practical, never did anything to excess, and probably had been drinking more water than alcohol. And yet, the urge for me to see after Emmy myself was so fucking strong. I'd only had two beers—despite my original intent to get drunk—and I could drive.

"Emmy." Her gaze met mine, and she smiled warmly, the kind of look she'd never have given me sober.

And fuck, if the look didn't shoot straight to my dick.

She leaned over and patted my cheek. "West. When I drop my keys, you should pick them up."

I frowned, but Katie laughed. I glanced at her, but she shook her head. "Don't ask."

"Fine. But get out of the way, all of you." I growled for good measure.

Abby rolled her eyes, now back with Emmy's purse. "You could just ask nicely."

Ignoring my sister, I carefully scooped Emmy into my arms. She instantly put her hands at the back of my neck, and once I stood, she stared at me, smiling again. "You're so strong. I knew it, with shoulders like that."

Her fingers played with the edge of my hairline, each pass sending a rush of heat and longing through me. Because, fuck, I wondered what her fingers would feel like on my chest, my arms, and even gripping my ass as I took her.

Stop it. She was drunk, and I was a fucking gentleman, despite my grumpy exterior.

I looked at Abby. "If you can unlock the car, I'll put her in and drive her home. Are all of you coming too?"

Abby opened her mouth, but Katie beat her to it. "Nope. We're staying a little longer." Both Amber and Abby blinked, but Katie kept going. "My brother, Kyle, owes me a favor, and he can come get us. Just make sure Emmy gets home safe, okay?"

"Of course I will."

Beck's voice came from behind me. "I'd go with you, but I need the truck tomorrow and can't leave it here overnight. But I can take any of you girls home, if you want."

They all murmured yes, and soon, Abby was leading me to Emmy's car. Luckily, it was an SUV so I could easily slide her into the front seat. Once I had her seat belt on, I closed the door and faced Abby.

My sister handed me the keys and Emmy's purse. "Her bedroom is on the second floor, the first door on the right. Text me once she's safe."

I grunted.

Abby studied me a second and then smiled. "You're a good man, West. I wasn't sure when you first came back, but there's no doubt now." She kissed my cheek before I could say a word and then stepped back. "Goodnight."

My little sister left, and I merely watched her for a second. The longer I'd stayed away from Starry Hills, the more I'd worried how my family would view me. Would it be hate? Disappointment? Disgust at being a coward?

Maybe they felt some of those things, but more and more I wondered if I could mend the rift between me and my siblings after all.

The horn beeped, and I jumped. Emmy grinned from her passenger's window and waved.

Seeing her so free and letting down her guard made me wish I could help her be like this always. Maybe I could even help ease whatever burdens she carried.

Not your problem, not your job.

Before she could honk the horn again, I slid into the other side and started the car.

Emmy patted my arm and said, "'Bout time. I'm ready for bed."

I glanced over, only to see her lean her head against the window and close her eyes. Just how many drinks had she consumed? I'd never seen her like this at any of the family dinners, and we always had wine.

And even though the situation brought back memories, I knew this wasn't the same as with my late wife. For one, Emmy hadn't argued or cursed me out. I also knew she was too fucking busy with her weddings and shit to go out on benders night after night.

As she started to snore softly, the streetlights highlighted her face, and my chest ached. I wanted to caress her cheek and nose and the softness of her bottom lip until I memorized every feature. Then I'd move her over to lean against me, wrap my arms around her, and keep her safe. Always.

She could be mine, if I wanted.

What, what the fuck? No. I was taking care of her because she was close to my family and my kids liked her, and for no other reason. None at all.

Tearing my gaze from her face, I reversed out of the parking spot and turned onto the street. The entire drive, I kept my eyes on the road lest my thoughts turn dangerous again.

After arriving at her house, I slowly maneuvered her out of the car and into my arms again. She'd barely woken up to help me, but within seconds, she laid her head on my shoulders and snored softly.

The weight of her, the feel of her heat against me, and her soft breaths against my neck only made me hold her closer. I might have even leaned down to prop my head against hers, closed my eyes, and pretended for a second that my life had ended up with this woman instead of Andrea.

With a woman who was kind and generous. A woman who encouraged my children instead of ignoring them.

A woman who'd let me take care of her while also being a true partner, one I could share anything with, just like back in the pool.

Since my thoughts were dangerous, I opened my eyes and slowly packed away my longing and desire and wants. Unlike when I was younger, I had children to think of. And I simply couldn't risk them getting hurt if I dated and things went badly.

All I could take were a few stolen moments and nothing more.

I carried Emmy to her room and laid her on the bed. But as I tried to untangle her arms, she only tightened them and murmured, "No. Don't go."

"No, Emilia, I can't stay. Now, let go, love. Please."

She must've heard me because I got free of her right after that. And once her shoes were off, I tucked her into bed and moved a trash can near the mattress, just in case.

I lingered for a few seconds, brushing the hair from her forehead, and wondered what it would feel like to crawl into bed and simply hold her. To wake up and take care of her hangover while also making fun of her for drinking too much.

To have Avery try to cheer her up while Wyatt went

to pick her some flowers and make her smile in his own way.

My thoughts were in fucking dangerous territory, so I hurried from the room and locked up, leaving the keys in a secret spot. I texted Abby to let her know Emmy was safe and where to find the keys and then walked home in the moonlight.

All the while remembering how it'd felt to have Emilia Mendoza in my arms, her heat and scent surrounding me, and her trusting me to look after her. For once, I wished I didn't have a shit-ton of baggage and trust issues weighing me down.

But even if I weren't so damn cynical, my kids were my everything, and I couldn't risk the tentative happiness I'd created for them, not even for someone as kind and smart and beautiful as Emmy.

No matter how much I wished it could be different.

Chapter Fifteen

Emilia

Katie: So what happened last night after you left the bar?
Me: Nothing. And don't you dare call me right now. I have the hangover from hell.
Katie: Then give me some details. I didn't arrange for him to drive you home alone for nothing.
Me: I remember a drive and then I woke up in my bed.
Katie: Alone?
Me: Yes, alone!
Katie: Damn. What a waste.
Me: Go away.
Katie: Someone's grumpy this morning. Next time, no tequila for you.

Me: I'm not going to drink it ever again. <puking emoji>
Katie: That's what you said last time. <laughing emoji>

As I finally trudged into the kitchen the next morning, my head throbbing as if a thousand tiny hammers were pounding nails into my skull, I found Abby with a cup of coffee and her tablet. She looked up at me and grinned. Her voice was extra loud as she said, "Good morning, sunshine."

I scowled, gave her the finger, and went to the coffeepot. "You're too damn loud."

Abby turned toward me, amusement in her eyes. "When did you become such a lightweight?"

I grunted, blew on the coffee in my cup, and took a sip. It wasn't nearly enough, but the hot liquid helped a little. "I usually only drink wine these days. And tequila always hits me hard."

I swallowed more coffee, and more, until it was nearly gone. After pouring another cup, I went to the kitchen table and sat down, laying my head on my arms.

Seriously, kill me now. I must be getting old, since I never had this problem in my late teens and early twenties.

Abby asked, "What do you remember about last night?"

As I tried to piece it all together, I mentally scolded

myself. I was too old to drink to the point of fuzzy memories anymore.

Then something about asking West to pick up my keys entered my brain. I groaned. Had I really asked him that?

"That sounds like you remembered something. Maybe about wanting to see my brother bend over so you could stare at his ass?"

I groaned again. I really had done that. "I remember West being there, dancing, and not much else. According to Katie, he took me home."

"Yep. West was the one who brought you home. He even carried you in his arms like some kind of hero."

It all rushed back to me—him carrying me, the feel of his warm, solid chest against my side, me touching him more than I should have.

"He's also the one who put you to bed."

I looked up. "Really?" She nodded, and I sighed. "It's going to be super embarrassing the next time I see him, then."

For a blessed minute, Abby was silent, and I thought she'd drop it. But then she had to speak again. "Do you want to hear my opinion about why you drank so much last night?"

I sighed, rubbing my temples. "Please spare me the two psychology classes you took in college."

She stuck out her tongue. "I've learned more since then. But regardless, I think alcohol gave you permission to be a version of yourself that we don't usually see, the one who'd probably be around if you ever forgave yourself."

I met her eyes and saw her concern. Years ago I had let slip to Abby about how I felt guilty for living when my parents had died. I'd refused to go into detail, but the damage had been done.

My silence didn't stop Abby, though. She pushed. "I know you won't listen to me about the crash and your feelings on it, but let me say this—I think you like my brother. Maybe more than a little. And it's okay, Emmy. If you don't give him a chance, you might regret it."

It was on the tip of my tongue to say it wasn't okay, for so many reasons. However, the doorbell rang, and I clutched my head. "Get that before I have to hurt someone."

Abby chuckled and went to answer the door. Soon Avery dashed inside, her brother right behind her.

But there was no sign of West.

Pushing aside the sting of disappointment, I smiled at the little girl. Avery stopped in front of me and held out a small paper bag. "This will help, my daddy said. He couldn't come today, but he wanted to make sure you'd feel better soon."

I gingerly took the bag, but before I could look inside, Wyatt walked up to me and held up a bunch of orange lilies, one of my favorites. "Dad asked Auntie Lori what flowers you liked, and then went and got these. I was super careful not to squish them too."

Taking the flowers, I tried not to read too much into West asking about my favorite anything. He probably just wanted to keep up his pool privileges.

I smiled at Wyatt. "Thank you. The bright orange

just screams happy to me, and I already feel better. You did an awesome job not squishing them too."

He beamed at me, and my heart warmed.

Avery gestured toward the bag. "Look inside!"

I did and took out some ibuprofen and a few sticks of hydration drink mixes.

As I stared at the get-well gifts and tightened my fingers around the lilies, I struggled not to cry. Why had West done all of this? He couldn't truly be interested in anything with me, could he?

No. He was just a nice guy. Yes, that had to be it.

Avery spoke up again. "You have to mix the packets with water. Me and Wyatt have them sometimes, when it's really hot outside. But Daddy said it should work for your illness too. Although I hope it's not too bad. I had strep throat once, and I thought I'd die."

I took Avery's hand and squeezed gently. "No, it's nothing serious. I'll be better soon, especially after taking what your dad sent me."

"Good." Avery leaned over and whispered, "I didn't know if we could swim today or not, but I wore my bathing suit under my clothes, just in case. I know you're really busy, but I'm going to do that every day until you have some free time, and you can give me another swimming lesson."

How this girl's mother could have ignored her and not loved her fiercely, I had no idea. Because I'd only known Avery briefly, and I already felt like I'd kick the ass of anyone who dared to hurt her.

Not wanting to think about the significance of that thought, I smiled and said, "Let me see how I'm feeling this afternoon. Oh, and did Wyatt bring anything to swim in?"

Wyatt sat with Abby, showing her pictures on his phone. He really did love taking pictures of animals and scenery. I wondered if his dad had thought of getting him an inexpensive digital camera.

Wait, no. These weren't my kids. I needed to remember that.

Avery replied, "Yeah, he has swim shorts on. I think it's so unfair that boys can just wear regular-looking clothes for bathing suits. Mine always goes up my butt, and I hate it."

I bit my lip to keep from laughing. "There are girl ones with shorts these days, or some types that are better at staying in place. I'll show you later, once I'm dressed and feeling better, and maybe I'll get you one. Because I know how much it sucks to get a swimsuit wedgie."

Avery threw her arms around my neck, and I hugged her back, the contact somehow helping my hangover, which wasn't exactly scientific, but I didn't care.

Once she pulled away, she said, "Get better, Emmy. I don't like it when you don't feel well."

My throat closed up with emotion. "You have a kind heart, just like your dad."

"Yep. He pretends to be grumpy, but he's not, really." She looked over at her brother. "Come on, Wyatt. Emmy needs to rest so maybe she can take us swimming later."

The little boy gave me a tentative smile before following his sister out the back door and into the children's play area I used for my business.

Abby sat across from me. "Hmm, why would West send you a care package?"

"He probably just feels sorry for me after carrying my butt up the stairs."

Snorting, Abby picked up her coffee and drank the last of it. "Maybe. The wedding expo should be interesting."

Oh, damn. I'd temporarily forgotten about that.

About us working together, in close quarters, for days in a row.

At least the expo wasn't for ten days. Between preparing for that and the Summer Star Festival—which was the week after the expo—I had plenty to keep me busy and away from Weston Wolfe.

Not only because it'd be embarrassing to face him after he'd carried me into the house, but I might also go all soft and starry-eyed at him. And if he gave the slightest indication he was interested, like Abby hinted, I might cave and let him kiss me.

And I couldn't do that. Ever. Because eventually I'd hurt him and his kids, and I'd rather die than do that.

I just had to make sure Wyatt and Avery were always around, and we were never alone.

Yes, that was the safest way to go.

So after putting the flowers in some water and then mixing the hydration drink, I thought of everything I needed to do in the next couple weeks and how I'd be too busy for Wolfe family dinners, let alone spending one-on-one time with West.

Chapter Sixteen

Weston

Aunt Lori: Make sure to have some fun over the next three days in Reno. <dancing emoji> <beer emoji> <tiger emoji>
Me: ???
Aunt Lori: Let your hair down and go get 'em tiger.
Me: ...
Aunt Lori: <crying emoji> You're no fun. Give me something.
Me: <thumbs up emoji>
Aunt Lori: How rude! <sighing emoji>
Me: <thumbs up emoji> <smiley face emoji>

Somehow I managed to avoid being alone with Emmy for ten whole days. I was polite enough and didn't purposely try to be an asshole, but after having her in my arms and feeling her warm body against me, I'd had way too many fucking dreams about her.

One where she was on her hands and knees, with me gently tugging her hair and claiming her sweet pussy from behind.

One where she sat on my face and I drove her crazy with my tongue and teeth and fingers until she fell apart, screaming my name, and I lapped up her orgasm liked a starved man.

One where she slept half on my chest, her soft breaths dancing across my skin, and I held her in my arms, hugging her tight against me, as if she were the most precious thing in the world.

Of them all, the last had scared me the most. Because having erotic dreams and waking up to jerk off some steam was one thing. Hell, I'd been doing that since I was a teen.

But the idea of wanting to cuddle in bed with a woman, to maybe imagine having more with her than hot, sweaty sex, made me both wish for it and know I could never have it. At least not until my kids were grown, when I wouldn't have to worry about protecting their hearts from yet more rejection.

As I drove up to Reno, Nevada, where the wedding expo was being held, I tapped my thumbs against the steering wheel and tried to think of how I could avoid being alone with Emmy for the next three days.

Idiot. I couldn't, plain and simple. I had to help set up her booth, for one thing. Plus, I was sure Emmy and Abby would want to hang out for dinner at some point, and if I said no, Abby would start asking questions.

I arrived at the hotel and spotted Emmy's car in the parking lot. The place was only about half full since a lot of exhibitors wouldn't arrive until the next morning.

I grabbed my luggage and went inside to the reception area, where I noticed Emmy politely arguing with the front desk person. I may not want to be alone with her, but something was upsetting her, and I couldn't just abandon her. I walked up and she looked at me, frustration plain on her face, and I raised my brows. "What's wrong?"

She huffed. "They can't find my reservation."

The front desk employee said politely, "I'm sorry, Ms. Mendoza. I've checked and double-checked, but there's nothing under your name. And we're completely booked up for the wedding expo. I can call around to see if I can find something else, but I don't know if anything will be free nearby."

Emmy's expression was a combination of frustration and worry. I didn't like it.

I may not be able to wipe away her tears or crawl into bed with her, but I could certainly try to help. But first, I needed to check something.

I asked the front desk person, "Do you have a reservation for Weston Wolfe?"

The employee typed on their computer, nodded,

and looked at me. "Yes, a queen-sized bed for three nights."

"Can I switch it to two twin beds instead?"

The employee did some more typing but then shook his head. "Sorry, Mr. Wolfe. It's possible you could wait and see if anyone would be able to switch with you, but..."

"It's unlikely they would."

The employee shrugged.

I glanced at Emmy, but she didn't meet my eye. No doubt she was thinking what I was—that we could share my room, but there was only one bed.

My dick screamed yes, take it and then find a way to finally thrust into her hot, wet pussy and make her scream in pleasure.

However, the head on my shoulders asked the employee, "Are there any cots available to set up in the room?"

More typing. "Yes, I can do that."

I let out a mental sigh. Being in the same room as her would be fucking torture, but at least she wouldn't be mere inches away from me. "Then do that. Ms. Mendoza will need a room key too."

"Are you sure, West? I can always see if Abby's friend has somewhere for me to sleep too."

"It's up to you, of course. But I know you, and you'll want to get an early start tomorrow. But Abby may not, given she hasn't seen her friend in a while."

She bit her bottom lip, and it took everything I had to keep my gaze fixed on her eyes. She eventually sighed. "You're right. We'll have to share."

After finally meeting my gaze, she searched my eyes. I noticed nervousness and worry and...guilt? Why the fuck was there guilt?

I wasn't about to ask her in the middle of the reception area. Once we got our keys, I took her luggage for her—she tried to protest, but I wasn't having it—and we headed for the elevators. Silence stretched for the entire walk. But after the elevator doors closed and we were alone, she blurted, "Are you sure about this?"

I did my best not to scowl. "Yes, it's fine. I'll sleep on the cot, and you can have the bed. But maybe just give me a bathroom schedule, so I can shower before you get ready."

"I'll take the cot."

"No, you won't."

"But, West—"

"No buts. Let me be a gentleman, Emmy."

She bit her lip again and finally blew out a breath. "Fine. But I'm buying you dinner."

Shit, that meant we'd be eating dinner together. Maybe even alone. Like on a date.

I nearly laughed at that. I mean, we were going to share a room, for fuck's sake. I'd hear her breathing while asleep or I might wake up to her taking a shower. Which would only stir my imagination for what she looked like as water cascaded down her naked body, a drop lingering on her nipple, begging to be licked off.

Dinner was nothing compared to that.

The elevator doors opened. We walked down the hall until we stopped in front of our room and stared. It was almost as if we were about to cross some barrier, one we'd both tried to keep in place and failed.

Deciding I was being ridiculous, I inserted the card, opened the door, and gestured for Emmy to enter. I followed close behind her until she stopped near the bed, and I almost bumped into her.

She probably noticed the same thing I did—the bed took up most of the room, and there was barely a place to put a cot against the far wall, under where the TV hung on the wall.

Thank fuck for TVs being so thin these days. The giant boxes from my childhood would've taken up the space, meaning we'd have to share the bed.

Part of me wished for the old-school TVs.

Stop it. Not going to happen. I cleared my throat. "It's nice enough."

She went to the window, peeked out, and then finally faced me. Her expression was one I couldn't read, though. "I'm sorry, West. I really did book a room, I promise. I tried looking for the confirmation email, but I guess I deleted it."

Frowning, I stored the luggage on the little foldable stand things hotels always had. "Don't apologize. I plan to eat a huge-ass dinner, so it's not like you're going to be saving money in the end."

She laughed—a soft one, almost as if it'd caught her by surprise—and my day instantly became better.

You could try to make her laugh every day. Then you'd get to see that gorgeous smile all the time.

Emmy's voice cut through my thoughts. "Eat as much as you want. Truly. It's the least I can do."

She glanced away, and an awkward silence fell. It would be so easy to close the distance between us, wrap my arms around her from behind, and make her forget all about her worries.

But I couldn't do that.

The smart thing to do would be to keep up the awkwardness. The distance would keep us safe and stop me from doing anything stupid.

But as I watched her face, Emmy biting that lucky bottom lip again, I said fuck it. I could be friendly and still keep my dick in my pants. I couldn't promise my dreams wouldn't be dirty as hell, but I'd jerk off in the shower and be ready for the day, no one the wiser.

"What do you plan to do today?"

She blinked. "Um, what?"

I crossed my arms over my chest and leaned my shoulder against the wall. "We can't access the event space until early tomorrow morning. So what had you planned to do today?"

"I don't know. I just wanted to arrive before the rush and thought I could read or watch a movie or something."

I'd come early for the same reason since my tolerance for annoying people had its limit, and hotel check-ins always seemed to have a lot of them. But staying inside on a nice day wasn't in me. "I was going to drive down to Lake Tahoe, since it's an easy day trip from Reno. Have you been back since you were a kid, when both our families went together?"

I hadn't thought of that day in a long time. But I

remembered a little six-year-old girl smiling, chasing my sister, and swimming as if she were a fish.

That carefree girl's world hadn't yet crashed down around her. I wondered if any of her remained.

Emmy shook her head. "Only once. Abby and I went with Katie's family and stayed in a cabin, but that was more than ten years ago."

For a beat, I wondered what it would be like to book a cabin and stay for a few days with my kids and Emmy. They'd love that.

So would I, but I wasn't quite ready to admit that to myself. Not only because my heart had been stomped on before, but my mistake had also caused lasting damage to my children.

Not wanting to think of my late wife, I focused on the present and raised an eyebrow. "Want to come with me?"

She bit her lip again. I hoped it didn't turn raw from all the attention. I'd just have to find a way to make her less nervous around me.

"I-I don't know if I should."

"We could even brave the freezing-ass water, if you want. Or just hike or bike around it. I'm sure the sunset will be fucking gorgeous."

Damn, I was being chatty, wasn't I?

But as Emmy's eyes lit up at the mention of seeing the sunset, I decided being chatty for Emmy wasn't a chore. Not at all.

"I'd love that. Especially since..."

Her voice trailed off, and I grunted. "What? Just fucking tell me, Emmy."

She rolled her eyes at my tone, and my lips twitched. Being a grumpy asshole had chased away her nervousness.

"I love sunsets. I have pictures from the different places I've been, especially when I had to travel for my clients' weddings. But I never snapped one of Tahoe when I was younger. It's beautiful there, and I'd love to have that image to put in my office."

It was a small admission. And yet, hearing the words stirred an urgency inside me, as if I needed to do whatever the fuck it took to make sure she got that picture.

Maybe if my kids were here, they'd say something and distract me. But for the next three and a half days, they weren't. So I didn't have my usual buffer.

Which fucking terrified me.

"Then we'll get you one. Let's change, and I'll drive."

"What, you're saying I can't wear a sundress and flip-flips to go hiking?" she teased.

I snorted. "At least that's better than watching someone in high heels do it. I swear, if I see someone like that today, and they trip, I might temporarily forget to be a gentleman."

Emmy laughed. "I think that's allowed, from time to time, for stupidity."

We smiled at each other, and my heart warmed, forgetting all the reasons I should keep this woman at a distance.

Besides, merely spending the day with Emmy wasn't the same as my going down onto one knee again.

Clearing my throat, I went to my bag and took out

my hiking boots. "I'll clear out the rest of the stuff from my car while you get ready."

I left without another word and tried my best not to imagine Emmy stripping off her dress. Or how it'd fall to a puddle at her feet, revealing nothing underneath but her beautiful body.

Breasts I could cup, nipples I could pluck, and a pussy I could claim with my mouth, hands, and dick.

Blood rushed south, and I did my best to tame my erection. I couldn't let Emmy know how she affected me.

I unloaded the car and put everything into storage for tomorrow morning. As I waited, I ignored every reason I shouldn't spend so much time alone with Emmy today.

Because after hearing about how she wanted to add a Tahoe sunset to her wall, I couldn't back out. I wanted to make her smile and laugh and just be there for her when she was too stubborn to ask for help.

Fuck, it was almost like I wanted her to trust me and maybe even confide in me.

No. We were sort of friends now but nothing more. Being a dick to her was childish, and I wouldn't do that any longer.

However, the trick would be keeping my cock from noticing her and keeping my thoughts platonic.

Chapter Seventeen

Emilia

Abby: Are you free for lunch today? Stella's taking me to the best burrito place ever, according to her.
Me: Sorry, I can't.
Abby: Can't or won't? Are you drooling over a new book boyfriend? <overheated emoji>
Me: <eye roll emoji> You read the same books as me.
Abby: I know. That's why I can tease you! But a book boyfriend won't become real, no matter how much we want them to. Sigh.
Me: I'm not staying inside. I'm going on a day trip.
Abby: Where? Why didn't you invite me? <crying emoji>
Me: Well...

Abby: Spill. Otherwise, I'll unleash my inner Aunt Lori and go all naughty emojis on your ass. <peach emoji> See what I did there? <LMFAO emoji>
Me: <sighing emoji> Fine. Someone invited me.
Abby: Ooh, who! Tell me!
Me: West. And just shut up now.
Abby: <angel emoji> To be continued...

I wasn't sure why I agreed to go to Lake Tahoe with West. Yes, it was beyond gorgeous, and I'd wanted to go back for a while now. However, being alone with him for hours wasn't the best idea. Because if he started to show more of his softer side, the one that bought me my favorite flowers, my resistance would crumble.

Part of me wanted to give in. To touch West's hot, bare chest and run my hands over his muscled body. Maybe even as I rode him hard, digging my nails into his skin, watching his eyes flare with heat as I came around his cock.

Maybe he'd even then flip me over, hold my hips, and make me come all over again.

My cheeks heated as I changed clothes and laced my shoes. *You have to resist him. You can't get involved like that, for so many reasons.*

After a few deep breaths and fanning my cheeks, I grabbed my backpack and camera and went to meet

West at his car. I found him leaning against it, arms crossed, as he watched an airplane fly overhead.

Despite the years since the accident, the airplane reminded me of that day:

Mommy, Daddy, are we there yet? I want to see Rafe! Can you go faster? Please?

Hush, Emmy, sweetie. We'll be there soon.

Except we never made it to the airport.

West appeared in front of me, his brows drawn together. "Are you all right?"

I blinked and locked those memories up tight. "I'm fine. I just wondered if you were practicing poses for the upcoming Starry Wolfe wine photoshoot that Sabrina has planned."

His eyes narrowed, clearly aware I was lying my ass off, but thankfully, he didn't push. "Are you on Aunt Lori's side, saying we should pose shirtless?"

I snorted, having heard that discussion once during dinner. "If you have it, flaunt it, right? I'm sure you could make a new calendar—Winery Hunks of Sonoma, or something."

His lips twitched, and it made my heart rate kick up. West wasn't exactly a smiley person, so when he did—or nearly did—it was a big deal.

"Hunks? I haven't heard that word in a while."

"Well, you do have a few gray hairs, and I wanted to use words you'd understand."

His gaze turned heated, and I sucked in a breath. "There's something to be said about experience."

For a few seconds, we merely stared at each other, almost as if time stilled, and the rest of the world faded away. My heart thudded, and I wondered if his did the same.

Just what had experience taught him? Would he show me if I asked?

A car drove into the parking lot, snapping me back to the present. I pushed aside my dirty thoughts and asked, "Does your experience come from watching so much porn over the years that you think you know it all?"

"Haven't you ever tried reenacting a porn scenario, Emmy?"

My cheeks heated as I remembered one of the videos Katie had insisted I watch—she had no shame and zero fucks to give when it came to sex and orgasm fodder. The video had a producer needing to make extremely, extremely sure the woman was just what he wanted for the part. Her stripping and posing on command, him licking and lapping her clit and pussy and kissing every inch of her body before bending her over his desk and fucking her hard.

I pressed my legs together at the image of West doing that to me.

And it took every bit of strength I had not to glance at his crotch and see if he was thinking similar thoughts.

I finally found my voice. "No, I haven't. And if you think we're going to end up lost in the woods for days, with no hope of rescue, so we have no choice but to notice each other and go at it like rabbits, then you're going to be sorely disappointed."

I swore I heard West growl low in his throat. However, I turned and went to the passenger side of the car. "Are we going to Tahoe or not?"

My reaching for the door handle snapped him into action, and he rushed to open the door for me. Even if I knew Beck and Zach did this too, it felt different with West. Though who the hell knew why.

Once we were in the car, West got us on the road and switched on the radio. He had some alternative rock playing, and I smiled. "What? No country music?"

"I used to like it, but that was my mom's thing."

He didn't say anything else, but I filled in the rest—it was too painful to listen to it, because it reminded him of her.

"I get that. M-my parents liked oldies most of the time. The cornier the better. And I can't listen to them any longer either."

I couldn't believe I'd just shared that. I didn't talk about my mom and dad. Ever.

West, bless him, didn't treat it as a big deal, if he even knew it was one. "Well, thank fuck my kids are too old for all the annoying kids music. Even now, Baby Shark still haunts my dreams. Doo doo doo doo doo doo."

He said it so seriously that I couldn't help but laugh. Then he sang, "Haunts my dreams, doo doo doo doo doo doo."

When he waggled his eyebrows, I laughed harder, to the point I struggled to breathe.

When I finally got myself under control, I glanced at West. His full-on grin was devastating and made him go from beyond sexy to probably the handsomest man I'd ever met.

He definitely needed to smile more. For a split second, I wanted to try and make it happen every day.

But then I pushed that thought aside. He wasn't my concern, he wasn't my anything.

West chuckled. "While that song is evil—and don't ever tell anyone I said this—some of the kids music I actually liked. Mostly the Disney ones, but a few of the others as well." He shrugged. "I can't be the only dad like that, although most won't admit it. But I don't need to put the songs down, boast about my dick size, and hock a loogie to keep my man card. I'm too old for that toxic shit anyway."

The thought of West having to try to be manly made me smile—he just was. "Good. Because a man who's willing to sing 'Let It Go' from *Frozen* to his daughter when she's sick, complete with wearing a blanket cape, is more man than I'd know what to do with."

He glanced at me and then back at the road before groaning. "Avery told you."

"Yep. She said you have quite the voice. I can pair my phone to play the song, and maybe you can give me a private show."

As soon as the words left my mouth, I realized how a private show could be interpreted as sexual. I blurted, "For your singing. Of course."

His lips twitched again. Clearly, his mind had gone to the gutter like mine. "Maybe later. I'd rather not shatter the windows. Although, what about you? Can you sing and offer a private show?"

I refused to let him embarrass me. "No, I can dance but not sing."

"I saw your dancing at The Watering Hole. You have rhythm, unlike me."

I stared out the window, needing a break from this laid-back, teasing version of West. Otherwise, I might do something stupid, like ask about his experience again. "I danced a little in middle school and high school. It was a way to keep my mind occupied and body in motion when I wasn't swimming. I'm better now, but when I was a kid, I struggled to sit still."

"Why?"

I should change the topic. I really should. We were entering dangerous territory.

And yet, for some strange reason, I didn't want to. "When I was swimming or dancing or even riding bikes with the BFF Circle, my mind calmed and stopped the memories. And for a lot of years, I really needed that, or I would've gone crazy eventually."

Silence fell. But unlike back in the hotel room, it wasn't strained. No, it was as if West were processing my words and giving me time to change the subject, if I wanted to.

However, for once, I didn't want to. After never talking about this for so long, it was as if a dam was breaking. I should stop, patch it up, and protect myself.

But a part of me wanted it to break and relieve the pressure.

He finally cleared his throat. "Well, I get that, about

calming your brain. I've kept busy for nearly two decades now, otherwise, I might've screamed for no reason and scared the shit out of people."

I finally looked at him again, but he didn't meet my gaze. "Why would you scream?"

"At life. At the unfairness of it. At good people dying before their time. At broken condoms and hasty decisions. Take your pick."

I'd been really young when West had married and left Starry Hills, so sometimes I forgot about the reason he'd married in the first place—his late wife had become pregnant after a one-night stand.

I wanted to ask him about more of the specifics since what he'd shared in the pool had only scratched the surface. Maybe asking for more and him unloading his hurts would help him move on or be a little more at ease.

However, judging by his clenched jaw, he didn't want to talk about it. And selfishly, I didn't want to ruin the rest of the day. For now, at least, I wanted to bring back the lighter conversation. "When you're upset or mad at the world, scream into a pillow. I've done that, and it usually helps. Or if you don't have a pillow, yell against your arm or a hand covered with your shirt. You can do it right now, and I won't ever tell."

West finally looked at me, his expression unreadable, before focusing back on the road. "Maybe later. Right now, I don't feel the need to scream about anything."

My heart thumped inside my chest. Did that mean he liked spending time with me?

Wait, no. That shouldn't matter. Not at all.

I needed to focus on Operation: Friend Zone, and

ASAP. "When was the last time you went to Lake Tahoe?"

"Way too long ago." He gestured toward the radio. "Pick what you want. It won't be much longer until we arrive."

He turned the volume up pretty loud, a clear signal he was done talking.

Which was for the best. At this rate, I'd be blabbering on about killing my parents, or my brother being disgusted with me, or something else deeply personal and secretive and unflattering.

Needing to lighten the mood, I paired my phone with the car and put on a Disney playlist. West smiled but said nothing. Soon I started singing. He eventually joined in, and we both sang at the top of our lungs for the rest of the drive.

Which told me one thing—West did indeed have a nice singing voice.

Chapter Eighteen

Weston

Abby: What are you doing today? Want to grab some lunch?
Me: No. Can't. Busy.
Abby: Doing what?
Me: Stuff.
Abby: Really, West. You could give more details.
Me: Scowl. Grunt. Shrug.
Abby: <laughing emoji> You're hopeless. Have fun with Emmy!
Me: What? How did you know...
Abby: <blowing a kiss emoji> See you tomorrow and maybe I'll tell you.

. . .

We grabbed some sandwiches from a sub shop and got directions to a place for hikes and lookouts. The serious hikes were too far away for today, but there were some nearby that were a mile or three, and we finally reached one that was supposed to lead to some stellar views.

The incline wasn't too bad. No, my heart raced for an entirely different reason.

Because Emmy had decided to be the trailblazer, camera in hand, and it meant I had a view of her ass and thighs encased in tight, stretchy pants the entire way.

As if I needed more reasons to desire the woman. Her making me laugh in the car, and us grinning as we attempted a high note in a song but mangled it, had made me want to kiss her.

When away from work and Starry Hills, she was just so much happier. A little more carefree. In general, it was as if some weight had been lifted from her shoulders.

I suspected it had to do with either her parents or her brother. She lived in the house where she'd grown up, full of memories and constant reminders of what she'd lost. I doubted all her changes since inheriting had fully banished the past either.

Thinking about the transformation of her home from ranch to wedding business stayed with me. So when we finally found a pretty spot to sit on some rocks for lunch, looking over the deep blue water of the lake and mountains in the distance, I blurted as she took her first bite, "Why did you sell the cattle?"

She choked, and I thumped her back until she calmed down. Once she sipped the water I offered, she croaked, "Why are you asking me that?"

"Because I'm trying to understand why someone would take a well-established business with as stellar and desirable a reputation as Starry Dreams Ranch and toss it all away." She frowned at me, and I realized how harsh that might sound and added, "I mean, obviously you wanted to run your event business, and I get that. But the cattle portion is far enough away it shouldn't interfere. Not to mention it'd add authenticity to the rustic wedding scene."

She rolled her eyes. "Cow poop smells are not very romantic."

"Hey, some of them ride in on horses, right? You can't tell me no horse has ever taken a dump during the trip."

"Of course it happens. But it's not like I put it in the brochures."

I softened my voice. "But really, why the change? You could've hired someone to run it for you and then kept that steady income coming in, to grow your wedding business even faster."

One thing I'd deduced was that even if her brother was a millionaire many times over by now, she hadn't taken a cent. Or he hadn't given her any of his money. Although the latter didn't really match the boy I'd known growing up.

Of course, who the fuck knew what fame and fortune would do to someone. My brother Nolan was mostly the same guy despite being the current in-demand movie hero, but then Nolan hadn't enjoyed and embraced his fame like Rafe had. At least according to the papers and tabloids I'd seen.

Emmy looked out over the lake, watching some birds fly in the distance. Eventually she answered, "The cattle reminded me of my parents. And I couldn't handle it, West. Because the constant reminders only added to my guilt." She paused, but I waited. She finally met my gaze and continued, "And I carry enough as it is, and any more will break me."

Her voice cracked at the last word, and her eyes turned bright, as if she were about to cry. I moved to crouch in front of her, wondering if I should touch her or not—she might break down if I did. For now, I focused on her eyes. "Why do you feel guilty, Emmy?" She looked down at her hands, twisting them, and I put my hand over hers and squeezed. "You can tell me. After all, you could threaten to blackmail me for my car karaoke choices, and I'd never hear the end of it from my brothers."

She gave a nervous laugh. "You're ridiculous, Weston Wolfe."

I squeezed her hands again. "Sometimes. But I know what it's like to hold so much inside, to the point you feel like all you want to do is rage and scream and break things to try and feel better. I won't judge, Emmy. I promise."

"How can you promise that? I'm a murderer, West. I killed my parents."

I took a second to process her words, careful not to show any emotion. Surely she couldn't believe that, could she? She'd only been ten years old, for fuck's sake, when they died in a car crash. My family had told me that a drunk driver had hit the Mendoza car and instantly killed Mateo and Kim.

"I think there's more to that story. Tell me so I can be my own judge."

After glancing up, she searched my gaze, as if trying to decide something.

In this moment, she looked lost and broken and afraid. More than afraid—terrified.

And I didn't like it. For a second, I wanted to be the one to ease her terror and help fight her battles.

Maybe I couldn't do it forever, but for now, I could help lighten the mood a little. If she were a little more comfortable with me, she might finally unload some of the burden she carried.

So I wiggled and groaned. "Can these old knees get up from this crouching position before you say more? They're going to give out at any time now."

The corners of her mouth lifted a fraction. "Can't have that happening, can we? Because there's no way I'd be able to carry your heavy ass down that trail."

I grinned, exaggerated getting up with difficulty, and sat next to her on the rock.

For a while, we both stared out over the water. I didn't know how much time passed, our lunch long forgotten, before she said, "Okay, I'll tell you. But just, well, just don't interrupt me. Otherwise, I might not be able to finish."

I nodded. She must've seen it from the corner of her eye because she sighed and said, "Well, I was ten..."

Her voice trailed off, but I did as she asked and kept quiet.

Chapter Nineteen

Emilia

I didn't know how West got me to this point, to where I agreed to talk about the crash.

Maybe it was being far away from Starry Hills and all the memories there. Or maybe because he'd been so, well, nice and funny and even a little corny during the car ride here.

Or maybe I just wanted him to know, hoping he wouldn't think the worst of me.

Which, of course, was stupid. But there it was.

As I stared out over the water, I tried again. "I was ten when it happened. Rafe had finally worked his way up and became one of the starting strikers for his team in England at the time, Stonelake FC.

"He wanted us to fly to the UK to watch him play in

person, and my parents scheduled our trip during summer vacation. When they told me about it, I barely slept, excited to watch my big brother play in person. I didn't quite understand all the rules for soccer back then, but I still knew my brother was amazing and talented and always in the papers in the UK or on the sports channels."

I paused, needing a moment to gather the courage to keep doing this.

Not only because of what was to come but also because remembering how much I'd loved my brother was painful. Like how he'd always sent me clippings and jerseys. And even a little tea set he said was very English with little flowers on it and even a little knitted thing called a cozy to put over the teapot to keep it warm. He had always spoiled me.

Until it all stopped. I've never admitted it, but I still missed my brother so much it hurt.

The wind picked up, and it caused West's scent of male and woods to hit my nose, bringing me back to the present. Since the man had kept his word and remained silent, I needed to finish this.

And for the first time in my life, I actually wanted to get it all out in the open.

I plucked a nearby leaf from a bush and twirled it between my fingers. "Because I kept changing which stuffed animal to bring with me, we were late leaving for the airport. Even so, my dad said we had enough time. We had a red-eye flight, and so traffic to San Francisco International Airport was pretty much nonexistent.

"Still, I was impatient. I asked repeatedly when we'd

get there. I wanted my dad to hurry, because then we could see Rafe faster. They tried their best to calm me, patient as always. Treats, words, even music changes didn't stop my incessant questions, though.

"Eventually, I got frustrated and tossed my stuffed horse at my mom, wanting her attention. Just as she scolded me, it-it all happened so fast."

I closed my eyes, willing the images not to come. But to no avail.

The noise and screaming and blacking out. The coming to, crying and shouting. The silence until the highway patrol and fire department arrived. The tearing of metal and the ambulance siren.

I felt a hand cover mine, and I opened my eyes and turned my head. West looked at me with concern, not disgust as I'd expected.

He pointed to his mouth and raised his brows in question. And just like that, some of my terror faded. Not all, but a little. I nodded.

"If you don't want to go on, you don't have to, Emmy. It wasn't my intention to break you."

I swallowed and wondered if voicing the last part of that night would, in fact, break me.

For years, I'd thought it would. I hadn't handled it well for the first year or two, to the point that I'd stopped talking except to Abby and sometimes her mom.

But now, all these years later, saying everything out loud was almost...cathartic. Healing. Maybe even a little relieving.

I hadn't come this far to back out now. So after taking a deep breath, I said, "A drunk driver hit us. But I know if I hadn't distracted my parents, even throwing shit into the front seat, my dad would've been able to swerve in time. They would've survived. It's all my fault they're dead, West." A sob escaped my throat. "My fault. And my brother knows it too."

The tears I'd held back for years spilled over my cheeks, and I hugged my arms around myself as I started sobbing.

Because I missed my life before—my parents, my brother, how I'd been surrounded by love.

And I'd lost it. All of it.

But it was my fault and mine alone.

I sobbed harder, unable to hold back the grief any longer.

West pulled me against his chest, and I didn't think —I clung to him and let it all out. Partly because of the memories and the guilt and the loss of my brother. But also because I knew West was just being nice to a crying woman.

However, once we left this isolated spot and returned to reality, I knew he'd want nothing to do with me. He'd finally realize what I'd done and that I was a murderer.

And for some reason, that thought made me sob all the harder.

Chapter Twenty

Weston

Fuck, I was no psychologist, but I'd heard of survivor's guilt before, usually regarding natural disasters or war zones or mass shootings.

But to think Emmy had felt this way for so many years because a drunk asshole had hit her family's car? It made me angry and a little sad. Angry because why the fuck hadn't my family picked up on this shit? She'd lived with them for years, after all.

And I wouldn't even start thinking about asshole drunk drivers. Or if this one was still alive, I'd hunt him or her down to beat the shit out of them for causing Emmy so much pain.

But the sadness was greater. Because a cranky little girl doing what children did when they were tired thought she was the reason her parents had died. I wasn't naïve enough to think that me telling her she was wrong would convince her, though. She'd stewed in this shit for years now. More than a decade, in fact.

As she cried, I merely held her, stroked her back in slow circles, and murmured soothing words. She seemed so small and fragile, which made me hold her a little closer, as if my embrace alone could keep her from shattering.

Eventually, she quieted, but I didn't let go of her. I wouldn't until she asked me to. Both to comfort her but also because I wanted to keep her safe. At least for as long as she was in my arms.

It could've been minutes or an hour when she finally said, "If you just drive me back to the hotel, I'll get my stuff and see if I can find somewhere else to stay."

Leaning back until I could see her face—and damn, her red eyes and tear-stained face squeezed my heart—I asked, "Why the fuck would you want to do that? Yes, I'm told I snore sometimes. But you can just toss a pillow at me, and I should shut up."

"Y-you still want to share your room with me?"

Unable to resist, I brushed the messy hair from her face, wiped away her tears with my thumb, and then cupped her cheek. I fucking hated how much she was suffering right now.

I couldn't solve all her problems, but I could ease her mind on this one. "Of course I want you to share my room. We're friends now, right? And friends don't abandon friends when they're hurting."

Emmy searched my eyes, and fuck, friends didn't

seem the right word. Because despite every reason I shouldn't, I wanted to kiss her right now and help her forget her worries.

What the hell? Where had that thought come from?

Before I could panic, she moved away and retrieved her uneaten sub sandwich. "You don't have to pretend, West. I'm a big girl and just want the truth."

I blinked. "The truth?"

"Yes, stop being nice to me. If you want to run, go ahead. I understand."

Like hell I'd be running anywhere.

I stood and moved until she had to look at me. "You want to hear the truth, Emilia? Then here it is: you're as much a murderer as I am."

"Now you're not making any sense."

I leaned closer. "I am, by your logic. Think about it—maybe if I'd tried harder, or pushed Andrea's parents to do more, or even fucking moved cities to get away from her toxic friends, maybe my wife would still be alive."

She shook her head. "It's not the same thing at all. You tried to help her, and she didn't want it."

"Just like it was the drunk who got behind the wheel and sealed your parents' fate, not you. You were a child, doing what all tired children do. Not only that, you were their second child. Any parent should be able to handle a cranky kid after so many years. No, Emmy. Even if you'd been asleep, I doubt it would've made a difference."

Standing, she raised her voice. "You don't know that! I was irritating and whining and throwing a fit."

"Was it your dad or your mom who kept answering you?"

For a second, she paused. Then her voice was quieter when she replied, "My mom."

"And your dad was driving, right?" She bobbed her head. "Just like I thought. With two parents, it makes sense for one to handle the cranky kid and the other to focus on the road."

"But I was loud and probably screaming and being annoying! I was a distraction."

I gripped her upper arms. "It's the drunk driver who's to blame, Emmy, not you. And even if you don't believe it, that's what I believe. So, no, I'm not going to kick you out of my room and suddenly hate you." And even though it was childish, I added, "You can't make me."

She growled in frustration. "Why are you being so stubborn? Is it because you're too nice to tell me to my face that I killed them? Too nice to tell me how you can't stand to be around me, let alone believe you allowed me to watch your kids? And so you're just pretending everything is fine until we get back to the hotel, and then you can ditch me? I can take a lot, West, but don't you dare fucking lie to me. Just leave and I'll find my own way back."

Emmy tried to turn away, but I didn't release her. I lowered my face closer to hers, trying not to notice her hot breath against my lips. "I'm being fucking honest, Emilia Mendoza. Hate is the farthest thing I feel for you right now. And I'm not. Fucking. Lying."

We breathed heavily, staring at each other, and I wondered what else I'd have to say for her to believe me.

This frustrating and stubborn and unbelievably strong woman was so damn complicated. And I sensed that if I couldn't convince her I was telling her the truth—that I didn't believe she was at fault—I'd lose something I wasn't even sure I had.

She whispered, "I wish I could believe you."

Frustration raged inside me. I leaned an inch closer, and her breathing picked up. An idea hit, but it was wrong on so many levels.

And yet, it seemed right at the same time. It would certainly convince her I was far from hating her.

So I said fuck it and kissed her.

Chapter Twenty-One

Emilia

One second West was arguing with me, standing far too close, and the next, he lowered his mouth to mine and kissed me.

For a beat, I froze. I'd dreamed of this, more than once. And yet, it wasn't something I should allow to continue. No matter what West believed, I knew what I'd done. And I didn't deserve to be happy, not even a little.

Kissing West would make me more than happy.

However, as his tongue lightly stroked the opening of my lips, I couldn't resist. With a groan, I parted them, and his tongue slipped inside. The first stroke of his tongue against mine snapped something inside me.

I wrapped my arms around his neck and pressed myself against him. Weeks of longing and desire and wishing for what I shouldn't have rushed forth. I licked and stroked and suckled his tongue, loving how he groaned and guided my hips until my belly was pressed up against his hard cock.

The feel of it only made me hotter, and the kiss turned almost desperate.

When his hands went to my ass and lifted, I didn't even hesitate to wrap my legs around his waist. As he rubbed me against his hard length, I sucked in a breath. It'd been so long since I'd even made out with a guy, but this...this was different.

I was on fire.

As if sensing my brain was going to start working again, West nipped my bottom lip and claimed my mouth again. He wasn't gentle, our teeth even clashed at one point, and yet I didn't care. Every lick and stroke and suckle drove me insane. And combined with his jeans-clad cock pressing against my clit and pussy, I was so, so close.

I should stop him. I really should. Orgasms were something I really didn't deserve.

But then West's grip on my ass tightened, and he moved me faster against him. The friction built, and I fought it, I fought it hard. West took no mercy, however, and kept at it—kissing me, pressing me closer against him, and hitting just the right spot between my thighs.

I came with a cry, pleasure shooting through my body as my pussy clenched and released, made more intense by the fact that West never ceased tormenting me with his dick.

As my pussy stilled and I came down from my high, his kiss gentled. A light nibble here, a soft kiss there, until eventually, he laid his forehead against mine.

"Do you still think I hate you, Emmy? Because I'm willing to do that again and again until you fucking believe me that I don't."

It was on the tip of my tongue to say it was lust. Hate fucking was a thing, after all.

And yet, it felt wrong to use those words about West and what he'd just done. What we'd done.

Shyness came over me, and all I could think about was getting away from him. Because when he held me and kissed me and gripped my ass so possessively, it made me want to believe I could have this. That maybe I could try for something with West, get to see his kids every day, and possibly have a family of my own one day.

But then years of guilt and internal arguments crashed over me, and I knew wishing for any of that was ridiculous. Somehow, I'd end up hurting West. Just like I'd done with my parents and brother.

And the man deserved better. Much better.

"Put me down."

He paused but then did as I asked. I wobbled a bit until I found my footing and then retreated several feet away from him. "If you want to be my friend, I can't stop you." I finally met his gaze. "But we can't be more than that, West. I just can't do it."

Grabbing my backpack, I hightailed it back down the trail. I knew we'd have to share the car back to Reno, and I wouldn't get my picture of Tahoe at sunset, but I desperately need some distance.

And as I waited by the car, I knew that I could never be alone with Weston Wolfe ever again.

Because I didn't think I'd be able to resist him a second time.

Chapter Twenty-Two

Weston

It took every bit of restraint I possessed not to run after Emmy. However, I'd seen the mixture of guilt and surprise and longing in her eyes after she'd come grinding against my dick, and I didn't want to push her too far.

Especially since I didn't know what the fuck I wanted to do about the woman.

Kissing her, damn, it'd never been like that before. Yes, after my father died from a heart attack, I'd coped by going out and screwing as many women as possible.

But none of them, not even my wife, compared to how Emmy's kiss made me burn, turned my cock to stone, and left me both wanting more and scared shitless about doing it again. Because her kiss setting me on fire was only part of it—I wanted to help her find happiness again too.

Not in a friendly way either. I wanted to be the man at her side, the one she could lean on when needed. The one who could take her to bed, eat her pussy for hours, and make her forget about any shitty memories or nightmares.

No, no, no. That had to be my dick talking. I'd thought I had something with a woman once before, and it had gone horribly wrong. And Andrea may have had problems, but she'd never thought herself guilty of murder.

I ran a hand through my hair and stared out over the lake. My first thought was that Emmy wouldn't get her sunset photo to add to her office wall.

Then I reminded myself that I shouldn't even think about taking one myself and giving it to her. I wasn't her boyfriend or anything.

But, fuck, what was I going to do? I wouldn't kick her out of the room, no way. I didn't know if anything could happen between us, but I wouldn't give her any reason to think I hated her and thought her guilty.

As I gathered up my shit and headed down the trail, I realized Abby had to know about Emmy's guilt and the reason behind it. She and Emmy lived together and had been best friends nearly their entire lives. Would Abby have any suggestions to help?

Could I bring myself to ask?

When grief over my dad's death had made me flee Starry Hills, one of my biggest regrets had been leaving my family behind, especially my younger siblings. Abby had been nine, and the twins, Zach and Zane, had been eleven. They'd pretty much grown up without me.

Then I remembered something Aunt Lori had said to me several times since returning to Starry Hills: *"They'll forgive you, West, if they haven't already. But they'll never feel like family if you keep your walls up."*

Sighing, I picked my way down the last part of the trail and made a decision. Well, two of them.

One, I was going to talk to my sister and ask for her help.

And two, I would kiss Emmy again, no matter what it took.

I couldn't think beyond that, however. I was fucked up from my first marriage, and I was wary of having a relationship again, especially if it went to hell and ended up hurting my kids.

But something about Emmy drew me. Not just because I kept dreaming of her naked and under me, either.

No, Emmy needed someone on her side, someone to make her smile and laugh. I'd done it already, and I burned to do it again.

Apart from my kids, I'd never wanted so badly to make someone else happy.

And even when we argued, it was different from my first marriage. I doubted I ever would have to fight because she'd made my children upset or scared. Emmy loved my kids, and had even showed them more attention and care than their own mother had.

Plus, it was nice not being the silent, grumpy guy persona I always carried to protect myself. She'd cried in my arms, for fuck's sake. I could risk showing a little of myself.

Maybe.

The gravel parking area came into view. Emmy leaned against the car, her head back and her eyes closed, looking as if she were truly alone and miserable. The sight erased my doubts. I didn't like Emilia Mendoza looking sad.

I would find a way to make her happy.

Because I might not know if she was my forever or not, but for now, she was my woman to hold, protect, and take care of.

She just didn't realize it yet.

The atmosphere on the drive back to the city was the opposite of the ride to the lake. Emmy was silent, staring out the window, and would only give one-word answers to questions. I didn't push, or be too annoying, and gave up for a while. But as we got closer and closer to Reno, I knew we needed to settle a few things before we reached the hotel.

So at one of the last rest areas before reaching the city, I pulled in, parked the car, and turned it off.

Never looking from the window, Emmy said, "I don't need to use the bathroom. I'll wait here."

"I didn't pull over to take a piss, Emmy. As your friend, I have a few things to say."

She sighed, still avoiding my eyes. "I'm too tired for a lecture or another argument, West. I just want to grab my stuff, find somewhere to sleep, and focus on the wedding expo."

"You have a place to stay already."

With a growl of frustration, her dark-brown eyes finally met mine. "No, I don't."

"Didn't you say we were friends?"

"Yes, but—"

"Then as your friend, I'm telling you to just share my fucking room, Emmy. Because you'll probably have to get a hotel room in a casino, get tired driving back and forth from the event hotel, and then you won't be at your best, which means lost business. Then I'll get an earful from Abby, who will tell my aunt. And who the fuck knows what Beck will do once he finds out I was an asshole for making you find another room when there are two beds in mine."

Some of her earlier spark returned, and I somehow kept myself from grinning.

Emmy shook her head. "A cot isn't a bed. And I'm a grown-ass woman, West. If I end up tired and fail, it's my fault and no one else's."

"If you're a grown-ass woman, then why are you running away? I just want to help you, Emmy. It's not like I'm going to crawl into bed and seduce you. You believe me, right?"

"I know you wouldn't do that."

Well, I would eventually. But definitely not until she was ready for it.

"I promise not to get into your pants, or try to kiss you, or mention anything to do with your parents or brother. Just stay with me, Emmy." She looked torn, almost ready to give in. So I added, "Please, Emmy. You've helped me out so much already this summer with my kids. In return, let me help you for once."

I kept waiting for her to say I could find somewhere else to stay. And if she asked, I'd do it.

However, that was my last resort. Because, fuck, I wanted her to stay in the same room with me. I couldn't try to charm her in my grumpy-ass way if she was always avoiding me.

She crossed her arms over her chest and gave me a long look before saying, "Fine. But if you make any mention of *that day*, or my brother, you give me the right to kick you out, and I keep the room."

The corner of my mouth kicked up. "You'd kick me out, huh, and expect me to go?"

"Yes. And I know if I asked you to leave, you would, West. Because despite everything, you're a gentleman under that scowling exterior."

Well, at least she didn't think I was some awful, heartless guy who'd been unable to save his wife from herself.

Even if I knew I'd done all that I could—sometimes you couldn't save someone who didn't want to save themselves—I knew her parents and others back in Ridgefield blamed me for Andrea's death.

The fact Emmy probably didn't, judging by her words, meant more than it should have.

I cleared my throat and put out a hand to shake. "Deal."

She hesitated and then took my hand. Even though a jolt of heat rushed through me, I was careful not to react. I needed to build trust with Emmy before anything else.

As if burned, Emmy yanked her hand back. She said, "Oh, and you can order room service, and I'll pay for it. Abby asked me to dinner, and I said yes. But I won't back out of my offer to buy you dinner in exchange for letting me share your room."

Maybe it was from years of dealing with my strong-willed, stubborn daughter, but I had a sense of when to push and when to hold off. Tonight required the latter.

Although if Emmy thought she could avoid me for the entire expo, she was in for a big surprise.

Chapter Twenty-Three

Emilia

Me: Can I crash your dinner plans and join you?
Abby: What did West do?
Me: Nothing.
Abby: <face with monocle emoji> x3
Me: You once told me not to ask questions until you were ready.
Abby: <sighing emoji> You're right. I'll contact the restaurant. Dinner's at 6:30pm
Me: <heart emoji> <wine glass emoji> <people hugging emoji>
Abby: Oh, don't think I won't try again later. But not tonight.
Me: Fine. But even if you push, I don't have to answer.

Abby: We'll see, my friend. I know just how to push your buttons.
Me: <tongue out emoji> And I know how to resist you.
Abby: That sounds like a challenge.

Thankfully, West hadn't tried to strike up another conversation in the car or even in the hotel. He'd merely called his kids while I showered, changed, and gathered my stuff before leaving.

I wanted to ask how they were, but I was afraid to talk with him again so soon after the blow up on the trail.

Well, blow up and then make-out session. One that still made my cheeks heat whenever I thought about it.

And if he so much as smiled at me, I might be reckless and try to kiss him again.

So yep, I was a coward and fled as soon as possible, arriving early at the restaurant. Since work was a good distraction, I replied to some emails as I waited for Abby.

Eventually, someone knocked on my window, and I jumped. Abby raised her dark eyebrows at me.

After grabbing my purse, I opened the door, and she didn't waste time. "Why are you hiding out in your car? I'm early, which means you've been here even longer."

"I wasn't hiding. I was working." Abby looked unconvinced. Damn her knowing me so well. "Well, it doesn't matter. I didn't really eat lunch, so I'm starving. Let's head inside." I glanced around. "Where's your friend?"

Abby waved a hand in dismissal. "I made plans with her for tomorrow instead."

"Abby..."

"Don't 'Abby' me, Emmy. Something's up. And since you were always there for me after the Epic Douchebag Disaster, I'm going to be here for you as well. You need me."

"You got all that from a few text messages?"

"What can I say? I can read between the lines of yours by now."

I bit my bottom lip. I felt bad that she'd changed her plans for me. And yet, a little relieved because out of everyone in the world, I told Abby the most.

West was catching up when it came to knowing more about me, but I didn't want to think about that right now.

"Fine. Then let's get inside and order first, and then maybe I'll answer your questions."

"Oh, Emmy, you poor thing. You still think you can resist me? I'm a pro at getting what I want with family."

She grinned, and I snorted. "You're definitely the youngest."

"You're the youngest, too, so way to throw shade on yourself."

I stuck out my tongue, and we laughed. And for the next little while, the tension and tears and kisses with West faded away.

Except I knew it wouldn't last. As soon as we finished ordering, Abby leaned forward and said, "Spill."

I sipped my water and watched the condensation

run down the glass before I muttered, "I told West about *that day*."

Abby tilted her head. "And? He has the same opinion as me, doesn't he?"

This was a topic we didn't talk about often. Because we never agreed. "Yes."

The server brought our ice teas—tomorrow would require an early start, and we weren't risking alcohol—and as soon as she left, Abby spoke again. "Okay. So then what? I'm sure you argued with him about it. But why are you running away from him? Because I suspect you changed your dinner plans to avoid him."

My cheeks burned as I tried to gather the courage. West was Abby's brother, after all.

But if I was going to tell anyone about what had happened, it would be her. So I blurted, "We argued, and he kissed me to prove he didn't hate me."

"Did he now?"

I glanced up and didn't like the knowing look in Abby's eyes. "What the hell does that mean?"

"Do you want the truth?"

I nodded.

"I'm surprised you two haven't jumped into bed together already, if I'm honest. We've all felt the tension at the dinner table."

Blood drained from my face. Had we been that obvious? Had his kids noticed?

Abby reached across the table and patted my arm. "We know you best, Millie. Emmy. Speaking of which—he's the reason you asked to be called Emmy again, isn't he?"

I'd wondered how long Abby would take to ask me about that. "Yes."

"Interesting."

I took an ice cube from my glass and tossed it at her. She shrieked and then laughed.

I vowed to give our server a huge-ass tip to make up for my mess.

Abby pointed a finger at me. "You'll pay for that later."

"You deserved it, with all your vague-ass answers."

"I can't help it. I rarely get to tease you like this. And since I won't tease West—at least until you two are like making out in public or something—you'll get it twice as bad."

"We won't be making out in public."

"Why not?"

Such a simple question and yet so fucking difficult.

Our food arrived—we both had ordered fettuccine alfredo as a treat, since Beck had never been able to make it right—and I quickly took a bite. Both because I was starving but also to give me time to process how to answer her.

With anyone else, I'd probably chicken out and try to change the subject.

But Abby wouldn't let it die until she got a response. So after swallowing, I finally said, "You know I don't do relationships. And I most definitely don't imagine having a family one day."

I didn't know if I'd told Abby about how I didn't think I deserved a family of my own or not. I had some hazy, drunk memories from my twenty-first birthday but nothing definitive.

Abby shrugged. "Well, you don't need to have a relationship to fuck him."

I choked on my latest bite. It seemed I couldn't swallow properly to save my life today.

Once I could finally breathe again, I took a sip and said, "What?"

"Yes, he's my brother. And so kindly don't do it on the kitchen counter where I can find you because then I'll have to wash my eyes out with bleach. But West is lonely, you're lonely, and it might not solve all your problems, but some casual sex might do you both the world of good."

"Are you really telling me to sleep with your brother?"

"Why not? You guys have been undressing each other with your eyes for weeks now. So just lay out some ground rules, don't get caught by anyone, and then when you're ready, walk away. As a bonus, given how determined my brothers are, I'm sure he'll make you really, really happy too."

I groaned and put my face in my hands. "Did you really just say that?"

"If he wasn't my brother, I'd say more. But because he is, vague descriptions are all you're getting from me." She pointed her fork at me. "And don't even think of crowing about his dick after the fact. Talk to Katie or Amber about that, please and thank you."

I couldn't help but laugh at the ridiculousness of it all.

But could I do it, was the question. Maybe that was all West was looking for anyway—a casual hookup. He'd made no bones about never wanting to marry again. And he sure as hell wouldn't want to date if he wasn't serious, given his kids.

It could be dangerous, and yet the thought of all that warm, muscled man naked and over me made me shiver.

Abby said, her voice softer this time, "Just think about it, Emmy. We will forever disagree about what you deserve. But just promise me you'll think about it, okay?"

After a long moment, I nodded. "I will."

"Good. Now, have you heard back from Nolan's movie-star friend about planning her wedding?"

Work was neutral ground, and I could've hugged Abby for moving us back to safe territory. "No, although Zara promised to give me an answer by next week."

"Don't worry, Emmy. You'll get it. No one can plan country or rustic weddings like you can."

Considering how Zara was marrying her college sweetheart—who was from Texas—I was surprised she'd want something in Sonoma. The feelings and atmosphere between the two places were vastly different.

But Nolan had recommended me, had shown Zara some pictures of past ceremonies, and she'd been charmed. She was from Los Angeles originally and had mentioned how she couldn't stand the heat of Texas in the summer, and she wanted a summer wedding for next year.

I'd used the cooler weather as a stepping stone and put together the best proposal ever to try and win her.

Because getting the super popular and famous Zara Jones as a client would launch my business to a whole other level.

I finally replied, "Well, I can't do anything but wait for her answer, at this point. Although I thought maybe we could talk a little more about our expo cross-promo between Starry Wolfe wine and Starry Dreams Events and Weddings."

And so for the remainder of dinner, I forgot about West, our kiss, and Abby's suggestion.

By the time I returned to the hotel room, West snored on the way-too-small cot, somehow still looking sexy with his mouth open and making a racket. Part of me was relieved he was already asleep, but another part of me wondered if talking with him again would sway my decision one way or the other about hooking up. My vagina screamed yes, for the love of everything, do it. My brain, however, cautioned it was a bad idea.

Except given how I dreamed of West bending me over the bed and taking me hard from behind, smacking my ass as he did it, I had a feeling I knew which way the wind blew.

Only if he agreed to rules and boundaries, though. I mean, if he was lonely, then me having sex with him would make him happy, right? And that was always my goal?

Stop kidding yourself. I'd be happy too.

But it wouldn't be permanent. So I could justify it, through my weird web of logic.

The hard part would be suggesting it to him.

Chapter Twenty-Four

Weston

Me: Once we get home, can we grab drinks at The Watering Hole?
Abby: Um, okay. Why? You always go with Beck.
Me: Never mind.
Abby: No! Don't do that. Of course I'll go. But only if I get to order you a fruity cocktail and you promise to drink it.
Me: Fine.
Abby: I can just imagine your scowl. It's gonna be fun. I'm taking lots of pictures.
Me: ...
Abby: You can't back out now. I won't let you.
Me: ...

Abby: Love you too. <heart emoji>

By the time I woke up the next morning, Emmy was gone. Everything from her makeup pouch thing had migrated to the counter, taking up every inch of space, signaling she'd already gotten ready for the day.

How the fuck had she done that and not woken me up?

Trying not to think about how maybe I'd slept deeply because I trusted her, I showered and headed downstairs to grab some complimentary breakfast and got to work.

Abby hadn't arrived yet, so I retrieved all the stuff she needed for the expo from the storage space and put together the tables and displays for our booth. The wine wouldn't come out until tomorrow, and Abby would do the finer decorating, so it didn't take long to finish.

Which meant I needed to help with Emmy's space next.

My palms sweated like some nervous fucking teenager as I headed to the other side of the giant room. While I knew what I wanted, I wasn't sure how Emmy would act today. If she pretended that yesterday at the lake had never happened, it was going to take a fuck-ton more work to kiss her again.

When I finally approached her booth, she was bent over, rummaging through some storage totes, and I took a second to stare at her ass. So fucking perfect and soft looking, and I imagined biting one cheek and then the other as I slowly fucked her with my fingers.

Emmy stood, and I hoped like hell she couldn't tell I'd just been ogling her. She smiled, and I noticed how she had on a lot more makeup than usual.

"Hey, West. Good timing. I need your help." She walked up and put a hand on my bicep and squeezed. "You're definitely stronger than me, so I'm sure you can do it."

I couldn't stop from frowning. Not that I didn't want her hands on me, but fuck, was this some sort of sign? Or was I just hoping it was?

Then she leaned against me, her breasts pressing against my chest, and blood rushed to my dick. "Ready to help?"

My heart raced as my gaze darted to her lips. At least she didn't bite her bottom lip, or I might've done something fucking stupid, like kiss her before she was ready.

She moved away, and I instantly missed her heat. "Come on. I have this giant display thing that needs put together, along with a little archway. If you could do the archway first, I can decorate it while you finish the other."

Confused as hell about what was going on with her today, I willed my dick to behave and focused on the tasks she gave me. We worked in silence for a while until Emmy finished decorating the archway. Then she came near me and said, "I thought we could grab lunch together. The front desk recommended an amazing Mexican restaurant not far from here."

I glanced at her, trying to figure out her mood, but

she merely smiled. Not wanting to look a gift horse in the mouth, I replied, "Sure. Just us?"

"Yep. I owe you more than one meal for sharing your room with me. Especially given how uncomfortable you looked on the cot."

It had been fucking terrible, and the shitty thing would probably collapse soon from my weight. But I merely shrugged. "It's fine."

"It's not. But I may have a solution for that. And no, don't ask me now. We'll talk at lunch, when we're alone."

Okay, that was an about-face from the woman who'd insisted she needed to get her own room and stay far, far away from me.

Was she up to something?

The next few hours flew by quickly. I helped Emmy with some of her decorating—not the delicate stuff, because apparently, I had big, manly hands, whatever the hell that meant—and then did a few things for my sister at our booth too. Before I knew it, it was nearly one o'clock, and I found Emmy again.

She smiled as soon as she noticed me, and I couldn't wait until we were at the restaurant. Because I wanted to know just where I stood with this woman.

Important things, such as if I could kiss and hold her close again.

I drove us to the restaurant, and after we were seated and ordered, Emmy said, "I've been thinking."

"Yes?"

She cleared her throat, rearranging the silverware on the table, and I could tell she was nervous. Before I could tell her to just put me out of my misery, she blurted, "If you want, I thought maybe we could, um, well, enjoy sharing our room, and especially the bed. What happens in Reno stays in Reno. We set rules and boundaries, make no promises, and have no regrets, only some fun between the sheets."

For a second, I just stared at her. I'd started the day thinking I'd have an uphill battle ahead of me. And here she was, offering herself on a platter instead.

"You might want to close your mouth before a bug flies in."

Her words snapped me back to the present, and my mind started working again. "Where has this come from? Not that I wouldn't fucking love to kiss you again, but I need to know why the change in attitude from yesterday?"

She went back to adjusting her silverware on the table and avoiding my eyes. "Well, as I said, there would be rules." She finally met my gaze, and I hated the uncertainty there. "I don't know if you're looking for a relationship or not, but I can't do one. All I can offer is some fun while we're here and you're kid-free. But only if you agree we go back to normal as soon as we leave Reno, back to being sort of friends but nothing else."

My first instinct was to shout "Hell yes!" and to get our food to go.

And yet, while I had no plans to get married again anytime soon, or ever, I didn't like there being no future for us. I already wanted Emmy more than any woman in my life. Add in how she loved my kids and could put up with my family, and I wanted to see where things went.

But saying anything would probably spook her, and

amazing sex might not be enough for her to give us a chance. She'd probably just try to push me away again.

All I could do was find ways to convince her, somehow, some way, that she deserved to go after the things she wanted.

Well, that and do my fucking best to ruin her for all other men.

A warning rushed through my head about how I had my children to think of, that I needed to protect them.

And maybe with a stranger, it would be a concern. But Avery and Wyatt already loved Emmy. Plus, if my family trusted her, I should at least give her a chance.

I finally answered, "I can handle your rules, but I have a condition of my own."

Her gaze turned wary. "Which is?"

"When we're alone, we're completely honest with each other. No lies, no half-truths or omissions. Just honesty."

She frowned, and I nearly held my breath. I was asking a lot, and I knew it. But I wanted—no needed—some honesty. I'd had too many years of lies and deceit and cheating.

Besides, it would give me a better idea of how to maybe win her over.

Emmy sighed. "Fine." She put out a hand to shake. "Deal."

My lips twitched at her gesture. Since I was determined to win her over from the get-go, I took her hand in mine, brought it to my lips, and kissed her fingers like some gentleman of old.

"West," she hissed as she took her hand back. "We're not in private."

"No, but now that I know I can have you, I needed a taste to hold me over." I let all the desire I had for her show in my eyes, and she put a hand on her neck and swallowed. "Should we get the food to go?"

She squeaked, "Will I get a chance to eat it?"

I learned forward. "Yes. But not until I've tasted you first."

She nodded as she swallowed, and I smiled. It was nice dusting off my charm and seeing how the older, more experienced version of Weston Wolfe could win over Emmy.

I wasn't going to hold anything back.

Emmy didn't stand a chance.

Chapter Twenty-Five

Emilia

The entire car ride from the restaurant back to the hotel made me feel like I was in high school again. I'd sneak a glance at West, he'd catch me, and I'd look away. Then I'd try again, and he'd meet my gaze and only look away because he was driving.

I couldn't stop remembering his words, "Not until I've tasted you first."

Squeezing my thighs together, I wondered what it'd feel like to have West's tongue teasing me, torturing me slowly, as I threaded my fingers through his hair, and he finally suckled my clit and made me come.

Abby had been right about one thing—the Wolfe brothers were *very* determined men.

And I hope it extended to all areas of their lives.

West pulled into his parking spot, turned off the car, and leaned over, whispering into my ear, "I bet if I undressed you right now, you'd already be wet and swollen for me, wouldn't you?"

Heat rushed through me, and my already sensitive clit pulsed harder. "Yes."

"Good. Because as soon as we're inside our room, I'm going to spoil my lunch by having dessert first. I've dreamed for weeks of how sweet you taste, Emmy. So you'd better hurry your fine ass up to the room as soon as I open your door, or I might have to carry you."

I vaguely remembered being in West's arms before, when I'd had too much to drink. And from some part of me I didn't even realize existed, I said, "Is that supposed to be a bad thing?"

He lightly brushed my cheek with his fingertips—only for a second—and then pulled away. "Enough. I want you naked. I'll play with you more later."

His words felt dirty and thrilling and only made me wetter.

I might've gotten in over my head with this guy.

And yet, I couldn't seem to care.

West exited his side, dashed to mine, and opened the door. As soon as I was out, a new boldness washed over me, and so I walked quickly, swaying my hips, feeling powerful. I knew West would watch me, it'd drive him mad, and maybe it'd bring out some of the fierceness from yesterday.

Because I still thought about his desperate kiss back at the lake.

The elevator ride was torture since there were several people riding with us. Even so, West brushed his finger against one of mine. The light touch sent a jolt of awareness through my body.

From a finger, one fucking finger.

Yep, I was in trouble.

We finally reached our floor, and neither of us said a word. We walked quickly, with West behind me but never touching me.

I was starting to regret the "only in private" part of the agreement.

No, no, no. I needed that stipulation—sex in private and pretending we were nothing but family friends in public. That way it'd be easier to walk away when we left Reno.

We reached the door, and as soon as we were inside, West put the food on the desk, gently pushed me against the wall, threaded his fingers into my hair, and stared in my eyes. I searched his gaze, waiting. I licked my lips, and his eyes moved to my mouth.

"You've been driving me fucking crazy with that mouth of yours. I bet you've been doing it on purpose."

His gravelly voice rolled over me and I shivered. "No, I haven't."

With his free hand, he traced my bottom lip, back and forth, each pass making me burn hotter. "I have plans for this mouth, Emilia." He gaze met mine again. "So many plans. But first, I'm claiming what's mine."

His words should've sent warning bells through my head, but as his lips pressed against mine, I forgot about everything else but the kiss.

Our tongues tangled as I pressed against him, needing to feel his hard body against mine. He was so warm and solid, and I itched to run my fingers up his back.

Before I could snake a hand under his shirt, West grabbed my ass and rocked me against his already hard cock. I moaned, wanting more, so much more.

Without thinking, I broke the kiss and asked, "Why are we still dressed?"

West's eyes turned molten. "Let's fix that. Strip off your clothes, sit on the bed, and spread those pretty thighs for me."

The command should've irritated the shit out of me. I was my own damn boss, I'd been independent since I was eighteen, and I normally balked at men telling me what to do.

But here and now, with West gazing at me as if I were the most beautiful woman in the world, it seemed...right. Like if I pleased him, he'd reward me. In a big way.

I undressed faster than I ever had in my life. Years of changing in locker rooms for swim meets had chased away most of my modesty anyway.

But as I sat on the bed, legs spread and my pussy exposed to West's hot, possessive gaze, my stomach started to churn with nerves.

"So fucking perfect," he said, his voice husky and deep.

And just like that, I wasn't nervous any longer.

He walked over to me, leaned down, and ran a finger through my center. I sucked in a breath when he lightly pushed inside me and then cried out when he pulled away.

West licked his finger and hummed. "That's the best fucking thing I've ever tasted, and I need more. I want you dripping down your leg, Emilia. So touch yourself until I tell you to stop."

I'd never done that in front of a guy before. And yet, the thought of disobeying his command didn't sit right with me. I shyly moved a hand between my legs, stroked once, and looked up at West again.

His gaze was trained on me, hungry and almost wild. "Before I start eating that sweet little pussy, I need you to show me what you like, Emilia. To see if what I've dreamed about doing to you is what you need."

His words send a rush of wetness between my thighs.

Later, I'd ask about those dream. For now, I was too impatient so I dipped my finger into my pussy before lightly stroking my clit in slow circles. West tugged off his shirt, and I drank in the sight of his broad shoulders and muscled chest. What I wouldn't give to touch the dark hair trailing down to underneath his jeans and back up again. Maybe I'd tug his chest hair lightly to see if he growled.

West stroked over his jean-clad cock, and I increased the pace of my finger, my breath coming fast and labored as I imagined unzipping his pants, taking out his cock, and torturing him with my tongue. I'd lap and circle the tip until he grabbed my hair and demanded for me to take him into my mouth.

I'd take him deep, moaning around his thick length,

and he'd move his hips faster and faster until he was nearly mad with desire.

For me.

Damn. I was close, so close.

West shucked his shoes, jeans, and boxers, and my mouth went dry. His cock was long and heavy, deliciously thick. As he touched the wetness on the tip and began to stroke himself, I rubbed myself faster. It wouldn't take much more to push me over the edge.

"Remove your hand, Emilia."

I whimpered, and he added, "I'll take care of you, I promise. But inside this room, you'll only come from my touch and no other. Understand?"

Damn, that was hot, and I stilled my hand. "Yes."

He walked up to me and traced one finger against my cheek. "Good girl."

Two words that made me shiver, in a good way.

West went farther up the bed, rearranged the pillows, and said, "Lie back against the pillows and keep your legs open for me."

I did as he asked, without hesitation. There was something freeing about not having to be in charge of this aspect of my life right now. I'd hate for it to be this way with everything, but here with West, it was perfect.

He removed something from his luggage, and he tossed the condom packet next to me before crawling on the bed and stopping between my legs. I couldn't resist teasing him. "Someone was optimistic when packing."

The corner of his mouth ticked up. "I bought them yesterday, after you went to dinner. Because after that fucking kiss, I was hopeful."

"Oh."

He placed a finger under my chin and raised my face until I met his gaze. "If you want to back out of this deal, say it now, Emilia, and I'll leave."

The rational part of my brain said to take the out. Even just this brief glimpse of West alone and naked set off warning bells inside my head. He'd barely even touched me, and I was hotter than I'd ever been in my life.

If he actually put his mouth on me and then his cock inside too, I wasn't sure if any other guy would ever compare.

Don't think of the future. Take these few days and live life to the fullest while you still can.

"No, of course I don't want to back out."

Relief filled his eyes but quickly vanished, replaced with the hot, hungry look he'd been wearing ever since I took off my clothes. "Good."

He ran a hand up one inner thigh and then the other. His hands were warm and rough and felt delicious against my skin.

West pushed against my inner thighs, opening me wide, and his gaze latched on to my pussy. "Spread your pretty cunt for me and keep your fingers there." His gaze met mine again. "I want you to feel my tongue against your pussy, against your fingers, to remind of how you're helping me to eat you senseless."

My heart pounded at his words. Before I could stop myself, I blurted, "Do you teach classes on dirty talk?"

West chuckled, and the sound was just as delicious as the feel of his rough fingers against me. "Do you want me to answer that or to finally suckle your clit between my teeth?"

Oh god. I could just imagine what that felt like. "The second."

He chuckled again but settled on the bed, head between my legs, and he looked at me with an expectant expression.

I slowly ran my hands down my front, taking a moment to caress my breasts and roll my nipples, and West growled. "Fuck yes, Emilia."

His words emboldened me, and I spent more time pinching and plucking the taut peaks, moaning and spreading my legs wider.

"Enough for now. Open that sweet pussy for me, Emilia. I'm starving."

I moved my hands between my legs and did as he asked. For a second, I felt incredibly exposed. But West growled, "Mine," and finally laved his tongue up my center and then against my clit.

My hips arched off the bed at the warm, wet touch. And soon I was writhing and arching into his licks and swirls and suckles. Every once in a while, he'd run his tongue down my center, lightly fuck me with it, and then return to sweetly torturing my clit.

He was relentless, and it felt a little dirtier whenever he licked my fingers, reminding me that I spread myself for him.

Then he finally thrust a finger inside me, and I cried out. It felt good, but not enough, not nearly enough. "West."

"So hot and tight and damn perfect. I can't wait to be

inside you. But first, you're going to come for me, Emilia. And scream my name as you do. Understand?"

My pussy throbbed, and my clit pulsed, and I was almost desperate as I replied, "Yes."

"Yes what?'

"Yes, I'll cry out your name."

With a growl, he sucked my clit between his teeth and lightly nibbled. The mixture of pain and pleasure sent me over the edge. The orgasm crashed over me, the spasms so intense I screamed and cried out West's name. I also cursed him as he continued to torture me, drawing it out.

When he finally relented, I melted against the bed. It took everything I had to keep my hands in place, but I wasn't about to ruin all the hard work I'd done following his command.

West took one of my hands, brought it to his lips, and kissed the palm. He repeated the gesture with the other before leaning down and murmuring, "Good girl," and claiming my mouth.

This time it was slow, gentle, and I could taste myself on his lips. And yet, it only made me ache all over again, wanting more, so much more.

He pinned my hands to either side of my head and finally broke the kiss. His eyes burned into mine. "Tell me how you want me to fuck you the first time. Tell me your fantasy."

I searched his gaze. "How are you real?"

He nipped my bottom lip. "Tell me, Emilia. Because I'm so fucking hard and feel as if I'll die if I'm not inside you soon."

Maybe some women would lie and think slow and gentle and missionary was the only choice, to avoid being seen as demanding or bold. And yet, West would probably be able to tell if I lied. So I blurted, "Bend me over the bed and fuck me hard, West. That's what I want."

He kissed me, his tongue devouring my mouth for nearly a minute before he pulled away and got off the bed. I nearly cried out at the loss of his touch but resisted, his eyes telling me he wouldn't abandon me.

After picking up the condom packet and ripping it open, he took it out and rolled it over his cock. When done, he said, "Stand up and face away from me."

I did so, although my legs wobbled when I stood. West steadied me, his hands on my hips, and he lightly brushed his thumbs over my skin. Back and forth, in a slow, maddening rhythm.

I growled, and he chuckled before nuzzling my neck. "So impatient."

"You're the one who said you felt as if you'd die if you weren't inside me."

"True." He kissed the side of my neck. "Now, brace yourself on the bed, spread your legs, and let me turn that fantasy into reality."

Once I was in position, my ass in the air and my pussy on display again, West ran one of his rough hands over my ass cheek. Then I felt a light nip on the opposite one before he kissed the same spot. "You have such a fucking bitable ass, Emilia." He nipped the other cheek, and I moaned. Never would I have thought that teeth on my butt would make my pussy even wetter. But there was just something about this man that drove me wild.

After kissing my lower back, he stood, and I could feel his hard cock against my pussy. I arched my hips, desperate to feel him inside me. But he was content to rub the head of his dick through my slit, teasing my clit with little slaps, and then retreating before torturing me all over again.

Weston Wolfe had porn-star levels of control. Seriously. No guy before him had ever lasted this long, and I doubted anyone after would either.

The thought of being with another man sent a thread of sadness through my heart, but I pushed it away. Right here, right now, the future didn't matter.

West ran a hand down my back and up again. Then he pushed his cock inside me, and I moaned as he stretched and filled me. It'd been a while, I was tight, and he was so damn thick.

But eventually, he stilled and groaned. "Fuck, Emilia. It's as if you were made to grip me exactly the way I like it."

He held my hips in place and started to move. Slowly at first, and then he moved faster and harder, and I gripped the bedspread, moaning and arching into his touch. I moved my hips in time to his, loving how at this angle, he hit that spot inside me that felt so good.

Gripping my hair, he tugged lightly, and I moaned louder. West growled, "Who's inside you right now?"

"You."

"And who owns your pussy?"

"You."

"Squeeze me, Emilia. Let me know you're claiming my dick too."

It was hard to concentrate, as I was already getting close to coming again. But I squeezed my inner muscles, and damn, it made everything much more intense.

"Fuck, yes. There's my good girl. Keep doing that."

It was difficult, and I just wanted to let him claim me and take it. But I clenched and teased him, and he rewarded me by rubbing my clit. "Come for me, Emilia."

As he pinched my clit, I came, the orgasm even more intense than the first one, to the point that I cried out and screamed and shouted his name.

He released my hair, and with a grunt, he gripped my hips and stilled, his groan something I would never forget—as if he were both dying and happy at the same time.

When West finished, he leaned down and kissed the nape of my neck, the touch light and tender. "I thought you'd kill me with that surprisingly strong pussy of yours."

I giggled—actually giggled—and West laughed. He pulled out of me. I only had a second to lament the loss before he stood me up, turned me around, and pulled me up against him. He cupped my cheeks with his hands and kissed me tenderly. "When can we do that again?"

He sounded so damn eager, which only made me smile. "And here I thought older men needed more time to recover."

After nipping my bottom lip, he growled, "I love that mouth of yours. And I can't wait to stuff my dick inside it and have you suck me dry."

My earlier images came rushing back, and it sent a new rush of heat through me.

But my stomach decided to rumble that second, and West frowned. "You're hungry."

I waggled my eyebrows. "For many things."

He barked out a laugh and lightly slapped my ass. "Food first. Then maybe you can stuff your mouth with my dick."

"So bossy."

"And you love it."

He smirked, and I stuck out my tongue at him.

West took my hand and guided me to the table.

"Wait, we're eating naked?"

"More than that. You're going to eat while sitting in my lap."

"Why? I'll probably end up spilling something on you or me, and I'd rather not get chili anything in certain places."

"I'll protect your pussy with a napkin. As for anywhere else, that's what showers are for, Emilia. Just imagine—you wet and slippery, making it easy for me to tease you to a fever pitch. Then I'd kneel and lap between your thighs as you hold my head close, keeping me prisoner until you cry out my name again."

My cheeks heated. "You keep saying these things as if they're bad."

"Such a dirty girl. I like it." He kissed me. "But food first. And us both staying naked means we don't have to dress and undress all over again, wasting precious time. And I want all the time I can get with you in this room."

I knew he had to mean sex and more sex. Except a

small part of me wondered if I could have both the commanding man in the bedroom and the man who sang Disney songs in the car or who got into a water fight with his son.

No. I needed to stop thinking of the future. For so many reasons, it wouldn't work, wouldn't last.

West released my hand to retrieve a towel from the bathroom—his condom was gone when he returned—and lay it down on the chair. He grunted. "I don't want to know who else has sat their bare asses here."

"Maybe you should've brought a black light. That would've shown you everything that's gone on here."

"No way. I don't want to think of any other guy's cum on the bed, or wherever the hell they spread it."

He grabbed my hand again. Once he lowered down, he pulled me onto his lap so that I sat on one leg, with my legs between his thighs.

Which put my leg against his already hard cock.

For some reason, I couldn't help but laugh at the thought of eating naked with a hard-on. Not for the first time, I was glad I wasn't born a man.

West lightly tugged my hair. "Now what are you thinking about?"

Since we'd agreed on honesty, I didn't hesitate. "You're just sitting here, eating lunch with a naked woman in your lap, and a dick like stone just chilling there."

"The only time I get hard at a table is when you're sitting at it."

His gaze turned intense, and I remembered all the times I'd caught him staring at me over dinner at the

Wolfe place, and shivered. "I'm a sure thing for the next couple of days, so you don't need to keep dropping one-liners like that."

I reached for my takeout container as West said, "I'm just being honest, Emmy. You're so fucking beautiful and smart and kind. Why wouldn't I want you?"

It was on the tip of my tongue to say because I only brought trouble to those who loved me. Not that West felt that way about me, but it was all too easy to imagine dating and falling for him.

No. Wanting to distract him, I speared my fork with a bit of the burrito covered in sauce and cheese and raised it to his mouth.

West raised his brows. "You're feeding me?"

"Well, it's selfish, really. You need your strength if you're going to make me orgasm that hard again."

With a growl, he took the food off my fork as his hand caressed my waist. Such a simple touch, somewhere between possessive and comfort, in that way trusting couples had.

I quickly shoveled some food into my mouth.

Whether from hunger or just impatience to fuck again, we both fell mostly silent and ate quickly. I was beyond full and, without thinking, laid my head on West's shoulder and closed my eyes.

His hands went to my waist and back, caressing me softly, gently, adoringly.

I sighed, taking a second to memorize everything about this moment. It was one I'd remember for a long time, maybe even the rest of my life.

The peace didn't last, however, as my purse vibrated

strongly, over and over, meaning someone was calling me.

West nuzzled the top of my head. "Do you have a remote-controlled vibrator in there?"

I snorted and opened my eyes. "You wish." I hesitated and then thought screw it, and let the devil in me say, "I have one, though, and it can be fun."

As my phone continued to ring, West merely groaned—no doubt thinking of what I might do with said vibrator—and I maneuvered myself off his lap. His hand followed me, touching me as long as possible until I walked too far way.

I instantly felt cold and as if I was missing something.

My purse stilled, and I took out my phone. "Damn. Three missed calls from Abby and like ten text messages."

I opened the texts and read them:

Abby: Want to meet up for lunch?

Abby: Emmy? Where'd you go?

Abby: Did you finally seduce my brother?

Abby: I don't want details <vomiting emoji> but just a yes or no.

Abby: Okay, I'm assuming yes.

Abby: Hmm, are you getting married in secret?

Abby: If you won't answer, then I'll just guess. I think you want Elvis to walk you down the aisle. They do that in Reno too? I think?

Abby: If Beck finds out about this before me through West, I'll never forgive you.

Abby: I will. Maybe. But don't get too distracted by D.

Abby: Ugh, I can't believe I had to say that about my brother. Seriously, you owe me. And I'm going to even, gasp, call you now.

By the end, I was laughing. Abby and I usually answered each other quickly, especially at events we worked together.

That she'd guessed some of it—the hooking up part—didn't surprise me.

West pressed up behind me. He placed his hands on my hips and set his chin on my shoulder. "What's so funny?"

"Abby." I sobered a bit. "She's guessed about us, West. Just so you know."

"I wouldn't expect anything less. You two have always been thick as thieves."

Even if he'd never said it aloud, I knew he regretted the years he'd been gone, missing the chance to see his siblings grow up. His pained looks whenever Abby shared a memory were hard to miss. Well, at least for me.

I had been watching the damn man too closely for months now.

My phone luckily had that feature where it'd put the text of the voicemail for you to see. While not perfect, her calls basically matched her texts, except for one crucial detail. I swore.

West asked, "What?"

"Abby met the flower supplier I've been dying to talk with. The company I use now is great for simpler weddings but wouldn't be able to handle bigger events." I paused, biting my lip, debating if I should tell him about my plans.

Then he squeezed my hips. "Tell me."

I turned to face him. "Well, I'm trying to land a wedding from one of Nolan's friends, a famous movie star. And if she signs with me, I'll need a company who can handle things on a much grander scale."

He nodded. "Then you should go meet with this company."

I searched his gaze. He was right, of course. And yet part of me thought that if I walked out that door, he'd back out of our arrangement.

But I wanted West as many times as I could have him before we left Reno.

He kissed my nose. "Don't worry. I have plans for you tonight." He nipped my earlobe and whispered, "Part of them include you on your knees, swallowing my dick, and moaning as I coat your throat with my cum."

Just his words made heat rush between my legs. "Promise?"

He chuckled. "We're sharing a room, and there's only one bed. And before you say anything, the cot will be gone before you return. So you'll be stuck sharing that bed with me, Emilia."

After moving back enough so I could see his face, West cupped my cheek. He whispered, "A reminder of what's to come."

He kissed me, slowly at first before his tongue explored my mouth, teased my tongue, and then pulled back. "Now, get dressed and run your business like the boss you are."

I stared up at West for a beat, feeling confused and vulnerable and almost like I should run far, far away.

Because this man was a danger to all my plans and determination and beliefs about what I thought I wanted.

I'd just have to be really damn careful in the future.

And so I dressed, readied myself, and went looking for Abby so I could retreat and hide behind my work again.

Though how I was going to deal with the very large and tempting problem of Weston Wolfe after we left Reno, I had no fucking idea.

Chapter Twenty-Six

Weston

It'd been fucking hard to watch Emmy leave the room and not follow her. I'd barely had a taste of her, and she was already gone.

It wasn't just the sex—although that had been amazing—but the simple act of eating lunch with her and teasing her had been...nice. More than nice, in truth.

Weird as it was, it'd felt like we'd been dating for a while already, were comfortable with each other, and went from teasing to dirty in no time flat.

I ran a hand through my hair and sighed. Any pretense that I could resist her was out the fucking window now. Being with Emmy was what I'd always dreamed of having in a partner—sexy as hell in bed but a friend outside of it.

However, my cynical ass still had doubts about forever. Given my first marriage, it would be hard not to. There had been times, in the beginning, when'd I'd been so damn hopeful.

Regardless of my past, I was determined to try with Emmy. Because if the version of her who taught my daughter to swim could exist alongside the one who made me laugh one minute and then turned my cock hard the next, I might consider the big M word again.

Marriage.

But I was getting ahead of myself. The next couple days were about fucking Emmy as much as possible and wooing her a little when we weren't. Long-term plans would have to wait.

Too bad real life would take up most of our time in Reno.

After I cleaned up, I went to the secure storage area to catalogue the wine for the event. Once done, I knew Abby and Emmy would still be a while yet. So I took out my phone to call my kids, only to see texts from my aunt. With a sigh, I read them:

Aunt Lori: Avery wants to text you some emojis but said she's not allowed. So the next message will be from her, with my permission.

Aunt Lori: <unicorn emoji> <cat emoji> <fairy emoji> <pirate flag emoji> <lizard emoji> <horse emoji>

Aunt Lori: Me again. She said that's her day so far and wants you to make a story from it later.

Aunt Lori: Try to have some fun and don't do anything I wouldn't do. <winking emoji>

I chuckled, just imagining what kind of adventure Avery and Wyatt had experienced today. And I instantly missed my kids.

Needing to hear my kids' voices, I dialed Aunt Lori, and she picked up on the second ring.

"The twins don't take naps anymore, so you're a little early for story time."

"I'm aware. Is Avery or Wyatt around?"

"No, Zach took them into town to visit the All Things Shop. Probably to get some ideas for their birthday this fall. We're going to have a huge party, by the way, since it's their first one in Starry Hills."

Wyatt, in particular, didn't like to be the center of attention. "Do they even want one?"

"I asked, and even Wyatt said yes after a private conversation with his sister."

Which meant Wyatt might not actually want a party but found it hard to say no to his twin.

"Well, if they want one, let me know what I need to buy. No bouncy castles or clowns or shit like that, though."

"They're going to be eleven, not five."

I hesitated and then remembered my aunt's words about not keeping my family walled off. "They've never had a party before so just don't overwhelm them."

"Why not?"

"Their grandparents wouldn't allow it. And no

amount of arguing from me would change their minds either."

My aunt paused a few seconds before saying, "Well, I'm glad you three are back home with us. I'll make sure to spoil you all for the foreseeable future."

I smiled. "Thanks, Aunt Lori."

"Think nothing of it. Just don't forget to buy me a tacky Reno mug while you're there."

Aunt Lori loved the weirdest, tackiest mugs from tourist destinations, saying they were like ugly Christmas sweaters you could show off all year long. "I'll buy the ugliest one I can find. Talk to you later, Aunt Lori."

"Love you too, West."

She hung up, and I stared at my phone. I didn't know why I had trouble saying those words to anyone but my children, but I did.

Probably because the last time I'd said them to Andrea, she'd thrown them back in my face.

"If you loved me, you would let my parents raise the kids and give me all your attention. I'm your wife. I was first. But you won't do that, so you don't love me at all."

Not wanting the past to ruin my time in Reno, I locked that shit up and went to do a few more things on my list for the expo. The earlier I could sneak back to the room, the more time I could prepare for Emmy and what I planned to do with her.

Chapter Twenty-Seven

Emilia

Katie: So, have you boned West yet?
Me: WTF are you talking about?
Katie: Oh, come on. I heard you're sharing a room now. It's bound to happen. I mean, I have eyes and I've seen how you guys mentally undress each other.
Me: Abby. <swearing emoji>
Katie: She might've had some wine and texted me last night. I'm innocent. <angel emoji>
Me: Says the woman asking me if I boned West.
Katie: So, have you? He's hot, in a scowly-hairy way.
Me: He's not hairy.
Katie: Aha! You've seen him naked.

Me: He swam in my pool. And it's not the 1800s, when he'd have a full-body swimsuit.
Katie: Right. Well, you'll talk eventually. Abby won't want to hear about West's dick, but I will. Strictly for research purposes, of course.
Me: <lying Pinocchio emoji>
Katie: <blowing a kiss emoji>

Once Abby and I finished our meeting with Maria Hernandez, the premier flower vendor in Northern California, and were alone again, Abby hugged me. "You did it."

I smiled. "You helped."

"Still, Maria's very picky about which clients she takes on. And yet you made it seem easy to win her over."

I shrugged. "Well, I'd done my research beforehand. And if you come prepared, praise with honesty, and have a business proposal in mind, it's a lot easier to get what you want."

Abby sighed. "All of this reminds me why I wanted to be a teacher. Business doesn't come as easily to me as it does for you."

"And I'm sure you'll be in a classroom again soon, Abby. Your dream job is out there."

Abby scrunched her nose. "I don't know. I get asked in interviews why I turned down the job in San Jose, and it's not like I can say my mentor teacher took advantage, used me as his fuck toy, and then tossed me away when it was convenient."

The story was a little more complicated than that, but I knew what she meant. "That douchebag will get what's coming to him eventually, Abby. But you're an amazing teacher, and I won't let you give up your dreams because of that loser. Even if I love working with you and having you as a roommate, I know it's not what you want to do forever."

"Yeah. I'm super grateful for the job, but it's definitely not my passion."

I hugged Abby. "I know. But for now, though, we're kicking ass and taking names. If we get the Zara Jones account, the sky will be the limit."

Abby studied me a second, and I knew what she would ask. To be honest, I was surprised she'd lasted this long without blurting it out. "So you and my brother are a thing now, huh?"

"That obvious, is it?"

"Well, you had that I've-been-fucked-good look when we met up earlier."

"I hope only you noticed it and not Maria."

"Don't worry, it was just me. She probably just thought you were in a good mood. And you were, by the way. Does that mean you're giving West a chance?"

"Only while we're in Reno, and then things go back to the way they were."

"Hmm." I opened my mouth, but Abby beat me to it. "I'm not going to say another word. But just give West a chance, Emmy. He's had a shitty time so far and could use a little fun and laughter in his life."

His difficult past was exactly why he should stay far away from me. Because I'd probably end up hurting him eventually, making his life shitty again.

Speaking of the devil, West texted me:

West: Come on up when you're ready. We're dining in tonight.

I smiled, and Abby snorted. "That smile speaks volumes. Just go. And don't be late for tomorrow morning! Even if most of the prep work is done, the doors open at ten a.m., and you don't want to miss it."

"Yes, Mom."

Abby stuck out her tongue, and we both laughed. I waved and did my best not to run to the elevator.

By the time I reached our room, my heart thudded in my chest, and my palms sweated a little. Both in anticipation and nervousness.

What did he have planned for us?

I knocked, and the door swung open. West stood there in an untucked button-down shirt, dark jeans, and brown cowboy boots. He'd also shaved, and his hair was still damp from a shower.

West always looked sexy, but my mouth turned dry at him all cleaned up.

He grabbed my hand and tugged me inside. "I wish I had some M&Ms or something so I could toss it into your mouth. It's hanging wide open."

His words snapped me back. "It's just shock from you actually wearing a nice shirt."

"Not all of us have jobs where we can dress up and stay clean until the end of the day."

"Thank goodness. I like you a little disheveled and dirty."

His eyes turned heated for a second before he shook his head. "Stop that. I'm trying to be a gentleman and give you a nice dinner." He leaned in and whispered, "Making you beg and scream my name comes later. If you're a good girl."

He pulled back, and it took everything I had not to reach for him, haul him closer, and kiss him. But it was also fun playing with him a bit, with our clothes still on. "Someone's cocky."

He put his hand to his ear. "What? You're asking about my cock and heard about how big it is?"

After he winked at me, I laughed. "Maybe you are getting old and hard of hearing."

With a growl, he pulled me close, and I gasped as he pressed his knee between my legs. He continued to rock me on his firm, muscled thigh as he said, "I have a fuck-ton of patience, Emilia. And I plan to put it to use later. Every time you say I'm old, I'll just have to keep you teetering on the edge that much longer."

I had to grip West's forearm to keep from falling over as he moved my hips, grinding me against his leg. I was close, so close.

Then he stepped away, and I growled. "What the hell?"

Amusement danced in his eyes. "Had to rest my old joints for a bit. Sorry."

I stuck my tongue out at him. "You're mean."

He smirked. "You started it."

Well, true. But now it was war.

So I lifted the hem of my dress, showing him I had no underwear on, and then I dipped my finger to gather some wetness before I circled my clit. With his scorching eyes watching, it took me less than a minute before I cried out, and the orgasm washed over me.

West was there to steady me as my legs gave out. His breath was hot as he whispered into my ear, "Now who's being mean?"

I dropped my dress and stood on my tiptoes to press a kiss to the corner of his mouth. "I can be much, much meaner."

He tried to pull me close, but I managed to wiggle away and dashed for the bathroom. Before I could reach it, he snagged me around the waist, carried me to the bed, and tossed me down. In the next second, he had my wrists pinned to the bed and his body over mine. Our breaths mingled as he stared at me.

The mixture of heat and amusement did something to my insides. I'd never imagined being able to have fun like this, let alone with a guy. One I liked more and more, the longer I was around him.

West bit my bottom lip and then took my mouth in a searing kiss. His tongue wasted no time in caressing my tongue, all while his hips ground against mine.

I was so lost in his heat and taste and scent that I

blinked when he finally pulled away and rose to his knees.

Then I saw him undo his fly, remove his dick, and take the condom from his pocket. Once it was on, he leaned down, whispered, "I can't wait," and then kissed me as he thrust his cock inside me.

I moaned, arching into him, as he pinned me again and thrust hard. Again and again. The bed shook, and he swallowed my moans with his mouth.

It was rough and needy and raw.

Like if he didn't fuck me, he'd die.

He released one of my hands and strummed my clit, still taking me with hard, quick thrusts, and soon, I cried out again. West followed right after and laid his forehead on my shoulder.

We lay there for a minute, catching our breaths. It was strangely erotic to be mostly dressed with West still inside me, highlighting how he'd wanted me so badly he couldn't even take the time to get naked.

He kissed up my neck, my jaw, my cheek, forehead, and eventually my mouth again. Part of me wanted to read more into his tender kiss. But I refused to do so.

West pulled back so he could see me. He moved a hand to brush hair back from my face. "You're so fucking beautiful, Emmy. I don't tell you that enough."

His eyes were sincere, and my throat closed with emotion. If I didn't do something, I might start crying.

And since this was supposed to be a no-strings-attached few days of sex, I needed to get my shit together. He wasn't my boyfriend, could never be, and I needed to be strong and independent and responsible like I'd been for so long. Even when I'd lived with the Wolfe family, I'd almost always kept up appearances of being happy and content.

I pushed against his shoulder. Even though he frowned, he moved away and let me up.

I asked, "So, what's this night you have planned for me?"

His brows came together for a second but then eased. "Give me a second."

He walked into the bathroom. When he returned, his jeans were done up again, and he carried a wet washcloth. "Spread your legs."

Frowning, I did. When he gently cleaned between my thighs, my throat grew tight again.

How the hell was this man real? And how had his late wife not appreciated him?

Not your concern, Emmy.

Once he'd discarded the washcloth and returned to the room, he pulled out a chair at the table. "Your dinner will arrive soon, madam."

"Madam? That makes me sound about fifty and really old."

"Well, if you're old, then I'm about to expire any minute now."

He winked, and I couldn't help but laugh. As I slid into the seat, he pushed it up and sat across from me.

I propped my chin on my hand. "It's weird to see this side of you. Who'd have thought that the guy who grunts all the time could tease me so much?"

West lifted one shoulder. "Sometimes we hide who we are to protect ourselves. I think I did that once my marriage fell apart the first time, and every time after that."

Things had just turned deadly serious. And yet, I didn't want to brush past what he'd shared.

So I dared to ask, "What I never understood was why you left with her? I get that you married her because she got pregnant. But surely you knew your family would've stood by you?"

There was a knock, and West went to answer it. I crossed my arms, a little irritated at the interruption.

He returned with takeout bags. The smell of tomatoes, chili, and garlic filled the room, and my mouth watered. Had he really ordered one of my favorite foods?

As soon as he put the opened container of arrabbiata pasta in front of me, then the salad, garlic bread and even wine—Starry Wolfe wine, of course—I stared at him. "Did you know this is my favorite, or did you just make a lucky guess?"

"The one time Beck made this dish and we were both there, you made little moans and sounds of pleasure as you ate it. I figured you liked it."

My cheeks heated at the thought of West noticing my weakness for spicy, tomato noodle goodness. "I do. It's just that I can never make it from scratch quite right, and the jarred stuff is never as good as homemade." I paused and then added softly, "My mom made the best kind. It still reminds me of her."

I stared down at my food and remembered my mother placing a giant bowl of pasta on the table with a flourish. Her apron had always been dirty with sauce and who knew what else—she'd not been a tidy cook.

But my dad, brother, and I had always competed to make the loudest sounds of pleasure with smacking lips or hums or whatever ridiculous thing we thought of until my mom would laugh and tell us to stop being silly.

I swallowed. I hadn't recalled those memories in years.

For years, I'd been able to pack away those memories and keep them from escaping. But for some reason, West kept bringing them out.

His hand covered one of mine, and I met his gaze. The understanding in them made my eyes heat with tears. "I know what it's like to miss a parent, Emmy. My aunt has been encouraging me to treasure the memories I have instead of always trying to keep them locked up. I'm stubborn as fuck, but I'm slowly starting to think she's right. Don't tell her that, of course, or I'll never live it down."

Needing a distraction from my own memories, I focused back on West. "You never answered my earlier question. Your family loves you, so why did you leave Starry Hills?"

He sighed, removed his hand, and twirled his fork in the pasta.

I sensed he was gathering his thoughts, so I didn't push.

Once I'd eaten a little and picked up my wine glass, he finally said, "Everything reminded me of my dad. I'm the oldest, and Dad had spent the most time teaching me how to run the winery and vineyards. He'd made big plans, saying one day I'd take it over. Then, like now, I wasn't sure if that's what I really wanted. And being young and stupid, I figured if I could prove to him I wasn't responsible enough to take it over, he'd leave me alone."

West fell silent, and I studied him. I'd never really considered if he wanted to run the family business or not.

"Did you ever tell your dad the truth?"

After shaking his head, West met my gaze again. Regret blazed in the blue depths. "I should've stepped up. But I was so fucking young, only twenty when he died." He paused before replying so softly I barely heard it, "I was supposed to be there with him and Beck, inspecting the orchard, when my dad had his heart attack."

The death of Jeremy Wolfe had come not long after I'd lost my own parents, and most of that time had been a blur for me. I wondered if I hadn't been in the car crash, then would I have noticed how the death of West's dad had affected him.

He sipped his wine before continuing, "Me dicking around, always staying out late and shirking my responsibilities, probably added to his stress load. I sometimes wonder if I'd just been the good son, or maybe talked to him like a grown-ass man, he wouldn't have had the heart attack that killed him."

"Oh, West."

He smiled wryly. "I know it's fucking stupid to think me merely showing up one day would've changed everything. Or that the stresses of the business or all my siblings probably contributed to his heart problems, not to mention genetics and his love of bacon and greasy shit. I recognize that all now. But back when I was twenty? Andrea showed up, saying she was pregnant, and I saw my chance to run from it all. Then I wouldn't have to wonder if my mom looked at me with anger, wishing I'd been a better eldest son. Or I could avoid Beck looking so damn haunted, after watching our dad die right before his eyes. Not to mention how confused Abby, Zach, and Zane had been, not understanding that their dad would never come home." He drank some more wine. "I was a fucking coward, plain and simple. I justified it, saying I was doing right by Andrea, marrying her even if I didn't love her. And I vowed to be the best fucking dad ever, to make up for being such a shitty son."

West looked so sad and lonely that I couldn't help but get up, walk over, and get him to push back so I could sit in his lap. His arms wrapped around me, and I held him close.

For a man who always tried to look strong and unaffected to strangers, he was deep and vulnerable and just a little broken.

A little broken like me.

We sat that way for a few minutes, me just wanting to comfort him until he was ready.

Eventually his angry laugh startled me. "If that wasn't bad enough, I didn't even visit my mom when she got really sick. I was too busy trying to help Andrea when she didn't want it. At the time, it felt as if saving Andrea meant I could save myself, in some weird-ass sense of logic. But I failed at that too. I sometimes think that's all I'm good at—failure."

"No."

He looked at me, and I added, "You're an amazing father, West. Don't even try to deny it. You love Wyatt and Avery so very much. Even when I couldn't stand you, that one thing always stood out to me. You're a good dad."

His gaze softened. "I try. Though sometimes I don't know what the fuck I'm doing. And in a few years, they'll be teenagers, and I'm going to have more gray hairs than I know what to do with."

Part of me wanted to say I could be there. I could help. And yet, that meant thinking of a future, of allowing myself glimpses of happiness.

It should be easy, and yet, I still felt responsible for my parents' death.

They'd want you to be happy. Maybe. But in this moment, I didn't quite feel worthy of that.

Although for the first time in my life, West made me question if I should take a chance and hope I didn't hurt someone else I cared for.

West squeezed me gently for a second before moving a hand to my cheek and caressing it with the back of his fingers. "That's why I left, Emmy. Coming home was so fucking hard, but you've made it easier, both for me and my kids. So, thank you."

I searched his gaze, unsure of what to say to that.

So I kissed him gently before getting off his lap. He let me go, watching as I sat across from him.

We ate in silence for a little while. Not really strained but almost as if we both had a lot to think about. West, about his family and probably his future. And me, about if I wanted to risk hurting a man who'd been hurt so many times before, if things didn't work out between us.

And honestly? I hadn't the faintest idea of what to do. So I attacked my food and drank my wine, hoping an easy answer would come to me.

Then an upbeat ringtone blared through the room, and West shook his head. "That would be my kids. Sorry, I need to take it."

I shook my head. "Don't apologize."

He answered the call, and I watched as love and happiness filled his eyes. What I didn't expect was for him to soon switch it to speakerphone and for Avery to ask, "Will you help us make up a story tonight, Emmy? Please?"

Chapter Twenty-Eight

Weston

To say the night had turned heavy was an understatement. I never talked about my dad, let alone about how I'd acted out, trying to disappoint him so I wouldn't have to run the vineyards and winery. Revealing the reasons to Emmy about why I'd run away with Andrea had even surprised me.

When Emmy had sat on my lap to hold me, something had shifted inside me. I couldn't imagine her ever ignoring my kids, or asking me to send them away so I could pay attention to her, or even going out screwing every guy she came across, in some weird way of trying to make me jealous.

I was fucking terrified, but I wanted this woman to be mine. And for more than a few days in Reno.

As I sat thinking about how I could make that happen, my phone rang. It was early for my kids' bedtime, but no doubt they were excited. I picked up and said, "Hello."

Avery answered, "Daddy! You'll never believe what we did today with Uncle Zach! Not only did we find some amazing stuff for our birthday this year, but there was a sign-up for swim lessons! We're going to swim with the other kids. And maybe Emmy can help me learn a little faster, so I can be the best."

I smiled. "We'll see, love. I'm having dinner with Emmy, so I can ask her later."

Fuck. I hadn't meant to let that slip.

But my daughter caught it and said, "Then put it on speakerphone! Unless you're at a restaurant or casino or something?"

"What do you know about casinos?"

"Uncle Zach told us all about them. I want to visit the circus one."

I nearly muttered that her uncle could take her, then.

"Daddy? Are you still there?"

"Yes, I'm here. And yes, I can put you on speakerphone." I punched the button and said, "Go ahead."

Avery asked loudly, "Will you help us make up a story tonight, Emmy? Please?"

Emmy blinked at me, understandably. I explained, "We sometimes make bedtime stories together, each of us taking a turn to add a little bit more to the tale. But we only do it if both Avery and Wyatt agree to participate. Is Wyatt there?"

"I'm here, Dad. And as long as Avery stops hogging the phone, I want to make one tonight."

I said, "Share with your brother, Avery."

She sighed dramatically—heaven help me when she became a teenager—and answered, "Fine. So, Emmy, will you help?"

Emmy stood and walked over. Without thinking, I took her hand and pulled her to the bed.

As we sat down, side by side, she said, "I'll try. I don't have the best imagination, though."

Her hand was still in mine, and I squeezed it. "Well, we'll go Wyatt, Avery, me, and then you. That way you can see how it's done."

Emmy smiled. "Okay."

The image of us doing this with my kids in person flashed in my head, and longing washed over me.

Knowing that Wyatt would need a little prodding to get started, I focused on the phone and the story. "All right, Wyatt. Kick us off."

After a few beats, he finally spoke. "There once was a pirate family who ruled the seas. Their ship was bigger than anyone else's, the most powerful, and no one could ever defeat them. But one day..."

I watched Emmy's face as Avery picked it up. "But one day a fairy queen rode a giant horse on the water, with a fire-breathing dragon on her shoulder. The little dragon flew around the ship and..."

Amusement danced in Emmy's gaze, and I only wanted to add to it. "The little dragon could breathe fire like a fire blade, and he cut off all the sails, so they fell into the water. Without the wind, the ship couldn't move, and..."

Emmy bit her lip a second—which I did my best not to notice but fucking failed—and then finally spoke. "The ship couldn't move and was stranded. But once the fairy queen left them, the little girl and boy called for their friends, the ones who lived under the water. Then..."

She was much better at this than she'd let on, that was for sure.

Wyatt grunted, paused, and then took his turn. "Then the water cats rose to the surface. Instead of fur, they had scales and little spikes. Oh, and their tails had fins on them. Since the kids always fed them treats, they were friends. The kids said they'd give the water cats more treats if they would..."

Avery's voice became fast, like it did when she was excited. "They'd give them more treats if they went down to the deepest part of the ocean and called on the ruler of the seas, who was..."

I jumped in. "Who was busy decorating the ocean, making sure all the shells and coral and plants were in place. So instead she sent her pet unicorn, who, instead of hair for her tail, had little tentacles with fins. The giant sea unicorn came to the surface..."

Emmy mouthed, "What the hell?" And I bit back a laugh. I could've made it easy for her, but nah, that wouldn't be any fun.

Avery said, "Come on, Emmy! You can do it!"

Emmy laughed. "Okay, okay. Well, the unicorn asked the sea cats to make some really special sails out of the strongest seaweed, a kind that the humans had never discovered. The unicorn helped the sea cats attach the sails to the masts with all her tentacles and then..."

Wyatt jumped in, "And then, as the pirate parents got the ship moving again, the sea unicorn let the kids ride on her back. Soon they caught up to the evil fairy queen and..."

Avery said, "The parents asked the sea cats to attack the evil queen. They did, and once the fairy queen fell off her water horse, she turned into foam and died. The horse's spell was broken, along with the little dragon, and..."

I decided I wouldn't be a dick and would help give them the ending they wanted. "They thanked the pirate family for their help and decided to travel with them. And so..."

Emmy smiled at me. "And so the pirate family continued sailing the ocean as a family, stealing from those who were evil and helping those who needed it. They became super famous and beloved. The end."

I brought Emmy's hand to my lips and kissed it. I mouthed, "Thank you."

Avery clapped. "You did amazing, Emmy! You have a great imagination. I hope you can help with our stories again in the future. Maybe Daddy can invite you over for dinner, and you can stay the night, like a sleepover."

I wanted that so badly—although a very adult sleepover, after the kids were asleep—but Emmy's expression turned unreadable.

I quickly said, "We'll see, Avery. Now, we have some

stuff to do before bed, and then we have work tomorrow. Listen to what Aunt Lori says and get ready for bed."

"Love you, Daddy! And you too, Emmy!"

I felt her stiffen beside me.

Wyatt grunted. I decided it was time to end the call. "Love you both, and I'll talk to you tomorrow. Goodnight."

Once they murmured goodnight, I clicked End and placed the phone on the nightstand. "Sorry they interrupted our dinner."

She shook her head. "No, it's okay. I was mostly finished anyway." She stood. "I'm going to get ready for bed."

I cleaned up our meal and then lay on the bed, waiting to see Emmy's mood when she came out. However, I fell asleep, and by the time I woke up the next morning, she was gone.

I couldn't believe I'd slept next to her and never woken up. But her absence made me wonder if last night had pushed her too far, scaring her. After all, we were supposed to have a few days of sex and nothing else. Making up stories with my kids had felt more like we were dating.

With a sigh, I readied myself for the morning and tried to figure out my next move. Because I wasn't giving up, not even close.

Chapter Twenty-Nine

Emilia

Amber: I finally got the ingredients for your special-order cake. Do you want to do a tasting after you get back?
Me: Sure.
Amber: Then in two days?
Me: Okay.
Amber: Is something wrong?
Me: No. Yes. I don't know.
Amber: You can always talk to me, Emmy. <heart emoji> I know how to keep secrets.
Me: I know. And I might take you up on the offer. Right now, I just need to think.

Amber: Then I'll try to distract Katie today so she'll leave you alone.
Me: You're the best. Love you. <heart emoji>
Amber: Love you too. And don't stew too long. I won't allow it.
Me: <laughing emoji> I know better than to bring out your determination. It's better than your temper, but not by much.
Amber: <tongue out emoji> Remind me why I'm helping you again?
Me: Love you, truly. <heart emoji> Talk to you soon.

Thank goodness for work and the need to focus on the expo. It kept me from thinking about last night.

I'd barely gotten any sleep, and not because West had been busy fucking me and making me orgasm.

No, I'd laid awake thinking about storytime with the twins. It'd been so perfect and made me want things. Things that I shouldn't really want.

And yet, I did.

Luckily, we'd be in Reno today and tomorrow still, and I could have West to myself for a little while longer. I loved his kids, but I also needed to know the man if I was going to risk anything.

As I tried to focus on the last-minute arrangements of everything in my booth—from pamphlets, to cards with QR codes, to sample flower arrangements and photo albums of past weddings—Abby walked up and held out a brown paper bag. It was one of those bakery ones, where you could see some of the grease from what I hoped was a muffin inside. And opening it, yep, the blueberry muffin smelled amazing.

But it also made me skeptical. "What are you buttering me up for?"

Abby put her hands up in surrender. "I figured you'd need some sugar after last night." She sighed. "And can I say how crappy it is that I can't really tease you since you hooked up with my brother?"

"The loss is yours." Wanting to tease her, I waggled my eyebrows.

Abby made retching sounds. "Stop, please. Just stop."

"You know you deserve it." I noticed a wariness in Abby's eyes. "Is something wrong?"

She looked away, took a deep breath, and then met my gaze again. "Yesterday, Rafe was injured bad, real bad, and they're not sure if he'll ever play again."

I had all sorts of mixed emotions about my older brother—regret, longing, sadness, and even love. But despite everything, I didn't want him to be hurt and in pain. "What happened?"

"Some sort of dirty move by another player. It's his knee, the one he injured before. There's not much more information than that, but if he can't play soccer anymore then, well, he might...."

Come home, was left unsaid.

I'd inherited the ranch—I never found out why I was

the sole heir—but Rafe had a few properties elsewhere in the Starry Hills area.

So it was entirely possible he'd return.

Except I knew, from Abby, that he was super popular in England, had a reputation with the ladies, and was a bit of a player. Not as much as his younger days, since Rafe was thirty-five now, but even if half of it was true, he'd be bored out of his mind in Starry Hills.

Not to mention that if he came back and finally confronted me about our parents, I wasn't sure what would happen. Would he yell? Ignore me? Be all fake politeness for the sake of keeping the peace since we lived in the same the town?

Abby placed a hand on my arm, bringing me back to the present. "I'll keep an eye on the headlines and keep you updated. I know normally you don't like to hear about him, but I figured this was important."

"Yes, thanks for telling me, Abby."

She shrugged. "It's not like I'm doing something out of the ordinary."

That was true. Oh, she'd cursed Rafe out when he'd left right after my parents' funeral. But still, Abby had always kept up with what he was doing, who he played for, the wins, you name it.

An announcement blared, saying the doors would open in five minutes. Abby gave me a hug and then dashed off to her booth.

Taking a deep breath, I willed my professional business face into place, complete with a smile and the friendliest look I could manage.

Standing out and getting noticed at live events

meant giving it your all, making eye contact with those who walked by, and never being passive, like looking at my phone and waiting for people to come to me. So I put on the final touch—a flower wreath around my head, which was popular with brides this year—and waited for people to ask me about it. Then I could slowly ease into my mini-pitch.

Soon I was doing what I did best, chatting with engaged couples or seriously dating couples, and forgot all about my brother, West, and the future beyond getting people interested in booking my business.

Chapter Thirty

Weston

Me: I hope you kick ass today.
Emmy: Thanks! You too.
Me: I can't wait for tonight. <smiling emoji>
Emmy: I bet. If you don't pass out again tonight. I really should call you an old man.
Me: Making you come with my mouth takes work.
Emmy: But you didn't do that last night.
Me: Then your pussy drained me.
Emmy: What, of your life essence? Really? <eye roll emoji>
Me: I've never been that tired after fucking someone, so yes.
Emmy: Are you calling me a succubus?

Me: Um, no.
Emmy: I think you are.
Me: I hope not. Because then you'll literally fuck me to death.
Emmy: Isn't that like a guy's fantasy?
Me: No comment. I gotta go. See you later.

I had worked nearly two decades at my in-laws' cattle ranch, and the work could be brutal. And yet somehow, working the winery booth for eight hours with my sister left me feeling more exhausted than I'd been since my kids had started sleeping through the night.

As the last attendees were herded out the door, Abby lifted a small cup of cabernet sauvignon toward me. I took it, and she tapped her paper cup against mine. "To surviving the first day, old man!"

I grunted but couldn't keep a smile from my face. Watching my little sister charm the visitors, enthusiastically chat about Starry Wolfe wine, and sign people up for sample boxes or for our mailing list had been illuminating. She liked talking to strangers and could put on a show.

Which made her being overly quiet at home all the more mysterious. When she was little, she'd been outgoing and charming, kind of like Zach. I thought maybe she'd just grown up. However, after today, it made me think something had happened to her in the years I'd been away.

Maybe if we finally got a drink together, I could broach the topic with Abby.

My sister scrutinized my face a second before saying, "We don't have to wait until we go to The Watering Hole to talk, West. We can do it while we clean up, if you want. Knowing how Emmy will want everything arranged perfectly and in its place for tomorrow, we have about half an hour before she comes over."

I downed my little cup of wine, tossed it in with the others to be recycled, and raised my eyebrows. "I'm guessing you know we're sort of together for our stay in Reno?"

Abby nodded, and I hesitated. Was I really going to talk to my little sister about this?

"West, just spit it out already, for fuck's sake. You want more than Reno, don't you?"

"Yes."

Abby smiled. "I knew you guys would get together."

"It seems like everyone thought so."

"I don't know. Sometimes Zach can be pretty clueless when it comes to noticing someone's into him, and others, for that matter."

Given how he had never noticed that Amber was in love with him since forever, that didn't surprise me.

"It's just fucking complicated. Her past, my past, my kids." I sighed. "Rationally, I know I should take the Reno hookup and forget about anything else. But..."

"But which wants her more—your penis or your heart?"

"If I never hear the word 'penis' coming from your mouth again, I'd die a happy man."

She rolled her eyes. "I'm an adult. At any rate, I'm on your side, West. If I can help, let me know. My gut says you two will work."

"Why are you on my side, though? Yes, I'm your brother, but let's not beat around the bush—I ran away when I should've stayed to help the family."

She shrugged. "We each dealt with the death of our parents and our grief in different ways. When I was struggling to figure why so many of you left and kept leaving, Aunt Lori helped me to understand that you weren't abandoning me but trying to cope with it all."

"Abby."

She put up a hand to silence me. "But I'm not the center of the universe, and I'm also not a little girl any longer. Last year I finally understood how running away might feel like solving your problem, even if it doesn't help at all." She cleared her throat, making me want to ask what she was talking about.

However, Abby didn't let me get a word in. "At any rate, I'm sure you understand what keeps Emmy back from wanting more than a few days with you. But my best advice is to just be stubborn." Her lips twitched. "Which should be easy, given how you're a Wolfe."

I rolled my eyes. "Being stubborn isn't a problem. I'm good at that. But will it help?"

"It's the only way our family and the BFF Circle stayed in Emmy's life. I won't spill all her secrets, but she tried to push away everyone who cared about her when she was little. So my advice is to be stubborn, West. And be sure, very sure, that she's what you want."

"I am," I answered without hesitating. "I'm fucking terrified, but I sense that if I don't go after her, I'll regret it."

"Good. And West?"

"Yes?" I asked carefully.

"I'm glad you came back." Abby hugged me, and I stilled for a second before awkwardly patting her on the back. When she released me, she said, "And I hope you plan to stay."

Despite everything, despite me leaving all those years ago, Abby didn't hate me for it. And I hadn't realized until this moment just how much I needed to know that.

After clearing my throat, I replied, "Starry Hills is home for me and my kids, and I have no plans of going anywhere."

"Good." She glanced around me and then smiled. "Someone finished early and is coming this way."

I turned, and my gaze met Emmy's. When she smiled, all of my tiredness melted away.

I met her halfway and barely restrained myself from kissing her. We'd agreed not to show affection in public. "Did you have a good day?"

She lit up, and I sucked in a breath at how fucking beautiful she was. Somehow I managed to listen to her answer and not just stare at her mouth. "An amazing day, for sure. I don't know how many people who stopped by will become actual clients. But a lot of people loved my barn, the lavender fields, the decorations, and even the option to ride a horse to the ceremony. If it keeps up like this tomorrow, and people follow through, I might be booked up so far in advance that I'll need to start thinking of other locations."

I couldn't resist taking her hand and squeezing it. "That's fucking amazing, Emmy. And there's always the calving barn you could renovate for smaller events too."

Her brows came together. "Maybe." Her expression cleared as she released my hand. "I just need to talk to Abby for a minute, okay?"

"Sure."

As the pair chatted, I helped clean up the Wolfe booth while I waited. Soon everything was secure, and I walked up to Emmy as she said goodbye to Abby. My sister winked at me before leaving us alone.

After taking Emmy's hand again, I leaned over and whispered, "I know we said we'd keep our little arrangement to the room. But I had an idea..."

"Which is?"

My heart thumped harder at the fact she hadn't said no. "There's an adults-only pool. And I thought we could relax in it for a while, if you brought a bathing suit."

I held my breath, but she answered with a smile. "I always bring one. And relaxing in the pool sounds perfect. But while I'm always ready to dive into a pool, what about you? I don't think boxers will cut it."

"No, but they have some swimming trunks in the gift shop. I'll get one."

"If you're willing to buy an overpriced pair, then you must really, really want to go swimming."

I leaned over and whispered into her ear, "I'd do almost anything to see you wet and dripping."

"West."

Chuckling, I leaned back until I could meet her gaze. "What? I was talking about you in a swimsuit. Where did your mind go?"

She narrowed her eyes. "You most definitely weren't talking about a swimsuit."

I grinned, and Emmy laughed.

The sound, combined with her smiling eyes, shot straight to my cock.

But I willed the beast to behave. I wanted some time out of the bedroom with Emmy, to show her how good we fit, how we could be all the time if she would only allow it.

I tugged her along and bought my trunks before rushing to our room. I was eager to see Emmy in her swimsuit. Of course I was. But now that I'd firmly made up my mind to be stubborn and go after her, I was eager to get started.

Chapter Thirty-One

Emilia

Once we reached our room, I changed my clothes as fast as possible, impatient to see West's reaction. I always brought two swimsuits with me on business trips—one to actually swim in and one to lie out in the sun and feel sexy.

I put on the latter.

After taking one last look in the bathroom mirror, I exited, and as soon as West saw me, his jaw dropped. "Damn."

As his eyes took in my shiny gold bikini, I could almost feel his hands on my body, caressing me, making me want to say "Screw it," strip, and ask him to fuck me again.

But then I remembered how sweet it'd been for West

to ask me to go swimming, almost as if he'd been a little nervous, and I couldn't deny him. More than that, I wanted to relax with him in a pool, out in the open, and almost feel normal for a little while. Just a woman with a hot guy, not one with a sad, complicated past and a crap-ton of baggage weighing her down.

Determined to enjoy the night, I sauntered over and took his hand. "Well? Will this do?"

He guided my hand to his very hard cock. "This is what you and that bikini do to me."

West leaned down to kiss me, and I turned my head. "No, because if you kiss me right now, we'll never make it out of this room."

"And that's a bad thing because why?"

I snorted. "Come on. I want to cool down in the water first. Then you can warm me up again."

"I'm going to take that job very, very seriously. I'll start with my mouth between your thighs."

My pussy pulsed at his words, but I was determined to leave this room with my clothes still on. "Grab the towels and let's go."

He grumbled but did as I asked. After slipping on flip-flops, we took the elevator to the correct floor and then walked outside to the adults-only pool.

There were a few groups of people milling about but not many. The pool was bigger than I'd expected, in a large L shape, and few were at the deep end.

We found some empty chairs, and after ditching our stuff, I went to the edge of the deep end. I should just jump in, but I wanted to tease West a little. So I raised my arms over my head, leaned one way and then the other, before bending over to touch my toes, as if stretching. West's deep growl caressed my skin.

"Are you trying to kill me, woman?"

I stood and peeked over my shoulder. "Maybe. It's kind of fun."

His voice went even lower. "I think someone needs a taste of her own medicine."

He took a step toward me, and I said, "Well, if you want your revenge, you have to catch me first."

I dove into the pool and swam far away. When I surfaced, I searched for West but couldn't find him.

Then a familiar voice said behind me, "Gotcha," and I was pulled under the water.

West didn't hold me down but let me up. I turned, splashed him, and said, "Unfair."

The man looked so damn smug. "How? It's not my fault you didn't look behind you. And that's mild considering you were trying to seduce me in plain sight of like ten people."

"Seducing, huh?"

I batted my eyelashes at him, and he blinked. Taking advantage of his surprise, I placed my hands on his shoulders and tried to push him down. Since the water was deeper than I was tall, I didn't have much leverage, though, and West barely bobbed. He laughed, the sound deep and almost rusty. And damn, I wanted to make him do it again.

Before I could make my next move, West pulled me close and kissed me.

Kissing and staying afloat was difficult, but soon he

was devouring my mouth, grabbing my butt, and despite the cool water, my body was on fire.

I'd never had sex in a pool, but I wondered what it might be like. In my backyard, of course. Not here.

At some point, West must've guided us to the shallow end because his shoulders were above the water, and I had my legs wrapped around his waist. Just I started rubbing against his hard cock, he pulled back but kept a possessive hand on my ass. "None of that. It's an adults-only pool but not an X-rated one."

I stuck out my tongue. "You're no fun."

West laughed again, and I decided to play dirty. I moved a hand down between our bodies until I could stroke his dick through his trunks. West sucked in a breath. "Stop, Emmy. I don't want to be kicked out of the hotel for coming in the pool."

I stilled my hand and removed it. Seeing as our make-out session was over, I decided to get even with him while he was distracted.

So I unwrapped myself from his body, dove down—the water was still five feet deep—and I tugged at his ankles.

He slid into the water, and I swam away. When I surfaced, I saw a very tall, very wet, and very irritated West not too far behind me.

"I see how it is. This means war, Emmy."

He came after me, and I squealed. For the next five or ten minutes, we each tried to catch and dunk each other.

Eventually, we ended up in the shallow end, with no one around, and West lifted me and settled me on the side of the pool. He stepped between my legs, cupped my cheek, and stroked my skin.

I loved the mixture of heat, amusement, and happiness in his gaze. It was hard to believe that at one time he'd only glared at me.

When he was relaxed and temporarily free of his worries, he looked so much younger. It made me wonder if he'd ever had someone to simply have fun with. Oh, of course he had fun with his children. But sometimes it was nice to tease and banter with someone closer to your age.

For a second, I wanted to be that person. The one who could make the usually scowling, growling man smile and laugh.

Don't go there.

Needing a distraction, I placed my hand on his chest, running my fingers through his chest hair, and reveled in his head and hard muscles.

He continued to stroke my cheek with his thumb, his gaze never leaving mine.

Everything and everyone faded away right then. It was only West and me.

No past, no future, just the here and now.

Two people with sad pasts trying to have fun and forget, if only for a little while.

The urge to touch more of him raced through me. So I raised my other hand to stroke his jaw.

He took my hand and kissed my palm. "Emmy."

"Hmm?"

He put a hand over mine on his chest, his skin warm.

His eyes looked unsure, and I wondered what this strong man had to worry about.

He cleared his throat. "I know we agreed this would end when we left Reno, but I have to ask—would you go on a date with me in Starry Hills?"

I should just deny him. That would be the safest route, of course. Because if we went on a date, it would mean we were a thing, like a couple.

And even if I didn't want to, I could end up hurting this man and his children. And West, Avery, and Wyatt didn't need any more pain and grief in their lives.

As if sensing my worry, he stroked my cheek. "Just give us a chance, Emmy. Fuck, I never thought I'd ever want to date anyone ever again. I'd sworn off women. But then, well, I met you. You're amazing with my children, smart with your business, playful when you want to be, and so fucking beautiful it hurts." He leaned forward and kissed me gently. "Just one date. That's it. And I won't tell my kids about the date, so you won't get any pressure from them. Although..."

"Although what?"

"Their bedtime stories have featured a lot of single dads getting married lately, so I can't say they won't make comments or drop hints as subtle as a jackhammer. I hope you'll still see Avery and Wyatt, but they won't be involved in whatever this is between us until we're ready. If we're ever ready." He stroked my cheek a few more times before whispering, "I want to try with you, Emmy. Tell me you want to do the same."

I searched his gaze, and it was on the tip of my

tongue to deny him. To tell him that I'd probably hurt him.

Not to mention if I said no, then I wouldn't have to risk my heart breaking.

And yet, I couldn't do it. As I searched his blue eyes, so eager and unsure at the same time, I wanted the chance to sit in his lap again, play with him in the pool, and hold him close as he came inside me.

I wanted Weston Wolfe. I wanted to try with him, even though the thought of getting close to someone again, maybe even eventually loving them, terrified me.

Plus, for so many years, I'd carried a soul-crushing amount of guilt about the car crash, which could complicate things too.

But the more I thought about what West had pointed out—that I'd dealt with my mom, and my dad had been driving—the more I started to wonder if it would've been the same outcome, even if I'd been asleep.

I wasn't a hundred percent sure I could forgive myself. But that I even questioned what had happened was thanks to this man standing in front of me, currently asking me on a date.

Was he worth the risk? A resounding, "Yes" rang through my head.

Before I could change my mind, I blurted, "Yes."

His eyes lit up. "Yes, you'll go on a date with me?"

I smiled and wrapped my arms around his neck. "I'm at like ninety percent yes. I might need a little more persuading, though." I leaned forward, nipped his earlobe, and whispered, "Make me come a few more times, West, and I will most definitely go on a date with you."

With a growl, he kissed me. His lips were warm, soft, and demanding. When he touched his tongue to the seam of my lips, I didn't hesitate to open. He licked and tangled and devoured me until we both broke the kiss to catch our breaths.

A playful glint entered his eyes before he used those wonderfully broad, powerful shoulders and arms to push himself out of the water, stand, and then yank me up. The next thing I knew, he tossed me over his shoulder and dashed to our chairs.

I couldn't stop laughing as he picked up our stuff and headed for the elevator. People were staring, and yet I didn't care.

Once inside the elevator—thankfully, it was empty—he lowered me slowly down his front until he could kiss me again briefly before saying, "I only put you down because I needed to find our keycard."

I snorted. "See, you should've just had me find it while I was still over your shoulder." He made as if to pick me up again, and laughing, I backed away. "I had one head rush already, and I don't really want another one."

As soon as the elevator doors opened, I dashed down the hallway, knowing he'd chase me. The hole in my plan became obvious, though, since I could do nothing but stand by the door. West opened it, tossed our stuff inside, and then picked me up in his arms, one hand under my knees and the other behind my back.

He kicked the door closed, entered the bathroom,

and put me in the tub. "Strip for me, Emilia. Between the hot water and my tongue on your pussy, I'll have you warmed up in no time."

I didn't hesitate to take off my bathing suit. And soon, with the hot water spraying down on us, West did exactly as promised and made me scream his name.

In fact, West had made me come twice more on the bed before we both just lay there, my head on his chest and his arms around me, in a post-orgasm haze. I took the opportunity to run my hand through his chest hair and chuckled when I noticed a few silver ones among the dark ones.

He lightly swatted my butt. "Now what are you laughing at?"

I propped my head on his chest and smiled up at him. "Nothing. I'm just studying and learning more about your body."

He frowned. "And yet you found something to laugh about. It'd better not be my tattoo. I got shit enough about it back in Ridgefield."

I vaguely knew he had ink on his upper left arm but moved to straddle his waist so I could get a better look at it. He easily moved his arm and torso so I could see it more clearly.

There was a fierce wolf standing and howling at the moon. It looked a lot like the ones I'd seen inked on Beck and Zach, when we'd all gone swimming. But just below the howling wolf were two little pups, playing with some butterflies and ladybugs. One of the little wolves was at a distance, crouched down, waiting to pounce. The other was in mid-twirl with a butterfly on its tail and a ladybug on its nose.

"It's me and my children. I got the big one with Beck one night, when we were drunk. Later, I added the two little ones. That way, I would always be able to see my family, remember my kids, and let them know how much I always wanted them near me."

My voice was scratchy as I said, "That's beautiful, West."

He grunted. "It made Wyatt and Avery happy, and that was enough for me. I've gotten shit for the butterflies and ladybugs, though. But Avery loves them, so I got them for her."

I traced the wolf in mid-twirl. "Avery." And then the one waiting patiently to pounce. "And Wyatt."

"Yes."

I moved until I lay on West's chest, took his face in my hands, and kissed him. "You grunt and scowl, but deep down, you're a big softie." He grunted extra-long on purpose, and I laughed. "Still a big softie."

West rolled me onto my back and pinned my hands above me. He took his time nipping my bottom lip, lightly kissing the corners of my mouth, and then finally took my lips in a searing, devouring kiss.

I wrapped my legs around his waist and rocked against his hard cock.

He groaned. "I'm going to need another condom, aren't I?"

Part of me wanted to say no, and yet, I'd sworn off

men last year and stopped taking birth control. As much as I hated remembering to take it, I would start again. Because the thought of West inside me with nothing between us made me want to moan.

Not tonight, though. So I kissed him and said, "Yes."

After sliding his dick through my pussy lips a few times, he finally released me with a growl. Once he'd put on a condom—we'd probably need another box for tomorrow, at this rate—he came back to the bed. He pushed my thighs wide, positioned his cock, and thrust slowly inside me.

I was a little sore after so much sex, but he kissed my mouth tenderly, rocking against me slowly, and I forgot about everything but the man above me. We stared at one another, saying nothing, and I held on to his shoulders. Something about his gaze was intense and heated and almost tender.

It would be so easy to fall in love with Weston Wolfe.

No. I wasn't thinking that far into the future. So I leaned up to claim his mouth, and West moved faster, angling my hips up to make me moan harder.

When his hand found my clit and stroked, it was too much. As I came, West stilled and shouted my name.

He rolled onto his back and pulled me close, his heart beating under my ear, and soon it lulled me to sleep, complete with dreams of what my life would look like in the future, with West and his kids as my family.

Chapter Thirty-Two

Weston

Aunt Lori: Did you let your hair down in Reno? <dancing emoji>

Me: My hair is short.

Aunt Lori: <unamused emoji> And sort of gray now. But that's not what I meant, and you know it.

Me: I guess I could put a barrette in and then take it out. That would be letting my hair down.

Aunt Lori: Are you...being funny? <surprised with mouth open emoji>

Me: It happens from time to time.

Aunt Lori: Who are you and what did you do to my nephew?

Me: I'm not an alien. It's just me. Be nice, or I won't give you the mug. It's a good one.

Aunt Lori: <thinking emoji> I want my mug. But I'm

not giving up until I figure out the change. Maybe Abby will know.

Me: I'll be there soon to get my kids.

Aunt Lori: Changing the subject, I see. Abby is the key. <smiling devil emoji>

Me: Just make sure my kids don't burn down the house. See you soon.

Waking up with Emmy in my arms had been like heaven. She kicked the blankets off during the night and moved more in her sleep than even my kids did, but I didn't care.

The second day of the wedding expo had been busy, though, for Emmy. In addition to the expo hours, the rest of her free time had been spent meeting with suppliers and businesses in the area. Our only time together had been late. So we'd only had a quick fuck that night before falling asleep.

Today we were headed home. I wished we could've shared a car, but it wasn't possible since we both needed ours back in Starry Hills. After giving her a long, possessive kiss, we hit the road.

I tried not to worry that the happiness of the last few days would end once we were back home. In the first few weeks of my marriage, I'd had a brief bubble of bliss with my wife too. But that had only been lust, which hadn't lasted long.

However, I refused to believe what I had with Emmy was merely lust. The fun we'd had in the pool still made me smile, and I'd never been able to laugh so easily one minute and then be turned on the next.

I spent most of the drive remembering the last few days, a stupid smile on my face, and before I knew it, I pulled into the back of the main house where the family lived and parked. I hadn't done more than exit the car when I heard Avery shout, "Daddy! You're home!"

She ran toward me, and I crouched down to engulf her in my arms. "I've missed you, baby girl."

After squeezing me hard, she pulled back. "I missed you too, Daddy. Can we go for ice cream now?"

I blinked. "What?"

"You always say we can go for ice cream later, and it never happens. Can we go now?"

Wyatt finally joined us. He didn't race into my arms, but I pulled my son in for a quick hug and then ruffled his hair. Wyatt said, "I want to go too, even if Aunt Lori said it was too close to dinnertime."

I stood and put a hand on each of their shoulders, gently prodding them forward. "You know better than to keep asking adults the same question until you get the answer you want."

Avery looked sheepish. "I know, but I just want to spend time with you, Daddy."

"Then we can spend time helping Aunt Lori or one of your uncles with something."

Avery tapped her finger against her chin. "Or we could go visit Emmy! It's been days since we went to her property."

Emmy and I had discussed how to handle my kids. We'd act like before until we were more certain of the future. Avery got attached easily, and I didn't want to get my daughter's hopes up and then destroy them.

"You can go over there tomorrow. Tonight, she needs to rest. She has another wedding in a few days, and the expo was really busy."

In fact, between her weddings and the Summer Star Festival next week, I wasn't sure when I'd finally get to take her on a date.

Which dimmed my mood a little.

But I kept up a smiling face for my kids and enjoyed dinner with my family, especially when Aunt Lori proudly used her new mug for coffee with dessert.

Once it was over, though, Beck asked to have a private word with me in his office.

Aunt Lori said she'd put my kids to bed. So after I hugged them both, I followed Beck into the small room he and I shared as an office. Beck hated being indoors—so did I, truth be told—so it was fairly spartan with a desk, three chairs, a computer, a laptop, and a printer.

Beck gestured toward one of two chairs in front of the desk. Once we both sat, I asked, "What is it? You look all serious, which fucking makes me nervous."

Beck said nothing for a second, the bastard, and then he snorted. "It's nothing bad, I promise. But how often do I get to make you squirm?"

"I wasn't squirming."

"Yes, you were."

I glared but decided to be the older brother for a change. "Just tell me what's up, Beckie."

He hated the nickname, and his smile disappeared.

"Fine. The sample and monthly box orders from the expo are better than I'd hoped for."

"That's because of Abby."

He shook his head. "Not entirely, from what I heard. She answered questions and described the wines. But you were the one giving sales pitches, West."

I shifted in my chair. "I had to do that back in Ridgefield. I can never be charming, but I can be polite and persuasive without being creepy as fuck about it."

Beck chuckled. "I'd like to see that. But in all seriousness, I worried at first, you know. That you wouldn't try your hardest to learn about the business and put your heart into it. But I was so fucking wrong, West. So much so, Zach and I talked about the future."

Even if each of us had a small stake in Starry Wolfe wine, Beck had the largest share, followed by Zach. The rest of us had sold most of our shares to them long ago.

"And what did you two decide?"

"We'd like to give you more responsibility, West. And if you handle it well, more say in the business."

I stared at my younger brother, shocked. "I haven't been here that long."

Beck shrugged. "I know. And it's not like I'm going to hand over everything tomorrow. However, Dad wanted the winery to remain in the family, and you're family. If you want to stay and help us run the place, you should get the chance."

My throat grew tight with emotion. Despite me running away, abandoning my family when they needed me, and even having to ask them to look after my kids for an entire summer while I dealt with my late wife, Beck didn't hold a grudge.

I should be happy, ecstatic, and jump at the chance. I'd be an even bigger part of the family, not to mention possess a steady job and a future for my kids.

And yet, the thought of this being my life forever, growing grapes and making and selling wine when my heart wasn't in it, made me hesitate.

Beck searched my gaze and said, "Take some time to think about it. Your life has changed a lot in recent months, and this is yet another change. A big one. But just know that I *want* you to work alongside us, West. No one is forcing me to do it."

"I know. And I'm really fucking grateful. I am. Just..."

Beck put up a hand to stop me. "It's all right, West. Get your kids settled, find yourself a place to make your own, and then we'll talk again."

I nodded. "Thanks, Beck."

I moved to stand, but Beck motioned for me to stay put. "Don't leave just yet. Avery and Wyatt are distracting Aunt Lori, and I'd like some peace for a little while longer."

I chuckled. "Scared of a tiny woman in her sixties?"

He scowled. "Being short has nothing to do with her personality."

I laughed, and then we shared a smile, one full of love for the force of nature who helped keep the family together.

Then my smile faded as I remembered I hadn't been here when Aunt Lori had.

Beck stood, walked over, and put a hand on my shoulder. "You came back, West. And that's all that matters now."

I looked up at the face that was a lot like my own and yet not. "Thanks."

He released me and then leaned against the desk, crossing his arms. "So, you and Emmy, huh?"

"Abby talked to you, then."

"Yes and no. Whenever Emmy's name came up at dinner tonight, you went all starry-eyed. It's not that hard to figure out. Especially when Abby said she'd be watching your kids in a few days and staying the night here while you went out. Probably all night."

Subtle wasn't the best way to describe my little sister.

I stood. "Just don't mention it to Avery and Wyatt yet. I don't want them to get their hopes up."

Beck nodded. "I get it. And if you ever need some advice about women, I'm your man."

"Says the guy who pretty much scowled and grunted and scared away most of the women in town for years."

"Hey, I'm a changed man. And Sabrina says I'm romantic."

"Oh, Beck, how the mighty have fallen."

"And glad to have done so."

As I smiled with my brother, I was glad that he was so fucking happy.

It gave me hope for myself.

The thought startled me, but I pushed it aside, and I lightly punched my brother's arm. "I'll remember that. And when I have an answer for you, I'll let you know."

"Good. I'll see you tomorrow."

As I watched Beck leave, no doubt to go to the little guesthouse he lived in with Sabrina, I still had trouble believing all the changes to my brother since finding love. He was more like the teenager I remembered, before our father died and changed everything.

Thinking about what I'd missed during the years after that darkened my mood a little. In retrospect, staying away from my family all these years, trying to fix my life by myself, seemed kind of stupid.

I couldn't change the past, but I could work on the future. Not just with my family but with Emmy too. I was still fucking terrified of falling for her and then having my heart broken.

But she was worth the risk. Not because I was married to her and felt like it was my responsibility. No, I liked her. A lot. And seeing her sad tore my heart in two.

Not to mention how much my kids loved her, and I was pretty sure she was fond of them too.

Maybe I could have a true family one day.

Laughing at how sentimental I'd become, I went upstairs to check on my kids. And once I finally fell asleep, I dreamed of a certain woman with dark-brown eyes, dark hair, and the softest skin I'd ever touched.

Chapter Thirty-Three

Emilia

West: My bed was cold last night.
Me: Maybe you should buy an electric blanket.
West: I'd rather have a warm woman I can make scream my name before bedtime.
Me: Hmm, I think you're getting cocky again.
West: I knew you wouldn't forget about my cock any time soon.
Me: This again? I really think you need reading glasses.
West: Do you have a professor fantasy? I can keep you after class and give you a stern lecture.
Me: Will that lecture include some spankings?
West: Fuck, you want that?
Me: Yes please. <overheated face>

West: Then the next time I have you alone, I'll have to bend you over my knee until you promise to be a good girl again.

Getting back into my routine was hard, so much harder than I'd thought. I'd never really taken a vacation over the last three years, and even if I had technically been working during the expo, the evenings with West had felt like a vacation.

I couldn't stop smiling whenever I thought of him.

I still felt guilty for being happy, and I wasn't about to make any long-term plans. However, I didn't want to push him away and hide. I wanted to give us a chance.

Once I put my phone in a drawer to stop looking for more of West's dirty texts, I worked my way through some of the emails I'd received from visitors to my expo booth. I'd barely made a dent when Abby burst into the office we shared.

"Did you see it?"

"See what?"

Abby handed over her phone, and I saw it was an email, one to the address I used for word-of-mouth recommendations and not the generic one for events.

I hadn't checked that inbox yet, but as soon as I read the message, I stopped breathing. It took a second for my brain and mouth to start working again. "Zara Jones wants to hire us."

Abby raced over and hugged me around my shoulders. "Yes! She was impressed with your proposal and charmed by the location. Her fiancé even said he loved the working dairies and farms nearby, making it more authentic."

I stood and hugged Abby again. "I can't believe it!" I leaned back to look at Abby's face. "We're going to plan a wedding for a movie star!"

As it hit me how ridiculously huge that was, I sat back down. Abby sat on the edge of my desk and said, "You're going to have to start hiring more people, Emmy. There's no way the two of us can do it with only a few caterers to help, not even with your workaholic tendencies."

Since it was true, I didn't deny her words. "Thank fuck her wedding is next year. It gives me some time to figure things out."

Abby frowned. "But didn't you catch the part where she wants to move it forward to September this year? Apparently, there are reasons she wants it sooner rather than later. I wonder if she's pregnant and wants the wedding before she shows too much."

I scanned the email again and true enough—she'd added it right at the bottom:

I hope you can manage the wedding by the end of September at the latest. It's short notice, but something has come up, and we need it by then. Let us know ASAP if it's possible.

. . .

A wedding this important in less than three months? I wanted to scream it was impossible. And yet, this was the biggest break of my life.

Abby kicked her foot against mine. "Emmy." I meet her gaze again. "We can say no. But if you want to say yes, we need to hire and do it soon. They want a gazebo built for the ceremony, several arches, and even a custom-built stage, in a rustic style. Not to mention the flowers we'll need to order from Maria in the next few weeks. Plus there's the catering, and most importantly, meeting with Zara and her fiancé. What do you want to do?"

"Of course we'll say yes. And before you ask, yes, I'll hire more people to help us."

I even had in mind a certain guy who was rather skilled with power tools to build things for me.

Would West want to help me, though? Mixing business and pleasure could be a disaster of epic proportions. And yet, it could be the best thing ever. Besides, he could use the extra money for his kids. Of course I'd ask him.

I pulled up a blank document on my computer and drafted my response. "I'll send her a reply, schedule a time to go over the contract, and start making lists. As soon as the contract is signed, I need you to arrange the flowers and start hiring help for the day."

"And building the things they want?"

"I'm going to ask West if he'll do it."

I held my breath to see if she'd say it was stupid. But Abby nodded. "He likes that kind of stuff. Nearly as much as raising cattle."

I knew he'd worked at his in-laws' cattle ranch, but I hadn't known he'd liked doing it. The fact I didn't know that detail irritated me.

There was so much I didn't know about West.

And now, with this job? I was worried about being too busy to date him.

Regardless of how busy it would get, I would go on the one date I'd promised him. After that, I'd have to see.

Because work was my safe place, the one thing constant in my life. I wanted to hope for more with West, wanted to think I wouldn't mess things up and could accept some happiness without drowning in guilt.

And yet, nothing was certain. Definitely not at this point.

But my work was. It always was.

So I dove into what I did best, ignoring the slight pang in my heart about not having more of what I'd had in Reno.

It was early evening by the time I had scheduled a meeting with Zara for the next day. Between that and the work for an upcoming wedding, I didn't have time to eat.

So when someone knocked on my office door, I was grumpy, tired, and hangry. I barked, "Come in."

Avery and Wyatt dashed inside, with West not far behind him, and my irritation faded at the sight of them. He carried two pizza boxes, and as soon as the cheesy, greasy smell hit my nose, my stomach growled.

Avery spoke first. "Daddy said we could help deliver your dinner, but we couldn't stay very long. You're super busy, and we can't bother you."

I smiled at Avery. "I can take a break for dinner, if you three can stay?"

Looking at West, I was unsure of what to expect. Even if we weren't telling his kids about us maybe being a thing, I still wanted to spend time with them.

West smiled at me, and I let out a breath of relief. "We can stay for dinner. Just not too late, though. Avery and Wyatt have swim lessons in the morning. Although why the fuck it has to be at nine a.m., I don't know."

Avery tutted. "Bad word, Daddy!"

I bit my lip to keep from smiling. I suspected it was more a game West and Avery played than any real scolding.

West sighed. "Yes, I know." He held up the pizza boxes. "Shall we?"

I stood, and we made our way to the kitchen. Avery chatted about riding Beck's horses when we'd been away in Reno, and even Wyatt had jumped in to talk about their ride.

As I retrieved some plates, I asked Wyatt, "You love horses, don't you?"

He nodded. "Some of my friends in Ridgefield dreamed of motorcycles or sports cars. But I just want to have a few horses of my own. Maybe breed them someday too. One girl in my old class, her mom and dad did that."

Since Wyatt was rarely this chatty, I decided to keep him talking. "Would you want to learn some more about horses? Because I might know someone who could teach you."

"Yes, that would be awesome."

"Well, the King family has a big stable of them, and the brothers know just about everything to do with horses. Maybe I could ask my friend Amber if her brothers would take you on a tour and you could meet some of their animals?"

Wyatt's eyes lit up. "I'd love that." He looked at his dad. "Can I go if they say it's okay?"

I glanced at West, and the soft expression on his face, as he stared at his son, did something to my heart.

After clearing his throat, West replied, "If they say yes, then of course."

Wyatt beamed at his father. "Thanks, Dad."

I helped dish out the pizza, the kids busy inhaling it like they hadn't eaten in days. I shared a smile with West.

He shook his head. "I hate to see how much Wyatt will eat as a teenager."

Avery piped up. "Me too! Aunt Lori says I might be as tall as Aunt Abby. And I'll need to eat a lot to get that tall."

Her dad replied, "We'll see, Avery. Your grandma isn't that tall, right? So maybe you'll take after her."

Avery scrunched her nose. "I don't think so. She's very strict and serious and doesn't laugh. I don't want to be like her."

West looked torn, knowing he shouldn't talk badly about their maternal grandparents and yet he had reasons to dislike them. Ones his kids didn't know about.

Maybe it wasn't my place, but I felt like jumping in and sparing him. "No matter who our relatives are, we're all different and unique. Your Uncle Zach and your dad have the same parents, but they have very different personalities, right?" Avery bobbed her head. "So I think you're just Avery Wolfe, and if you ever stop laughing and being chatty, I'll eat all the lavender in my fields."

Avery giggled, and Wyatt snorted. Avery said, "That's ridiculous."

I shrugged. "I know you pretty well by now, and I'm sticking to my words."

West lightly tapped his foot against mine under the table, and I met his gaze. He mouthed, "Thank you," and I nodded.

The rest of the meal went smoothly, us talking about the upcoming festival, the kids' swimming lessons, and how Avery and Wyatt couldn't wait to visit my overgrown pasture fields again. But right as I was cleaning up the plates, Wyatt asked, "Are you going to get cattle again someday? I mean, you have so many fields and so much space. They'd like it here."

I froze for a second and then found my voice. "I don't know."

"Why?" Wyatt asked.

Such a simple question with such a difficult answer. West looked about ready to intervene, but I beat him to it. "It would take a lot of work to start from scratch again. I sometimes miss them, but I can't both plan weddings and run a cattle ranch. So I let the fields grow and let two little kids play in them instead."

"But Dad could watch your cattle for you. He ran

our grandparents' place. He cursed sometimes if they were mean or would kick or be stubborn, but usually, he laughed about it afterward."

West jumped in. "Wyatt, we don't tell other people how to run their businesses or their lives. Emmy has a wedding and event business, and she loves it. That's all that matters. Whatever she does with the rest of her land is her choice."

Wyatt replied, "But, Dad, you know everything there is to know about cattle. And you hate the grapes. You said so."

West muttered, "I didn't think you'd heard that."

His kids must have supersensitive hearing because Wyatt replied, "I did. You talk really loud sometimes."

I could tell he wanted to drop it, and yet I remembered Abby telling me how West loved power tools nearly as much as cattle, and I blurted, "Is that what you want to do one day? Run your own ranch?"

As soon as I said the words, I wanted to take them back. He'd probably think I was asking him to come work for me.

Eventually, he shrugged. "Maybe someday. But for now, I'm helping my family."

I burned to ask more questions, to learn more about West's dreams. But Avery yawned, and West pounced on the excuse. "I think it's time to load the dishwasher and head home."

"No, you guys can go. I'll do the cleanup."

West frowned. "Are you sure?"

"Yep. You have the drive home still."

"How do you know we didn't walk?"

I raised my brows, nodding toward the pizza boxes—he wouldn't walk that far without them getting cold—and he chuckled. "True. I prefer walking, but I'm not that fast."

Avery nodded. "You don't have any superpowers, Daddy. It would be amazing if you did. But sadly, you don't."

I bit back a smile as the two kids came over to me and each gave me a hug. Avery said, "Thanks, Emmy. We should be back to play the day after tomorrow."

Wyatt jumped in. "Yeah, I want to find another salamander. And you can tell me if your friends will let me see the horses."

West said, "She's busy, Wyatt, and it may take a few days."

"No, no, it's okay. I'll see Amber and my friends tomorrow for lunch. So I'll ask then."

Wyatt smiled, looking happier than I'd seen him since the water fight with his dad in my pool. "Thanks, Emmy!"

He gave me another hug. Not to be outdone, Avery did the same. Then they raced to the front door and waited for their dad.

Alone, West came up to me and gave me a quick, gentle kiss. I leaned toward him, wanting so much more, and yet I knew I couldn't have it tonight.

He whispered, "Are we still on for dinner in three days?"

Despite everything looming with the Zara Jones wedding, I wouldn't give up this one thing with him. "Damn straight it's still on." He smiled, looking even sexier, and I growled. "Go before I do something rash, like jump you, uncaring if your kids find us."

Laughing, he caressed my cheek with the back of his fingers and then headed toward the door. "Goodbye, Emmy, and sweet dreams. Maybe you can share some of them with me via text."

His wink made me laugh, and once they had gone, I leaned against the front door and sighed. It hadn't been the first time I'd eaten with his kids, or even West for that matter. But all of us together, in my kitchen, had seemed familiar, like we'd done it a million times already.

And I wanted more of it.

I only hoped West wouldn't lose interest over the coming months, when I couldn't spend as much time with him and his kids. Because even if I'd mostly kept my heart protected, it would still fucking hurt if what I had with West and his kids all came crashing down.

Chapter Thirty-Four

Weston

Emmy: Are you really not going to tell me where you're taking me tonight?
Me: Nope.
Emmy: <sighing emoji> I'm not sure I like surprises.
Me: You'll like mine.
Emmy: And the ego comes out to play.
Me: There's nothing wrong with confidence. You like it. Admit it.
Emmy: I plead the Fifth.
Me: I have more confidence for you—I'm going to make that dream of yours come true, and you'll be a boneless heap of pleasure by the end of it.

Emmy: I can't really see you doing role-play, Mr. Wolfe.
Me: Do you want to wager on it?
Emmy: What will I get if I win?
Me: I'll fix the wobbly chair in your kitchen.
Emmy: You'd do that anyway. But fine. If I lose?
Me: Then I get to tie you up, blindfold you, and have you at my mercy.
Emmy: That doesn't really sound like losing to me. <overheated emoji>

Three days later, as I knocked on Emmy's front door, my heart raced. It was fucking ridiculous, as I was thirty-six years old with two kids.

But I hadn't taken a woman out on a date in years. Plus, Reno had been its own bubble, sort of a break from reality, and I had no fucking idea how things would play out, where people we'd known our whole lives would see us.

The door opened, and my mind emptied of everything but the beautiful woman in front of me. Emmy wore formfitting dark jeans and a dark-red top that revealed a hint of cleavage, and her nearly black hair danced around her face and shoulders. Then she smiled at me, and it took every bit of restraint I had not to push her inside, kiss her, and say screw the date and take her to bed.

Emmy's gaze turned heated as she gave me a once-over. "I can't decide if I like it better when you're all cleaned up or slightly dirty after a day's work."

"I can show up dirty next time, if you want." Something flickered in her eyes, but I decided it was just me being paranoid. So I leaned in, kissed her gently, and offered my hand. "Come on. I can't wait to see how you like my surprise."

After she locked up her house, I took her to my truck and opened the door for her. She slid inside, and I raced around. Once I was on the road, she asked, "So, do I get any hints? Maybe we could play something like twenty questions, and you'll let me know if I'm right?"

I smiled and glanced at her briefly before focusing back on the road. "You were the kid at Christmas who'd wake up early, and then at exactly the time your parents said you could bother them, you'd jump into action, weren't you?"

As soon as I said the words, I regretted them. I didn't want to make her think of her parents.

However, she laughed, and I relaxed a little as she answered, "Yes. Before I could tell time, my parents drew 7:00 on a piece of paper and said when it matched the clock in my room, I could wake them up. But not before." She hesitated and then added, "I had to wake my brother too. Since he's ten years older than me, he never got as excited for Christmas. Although..."

Her voice trailed off. A quick look assured me she wasn't about to break down and that maybe she wanted to talk about her brother and parents. So I asked carefully, "Although what?"

She cleared her throat. "They said I helped

everyone feel young at heart again with my enthusiasm. I don't know if you're aware of it or not, but I was a surprise baby for my parents. They had a hard time conceiving Rafe and had accepted they wouldn't have any more kids. But I came along when they least expected it and always said I was their little miracle, one to make them see life through the eyes of a child again."

Since I wouldn't need to shift gears any time soon on the empty stretch of road, I reached out and took one of her hands.

She squeezed and held on tight to me. "I miss my parents, but I know they won't be coming back. But when it comes to Rafe...he's still alive, and I miss him so much. And yet, I completely understand why he doesn't want to talk to me."

I tried my best to keep my voice calm and not let my anger show. Because if Rafe Mendoza blamed his little sister for the car crash, he was a fucking idiot. "Have you reached out to him?"

Her voice was so low I barely heard it. "No."

"Maybe you should."

Her head whipped around. "What?"

"Look, I don't know everything that's gone on between you and your brother. And you can tell me to fuck off and mind my own business, if you want to. But take it from someone who ran away and didn't talk to his family for more than a decade, all because he was too stubborn and thought he knew best." I paused, glancing at her. "I was wrong, Emmy, about my family, and what we all needed. And I wish I'd reached out to them sooner. Maybe you should try with Rafe and at least get some closure with him."

She sat silent for a long while, and I had to let go of her hand to change gears.

Eventually, she spoke again. "He set up a trust fund for me, not long after my parents died."

We were nearly to town, but I still pulled over to the side of the road, shut off the car, and turned toward her. "What?"

She looked out the window, although I could see her reflection in the glass. Her eyes were sad, so fucking sad. And yet, I sensed she didn't want me to pull her close and hold her right now.

Shrugging one shoulder, she said, "I haven't touched it. I don't know if he felt like he had to give me money, since he didn't want custody of me, or if it was a way to ensure I never talked to him again. An allowance had been offered to your parents—which is how I learned about it in the first place—but they turned it down. My mom had been your mom's best friend, and she said she'd never take money for helping her friend's daughter." She smiled sadly. "It was very like your mom."

It was. My mother had always possessed the tendency to help anyone who needed it, be it animal or human.

Not for the first time, I missed her and wished I could've been there when she died.

But right here, right now, it was about Emmy and not me. So I dared to take her hand. When she held it tightly and turned toward me, I inwardly sighed with relief. "Do you *want* to talk to your brother? It's all well and good for me to suggest it. But what do you want, Emmy? Tell me."

"Honestly? I miss my brother so much. And yet, it's been so long, and we've both changed. Plus, he thinks the accident was my fault, and I don't know if he'd ever want to talk to me again."

"You keep saying that, but why? Did he tell you he blamed you specifically?"

"Yes and no."

When I was younger, I hadn't been very patient. But after being a father for nearly eleven years, I'd learned the trait, for the most part. And I could tell Emmy needed a moment to gather her thoughts.

I was eventually rewarded.

"Rafe avoided me at the funeral. All I wanted was for my big brother to hug me and cry with me and reassure me everything would be all right. But all I really remember was him telling me that I would live with the Wolfe family, and that he'd be too busy to visit me."

Rafe would've been nineteen at the time, and still young, but anger churned in my belly at how he'd handled the situation. The boy I'd known as a kid never would've abandoned his sister that way.

What had happened to him?

"Emmy."

She finally met my gaze again.

"It was harsh, I'll agree. But it doesn't sound like he blamed you."

"Then why wouldn't he look at me? Or when I tried to hug him, he kept me at an arm's length and foisted me off on your mom? Because he knew it was my fault! Of course he wouldn't want to comfort the person who killed our parents."

"Emmy, you didn't kill them. I looked more into it, and the guy who hit your parents was four times the legal limit. He was blind drunk and driving so fast no one would've been able to swerve around him."

Even in the dim light, I saw her eyes wet with unshed tears. "Why are you so insistent about this, West?"

"Because it fucking rips my heart in two to see you punishing yourself for something you didn't do. You were a kid, Emmy, and the asshole who hit your car probably wasn't far from passing out. As for your brother..."

Something clicked together in my mind, something I hadn't realized before.

But it made a lot of fucking sense.

"What about my brother?"

"You were going to see him play, weren't you?"

She frowned. "Yes. It was the first time we could fly to England and see one of his matches in person."

Fuck. I was even more confident that my hunch was right. But how could I convince her to believe it?

All I could do was voice suspicions. "Maybe Rafe blames himself for what happened."

"What? No, that's ridiculous."

"Just listen for a second, okay? Your dad was driving you guys to the airport to see Rafe. He was the one who asked you guys to visit him in England, right?"

"Yes, but—"

"If he hadn't asked you guys to come, then you never

would've been on the road that night and never would've been hit by the drunk driver. Think about it—if he felt even a sliver of the guilt you've felt over the years, and your roles were reversed, would you have thought it better for him to live with my family than with you, if you blamed yourself for destroying your family as you knew it?"

I expected Emmy to argue. After all, she'd been blaming herself for more than a decade and probably had a web of logic I would never fully understand.

But she merely sat quietly, staring out the window, thinking.

Life was always full of what-ifs, but if only Rafe and Emmy had talked to one another all those years ago, they could've avoided years of pain.

Because the more I thought about it, the more my theory about Rafe made sense.

"Change of plans." I started the car and pulled back on the road.

"You should take me home, West. I'm sorry to cancel our date, but I'm tired."

"And I will. But we're going to swing by a drive-thru and grab some food. Then I'll take you home. If you want me to leave, I can. If you want me to stay, I can do that too. It'll be up to you."

As she continued staring out the window, my heart ached for her.

At the same time, I wished I knew how to call Rafe and demand some answers.

After picking up some burgers and curly fries, I

drove back to Emmy's place. She'd turned the radio to some Top 40 station but didn't look at me.

Once I pulled in front of her house, I offered her the food. "Just promise me you'll eat something. Abby says you've been super busy lately and not eating regular meals."

She stared at the bag and took it. "I will."

I waited for her to invite me in, but she didn't. When she moved to open the door, I shook my head. "Wait."

I raced around, opened it, and helped her down. For a beat, she stared up at me, her expression unreadable.

I wanted to take her inside and make her laugh, or at least smile, and then make her forget about her problems, even if only for a few hours.

But I wasn't her boyfriend, barely more than a friend with benefits, and didn't really have that right.

Even if I fucking wished I did. I wanted to be there for her, take care of her, be her person, the one she could lean on whenever she needed.

To make her mine and let the world know.

Because some how, some way, I was already falling for this woman.

But after tonight, I wasn't sure if I'd ruined my chances because of my thoughts about Rafe.

I still stood by my guess about her brother. And yet, she'd spent so many years blaming herself, she might not want to hear a different point of view. I never wanted to cause her pain, but I hadn't been able to let her continue to punish herself.

Eventually, she touched my face, and I leaned into it, hoping it wasn't the last time.

She whispered, "Good night, West."

She turned and walked inside her house, and I watched her, memorizing the movement of her hips, wishing I could run after her and ask to stay.

After so many years of thinking I'd never want anything to do with a woman and then getting a little taste of what it could be like? Fuck, it was hard giving her space when she needed it.

I sighed, climbed into my truck, and gripped the steering wheel so tightly that my knuckles turned white.

Maybe this was proof I shouldn't date or try to let someone close to me. For the second time in my life, I felt I couldn't help a woman I cared about.

And the scary thing was that my feelings for Emmy were already more than I'd ever had for Andrea. If Emmy rejected me? It was going to fucking hurt.

At least I hadn't brought my kids into this relationship yet.

As I drove home, I still held on to the hope that Emmy merely needed time to think and that I hadn't fucked things up for good.

Chapter Thirty-Five

Emilia

Abby: Where did he take you?
Me: Er, we never made it to the date.
Abby: There's more to the world than the bedroom.
Me: No, it wasn't that...
Abby: Something's wrong. I can get my aunt to watch the kids and come over, ice cream in tow.
Me: No, no. I need to be alone right now.
Abby: Are you sure?
Me: Yes. Just like you needed time by yourself after coming back from San Jose, it's the same for me now.
Abby: Well, we'll talk tomorrow. That's long enough, and I won't let you hide.

Me: I know, and I love you for it. <heart emoji> See you tomorrow.
Abby: <heart emoji> back at you.

Sitting inside my father's former office, I held the photo of me, Rafe, and our parents, all of us smiling as my brother held up his soccer jersey. It'd been taken a few days before he'd left to train with his new team in England.

It'd been such a happy day. We'd eaten at the barbecue place in town, had gone for ice cream afterward, and had sat together playing Uno and laughing every time someone got stuck with a bajillion cards.

Once Rafe had left for England, the house hadn't been the same. My parents had tried their best, though, to give me extra attention and encouraged me to play with my friends over the summer. Eventually, helping them out with the ranch bonded us and reshaped my childhood.

But I'd always missed my big brother's smiles, teasing, and how even if he was so much older, he'd still play with me. So when I learned about getting to see him play, I'd been beyond excited. I'd never been on an airplane before and learning how we would see castles like in the fairy tales made me even more impatient.

Then the crash had happened, and everything else had faded away.

At first, I refused to believe West's words about my

brother. Rafe had been so distant at the funeral, hadn't even visited me for his brief stay in Sonoma, and had fled back to England as quickly as possible.

I'd always viewed it through the lens of my own guilt, though.

Had Rafe blamed himself? Was that the reason he'd never looked at me, or hugged me, or tried to comfort me back then?

I stared at my brother's smiling face in the photo and tried to imagine if things had been reversed. If I had asked them to visit me, would I feel responsible?

Maybe.

I sighed. Had we both carried guilt unnecessarily, all because we'd never talked to each other?

And could I really accept that a drunk driver was responsible, and I hadn't killed my parents?

I rubbed a hand over my forehead, closed my eyes, and wished I hadn't sent West away. Not only because he was a lot more logical about the past, but because things always seemed a little more bearable whenever he was near. There was something about his strong arms around me, or the sound of his heart beating under my ear, or just his heat and scent surrounding me.

Longing rushed through me. I missed his voice, his presence, his everything.

After opening my eyes, I stared at my phone. I could ask him to come back. I probably wasn't strong enough to truly talk this out just yet. But once he wrapped his arms around me, I'd just feel better.

Before I could change my mind, I found his name

and hit Call. I knew he didn't really keep track of texts that closely, and I wouldn't be a coward that way.

After three rings, his voice came over the line. "Emmy? What's wrong?"

I took a deep breath, determined not to cry. "Can you come over? I know it's late, and you were just here, but..."

"Of course. I'll be there as soon as I can."

"Thank you."

He grunted, which made me smile, and he hung up.

I stood, the photo still in my hand, and closed the office and locked the storage facility before returning to my house.

Needing some fortification, I took out two wine glasses and a bottle of Starry Wolfe chardonnay and waited.

After what had to be a record-breaking drive, someone knocked at my front door. I opened it, and West pushed his way inside, shut the door, and then pulled me into his arms. I closed my eyes, breathed in the scent of male and something woodsy, and took strength from West's solid presence.

I didn't know how long we stood that way before I started crying. But once I started, I couldn't stop, and soon I was sobbing.

Sobbing for how much I missed my parents.

Sobbing for how much I missed my brother.

And sobbing for all the years I'd lost, weighed down by the guilt of my parents' death. Which I was only starting to believe hadn't been my fault.

West merely stroked my back, murmuring soothing words. At some point he guided us to the sofa in the living room, pulled me onto his lap, and held me close.

When I'd cried myself out, I sat silently, cuddled against West's warm chest, and listened to his heartbeat. Steady and strong, much like the man holding me.

It hit me then how much I wanted more of this. To have him around always, being my rock when I fell apart, and for me to be there for him when he had tough days too.

I also wanted to be there for his kids, who were starved for attention from a mother-like figure and needed someone to love them and be proud of them and help tell them bedtime stories.

Could I do it, though? Really accept it was okay for me to be happy? To risk my heart for him and his kids?

My heart screamed yes, but my brain was still muddled.

As West's arms tightened around me, I sighed. I didn't have to decide about forever right now. I just wanted to enjoy the present.

I finally sat up and looked into West's blue eyes. They were full of concern. For me.

After raising a hand to his face and brushing his jaw, I finally croaked, "Thank you for coming."

He wiped away the remaining tears from my cheek and kissed me gently. "Anytime, Emmy. I'm just glad you don't hate me."

I frowned. "Why would I hate you?"

"Well, I'm not good at being gentle and subtle. I

could've maybe told you my thoughts about Rafe a little less forcefully."

The corner of my mouth ticked up. "But that wouldn't be you." I stroked his cheek, loving his late-night stubble under my fingers. "And I need some honesty every once in a while to break through my stubbornness." I paused, took a deep breath, and reminded myself I'd wanted him here and needed to stop keeping things from him. "I'm starting to think... well, maybe there was nothing I could've done that night."

He didn't crow about being right. No, the wonderful man merely kissed me and tightened his hold on me. "Does that mean you'll reach out to Rafe?"

"Maybe, but not right now. I'm still trying to convince myself it wasn't my fault and to not feel guilty."

He kissed the top of my head. "The last thing I'd ever do is pressure you, Emmy. But just promise me one thing—if you need to talk about it, or to go over the facts of that night to maybe help convince yourself of the truth, then call me. Anytime. I don't want you to be alone in this."

West was too good to be true. I couldn't believe how any woman would want to cheat on him like his late wife had.

And yet, I knew the upcoming months would be busy. West might not be that patient or want this to work as much as I did. Still, I was done keeping things from him. "I have something to tell you."

He placed a finger under my chin and lifted my gaze to his. He raised his brows and grunted.

I snorted. "I thought with me, at last, you were using your words more."

And then West did something I'd never have expected—he stuck out his tongue.

I broke into giggles, and he chuckled, and it took us both a few minutes to calm down. When I had myself under control, I cupped his cheek. Staring into his eyes, I realized my feelings for this man were intense, and I wasn't quite ready to face them.

After pushing them aside, I bit the bullet. "I want to date you, West. I do. But I snagged this wedding, you see, and..."

He listened as I told him about Zara Jones and the short notice for her wedding. When I finished, I waited to see what he'd say.

West kissed my lips before murmuring, "I know your business is important to you, Emmy. But I can't not see you or bed you or touch you for that long."

My heart plummeted, and I moved to rise from his lap. But his strong hands kept me in place as he added, "Let me finish."

I nodded, unable to look at him as he said, "I suggest a compromise. Once or twice a week, I can come over late, after my kids are asleep, and spend the night with you. Even if it's just holding you in in my arms as we sleep, I'll take it. Although I'd be lying if I didn't say I wanted to strip you and lick your perfect pussy every now and again too."

My eyes shot to his. "So you don't want to give up on me?"

He frowned. "Of course not. If I were the type of

guy to scoff at supporting your career, then you should rightly kick my ass to the curb. But I think a few breaks to yourself, a couple times a week, is reasonable. It'll also give my hand a break in the shower, in my bed, and everywhere else I can squeeze in a few minutes of privacy."

He winked, and I kissed him. He wanted to support me, stand by me, and not give up at the first sign of difficulty.

Our kiss soon turned heated, his tongue stroking against mine, his teeth tugging at my bottom lip, and his groans shooting straight between my thighs, making me ache for more, much more.

Eventually, I broke the kiss to catch my breath and laid my forehead against his. "Thank you."

"More like I should thank you. You'll be helping out my poor cock, giving it some much-needed attention."

I lightly swatted his chest. "You're being silly."

He grunted and then pressed his groin more against my side, proving his very hard cock was at the ready. "Won't you give him some loving?"

I laughed. "It's a he, huh? Does he have a name?"

"Of course it's a he. And no, there's no name." I smiled slowly, and West shook his head. "Oh, hell no. You're not naming my dick."

"Are you sure? I mean, it could be something strong like Stone or Brick or Axe."

He raised an eyebrow. "Stone, really? Not going for subtlety, are you?"

I moved a hand and stroked his rather stonelike cock. "Well, I thought at your age, a little encouragement might help. I mean, the fewer little blue pills you have to take, the better, right?"

"I'll show you what this old man can do."

With a growl, he had me on my back, and I laughed before he kissed me and started rubbing his jeans-clad dick against my clit. Soon I moaned and arched into him and forgot all about names for his cock.

Eventually, he broke the kiss and said, "For fuck's sake, please tell me you have some condoms because I wasn't expecting this."

"Yes. In my bathroom upstairs."

"Which is attached to your bedroom. How convenient."

Without another word, West hefted me into his arms and carried me up the stairs.

Part of me loved it when he went a little caveman-like.

All too soon he placed me on my bed and went to get a condom. I stripped my clothes off. And when West returned naked and already wearing a condom, I smiled. "You're impatient, too, huh?"

He lowered over me on the bed, propped on his forearms, and nuzzled my cheek. "I will always be impatient to see you naked, Emilia. Always."

I lightly ran my nails down his back. "Well, I'm impatient for a lot more, West. I never thought I'd say this, but stop talking."

He snorted, but then he kissed my jaw, my neck, and finally he took one of my nipples into his mouth. As he suckled and nibbled gently with his teeth, I threaded my fingers through his hair and moaned. Each tug of his mouth only made me wetter, and when his fingers brushed my clit, I cried out.

West lifted his gaze, one full of heat and wanting and something else I couldn't identify, and said, "I'm desperate to be inside you, Emilia."

"Then what are you waiting for?"

West thrust into me. I gripped his broad shoulders and dug in my nails as he moved his hips, fucking me hard and swift, almost as if he'd die if he didn't, and I soon met his movements with my own. I moaned and cried out, glad we were alone because I couldn't be quiet if my life depended on it.

The erotic sound of flesh slapping against flesh grew louder, and West took my mouth in a brutal kiss, claiming it at the same time as my pussy. I was close, so close, and if only...

And then he changed the angle so he rubbed against my clit with each swift thrust. Lights danced before my eyes before pleasure exploded throughout my body, my pussy convulsing around West's cock. Soon he stilled, giving the deepest, most desperate groan, and collapsed on top of me.

I held him close, wrapping my legs around his waist and arms around his back, wanting him to stay with me a little longer.

Maybe to stay with me forever.

I was already so close to loving this man, it wouldn't take much more to push me over the edge.

I wasn't sure how much time had passed when West rolled onto his back, taking me with him, and he said, "So I'm guessing this is a yes to my plan?"

Focusing on how happy I was in this moment, I forgot all about my worries and fears. "Yes. And maybe if we survive my hectic schedule, then..."

I mentally cursed. Why was I bringing up the future now?

West gently turned my head until I could see his eyes. "Then what, Emilia?"

I finally realized he called me my full name whenever we were naked together. And despite my earlier protests to him, I actually liked it. Because he was the only one to do it, making it special.

He gently poked my side, and I sighed. "Fine. Maybe if we're still doing okay after this wedding is over, we could tell your kids? That way we could all spend more time together?"

His eyes lit up, and he kissed me. "I think that can be arranged." He pulled back a little. "By then it'll be necessary. Stealing moments alone is one thing, but my kids come with me, Emmy. And they will always show up when you least expect it, will need a lot of my attention and love, and come first like ninety-eight percent of the time."

I knew he only said these things because of his late wife's attitude, and I didn't take offense. I cupped his cheek and stroked his skin. "I love your kids, West. And as long as that two percent is for us, I'll be fine."

He scowled. "You say that now..."

"No. I've been getting to know Wyatt and Avery over the last few months. I know them. I do. Avery can be outgoing and restless, and yet sometimes she gets really insecure about things and needs encouragement.

Wyatt is shy and thoughtful, but once he gets something in his head, he really gives it his all, and he needs help focusing that determination."

He brushed some hair from my face. "If the four of us end up a team, then things will change a little, though. You'll have to be more than their occasional friend. Raising kids can be messy and frustrating and amazing, all at the same time. Do you want to sign up for it, even knowing it won't always be easy?"

"Yes. I already want to kick the ass of anyone who hurts them, and maybe I can actually chase people away if I'm dating their dad."

"Ass-kicking is usually a last resort. Only because you don't want to end up in jail."

I rolled my eyes. "I know that. I might not have any parenting experience, but I love your kids, West. The rest I can learn."

West's gaze softened. "You're amazing and beautiful and so much better than I deserve."

I rose and straddled his hips, leaned down, and took his face between my hands. "No, you're much better than I deserve. But I'm selfish and want to keep you all the same."

I kissed him, and it was sweet and tender at first before growing heated and fierce. Soon West was running for another condom, taking me this time from behind as he gave me the spankings I'd wanted, and I screamed his name as I came.

As we fell asleep in my bed, I couldn't stop smiling. When West had showed up in my life again five months ago, I never would've guessed that he'd end up being what I always wanted.

A man I could grow to love and who could grow to love me.

More than ever, I was determined to make things work in all areas of my life. Maybe fate was changing, and I finally had a chance at happiness.

Chapter Thirty-Six

Weston

Emmy: When is Avery's swim class graduation?
Me: Tomorrow, at 3pm. But like I said, if you're busy, I'll just take a video and share it.
Emmy: No, I'm going to try my best to be there and cheer her on. I might even make a sign.
Me: She'd love that. And maybe...
Emmy: Hm?
Me: Did you want to get ice cream afterward with us?
Emmy: I never say no to ice cream.
Me: If you have the time.
Emmy: West, if I don't have the time, I'll say so. You've been super supportive, but it's okay to ask me if I can do things. I just can't always say yes.

Me: I'm out of practice.
Emmy: I know. <heart emoji> But even when I'm busy, I make time for what's important. I'll be there.
Me: Then tell me about this sign and I'll see if I can add to it…

At the end of August, Wyatt, Aunt Lori, Zach, Beck, Sabrina, and even Nolan sat inside the community center, at the poolside bleachers, waiting for my daughter and her classmates to come out.

It was the final swim class, when they would display their skills before receiving certificates to mark their graduation. The younger classes also got stickers or little toys, but the older kids got a pair of goggles.

Avery had been up at dawn and ready to go, long before I'd had a cup of coffee. She'd even woken up her brother despite the fact Wyatt was taking karate classes and wasn't quite as excited as his twin about the day.

As we waited for the kids to enter in their swimsuits, I kept glancing at the door, wondering if Emmy would make it.

The last month had been fucking amazing, and I'd never seen enough of her. Even with her being so busy, she'd made time to eat lunch some days with my kids, and we'd brought her dinner a few times.

The nights when I had her to myself, I'd done my best to ruin her for all men. I knew exactly how hard she liked to be fucked, or how I should use my tongue on her clit, or even how she liked it that I got a little bossy when naked.

To say I craved her was an understatement. But I was being a fucking adult and doing my best to support her.

Keeping it from my kids got harder by the day, though.

At least they'd be in school again next week and would have less time to ask Emmy when they could eat lunch with her again. She'd told me how hard it was to keep saying no. Not because she didn't want to eat with them, but her workload was off the charts.

The door opened, and Emmy's brown eyes soon found mine. I grinned and waved. She smiled as she made her way to us.

I patted the spot I saved for her. "Just in time."

She waved at my family—they knew we were dating, just not my kids—and sat next to me. "Sorry. I had a last-minute disaster I had to clean up with the caterer."

I wanted to kiss her so bad but settled on taking her fingers and squeezing them. "What, were they going to serve maple syrup spaghetti for dinner instead of chicken and asparagus?"

"I'm sure there's been an *Elf* movie–themed wedding before, but my movie star one isn't it. No, I just had to talk the groom's mother out of changing the meals. Again."

"This is why I work with plants—they can't talk."

She snorted. "But they can die, which ruins things too."

"Let's not talk about dead plants," I whispered in her ear. "I'm just happy to see you."

She released my fingers to lightly rub my thigh. "Me too. Just a few more weeks, and then I'll have so much free time that I won't know what to do with myself."

I kept my voice low. "Oh, I know how to fill the nights. I still have a naughty student to punish."

She sucked in a breath. "West, this is a children's swimming event."

"No one can hear us."

Nolan sat next to me, and he cleared his throat. "Some of us can."

I glared at my brother. "A gentleman doesn't eavesdrop."

"It's not eavesdropping when I'm merely sitting here, and you're loud." He leaned forward and waved. "Hey, Emmy. Still glad I recommended you to Zara?"

Emmy nodded. "Of course. It's a much grander scale than I'm used to, but I enjoy the challenge. Maybe one day I can plan another big one."

Nolan smiled wryly. "Probably not mine."

"Oh, I wasn't...I don't listen to gossip, Nolan."

"I know. But still, it's not true."

Nolan's name had been bandied about in the papers lately. His ex claimed they were engaged. No matter how often he denied it, the media and his ex's fans wanted to believe the fairy-tale wedding would happen someday.

I slapped Nolan's back. "Of course not. That means someone would have to wake up to that face every morning."

Nolan smiled but didn't reply. I was working on the relationship with my middle brother, but he was away so often that I hadn't had a lot of time to get to know him as an adult.

Emmy took my hand. "Look, here they come. Did you bring a sign?"

"Of course." I picked it up from the floor. "We all did."

Everyone in the room clapped and cheered the kids as they approached the pool.

Emmy and I stood, each holding our respective signs. Mine said "Avery's #1," and Emmy's said "Congrats Avery!"

Beck and Sabrina each wore a T-shirt that read "Avery's a Champ."

Even my aunt had made a sign that read "Go Avery! Whoo-hoo!" and held it up with Wyatt on her other side. My son's face was red, but soon Aunt Lori got him cheering too.

When Avery noticed us, she beamed, and my heart grew three sizes. Her family was here for her, supporting her, as they should be.

As my kids should've had all these years.

Not wanting my past to ruin the day, I continued whistling until one of the swim teachers spoke into a microphone, silencing us all.

"Thank you, everyone, for coming to our final class and showcase event! The students have worked really hard to get to this point and are a little nervous, so let's give them some cheers to pump them up!"

The whole Wolfe clan cheered and whistled and stomped our feet until the teacher spoke again.

"And first up is Avery Wolfe!"

Avery waved at me, and I waved back. Then she went to the deep end of the pool, took a second to breathe, and dove into the water. She came up for air and slowly swam to the other side, where a teacher waited for her.

It wasn't the Olympics, but seeing my little girl doing the breaststroke all that way, sluicing through the water confidently—if a little overenthusiastically—was both fucking amazing and a little sad.

I murmured, "She's growing up too fast."

Emmy leaned against me, her arm brushing mine. "That's what everyone says about their kids. You can't stop time, but I guarantee she'll never stop being Daddy's little girl."

I refused to fucking cry and merely nodded.

When Avery reached the other side, she ascended the steps and gave a little bow. The Wolfes all stood and waved our signs, cheering her on, until she grabbed a towel and went to sit on the sidelines.

Emmy threaded her fingers through mine and squeezed. Our signs hid the action, and part of me wished we didn't have to.

Her career-changing wedding is nearly over. Soon. Soon you can show her off as your woman and include your kids in the relationship.

I murmured, "I'm glad you're here."

Emmy glanced at me, her eyes warm. "Me too."

She all but begged me to kiss her, and I couldn't.

While frustrating, between the previous weeks of secretly dating her, as well as her presence here today when Avery needed it the most, I believed in her. Believed she could be the one.

She was nothing like my late wife. And the road ahead might be rocky as fuck, but we'd make it work.

Emmy and I held hands until all the kids finished, and they lined up to receive their certificates. We all descended the steps, and Avery rushed up to us, a towel tucked around her waist. She held up her certificate and her new googles. "I did it!"

Uncaring that I'd get wet, I pulled her into a hug. "You did, baby girl. I'm so proud of you."

Zach produced a little tiara from his backpack. "And now you're the princess of the pool."

Avery beamed and let her uncle place it on her wet head. "Soon I'll be the queen."

We all laughed, and after Beck, Sabrina, Aunt Lori, and Wyatt all hugged her, Avery walked up to Emmy. "Did you see how fast I was, Emmy? Did you swim like that when you were on the swim team?"

Emmy hugged her. "Not until I was a lot older. You're a natural, Avery. I bet you'll be even faster than I was, if you want to keep swimming, that is."

"Oh, I do. I love moving through the water. It's relaxing, kind of." Avery looked up at her dad. "Can I keep taking swim lessons?"

I chucked my daughter under the chin. "I think we can manage that."

Emmy jumped in. "You can use my pool any time to practice, as long as the weather's warm enough."

Avery nodded. "Thanks, Emmy. I don't know if I'll have a lot of free time once school starts, but maybe on the weekends. Will you watch me?"

I opened my mouth, but Emmy beat me to it. "I'll try. Until I finish my big wedding, it might be difficult."

Avery shifted her goggles to the hand that held the certificate and took Emmy's in her free one. "Are you going to get ice cream with us afterward?" She paused and added softly, "Unless you're too busy. Then I understand."

Maybe a stranger would think she was guilt-tripping or trying to make Emmy feel bad. However, I knew it stemmed from her mother always deflecting and not spending time with her.

Emmy swung their clasped hands. "I almost never say no to ice cream."

Avery's face lit up. "Awesome, I can't wait."

"Then you'd better go with your class and change. We'll wait in the reception area for you."

"I won't be long."

She waved at us before hurrying away.

And as Emmy started asking Wyatt about his karate classes and joking with Zach about how Wyatt might be able to kick his ass soon, I barely stopped myself from grinning. I was so fucking happy and hopeful and halfway in love with Emmy already that I couldn't wait for her big wedding to be over. After so many years of merely accepting my fate and making the most of it, I wanted to grab the dream hovering just out of reach and make it reality.

Chapter Thirty-Seven

Emilia

Me: Since I woke up so early and got a lot of work done, I have my night free.
West: Are you propositioning me at an ice cream parlor?
Me: Maybe. <blowing a kiss emoji> We have some unfinished business.
West: <dashing emoji> Me at 9 p.m. tonight.
Me: <laughing emoji> I'll make sure to have snacks.
West: Why? I plan on eating only one thing—you.
Me: Maybe it'll be ON me.
West: Are you trying to kill me?
Me: It's fun to try.

West: Okay, I'm going to try for 8:45. Be naked and waiting for me.
Me: So bossy.
West: Obey and I'll make it worth your while.
Me: <overheated emoji>

As I sat in my bathrobe on the couch, trying to watch TV but not really paying attention, I couldn't stop smiling as I remembered first the swim class and then the ice cream parlor afterward.

I'd always loved spending time with the Wolfe family. Yet today had been different because of West and his kids. Watching West smile and laugh with his children and siblings over stupid jokes, or me and Avery teaming up against West and Wyatt and teasing them about their ice cream flavor choices—pistachio and rum raisin—or even Aunt Lori organizing a big breakfast for the twins' first day of school had made me feel all warm and fuzzy.

And I'd felt happy. Happier than I'd been in a long time.

I wanted this future. One full of family and laughter and even kids squabbling as kids did. I never thought I'd be someone who wanted a ready-made family, and yet never seeing Avery or Wyatt again seemed unimaginable.

My usual enthusiasm for work was waning, too. But

I had less than a month of craziness to go before I could start being more than just a friend to Avery and Wyatt.

The doorbell rang, so I turned off the TV and jumped up. After peeking into the peephole and seeing West, I smiled and discarded my robe. I opened the door, and West growled. "Mine. All mine."

He rushed inside, pulled me against him, and shut the door. His mouth pressed against mine, and I opened up to him, welcoming his tongue. As he lapped and licked and devoured me, I dug my fingers into his hair and pressed my body against his. The roughness of his shirt pressing against my hard nipples made me moan.

West broke the kiss and ran his hands down my back, to my ass, and then he lightly slapped one cheek. "You're naked like I asked." He slapped me again, and wetness rushed between my thighs. "Such a good fucking girl."

I pushed against his chest, and he let me go. I swayed my hips as I walked to the kitchen, knowing he'd follow me. After taking out a can of whipped cream from the fridge, I held it up. "Did you want to put some on your dessert?"

He tugged off his shirt and tossed it to the floor, baring his magnificently muscled chest dusted with dark hair. "Fuck yes. Give me that and then get on the bed."

I'd learned how West liked when I skirted on the edge of his orders. After handing him the whipped cream, I ran my nails down his chest until I could lightly stroke just under the waistband of his jeans. "Don't take too many breaks on the way to the bedroom, old man."

He growled, swatted my butt, and I ran down the hallway, with West close on my heels.

I'd barely jumped onto the bed when West entered my bedroom. He set the whipped cream down so he could shed his boots and jeans. Like usual on our nights together, he was commando.

Staring at his cock, I licked my lips. I craved driving him wild with my mouth.

"Not tonight, Emilia. Tonight, it's my turn to make you lose your mind with pleasure."

He shook the can a few times, popped off the lid, and leaned down to blow air against my nipple. I moaned, arching my back, and he murmured, "Let's see just how hard and swollen we can get your nipples tonight." He met my gaze. "Don't move until I tell you. Understand?"

"Yes."

"Good girl."

I watched as he slowly, oh so slowly, lowered the whip cream can until it hovered just above my breast. One second passed then another. My heart raced, and my pussy throbbed.

When he finally sprayed it on me, I bit my lip to keep from moaning. The cold cream was a shock and oddly made me hotter.

He repeated the action with my other nipple before setting the can aside. West rubbed his hands over my stomach, my hips, and then up between my breasts and down my arms until he could take my wrists.

He pinned them above my head. "Stay like this, Emilia, so your tits jut out just for me."

After he released me, I stayed in place, my breathing heavy. But he didn't do anything but caress me with his eyes for at least a minute.

Damn, my nipples ached. I wanted him to touch me so very badly.

I didn't know how much time passed before he lowered his head and circled my nipple with his tongue, around and around, until he gave it a cursory lick. Just a light flick, and yet heat rushed throughout my body, ending between my thighs.

He teased with light flicks, never fully licking the cream away, almost as if he were savoring it. Savoring me.

Then he finally suckled my nipple, and I cried out, the heat of his mouth a contrast to my cold skin. He took his time sucking and nibbling and tugging until I had my legs spread wide, my pussy exposed, arching up. I needed more than his mouth on me. I wanted his cock.

He finally released my nipple, met my gaze, and licked his lips. "Delicious."

Damn. That one word nearly made me whimper.

West lightly traced the curve of my other breast. "So fucking sweet. Let's see if you like what I'm doing."

He ran a finger through my center before thrusting it inside me. I moaned, and all too soon, he removed the digit. After sucking his finger clean, he growled. "You're so fucking wet. Let's see if I can get you even wetter."

"West, please."

I offered my hips in invitation, but he pressed them down. "Not yet, Emilia. I haven't finished my dessert. Behave and I'll let you fuck me the way you want."

Which meant riding him.

I nodded, and he kissed me briefly. "Good girl."

I could barely revel in his praise before his hot mouth was on my cold nipple, torturing me slowly like with the other, until he finally suckled me hard. I wanted to dig my nails into his scalp, his back, his shoulders, but I somehow managed to keep my arms above my head. Not being able to move made me focus on every touch, lick, and nibble.

West finally released me and ran his hands up my sides until he could cup my breasts. "So fucking perfect. And now I can't wait to see these tits bounce as you take my dick and ride me hard."

"Yes. I want that."

He kissed me and rolled on his back. "Then put on the condom and fuck me."

After shivering at his command, I slowly sat up and caressed his chest, lightly rubbing his nipples. I could torture him like he'd tortured me, but I was impatient.

I swiped the condom packet from the nightstand and quickly opened it and rolled it on. Some nights it was fun to tease, but I was too wet and achy and desperate right now.

Once that was done, I braced my hands on his chest and straddled his hips. West's hands went to my waist as I positioned his cock and lowered slowly, inch by inch, loving how he groaned, how his pupils dilated.

I would never tire of how this man looked at me—as if I were the most beautiful woman in the world.

Once I took him to the hilt, I sat and clenched my inner muscles. West lightly spanked my ass, then again a little harder, the light sting making me squeeze his cock harder.

"Fuck yes. Do that again."

I did, and I loved how his eyes became heavy-lidded.

"Ride me, Emilia. Ride me hard."

Moving my hips, I never took my eyes from his, loving how desire and wanting and heat swirled in his gaze. As his dick stroked me, it wasn't quite right, so I changed the angle until I moaned when it finally hit the right place inside me.

"Fuck, Emilia. That's right. Take your pleasure, find it. Use my dick to make yourself come."

I was tempted to move faster, but somehow I kept my pace the same, loving how he growled and tried to move my hips. "Not yet."

West slapped my ass again. "Now who's being a tease?"

I gripped his dick again. "I learn from the best."

He chuckled, and I couldn't help but smile at him.

Then he moved a hand to my clit and lightly brushed me. Once. Twice. Three times.

My heart raced faster as my breathing grew faster. When he removed his hand, I cried out. "No!"

"Now you know how I feel."

As soon as I moved my hips faster, rocking back and forth, his fingers returned to my clit and stroked me slowly, back and forth. I wanted to close my eyes and chase the pleasure hovering just out of reach.

"Keep your eyes on me."

And so I did. We both grew sweaty and hot and

panted, but soon I whimpered, knowing if West only stroked me a little harder, I'd come. "Please. Harder."

"Grip me, Emilia."

I obeyed, and then he pinched my clit. Pleasure coursed through my body as lights danced before my eyes. West tensed and groaned, his hand on my waist gripping me tighter as he found his release.

Once my spasms stilled, I slumped against him. West wrapped his arms around me and kissed my temple. "Fuck, that was amazing, Emilia."

I smiled and played with some of his chest hair. "You weren't too bad yourself."

His chuckle rumbled beneath my ear. "Considering you were so fucking wet you were dripping before you rode me, I think I was pretty fucking fantastic."

"Cocky."

"You talking about my cock again already?"

I snorted. "You sure you don't need that hearing aid?"

He lightly slapped my ass. "I may have a few gray hairs, but you benefit from my patience, Emilia." His voice turned husky. "Remember that one night, when I kept you on the edge for an hour?"

I squirmed, and despite my recent orgasm, my pussy throbbed again. "That was just mean, and I still haven't had a chance to get you back for that."

He lazily stroked my back, my ass, my hip, and the action soothed me. "You'll have your chance before..."

"Before what?"

He paused before replying, "Nothing."

I propped my chin on his chest so I could look at his face. "Don't say 'nothing' because clearly it's something."

Searching my eyes, he asked, "Have you thought about how things will change once your big wedding is finished and we tell my kids about us?"

We'd sort of skirted around this conversation, for the most part. I knew things would be different, but my focus had been trying to get to know West better first.

Not wanting to freak him out, I kept my tone casual. "Of course things will change. I imagine Avery will constantly ask if we're getting married or if I'll be over for sleepovers, or anything goes, really."

"Yes, I'm worried about the same thing."

I sat up so I could better see his face. "Maybe we should think of what to say or how to handle it. The last thing I want to do is put pressure on you, but given Avery's romantic nature, she might try."

West sat up, pulled me onto his lap, and cupped my cheek. "I wouldn't be averse to sleepovers once in a while, provided you can keep quiet."

My heart thumped at his words. "Truly? You want me around that much?"

"Of course I do. And my kids already love you. We'll take it slow, but I also want to see how we all handle being in close quarters."

Was he really implying that maybe, just maybe, one day he'd want to move in together? Or even get married?

I was both happy and reluctant at the idea. Trying to accept I deserved happiness, that I hadn't caused so much pain to my family, and that I could care for and maybe even love someone without losing them was still difficult sometimes.

Stroking my cheek with his thumb, West murmured, "Where did you go, Emilia?"

"I'm here. Just thinking."

"About?"

I bit my bottom lip a second before replying, "I'm still working on deserving this whole happiness thing. The fact I'm so happy right now and it's not a dream is hard to accept."

He smiled. "I'm here. And I doubt you'd come as hard in a dream compared to what I can do in the flesh."

I lightly swatted his chest. "Be serious."

"I am. But regardless, we still have nearly a month before we talk to my kids. Let's just take it one day at a time, one night at a time, and I'll do my best to convince you this is your life now. Our life now."

I kissed him. "Okay."

West wrapped his arms around me, and for a few minutes, we sat in silence, basking in the warmth and presence of one another.

Finally, I broke the silence. "I still can't believe you made whip cream so damn hot."

He chuckled. "When I have trouble sleeping, I imagine ways to torture you slowly. That was one of the scenarios."

I lifted my head. "Do you, now? Instead of sheep, it's this position, that position, position fifty-eight..."

He tickled my side, and I yelped before scrambling off his lap. "What was that for?"

"If you kept it up, I would be tempted to try two

more positions tonight. But you're exhausted, Emmy. I can see it."

I tried not to yawn and failed. "I've been up since four a.m."

"All so you can support my kids and then see me."

"You and your kids are worth being a little tired for."

Something flashed across his eyes I couldn't read before he got up. "Then let me clean you up, tuck you in, and you can get some sleep."

I nodded, and he went to the bathroom. Once West finished, he gave me a lingering goodnight kiss before dressing and heading home.

As I lay on my side, staring at the empty side of the bed, I wished he could stay every night.

One more month and then we can see where this goes.

Holding that thought close, I fell asleep and dreamed of having my own little family with West, Avery, and Wyatt.

Chapter Thirty-Eight

Weston

Emmy: The gazebo you built is amazing. Maybe you should show off those skills at the next wedding expo.
Me: I built it for you. I don't want to do it for strangers.
Emmy: <heart emoji> I'll treasure it.
Me: Maybe we can even try Position 22 in it.
Emmy: <laughing emoji> That might require some acrobatics.
Me: I can build anything we need.
Emmy: Is this your way of saying you want to build sex dungeons for a living?
Me: Um, no.
Emmy: Hey, I'd be supportive. Just think, someone could start an underground sex club in Starry Hills...

Me: ...
Emmy: Everyone will have to wear masks to hide their identities. And there will be a secret password.
Me: Is that what you really want to do and being a wedding planner is just a cover?
Emmy: No. I like designing pretty events. Black and gold and red would get boring after a while.
Me: Those are your sex club's colors?
Emmy: Of course. I can tell you why.
Me: I think my kids are calling me. I'll see you later, beautiful.

The next three weeks flew by in a blur of happiness. My kids started school and made some new friends. I took Wyatt to the King stables a few times to visit the horses—with a promise from the King brothers to teach him anything he wanted to know about caring for and raising the animals. And Avery spent as much time in Emmy's pool as possible while the weather held, loving the new swimsuit that didn't keep creeping up her ass.

The nights I spent with Emmy continued to be some of the best of my life.

Even if she hadn't worked up the nerve to contact Rafe yet, she talked more and more about her parents and brother. And even I, not the chattiest of men, started telling her stories of when Beck and I were kids, before she was even born.

Occasionally, I wondered how the fuck she wanted to be with an older guy like me. But she did, and I was too fucking selfish to tell her she could do better.

I'd even started accepting side jobs for her wedding business and did custom builds. I enjoyed the work, more than what I did in the vineyards and winery, not that I'd told my brothers that yet.

Beck didn't hound me about his offer for me to become more involved in the business. I still couldn't bring myself to say yes, because deep down, I knew I wanted to do something else—probably raise cattle. But I was still too happy with Emmy and my family accepting me again to rock the boat. That time would come soon enough.

Today I had a rare day off, and since Emmy's big movie-star wedding was in less than a week—meaning she was too busy to eat let alone spend time with me and my kids—I asked Avery and Wyatt what they wanted to do.

They asked to go looking for animals near the creek on Emmy's land, and so here we were.

As Wyatt and Avery scoured the creek and nearby rocks—I was too big and loud and had been told to wait several feet away—I looked over the land again.

The grass was impossibly high now, wildflowers growing among it, and I wondered if Emmy planned to keep it fallow forever. It was good grazing land for cattle, and with some elbow grease, it could be turned into a ranch like before, with prized beef that would start bidding wars.

If she didn't want to do that, then maybe she'd sell

me the parts of her land she didn't need, and I could start my own ranch.

The only drawback was if I fucked up and she dumped my ass, we'd be neighbors.

Avery tugged on my hand, and I looked down. She grinned up at me as she held out her hand and showed me a ladybug. "Do you want to make a wish?"

This was something I'd passed down from my mom —whenever we found a ladybug, we'd make a wish and then gently blow on it until it flew away. I'd even put a few ladybugs in my tattoo to honor both my kids and my mom.

"No, you do it, love."

"If you're sure. I made the last wish on the tree in the orchard."

My family primarily grew grapes and made wine. However, at one time, our land had been covered in apple trees. Only a small orchard remained, and only because my mom and dad had loved all the traditions held there. There was a wishing tree near the center. Plus a lot of family proposals seemed to happen there too.

I cupped the bottom of her hand with my own. "How about we both make wishes? I'm sure the ladybug won't mind doing two at once."

She nodded. "Good idea."

I leaned down until our cheeks touched, and I murmured, "Make your wish." A few seconds passed as I made mine. Then I added, "On three. One, two, three!"

We both gently blew, and soon the ladybug flew away.

Avery whispered, "What did you wish for?"

"If I told you, it won't come true."

"Well, I had to try."

"Are you going to tell me yours?"

"I can't!"

I tickled her sides until she begged me to stop, and I sighed dramatically. "I guess you really are going to keep your wish a secret, aren't you?"

"Yep." She took my hand. "Come on. We haven't had any luck finding creatures by the creek, so Wyatt won't mind if you help us now."

"What are we looking for exactly?"

Wyatt looked up from his search. "I want to find a frog."

There were some—they sung at night in the summers—but having grown up in Starry Hills, I knew they were tricky fuckers. "We'll try. But if we can't find anything in twenty minutes, how about we go get some ice cream?"

Avery clapped. "Yes! And can Emmy come too? Or is she still too busy?"

Emmy being bogged down with work had affected Avery the most. She understood how the actor's wedding was important, but my daughter still missed swimming with Emmy over the last couple of weeks, once it'd become crunch time.

"She's still super busy, Avery. Just another week, and then she should be around more."

Not only around more, but things between me and her were so fucking good still that I couldn't wait for her to meet my kids as my girlfriend.

It was still weird to think about having a girlfriend at my age. But Emmy was mine, and I planned to do whatever I could to keep her.

I might even propose the M word again one day—marriage. Something I never thought I'd do for a second time.

But Emmy was just that fucking special and amazing, and I was falling hard for her.

Avery sighed, but Wyatt came and showed her a pretty rock. "I found one for your collection, Avery."

As I watched Avery's mood improve, I couldn't help but smile. Wyatt was nowhere near as outgoing as his sister, but he was so damn perceptive, to the point where it scared me sometimes.

If any of my kids were to guess something was going on between Emmy and me, it'd be Wyatt.

But he hadn't said a word to me. If he asked, though, I wouldn't lie. After all the lies their mother had told them, I'd vowed not to do the same.

Putting a hand on the shoulder of each of my kids, I pushed gently. "Come on. It's fucking hot out, and I want some ice cream."

"Bad word, Daddy!"

"You're never going to stop that, are you?"

Avery grinned. "Nope."

I tried to ruffle her hair, but she ran away and giggled. When I tried to do the same to Wyatt, he followed his sister, albeit without giggling.

As we walked past Emmy's house and barn, I couldn't wait for the day when we could spend time with her together. Fuck, if I was the luckiest bastard in the world, we might even live together one day.

Unlike months ago, the thought didn't scare me. Emmy wasn't Andrea, far from it. Yes, things could fall apart at some point. But I hoped not. Because I wanted things to work with Emmy and my kids so fucking badly, more than I'd wanted anything in a long, long time.

It was the day before Emmy's big wedding. I was just finishing up dinner with my family—Zach and my kids were teasing each other—when the doorbell rang. My aunt made to get up, but I put a hand out. "I'll get it."

I left the laughter behind and went to answer the rear door, used by the family. I looked through the peephole to see an unfamiliar woman dressed in a business suit. I opened the door, and she asked, "Are you Weston Wolfe?"

"Yes."

She held up a big envelope, and I took it. "You've been served. Have a nice day."

I barely paid attention to the woman leaving, shut the door, and opened the manila envelope. I scanned the contents and swore.

My fucking in-laws wanted custody of my kids.

As I kept reading, I got angrier and angrier. They accused me of neglecting my children, leaving them behind to have sex with women, and that the twins would do better under their grandparents' care.

By the end of it, I wanted to rip the papers into tiny

pieces and set them on fire. How dare they? Not only was it bullshit, but some of their accusations in the paperwork were fucking lies, such as saying they had a video of me screwing a woman in a public bathroom while my kids waited in the car.

How the fuck could they get away with that kind of shit?

No doubt it was because of their high and mighty judge friends, or the sheriff's office falsifying evidence as a favor.

Beck's voice came from behind me. "What is it?"

I turned and handed him the papers. It didn't take long for Beck to say, "Fucking bastards." He looked up. "Why would they do this? Pretty much all of this is bullshit and can easily be disproven."

"If only it were that simple. My mother-in-law comes from a rich family, one who rubs elbows with all the judges and politicians in the area. Plus, some of my father-in-law's family works in the sheriff's department. They're banking on those connections to win custody." I ran a hand through my hair. "It's going to be a fucking nightmare, Beck. But there's no way I'm letting them take my kids away from me."

Beck laid a hand on my shoulder. "Let us help."

Relying on anyone wasn't my strong point. But I wasn't about to alienate my brother. "If it comes to it, I will. But maybe I can get this thrown out and save us the trouble."

Which was wishful thinking. My mother-in-law had money, lots of it, which meant the best lawyers. I wasn't exactly poor, but I couldn't compete with that.

What if they managed to win?

My heart hurt just even imagining that. My kids were my life.

No. I wouldn't let anyone take them. Ever.

Beck motioned with his head down the hall. "Come on. Let's get a drink, and we can talk some more about it."

He took me to the kitchen, where Zach was putting things in the dishwasher. My brother turned. "Aunt Lori is putting the twins to bed. But...what the fuck happened?"

After I explained the gist to Zach, his eyes flashed with anger. Zach was the most optimistic and good-natured of us, so seeing him mad took me aback.

My little brother growled. "We'll help you, West. Anything you need, name it."

I'd never been close to Zach, partly because he was eight years younger than me and partly because I'd left Starry Hills when he'd still been a kid. Patching things up with Beck had been easier, but Zach and I kind of walked on eggshells around each other.

But seeing him this worked up and offering to help me when I needed it the most? Damn, it made me want to hug him. "Thanks, brother. But right now, I'm not even sure what I need."

Beck brought out some beers, and we all settled around the large kitchen island. "For now, alcohol will help." He took a swig. "When are you going to tell the twins?"

After a long pull from my bottle, I finally answered, "Not yet. I don't want them worrying that they'll have to leave and live with their grandparents. While they don't hate them, they're cautious around them. Mostly because the Grenvilles expect perfectly behaved children, more like little adults, and don't hold back their criticisms."

It was one of the many, many things I'd argued with them about.

And just when I'd started to think I was free of them and in control of my life, even maybe finding love for real this time, they charged back in and tore it all down.

"Fuck, what am I going to tell Emmy?"

Beck patted my shoulder. "Just tell her the truth. Extreme circumstances will put a relationship to the test, that's for sure."

He spoke from experience. Not only had his girlfriend's work rival burned down our bottling facility, but the bastard had later gone on to shoot Sabrina too.

I nodded. "I'll tell her after the wedding tomorrow. I won't ruin the big day for her."

I finished my beer and rubbed my eyes with my hands. "Speaking of which, I need to help set up some of the stuff tomorrow morning." I lowered my hands. "Even though my in-laws will say I'm neglecting my children, can you keep an eye on them? I wouldn't put it past the Grenvilles to hire someone to take them."

Zach and Beck both looked alarmed, but Zach spoke first. "You have to be joking."

"I wish. I doubt they'd risk it, if they want a chance in hell of this case going forward. And yet, they hate it when people stand up to them or say no. I swear they're like fucking spoiled children sometimes."

Beck said, "Of course we'll look after them. And fuck whatever they try to make it out as. You're a single parent who needs some help, and we're their uncles. If that's neglect, then I'm a rainbow-farting unicorn."

Zach snorted. "Those were the last words I'd ever think to come out of your mouth."

Beck grunted. "Blame it on Sabrina and her friend. The things I hear at the baseball games."

He sighed dramatically, and I cracked a smile. I wasn't sure if Beck was trying to make me feel better on purpose or not, but I appreciated it all the same.

"Thanks, guys. I'll try to finish setting up tomorrow as quickly as I can, but I can't bail on Emmy on such short notice. And it is a paying job, so at least my in-laws can't accuse me of going over to fuck a woman because I can't control my dick."

Zach spoke again. "Even if you've been away for a while, this is your home, West. Most of the town will help out if you ask them."

I wasn't as sure about that as Zach, but I nodded. "Thanks."

Glancing at my brothers in turn, my throat tightened. There was something I needed to say, which was long overdue. It was time to own up to my past.

I cleared my throat. "I'm sorry I abandoned you guys when Dad died. And then for staying away, not visiting, and keeping you out of my life. At first, it was because I felt guilty for giving Dad stress with my crazy antics. But later, I was so damn focused on trying to save a woman who didn't want saving that I forgot it's not a weakness or a failure to ask for help."

Zach spoke first, his voice quiet. "I was fucking mad at you for years, West. I idolized you a little growing up, and it hurt like hell when you left. But as I got older and better understood about you and Andrea, I started to forgive you. By now, I do. Just don't fucking disappear again, okay? Because I'm older now, and I'll hunt your ass down and make you talk about feelings and shit. Which I know you love."

His last sentence had been teasing, and he winked at me.

I smiled. "I'm trapped in Aunt Lori's group texts now, so there's no escape, even if I wanted to."

Beck sighed. "Tell me about it." He sobered. "Have you apologized to Aunt Lori too?"

I nodded. "Yes. I don't know if I ever would've come back to Starry Hills if not for her."

Zach said, "Which is why you put up with her excessive emojis better than Beck does."

I peeled some of the label off my beer bottle. "Yeah." I looked up. "I still have Nolan and Zane to apologize to, though. Nolan will be here for the wedding and stay a few days afterward. But have you heard anything from Zane, Zach?"

The twins had been extremely close as kids, but I didn't know if they still were or not. It was yet another thing I'd missed out on.

Zach shrugged. "Every once in a while he sends an old-fashioned snail-mail letter. Something to do with security. But he doesn't really say much of anything and never mentions coming home." Zach paused and then added, "I'm afraid he'll get himself killed with the risks he mentions to me, and I'm afraid of the ones he can't."

"Well, he's a SEAL, so he's made of tough stuff."

Zach voice was quiet as he said, "So was Uncle Tim."

And he'd died at a young age, during the Gulf War.

It was more than thirty years ago, and still, Aunt Lori had never remarried. I wondered if she ever would.

Beck shook his head. "I refuse to believe Zane's a dead man walking. He'll be back again, if only to visit Mariah Fraser-Williams and her son."

I frowned, vaguely remembering Mariah as being in my sister's class years ago. "Why?"

Zach filled in. "Zane and Darren Williams signed up together, when they were both eighteen. But Darren died several years ago, leaving Mariah a widow. Knowing Zane as I do, he probably made a promise to look out for Darren's wife and child."

Yet more stuff I'd missed out on.

Aunt Lori walked into the room and raised her brows. "Am I interrupting a boys' club heart-to-heart?"

Beck rolled his eyes. "It's a manly chat. Complete with beer."

Aunt Lori snorted. "Sure. But I'm just glad you three boys are getting along again. It's about time." She hugged me, then Beck, and finally Zach before sitting down on an empty stool. "So, West, when are you going to marry Emmy and have some more adorable great nieces and nephews for me to spoil?"

I'd been drinking my second beer at the time and choked. Eventually, I calmed down and looked at my aunt. "Why are you asking me? You should be bothering Beck and Sabrina."

She grinned. "Oh, but I do. Don't I, Beckie?"

At Beck's exasperated look, I chuckled.

Then Aunt Lori looked at Zach. "It won't be long for you either, lad. I can feel it."

Zach never looked away from his beer bottle. "I don't think so."

Aunt Lori clicked her tongue. "We'll see. But at least I'll have nearly all of you together this weekend. Nolan's going to stay a few weeks before heading out again. It's the longest he's agreed to stay in forever. Probably because of the rumors."

I frowned. "Don't tell me his ex is still stirring shit up."

"Yes she is, the cow. I met her once, and she basically looked down at me the whole time, as if I were a peasant. At any rate, I plan to talk to Nolan and see if we can help him in any way."

Beck muttered, "He's a grown man and will ask when he's ready."

"Perhaps. But I promised your mom I'd do everything in my power to make you all happy, and I plan to see it through." My aunt scrutinized me. "As for you, what happened? Was it the person at the door?"

I had wondered how long Aunt Lori would avoid asking.

After explaining what my in-laws had done, my aunt slapped her hand on the counter. "Well, they don't know who they've messed with, have they? One Wolfe is stubborn, but all of us together? They don't stand a chance."

I was so touched that I didn't dare say that Aunt Lori was a Wolfe by marriage. "Thanks."

She placed a hand over mine, squeezed, and stood up. "But that's enough about those awful people for tonight. Tomorrow's a big day, so let's have some ice cream to feel better, and then I'll send you boys off to bed."

Zach's lips twitched. "You are aware, Aunt Lori, that we're all grown-ass men? And with the exception of Sabrina sending Beck off to bed, me and West decide that on our own."

Beck flipped him the bird.

Which only made Zach grin harder.

Aunt sniffed. "I know, lad. But I have some ulterior motives. Because if you guys eat some of the ice cream with me, then I won't feel so guilty about it. Don't you want to help your beloved auntie out?"

It was such an Aunt Lori thing to say that my brothers and I laughed. Beck answered. "Of course we will. It won't be homemade ice cream, but let me see what we have."

As we ate and shared stories about when we were boys, some of my tension eased. I knew I had a fucking uphill battle against my in-laws, but with my family at my back, it might not be as bad as it could be.

How I ever thought staying away was for the best, I had no fucking idea. But I wasn't about to make that mistake twice.

Chapter Thirty-Nine

Emilia

West: You killed it today.
Me: Just barely. But I must've impressed some people because Zara's musician friend wanted my business card.
West: Soon you'll have so many famous people wanting to book, you won't know what to do with yourself.
Me: Maybe. I need smaller weddings in between, though. But I'm just happy it's done. Are we still on for dinner tomorrow, here at my place?
West: Yes. I can't wait to tell Avery and Wyatt. Getting them to sleep tomorrow night will be hell.
Me: Just tell them a long, boring bedtime story.
West: I can read them descriptions from your decoration catalogue thing.

Me: Descriptions of tablecloths might do the trick. I'll try to dig one out for silverware and plates.
West: By the end, will the dish run away with the spoon?
Me: <eye roll emoji> And the cow will jump over the moon. <cow emoji>
West: Now I need to get your cats a fiddle.
Me: Ugh, I'm too tired to be witty.
West: Good night, beautiful. I'll see you tomorrow.

The morning after Zara's wedding, I woke up with a smile on my face. The event had been exhausting and stressful—especially with her security team stationed everywhere—but in the end, almost everything had gone off without a hitch. Only one bridesmaid's dress had needed altered, and the caterer hadn't made enough fish dinners. Both problems I managed to solve just under the wire, making the wedding and reception look effortless to an outsider.

And while I was beyond thrilled that my business would probably get larger-sized weddings going forward, I was more excited about talking with West's kids tonight.

Then there wouldn't be any more hiding or sneaking around, and we could finally see how the four of us fit together.

Stretching my arms overhead, I grinned so widely it nearly hurt my cheeks. If I was going to clean up a little before West and his kids came over, then I needed to get my ass out of bed.

I just finished my shower and wrapped myself in a towel when someone pounded on my door, and Abby shouted, "Emmy? Wake up!"

The panic in her voice spurred me into action. I threw open the door, and my heart skipped a beat at the fear in Abby's eyes. "What is it?"

"It's Avery and Wyatt. They've run away."

My heart dropped. "What?"

"This morning West found their note when he went to wake them up and discovered they were gone."

"Do you know why they ran?"

I didn't like how Abby hesitated.

"Abby. Tell me."

"Well, Avery and Wyatt think their grandparents are going to take them away from their dad. So they ran away until they're sure they don't have to leave Starry Hills."

I frowned. "Why would they think they'd have to leave?"

"According to Beck, the in-laws filed a custody suit, and West learned about it the day before yesterday. The kids must've overheard him and Beck talking about it."

West's distracted attitude yesterday suddenly made sense. "Why didn't he tell me this?"

"He didn't want to ruin your big day yesterday. And..."

Another damn hesitation.

"Abby."

She bit her lip and then blurted, "Part of the reason

they filed for custody is because they accused West of neglecting his kids to have sex with tons of women. But of course there's only you, and it's ridiculous, as he loves his kids."

"What?"

"And it gets worse. Apparently, there are pictures and videos. Some might even be of you and him."

My heart thudded. "People were watching us?"

"I don't know for sure. But West is going to fight it, and we're going to help. After we find Wyatt and Avery, of course."

Avery and Wyatt were missing, partly because of me. Because I'd had a secret relationship with their father, his in-laws might've found out, and they'd use it against him.

I closed my eyes and took a deep breath. All of my happy, shiny dreams from less than an hour ago vanished.

Yet again I'd hurt someone I loved. And not just West but his kids as well.

This had to be the universe telling me that happy endings really weren't for me after all.

But I would process all of that later. Right now, all that mattered was finding Avery and Wyatt.

Opening my eyes, I turned and said, "As I get dressed, tell me what they're doing to find the twins."

Abby sat down on my bed. "The whole family is searching our land. I wanted to ask Katie and Amber to help, but right now, West doesn't want it going beyond the family. I did say I'd search here and ask for your help, and he didn't object. So if you can think of where to look for them, where they might hide, please tell me. The evenings and nights can be cool now, and..."

And the thought of two little kids out in it, probably without blankets or a way to stay warm, could be dangerous.

No. We'd find them. We had to.

As I got dressed, I shared my best guesses of where they might hide on my property. And by the time I was finished, Abby and I had a game plan and split up. I jogged to check the outbuildings first, hoping and wishing that Avery and Wyatt would be somewhere easy to find.

But as the day wore on, and eventually the sun sank behind the hills, the twins were still missing.

I hadn't seen West at all today, hadn't even received a text reply, but I hoped he was holding up.

This was my fault, all my fault, for ignoring my guilt and trying to go after some happiness. And if anything happened to his kids, I'd never forgive myself.

Chapter Forty

Weston

As the last rays of daylight faded, I was torn between shouting, crying, and wanting to hit something. I still hadn't found Avery and Wyatt, and it was getting harder and harder to keep my panic under control.

The words from their note still echoed inside my head:

Daddy,
We heard you talking about how Grandma and Grandpa wanted to take us away. But we won't go, we won't. So we're going to run away for now. Don't worry, we'll be

safe. Wyatt and I have planned to do something like this for a long, long time. Our grandparents always said they wanted to send you away from us, and we wanted to be ready.

But we want to live with you, Daddy. Until they promise to let us, we're going to stay away.

Love,
Avery and Wyatt

PS—I'm sorry we stole money and took your credit card from your wallet. I know it's wrong, but we'll pay it back. I promise.

The fact my kids had a runaway backup plan at all made me even angrier at my in-laws and their crusade to try to raise seemingly perfect, boring, shallow creatures their friends would approve of. Once I found Avery and Wyatt, I'd let them know in no uncertain terms that we'd fight. Even if I had to ask my brother Nolan for money to get better lawyers, I'd fucking do it.

Because nothing meant more to me than my kids.

My cell phone rang. I saw it was Abby and answered, "Did you find them?"

"Emmy and Max King found them inside the Kings' stables, in one of the empty stalls. And don't worry, they're fine."

I closed my eyes in relief. "They're still there?"

"Yes. They refuse to leave. Even if the King brothers could physically pick them up, it'd be a fight. They're waiting to see you before they'll leave willingly."

"I'm on my way."

I was on the outer edges of the Wolfe property and ran back to my parked car. Once inside, my heart raced as I drove as fast as I dared. I just wanted hug my kids, hold them close, and promise them I'd find a way for us to stay together.

The long gravel road to the farm meant I had to slow down. But as soon as I could park, I did, jumped out of the car, and raced toward the stables.

Amber King waited just outside and turned as I approached.

"Where are they?"

She motioned. "Follow me."

I barely paid attention to the horses. My focus was on the voices coming from the far end of the building.

When we were nearly there, I picked up Emmy's voice. "Your Daddy will never let you go, Avery. I promise he'll do whatever he can to keep you close. But running away only hurts those who love you. Next time, just talk to him, okay? He'll listen."

Avery murmured, "I know. But we were scared."

"And I get that, sweetie. I do. But the entire Wolfe family loves you and will protect you, no matter what."

"And you too?"

"And me too."

I finally reached the stall. Emmy sat on the hay on

the ground, a kid to each side, hugging them close. Both Avery and Wyatt had their heads on her chest and looked exhausted.

And damn, the picture of Emmy comforting my kids did something to my heart.

Emmy noticed me and smiled, although I couldn't miss the worry in her eyes.

"Avery, Wyatt." They both looked up. I squatted down and held out my arms. "Come here."

They ran to me, and I hugged them close, kissing each of their heads and simply enjoying the feel of them in my arms. They were safe, alive, and where they belonged—with me.

Emmy stood and made to leave but I looked up at her and caught her gaze. Something was definitely wrong. She looked sad, so fucking sad.

Then it hit me—Abby had probably told her about my in-laws' lies and accusations. And knowing her as I did, she probably felt somewhat responsible.

Well, fuck that. After seeing her here, comforting my kids when we hadn't even shared our relationship with them yet, had cinched it for me. I loved this woman, and I wasn't going to let her run away so easily.

Standing, I brought my kids with me. Then I reached out an arm, gently grabbed her wrist, and tugged her close. "Come here."

She hesitated and then moved closer. As soon as I could, I brought her into our hug. My kids didn't even hesitate, each hooking an arm around her, and I pressed my cheek against hers. I whispered, "Stay with us. Please."

After a beat, she moved to rest her head on my shoulder and nodded against my neck.

As I stood there with my kids and the woman I loved in my arms, I knew what I wanted for my future. And I was going to fight like hell to make it a reality.

Chapter Forty-One

Emilia

It'd taken me a while to remember how much Wyatt talked about the King stables before I thought of searching there. The walk was easily doable from my place, and Amber had ensured her brother, Max, was there to help us, in case the twins were hurt.

The second I saw Wyatt and Avery playing cards on the floor of a horse stall, I nearly sobbed with relief. They were safe.

And yet, I knew I needed to keep it together for their sake.

Their looks of uneasiness had gone straight to my heart. Still, they'd let me in, and I did my best to comfort them.

I didn't know how long we sat together on the ground before West appeared. The relief in his eyes had been palpable. And seeing him hold the twins close had brought tears to my eyes. The three of them were everything I never knew I wanted, and I would probably lose them.

Because I wouldn't be the reason West lost custody of his children.

I tried to leave, but West convinced me to be a part of their group hug, even asking me to stay.

It was on the tip of my tongue to say we should talk in private, but then he whispered for my ears only, "Don't even try to say this is your fault. I'm fighting for us, Emmy. Please stay. I love you."

At his words, a long-buried dream of finding someone to love me and be loved in return rushed forth. After so many years of thinking I'd never get that, never be so happy I felt I would burst, my knees went weak.

But the arms of West, Avery, and Wyatt kept me upright.

And I hugged them all the harder.

This was where I belonged.

It would take a leap of faith and a whole lot of stubbornness. Maybe even a little optimism. But this time, I wouldn't run or hide or try to rationalize something away. I would fight with West because losing him was unimaginable.

So I whispered back, "I love you too."

Then he surprised me by moving his head and kissing me, right in front of his kids.

Avery and Wyatt noticed and moved back. Avery

cheered, which should've made me want to stop. But West hugged me tighter, kissed me for another few seconds, and then laid his forehead against mine. "Then we fight this together?"

I couldn't stop smiling, even knowing the road ahead wouldn't be easy. "Yes, together."

I stepped back and glanced at Avery and Wyatt, who were both grinning. They rushed at me and hugged me.

Avery said, "Wyatt was right! He said Daddy loved Emmy. But I wish you would've told us sooner."

I met Wyatt's eyes, and he shrugged. "It wasn't hard to figure out."

I laughed. "Are you sure you're only ten?"

Avery said, "We'll be eleven soon."

"So you will be. As for why we didn't say anything sooner, your dad and I needed to be sure. That's all. Sometimes people don't fit together as well as they thought they would, and it's hard when it doesn't work out."

Wyatt nodded. "Like with our mom."

The way he said it so matter-of-factly broke my heart a little.

But I pushed the feeling aside and hugged each of them tighter against me.

I glanced at West, unsure of what to do next. He reached out a hand to cup my cheek a beat before speaking to his kids. "Let's go home and get you two into bed. We can talk more about this in the morning."

Avery asked, "Will you come over for breakfast, Emmy?"

Brushing some hair off Avery's face, I nodded. "I can, yes."

She leaned into my touch and yawned. "Maybe tomorrow you can also help us make another bedtime story."

"We'll see, Avery. We'll see."

Wyatt asked quietly, "We'll be able to stay with you, Dad, right? I don't want to live with Grandma and Grandpa. I like it here."

West gripped his son's shoulder and squeezed. "I won't lie—it might be tough while I deal with your grandparents. But just know there's no way I'm letting anyone take you from me. Ever. Do you believe me?"

Wyatt and Avery both nodded and said, "Yes."

West hugged Wyatt against his side. "Come on. You both need to apologize for breaking into the stables, and then we're going home."

Avery still clung to my side as we followed. The kids both murmured their apologies, and soon we were all inside West's car—I'd come back to get mine in the morning.

By the time we reached the Wolfe house, the kids were sleepy. Since they'd eaten sandwiches for dinner already, West and I helped them get ready for bed. Once they were tucked in, I turned to leave and let West say goodnight when Wyatt spoke. "Aren't you going to say goodnight to us, Emmy?"

His request touched my heart, and I went over to his bed. "I don't know what to do."

Wyatt smiled shyly. "My dad still kisses our fore-heads and tells us goodnight."

I brushed hair from the little boy's forehead, kissed him, and whispered, "Sweet dreams, Wyatt Wolfe."

He nodded. "That's good for the first time. It'll be nice when you can join in our stories all the time, though. Then you'll do even better."

My lips twitched. "I'll work on it in the future. I promise."

He took my hand and squeezed. "I hope you'll be our mom now."

I blinked back tears. I couldn't exactly tell him it was still early in the relationship and West might get tired of me. But for now, I merely touched his cheek. "Just go to sleep, okay? We can all talk more tomorrow."

He nodded. I moved to kiss Avery goodnight, and she whispered, "I hope you'll be our mom too."

Close to tears, I merely pet the cat sleeping next to her and went to the doorway. Once West finished saying goodnight to his kids, he shut the door and turned toward me. He pulled me close, and I didn't even hesitate to snuggle against his warm chest.

He murmured, "Thank you for today, for finding them."

I looked up and shook my head. "Don't thank me. I was worried, so worried, and I'm just glad they didn't get far."

He kissed me gently. "And I meant it before when I said I love you, Emilia. No matter what happens next, we fight it together, okay?"

For a second, I worried about what could happen if I stuck around, how his in-laws might twist what we had into something sordid.

But the love glowing in West's gaze wiped away all those fears. Or at least, most of them. "Together. Because I love you too."

He kissed me, slow and tender, until he eventually pulled away. "Stay with me tonight. I'm too tired to do anything but sleep, but I want to hold you in my arms, Emmy. Please stay."

"Yes, I'll stay."

The happiness in West's gaze made my stomach flip. He truly loved me, flaws and all.

Soon we were settled in his bed, my head on his chest, and the exhaustion of the day settled in. There was so much to talk about in the morning. But for now, nothing could beat falling asleep in the safe, strong arms of the man I loved.

Chapter Forty-Two

Weston

I woke up to light streaming through the window and a soft, warm figure snuggled against me. I breathed in Emmy's warm, womanly scent and sighed.

She loved me. And despite all the reasons my past had made me wary, I believed her and loved her too. I simply couldn't imagine my life without her. And seeing her say goodnight to my kids? Fuck, it'd made me love her even more.

The last threads holding me back, the cynical bastard inside me who'd been hurt by Andrea, had dissolved last night. Emmy would never be like my late wife and think that Avery and Wyatt were a burden instead of a joy.

The only thing standing in the way of the future I wanted was my fucking in-laws.

Emmy stirred. Her back was against my front, and her soft ass cradled my morning erection. Even though I burned to make love to her, I simply held her. As soon as we left this room, I'd have to face the reality of the custody battle. But I deserved a few minutes of peace and happiness first.

When she wiggled her bare bottom against my dick, I groaned. "Tease."

Emmy laughed. "Your cock poking me started it."

I moved and rolled her onto her back. "No, you started it by being so damn beautiful and smelling so good that my dick couldn't help but notice."

"Were you sniffing me while I was asleep, Mr. Wolfe?"

As I nipped her earlobe, she laughed. "It's not my fault if you smell good enough to eat."

I moved a hand between her thighs and growled at how wet she was for me already. "Maybe I should eat you for breakfast. It's the most important meal of the day, after all."

"Hmm, is it? Well, then you can't miss it, can you?"

With a growl, I kissed her mouth, taking my time to lick and nibble and savor her. As she arched against me, her wet cunt rubbing against my dick, it took every bit of self-restraint I had not to thrust into her.

No. I wanted to drive her crazy first, make her squirm, and then I could claim my woman.

Breaking the kiss, I trailed my lips down her neck,

stopping to bite where it met her shoulder, and then soothed the spot with my tongue.

"West, please."

Running my fingers through her center, I watched as her pupils dilated and her breath quickened. "Still not wet enough for me, Emilia. I need you dripping for me first."

She tried to speak, but I took her nipple into my mouth, and her hands went to my hair, her words forgotten. I fucking loved how her nails dug in, stinging a little, as if she couldn't bear for me to leave her.

I took my time laving her taut peak, blowing against it, and finally took it between my teeth and lightly bit her. She cried out, and her nails dug in harder.

Yes, my woman liked it a bit rough.

So I made sure to torture her other nipple while also rolling the already wet one between my thumb and forefinger. Emmy squirmed and arched and moaned beneath me, trying to rub her clit against my dick. But I made sure to move away before she could come.

"West, I need you."

Releasing her nipple, I took her mouth in a quick, hard kiss. "Then hold my head close and keep your eyes on me as I torture that sweet pussy of yours. Let me know you want it, you need it, with your gaze and I'll make you come so fucking hard, Emilia. Tell me you want that."

"Yes, West. Please."

I lightly caressed her cheek. "Good girl."

Then I kissed my way down, between her breasts, her stomach, and finally, I spread her thighs wide.

Leaning close, I inhaled and groaned. "You smell so fucking good everywhere."

She snorted, but then I ran my tongue through her center, and I watched as her eyes turned heated and she sucked in a breath.

Her desire made me growl, and I let loose, teasing her clit, licking slowly. Every time I stopped touching her hard bud and circled around it, she bit her lip to keep from demanding more.

Normally, I'd want to hear her sweet cries and moans and words. But there was something hot about her not being able to be loud while I tortured her with my tongue.

Wanting to drive her crazier with need, I thrust two fingers into her tight, wet heat and barely contained my groan. She was already dripping and so fucking ready for me.

But I wasn't quite done playing with her yet.

Never taking my gaze from hers, I removed my mouth and blew against her. She arched her hips before I curled my fingers inside her and she squirmed.

Her eyes told me just how damn desperate she was. I whispered, "Try to not scream, Emilia."

After she nodded, I suckled her clit between my teeth and nibbled as I laved, and she muffled her cries against her arm. Her pussy spasmed around my fingers as I continued to torture her, drawing it out, until Emmy relaxed against the bed.

Once I removed my fingers, I sucked them clean. "Now you're wet enough."

Emmy's rapid breathing only stoked my ego. "You could always do that again, just to make sure."

I chuckled, leaned down to give her one last proprietary lick, and then murmured, "I love you."

Her smile was blinding. "I love you too."

I would never, ever tire of those words from her.

Needing to feel closer, I moved up and kissed her again. Emmy arched her hips and rubbed against my dick, and I hissed.

"I want you inside me, West. Just you, with nothing between us."

Even a few months ago, those words would've sent me into a panic. But with this woman, I wanted everything. Needed everything.

Coming inside her would be just one more way to claim her as mine.

I met her gaze, needing to be sure. "I've seen the birth control pills in the bathroom, but..."

She stroked my jaw. "Yes, I'm clean, and I've been on them long enough. I love you, and I want you to come inside me without a condom."

"Fuck yes. And I'm clean too." I kissed her hard, my tongue devouring her mouth, and then broke it. I let my feelings show on my face as I positioned my cock and thrust inside her.

I groaned, loving how tight and wet and hot she was. "Oh, fuck, Emmy. I've dreamed of this. You're so damn perfect."

"I don't know about perfect, but you're mine now, and so you're stuck with me."

"Not stuck. I'm feeling pretty damn lucky."

Her smile brightened the room. "You're in the middle of getting lucky, so get a move on."

I chuckled, kissed her quickly, and then moved my hips. "So impatient. But as you wish."

Emmy clung to my shoulders as I raised her hips. I thrust in slow, quick movements, trying to draw it out for her. It was so fucking hard to hold back since she felt so good, but I needed her to come again for me, where I could feel every inch of her as she milked my cock.

When she started squirming, my control finally slipped, and I thrust into her hard and fast, loving how her tits wobbled, and I couldn't resist taking a nipple into my mouth. Emmy clenched her inner muscles as I did, and fuck, it made me want to let go already.

But no. I released her taut bud and kissed her instead. Our tongues tangled as I moved faster, deeper, and eventually, Emmy cried out into my mouth as her pussy clenched and released my dick. It drove me over the edge, and I stilled as I spilled inside her, a primal sense of satisfaction racing through me. It was yet another way I'd made a claim on her.

Which was only fair, as Emmy had claimed my heart.

I kissed the side of her neck and willed myself to move. But I couldn't do it, not just yet. Laying here while still inside Emmy, her arms wrapped around me, felt too fucking good.

Someone knocked on the door, and Avery said, "We're coming in!"

I had just enough time to move off Emmy and toss the blanket over us before the door opened. Avery looked at us and smiled. "Morning! You had a sleepover, Daddy?"

Emmy giggled, and I glared down at her. She shrugged a shoulder as if to say, well, it was true. And that I should've locked the door if I'd wanted to avoid this situation.

Note to self: always lock the bedroom door when alone with Emmy.

If Avery finding us wasn't bad enough, Aunt Lori stood in the doorway, a big grin on her face. "Another nephew has fallen, I see. Maybe this means more great nieces and nephews for me before I go completely gray."

I groaned as Emmy laughed silently against my neck.

Nolan then popped his head in from the hallway.

Fucking fantastic. Was my whole family here for the show?

Nolan smiled. "Avery, come on. Let's set the table for breakfast. Your dad and Emmy will come down soon."

I vowed to thank my brother later and tell him I owed him a favor.

Aunt Lori winked—because of course she would—and closed the door behind her. Once we were alone, Emmy laughed and laughed, until tears streamed down her face.

I grunted. "I don't see what's so fucking funny. Half my family just saw me naked with you in the bed. And given your I've-been-fucked-good hair, they know what we were up to."

She smiled up at me and cupped my cheek. "But it is

funny, when you think about it, though. We'll never forget this morning, for so many reasons."

Emmy kissed me, and I sighed, the contact erasing some of my irritation. "True. But we'd better get ready, or they might come back."

She sat up, placed a hand on my chest, and nodded. "At least you're more relaxed to face the day now."

I cupped her breast and played with her half-hard nipple. "Yes, I'll need you around all the time to help with my stress. A few times a day should do the trick."

She laughed. "Perhaps. But for now, we can't put off talking about the future." She stood and offered her hand. "We'll start today as we mean to go on—fighting together. Okay?"

Her words eased the worry I'd had in my heart. I took her hand. "Okay."

She tugged, and I got out of bed. I helped her shower too. Being the good boyfriend, I soaped her up and made sure she was clean everywhere. In the end, I even used my tongue between her thighs too.

But all too soon, we stepped out of the room and went to face the real world.

Chapter Forty-Three

Emilia

Katie: So you and West are officially a thing! We should throw a sex-toy celebration party. <party popper emoji>
Amber: It's not a bachelorette party.
Katie: Yet.
Me: Um, are you planning my imaginary wedding already?
Katie: Oh, it'll happen. I have a feeling.
Abby: Like the feeling you had about you and that motorcycle gang leader last summer?
Katie: Hey, he was hot. And we did hook up. But sadly, he needs to be free...

Me: More like he wanted sex and nothing else.

Katie: Still, my feelings have been right before. Cheryl married Michael from the garage repair shop.

Amber: They started dating when they were fourteen. It's hardly a feeling.

Katie: Stop trying to harsh my optimism. West and Emmy will work out. I know it.

Me: Um, thanks, I guess? But maybe hold off on the sex-toy party.

Katie: Why? Are you into kinky stuff? I won't judge.

Me: Help.

Abby: Let's focus on my niece, nephew, Zack, and Zane's upcoming birthdays for now.

Katie: Fine. But I want to help with the party planning.

Me: Of course, with veto powers.

Katie: <sighing emoji> I'll take what I can get.

By the time we'd showered and headed downstairs, West was a little less grumpy. Had it been embarrassing for Avery and the others to find us naked and in bed? Of course. And yet, he was the parent and had to know that sometimes kids barged in when you least expected it.

I stole a glance at West and wondered what it would be like to have kids with him. He'd admitted once, right before he fell asleep, that he loved having a big family growing up. I wasn't sure if I wanted five kids, even with two already half-grown, but I'd like at least one more.

However, none of that could happen until we dealt with his in-laws.

And the first step toward conquering that was to talk with his kids and figure out the future for us going forward.

We entered the dining room, where Sabrina was placing a bowl of scrambled eggs on the table. She smiled at us. "Good morning."

She glanced at West holding my hand and then at me, approval shining from her eyes. She added, "Beck's nearly finished making breakfast. Avery's been helping him with pancakes this morning, and Wyatt is on toast duty."

West grunted. "I'd better check on them. Wyatt gets distracted, and it wouldn't be the first time he burnt toast."

I sensed he just wanted to be near his kids, and given what had happened yesterday, I felt the same.

We entered the kitchen to find Avery frowning at the pan in front of her as Beck tried to tell her how to flip the pancake without breaking it.

Avery growled. "I've tried that before, and it always breaks."

"Patience, Tater Tot. Sometimes you just need to practice until you get it right."

West squeezed my hand, released it, and went over to Avery. I noticed Wyatt staring at the toaster, as if willing it to hurry up, and I walked over to him. "Do you have superpowers that make toasters work faster?"

He shook his head. "Don't be ridiculous. This isn't one of our stories."

"Well, it's kind of like watching a pot and wanting it to boil. It takes ten times longer for some reason. So how about this—in between batches, let's see how long you can keep a spoon on your nose."

"Why?"

I shrugged. "Because it's silly and fun and helps pass the time. And it's way harder than you think it is."

He frowned. "I don't think it'll be that hard."

I went to the silverware drawer, took out two spoons, and handed one to him. "Then let's have a competition."

It was almost adorable to watch Wyatt scowl—so like his father—each time the spoon fell off his face. I managed an entire toast time, and soon Wyatt listened to my advice. By the time the last round of toast was done, he'd managed to keep it on his nose for about fifteen seconds.

I went to grab the plate of food, but Wyatt beat me to it. "I'll carry it, Emmy. Otherwise, Uncle Beck might think I didn't do my task."

I bit back a smile. Not wanting to damage his pride, I nodded and put the spoons in the dishwasher.

Once we entered the dining room, I blinked at how many people were there: Zach, Nolan, Aunt Lori, Abby, Sabrina, and West. Avery and Beck were right behind me and Wyatt. The only family missing was Zane.

And your brother, said a small voice inside my head.

Determined not to let that thought ruin our meal, I sat beside West, and he took my hand under the table.

The meal went on as if nothing had happened

yesterday. Zach teased Avery and Wyatt, Nolan dropped quiet words at just the right time to make everyone laugh, and Aunt Lori said inappropriate things just to shock us.

By the time breakfast was over, Nolan herded everyone but me, West, and the twins away, as if knowing the four of us needed to talk. Nolan might be famous and always in the headlines, but he never acted like anything but one of the family whenever he was home.

West, the kids, and I cleaned up and then sat around the big island in the kitchen. West propped his forearms on the marble counter and looked at each of his kids in turn. "We didn't have a lot of time to talk last night, so ask me your questions now. I don't want you to worry or assume anything again. Because I promise you, I won't let anyone take you away from me. Do you believe me?"

Avery bobbed her head. "We do, Daddy. But why do Grandma and Grandpa want us to live with them? They always scolded us and usually didn't even say why, just that I was reckless and not acting like a lady should."

From the bits and pieces West had told me of his in-laws, they were old-fashioned and thought boys and girls should act certain ways. Girls, in particular, were supposed to be seen and not heard and should only think about finding a rich husband.

The thought of them trying to crush Avery's spirit only made anger churn in my belly.

I tamped it down and glanced at West, and he nodded, saying it was okay for me to take this one. "Sometimes adults want things for their own reasons, even if it doesn't really make sense, and they don't think about how it might hurt or upset other people."

Wyatt said, "That sounds selfish."

West jumped in. "It is. But in this case, all that matters is what you two want. And I think that's to stay with me, right?"

Wyatt and Avery nodded.

Wyatt replied, "Yes. And with Emmy." He looked at me. "You're staying with us, right?"

I smiled. "I hope so. I love you both very much."

Avery beamed. "We love you too, Emmy. And not just because you have a pool."

I laughed, and even West smiled.

Then he sobered and asked, "You're okay with Emmy being my girlfriend? I don't want you to think I love you any less. But I think we have enough room in our family for one more."

When Avery and Wyatt both didn't hesitate to say, "Yes, we love her," I blinked back tears. Not of sadness, but happiness.

Avery jumped up and came over to give me a hug. I held her close, not sure when I'd come to care for her so much it hurt. And yet I couldn't imagine never seeing either of the twins again.

When Avery released me, she smiled. "Does this mean we get a little brother or sister now?"

West choked, and I laughed before answering, "That all comes later, much later. Right now, we need to make sure our little family can stay together, right? After that we can talk more about the future."

Avery sighed. "Fine. But I hope I get a little brother

one day. I want to spoil him and be able to tell him what to do. Because Wyatt doesn't usually listen to me."

Wyatt rolled his eyes, and I bit back a laugh, noticing how West was doing the same.

West said, "Going forward, if either of you ever have questions, or you think you hear something scary and panic, promise me you'll talk to us, okay?" They bobbed their heads. "And no more running off. Promise me."

He extended both of his pinky fingers. As his kids hooked their own around his, they both murmured, "I promise."

After his kids released his fingers, West reached out and ruffled their hair. "We're going to spend the day together, just the four of us. What should we do?"

Avery asked, "Can we go swimming today? It's one of the last warm days of the year, and I don't want to waste it."

I glanced at West, and he shrugged. I answered, "Sure. Maybe we could have a barbecue for dinner."

Wyatt asked, "Can the rest of the family come to dinner too? Uncle Nolan promised to kick a soccer ball around with me. Uncle Zach can't, because his leg is still weak. But I want to play some soccer today too."

Soccer always reminded me of my brother. However, I couldn't ignore Wyatt's passion just because my brother also liked it.

It was kind of like a new-parent lesson—learn to be interested in what your kids are, even if you're less than enthusiastic about it. "I can try kicking the ball around. Beck might do it too."

Wyatt looked at his father. "And you, Dad?"

West grunted. "Are you sure you don't want to play baseball instead?"

Wyatt shook his head. "Baseball is boring."

I nearly laughed at West's bewildered face. "I'll take you to a game next year, and maybe you'll change your mind."

"I doubt it. But if we go together, I'll give it a try."

Avery jumped in again. "Just don't forget about our camping trip next year. I want to go with everyone."

West sighed. "No one has agreed to do that yet, love."

"But we should! I want to swim in the lake."

I spoke up. "Well, let's enjoy the pool for now. We can always talk about camping later."

West mouthed, "Thank you," right before Avery replied, "I suppose. I might need new goggles by then, though. Mine are getting all stretched out."

I stood and put an arm around Avery's shoulder. "I have a few pairs you can try out. So let's get changed and head over to my place. By the time we get there, it might finally be warm enough to go swimming."

"Come on, Wyatt! Let's hurry!"

The pair dashed off, their steps thundering on the stairs.

West pulled me against his side and kissed my forehead. "If you ever get overwhelmed, let me know."

"I will. But even if I've never been a parent before, I've had to deal with kids of my clients. Or watch how the parents deal with them. Your kids are angels compared to some."

"You say that now. But if Avery gets tired, she gets

cranky. Wyatt will also get defiant if he's hungry and often wants the opposite just because. So prepare yourself."

I raised my face toward his. "Consider me prepared. For now, let's just enjoy this day."

Because the battle with his in-laws would intrude soon enough, was left unsaid.

West kissed me gently, and then we went to help the kids get ready.

It was after the kids had gone to bed that West and I sat out on the veranda that surrounded the Wolfe house, me in his lap, as we looked up at the stars. It was chilly, but we'd needed some peace and quiet. Besides, between the warm man around me and the blanket we shared, it was nice and toasty.

He played with my hair, his body tense. Now that his kids were asleep, he was probably thinking of the battle with his in-laws.

I'd been thinking about it too, off and on, all day. And while I had thought of something that might help, I didn't know if West would balk at my offer.

I would just have to get the conversation started and see what he thought. "Given everything you've told me, you're going to need really good lawyers. And they'll be expensive."

"I know."

I bit my lip, hesitating. Men and their pride were a

fragile thing, and yet I couldn't not offer. "I want us to use the money Rafe gave me to fight your in-laws."

After he gently turned my head until he could see my eyes, he said, "I don't want to take your money, Emmy."

"It's not taking if I offer it. Besides, I wouldn't touch it if it wasn't important. And your kids are pretty damn important, West."

He fell quiet, and I tried to read his expression but failed. This was the man I rarely saw anymore, the one who hid everything behind a stony facade.

And I didn't like it.

I turned, straddling his legs, and took his face between my hands. "I want to do this for us, for your kids, for the future. I still don't know why Rafe gave me the money, but if I was going to use it for anything, it would be for our future. Please, let me help you, West. Let me help your kids."

He took a deep breath, searching my eyes, and finally let it out. "Are you sure? I'll find a way to pay you back eventually. I promise, Emmy."

"If we're to be in an equal relationship, then we shouldn't need to keep score like that." The stubborn man grunted, but I pushed on. "Look, I know how little your in-laws paid you while you ran and expanded their ranch. They took advantage of your distractions and guilt and who the hell knows what else. I can't go back and make them be fair people, but I can do this."

He still looked unsure, but I had one more card to play. "Besides, I want you to help me start up a small ranch on my property again. If you agree to do that, then we'll both be helping each other, right?"

He blinked. "You want me to do what?"

"Help me set up the ranch again."

West searched my gaze. "Of course I'll help you, but why do you want to bring it back now?"

I played with the edge of the blanket. "Well, I sold everything when I inherited the place because the cattle reminded me of my parents. Seeing them every day only made my guilt ten times worse, and I couldn't bear it. However..."

"However..."

After moving my hand to his cheek, I said, "A certain guy helped me to realize I wasn't the one at fault for the car crash. While some of the guilt still lingers, I think it'll get easier for me to accept the truth over time."

"I'll make sure of it, Emmy. I'll help you in any way that I can."

I kissed his cheek. "I know. But that's only part of the reason I've changed my mind."

"Tell me the rest, love."

His hand stroked my hip, and I relaxed a little. "Well, when I went inside the calving barn and saw what you'd done to the place, it reminded me of all the happy times I had with my parents. Times I would love to experience again, especially with you and maybe your kids too."

"My kids would love it, for sure. And running a ranch would be my dream job. But what about your event and wedding business? I don't think couples want to smell cow shit on their special day."

I lightly smacked his chest. "It wouldn't be right next to the barn. Besides, the Starry Evans Dairy Farm is one of my neighbors, so eau-de-manure is already there. The new ranch would have to be a much smaller operation than when I was a child—at least at first—until we learn how to balance everything."

His hands tightened on my waist. "Want to know the truth?" I nodded, and he continued, "I'd already been thinking of buying your fallow pastureland and starting my own place. Oh, I didn't have all the details figured out yet, but the one good thing I learned while living in Ridgefield was that I fucking love raising cattle and running a ranch. I need the physical challenges, the interactions with the animals, the ability to try to be the best at something."

I wrapped my arms around his neck. "So is that a yes, then?"

"A hell yes. I'd be honored to help you start it and raise the best damn cattle in all of Sonoma. Hell, all of California, if given enough time."

"So you dream small, huh?"

He chuckled. "Well I have one of my dreams sitting in my lap right now, so I need a new one."

"West."

After kissing me briefly, he replied, "But I do have to make sure of one thing—are you doing this because you want to? Or because you're trying to make me happy?"

"Both. Because your happiness matters to me too."

"Emilia." He stroked my cheek a few times. "Damn, I love you."

"And I love you." He leaned in to kiss me, but I

placed two fingers over his mouth. "Tell me first: Will you let me pay for the lawyers?"

He blew out a breath, and I removed my hand so he could reply. "It stings my pride a little, but I'd do anything for my kids. So yes, I'll let you help me with the lawyers."

I leaned forward until our faces were inches apart. "I think all of this requires a little celebrating." I rocked against him, and West sucked in a breath.

One of his hands moved to my hip, over my belly, and then stroked between my thighs, pressing my jeans against my clit. I muffled a cry, finding it hard to concentrate on his words.

His husky voice made me shiver. "Most definitely. I think you should ride my cock right here, right now, and do your best to keep quiet."

Heat flooded my cheeks. "Here? Outside?"

"Yes, Emilia. Take off your pants, take out my cock, and take me inside you."

I could protest and try to be serious. But I knew even if I refused to have sex on the veranda, West would agree to let me help him.

And yet, anticipation ran through me. I wanted to do as he said. Every time he gave commands when it came to sex, it made me so wet.

After ensuring no one else was out on the veranda, I stood and stripped my jeans and underwear off. It was chilly, but as West stared at me, I barely noticed.

I slowly undid the fly of his jeans, reached inside, and took out his already hard dick. I stroked it a few times before he growled, "I want inside you. Now."

Releasing him, I straddled his waist, took his cock again, and slowly sank down on him. He rubbed my thighs with his warm, rough hands, and it only sent more wetness between my legs. "Now, ride me, Emilia. Ride me hard."

Never taking my gaze from his, I clutched his shoulders and moved slowly at first before I found a rhythm. West's gaze trailed down my body, down to where we were joined, and he growled, "Faster."

I obeyed, biting my lip to avoid moaning. There was something erotic about having to keep quiet while having sex in public.

West soon placed his hands on my hips, taking over the rocking of my body, and stated, "Kiss me."

I did, wrapping my arms around his neck again and stroking my tongue against his. We both tangled and fought for control, desperate to taste and claim the other. The kiss was a celebration of its own, almost like it sealed our deal. Sealed that we would forever be partners in the future, never overshadowing one another.

Eventually his fingers found my clit. He rubbed and pressed and soon I cried out into his mouth as I came, pleasure shooting through my body. It wasn't long before West kept me in place as he groaned and spilled inside me.

He'd been the only man to ever do that, and I hoped would be the only one for the rest of my life.

He eventually broke the kiss, nuzzled my cheek, and whispered, "You're such a good but dirty girl, aren't you?"

"Yes."

"And I love it."

I smiled and laid my head on his shoulder. West held me close for a while, until I started to shiver. He took me inside, cleaned me up, and soon we lay in bed.

I murmured, "I love you," and then fell asleep, more hopeful than I had been in a long time.

Chapter Forty-Four

Weston

Emmy: We're off to get decorations for the big birthday bash. Avery wants unicorns but Wyatt wants frogs. I thought maybe we could do frogs riding unicorns.
Me: ...
Emmy: It's better than Avery's suggestion of frogs speared on a unicorn horn.
Me: ...
Emmy: These are your children. You can't be surprised.
Me: No. But...
Emmy: But?
Me: I miss when balloons and streamers were enough.

Emmy: Oh, we're having those too. But the streamers will be used to tie up each other for a game.
Me: ...
Emmy: Not like that! But I'm not against you tying me up soon and having your way with me in private. <overheated emoji>
Me: See, that's my kind of party.

Even though I agreed to take Emmy's money, it still made me a little uncomfortable.

It wasn't entirely about my pride, though. I'd always had to be the responsible one and take care of my late wife, so it was weird to have someone who wanted to be a true partner. Not just with money but also with life and even my kids.

Like today, Emmy had taken the twins to town, saying they needed some bonding time. And she'd planned it all without blinking an eye, even rescheduling a meeting to be with Wyatt and Avery.

She was so fucking wonderful. I'd always wonder how I deserved her.

But since she'd taken the twins for the day, it gave me time to seek out Nolan and ask him something.

And of course he had to be in the orchard.

I approached the cluster of apple trees, both nostalgic and reluctant. My dad had died inside the orchard, when I should've been there with Beck.

Part of me wanted to run, afraid that my guilt would come crashing down.

However, I knew if I wanted to settle things with my siblings and truly find peace with the past, I had to stop running. I didn't want any ghosts or demons lingering to poison the future with Emmy and my kids. So I picked up my pace and headed into the orchard.

When I was nearly to the center of it, I saw the old stone arch, bench, and giant wishing tree. But there was no sign of Nolan.

Or so I thought until I glanced up and spotted my brother halfway up the wishing tree, sitting on a branch, twirling a leaf between his fingers.

"Don't you have a fancy contract where you can't do dangerous shit like that?"

Nolan glanced down and shrugged. "What my agent doesn't know won't hurt her."

He climbed down and jumped to the ground. As he dusted off his hands, Nolan tilted his head and asked, "What is it?"

Nolan didn't tease and beat around the bush like Zach did. No, he always knew how to get to the heart of things. Even as a kid, Nolan had been so fucking mature for his age.

I leaned against the wishing tree and crossed my arms over my chest. "First, what are you doing here?"

"Making a wish, of course. And no, I won't tell you what it was."

"Out of all the wishes we've made over the years, how many have actually come true?"

"Not many. But hey, I figured it couldn't hurt asking for one more."

I studied my younger brother. All the Wolfe siblings had dark hair and were tall. Nolan's eyes were more hazel than blue, though, and always seemed to hold secrets.

If I were closer with him, I might've pushed. But as it was, I needed a favor, and I didn't want to piss him off. So I changed the subject. "Your friend Adriana became a fancy lawyer in San Francisco, didn't she?"

Nolan sat on the stone bench and placed his hands on his knees. "Yes. But she doesn't deal with custody battles, West."

"But I'm sure she knows someone who does. I need a good one, no matter how expensive, to ensure I win."

Nolan studied me a second and smiled. "You wouldn't let me help you pay for the lawyers, but Emmy is going to, isn't she?"

"Yes. And it's not that I didn't appreciate your offer, Nolan. But..."

Glancing down at his hands, Nolan rubbed his legs. "It's funny. I didn't set out to become a famous actor for the money. It's nice, of course. But it's frustrating as hell when your family won't let you help them, no matter how often you offer to do so."

I sat beside him on the bench. "We're all stubborn fools, Nolan. You know that."

He glanced at me and said dryly, "That's the understatement of the year."

I laughed, and Nolan finally smiled.

I said, "But you do help people you care for. I mean,

what you did by recommending your friend to Emmy, Nolan, well, she'll never forget it. Not to mention all the videos and ads for Starry Wolfe Wine you've made, which has most definitely helped the winery. You *are* helping your family, more than you know."

"I suppose." He studied me for a second and then added, "It's nice to have you back, West. I know I was a pain in the ass back when we were kids, but I looked up to you. You didn't put up with Beck's shit, and yet you still had soft spots for the twins and Abby. I wish you would've come home sooner, but better now than never, right?"

In retrospect, I wished I would've taken more time for Nolan when we were kids. He was five years younger than me, three younger than Beck but nearly five years older than the twins, and seven older than Abby—meaning he'd never really had a chance to grow close to anyone because of the age differences. Maybe if things had been different, he and Beck would've been closer. But Beck had been forced to grow up when our dad died, leaving Nolan without a sibling close enough in age to be a real friend.

Well, I couldn't change me leaving and forcing Beck to step up for the family. All I could do was try to get to know my brother now.

Which meant being honest. "How do you come here and not think of Dad?"

"Oh, I do. But Mom made a point of taking us here a lot after he died so that we wouldn't associate the orchard with death. Beck managed to stay away, but the rest of us were too young to really resist." He lifted one shoulder. "Plus, I had my first major make-out session in this orchard. And for a teenage boy seeing boobs in the flesh for the first time, well, that memory outshone any others."

I chuckled. "It's hard to imagine you making out here in the open."

"It was easier back then. Now, people have this vision of me that's not quite real, and I'm seen as a conquest." He sighed. "So much so, people play games to try and snag me."

"That fucking woman is still saying you're engaged?"

"Yes. I dated Wendy for a month until I saw how shallow and possessive she was. But she won't let it go and is trying to force my hand. Or at least she's trying to make me look like a heartless asshole, like I led her on and she's the victim in this whole thing."

"What are you going to do about it?"

He sighed. "I'm working on it."

"Can I help?"

"No, but if I do need any help, I'll promise to ask you, okay?"

I grunted. "You'd better. I don't care how fucking famous you are. You're still my little brother. And if I need to kick some ass, I will."

Nolan laughed. "I'll remember that." He stood. "I have a video call I need to make. But I'll ask Adriana to recommend a good lawyer for you, provided you also promise to ask me for help if you truly need it. Because that's what brothers do, and it's about time we all start acting like a family again. You may have been the first to leave, but you weren't the only."

I stood and clapped him on the shoulder. "I agree. Something's up with Abby, and I haven't even been here that long."

We started walking back toward the house. "We've tried to figure out what happened, but to no avail. All I know is that she wants to give up teaching, so I think something happened at her old school." Nolan's gaze turned hard. "If I find out some asshole hurt her, I don't care what it does to my public image, I'm hunting him down and teaching him a lesson."

"And I'll be right there with you."

As we planned ways to scare the shit out of some make-believe guy, Nolan and I bonded a little. It was easier now that we were older.

Not that we were best friends, but by the time we reached the house again, we'd made plans to go out for beers and watch the latest football game.

Little by little, I was getting my family back. And hopefully, soon enough, I'd secure my new one with Emmy too.

Chapter Forty-Five

Emilia

Katie: I can't wait for this birthday party in two days! The twins are going to love my surprise.
Me: Um, what surprise? You're supposed to help with the setup and watch the kids during the party.
Katie: Oh, I'll do that too. But I have a surprise, one they'll love.
Amber: They barely even know you.
Abby: They're my niece and nephew, and I don't even have a surprise, just a present.
Katie: It's like a Welcome to Starry Hills gift. Don't worry. It's not outrageous.
Me: That doesn't really soothe me much. This is my

first birthday with the twins, so please be on your best behavior.

Katie: Blame Zach if things get wild. He always, always tries to provoke the four of us.

Amber: Not me.

Katie: Fine. The three of us.

Me: No pranks, no flash mob dances, no paintball guns. Keep it low-key.

Katie: You think so little of me. I look forward to your apology later.

Nearly three weeks after West hired a lawyer, I was sitting in my living room with him and the kids, playing a bloodthirsty game of Monopoly, when the doorbell rang. Since it was a little after seven p.m. and we weren't expecting anyone, I frowned. "Were any of your siblings coming over and you forgot to tell me?"

"No way. Monopoly has caused more fights and resentments in my family than any other game, and we're not allowed to play it together."

"What, did people flip up the board and start a fight?"

West remained quiet, but Wyatt asked, "Did you, Dad?"

He sighed. "One time. But only because your Uncle Beck cheated."

Avery sat up taller. "What did he do?"

The doorbell rang again. I waved for West to tell his kids the story and went to answer it. I looked through the peephole and stopped breathing.

No. No way. It can't be him.

With shaky hands, I opened the door to reveal the tall, lean form of my brother—same dark hair and dark-brown eyes, but his skin was tanned a deeper brown than mine. "Rafe?"

He shifted his feet, looking awkward, before his gaze turned stubborn. "We need to talk."

The command in his voice stirred my temper. "Why?"

If he noticed my tartness, he didn't show it. "If you won't talk with me, then I'll cut off access to the money I gave you. I know you finally touched it and probably need it. Just see me this once, and I'll never threaten you again."

I clenched the door handle in my fingers hard enough that my bones ached a little. On the one hand, seeing my big brother in the flesh made the little girl I'd once been want to hug him and patch things up.

The grown woman, however, wasn't about to just forgive and forget that easily. He'd abandoned me, and it still hurt.

My eyes prickled with tears, but I willed them away. I wouldn't cry in front of my brother. I just wouldn't.

I cleared my throat and raised my brows. "I think it depends on what you want to talk about."

He ran a hand through his short hair, and I noticed the tattoos peeking out from his short-sleeved top. I'd seen a few pictures of my brother over the years, but it was hard to match this much older version of him with the teenager I'd adored.

Rafe finally answered, "Fine, if you want to do this on the porch, we will. And I'll be blunt—my latest injury ended my soccer career, at least as a player. While I try to figure out what the hell I'm going to do next, I'm going to divide my time between England and one of my places here in Starry Hills. And, well, I figured I should let you know so I don't shock you."

"Wait, you can't play soccer anymore?"

He glanced away. "No. My body finally gave out."

I studied him and saw what he wasn't saying—he was terrified of what came next. Even growing up, soccer had been his entire life. When he'd signed with a team in England, it had become not only his life but also his career.

And now? His dream had crashed down around him.

The kids laughed at something in the living room, and Rafe frowned. "Who's that?"

I crossed my arms over my chest. "Why should I tell you?"

"I know you don't have any kids, Emmy. I'm just curious."

Rafe hadn't been around during the years I'd gone by Millie. And hearing my childhood nickname on his lips, so familiar and right, only reinforced that I'd been hiding when I'd asked everyone to stop using it.

I sighed, stepped out onto the porch, and gestured toward the swing. "Let's talk out here."

After I shut the door, we both walked over to the

porch swing, and I noticed Rafe's pronounced limp. Which only made me feel awful for keeping him standing so long.

Once we settled down, Rafe's legs were a lot longer than mine, and so he rocked us in silence.

Even as kids, Rafe had been the quieter one, so I knew I'd have to get the conversation rolling.

I blurted, "They're Weston Wolfe's kids."

He stopped rocking the swing and turned his gaze on me. "Why are Weston Wolfe's kids at your house?"

I sat up tall, unaffected by his firm tone. "West is my boyfriend now. I love both him and his kids."

Why I'd added that second part, I didn't know. But Rafe needed to know this was serious and not some fling.

He searched my gaze, sighed, and looked away. "It's not like I can say one thing or the other about it. I lost that right when I gave up custody of you."

"Why did you do it, Rafe? Why did you stay away? For so many years, all I wanted was for you to come back. But you never did." I paused, the swing creaked a few times, and I added softly, "I thought it was because you blamed me for the accident."

Surprise flashed in his eyes. "What? Why the fuck would you think that?"

Anger flared inside me. "Oh, I don't know. Maybe because my brother wouldn't even look at me at the funeral, let alone hug me. Or the fact you walked away and never even sent cards or called. Nothing, Rafe. For all these years, I thought you hated me so much that you washed your hands of me, couldn't stand the sight of me. And, and..."

To my horror, I lost control of my emotions and started crying and couldn't stop.

No matter what I realized now, for more than a decade, I'd believed my brother hated me for killing our parents. All those years of guilt and shame and sadness rushed forth, only making me cry harder.

At some point, my brother's arms awkwardly wrapped around me. But not for long, because the front door opened, and West looked at me and then Rafe.

His gaze turned furious. He walked up, plucked me up and against him, and growled, "What the fuck did you say to her?"

I tried to calm down, but couldn't manage it before Rafe replied, "It's none of your fucking business, Wolfe."

"It damn well is my business, Mendoza. Emmy's my girl, and anyone who makes her cry is going to answer to me."

As they glared daggers at each other, I sniffled and did my best to stop crying. Because if I didn't get myself together, my brother and West might do something stupid, like hit each other.

I finally pushed against West's chest, and he reluctantly released me. After threading my fingers through his, I turned back toward my brother. "Forget your dick-swinging contest with West. I just want to know why you stayed away all this time." Rafe hesitated, and I asked, "Is it because you blamed yourself?"

Rafe's eyes widened a fraction before his expression became unreadable. "My reasons don't matter. I'm so sorry I hurt you, Emmy. That was never my intention. I thought you would be better off with the Wolfe family."

He glanced at West. "I just didn't think you'd end up fucking one of them."

West growled, and I stepped between them. "That's enough, Rafe. This conversation is long from over, but it's probably best if you go for now. Well, after you give me your phone number because I'll be texting you. Once you cool down, we'll talk some more."

My brother studied me and then finally nodded. "Fine. Tell me your number, and I'll send you a text." I did. And once he was done, Rafe added, "I have to go back to England tomorrow, though."

"Tomorrow? So soon?"

"Yes. I'm still technically on the team back in the UK, for now. Once my contract with them is formally dissolved, I'll be dividing my time between Manchester and here."

Part of worried he'd never come back. "When will you be back in Starry Hills?"

Rafe shrugged. "I can't give a date just yet. But I promise I will be back, and when I am, we'll talk again. I hope."

Releasing West's hand, I went to my brother and hugged him. He froze a second before wrapping his arms around me. "You'd better come see me, or I'll have the entire Wolfe family hunt you down."

West grunted. "If I have to do that, then I might have to kick his ass."

Rafe released me. "I'd like to see you try. You lost the last time you challenged me."

"Only because you cheated."

Rafe rolled his eyes. "This again. It wasn't cheating. It was stealth."

"Whatever. If you hurt Emmy, I promise you'll regret it."

Rafe growled, and I bit back a smile. Even if they were posturing, their attitudes revealed a little of their former friendship when they were kids.

I wasn't entirely sure if my brother and I would ever be as close as we once were, but I hoped so. Maybe even West would get back his former best friend too.

Avery popped her head out. "Emmy, Daddy, who are you talking to?"

Wyatt's head also appeared in the doorway, but his mouth dropped open. No doubt because Rafe was one of his soccer heroes.

I answered, "Avery, this is my brother, Rafe. Say hello to him."

Avery ran out and stopped just short of my brother. "Hello, Rafe. Maybe one day you'll be Uncle Rafe, if Emmy ever marries my dad."

I groaned. Avery was like a dog with a bone when it came to me becoming her stepmom.

Rafe cleared his throat. "Well, nice to meet you, Avery."

Wyatt walked slowly toward us before whispering, "You're Rafe Mendoza from the Manchester Dragons FC."

"Er, yes. Do you like soccer?"

"Oh, I love it! My dad doesn't, but I try to watch highlights when I can. The games are at weird hours for us here, so I can't watch them live."

Hearing Wyatt being so talkative made me blink. I knew he'd loved soccer, but apparently, it made him gush unlike anything else.

Rafe smiled at Wyatt. "Well, thanks for watching. Maybe the next time I see you, I can give you a signed jersey. Would you like that?" After Wyatt nodded, Rafe asked, "Did you want one too, Avery?"

She scrunched up her nose. "Not really. You can give Wyatt mine."

West frowned but knew better than to bark at one of his son's sports idols in front of him.

After squeezing his fingers in mine again, I said, "Say goodnight, Avery and Wyatt. My brother needs to leave soon, and it's getting late."

The twins both said goodbyes and waved, Wyatt lingering a few seconds to stare at Rafe before Avery tugged him inside.

Once the front door closed again, I fixed my gaze on Rafe. "Promise me you won't stay away for years again, Rafe. I need to hear it."

"I promise, Emmy. I might not be able to come back for weeks or months yet, depending on the paperwork. But I'll come back to Starry Hills as soon as I can."

I searched my brother's face, memorizing how much older he looked and yet how he also looked the same from when we were kids. "Good. Then I'll see you then."

For a second, we all stood still. Then I decided screw it and wrapped him in another hug. Once I released him, Rafe spoke again. "Goodnight, Emmy, Wolfe. I'll see you again soon."

West glared at Rafe the whole time he walked off the porch and even as he climbed into his car. Only once my brother had driven away did West meet my eyes again. "He should've done a hell of lot more groveling before you hugged him."

"Maybe. But I think he's been hurting all these years, like me. And I wanted to show him that while we may have a crap-ton of unresolved issues, I don't hate him."

"If he hurts you, I don't care if he's your brother. I will kick his ass."

I placed a hand on his cheek. "Let's hope it doesn't come to that. And maybe I'm wrong, but something in Rafe's eyes told me he misses Starry Hills, misses me, and maybe even misses you."

West grunted. "Don't expect me to hug him anytime soon."

"I know, West. But I can hope."

After pulling me close, he nuzzled my cheek. "Supporting you is part of my job, unless you do something like get drunk and start doing lap dances for random guys. Then I will stop that shit in its tracks."

"I've never done that. Well, not since that one time when I was twenty-one."

"It's legendary in the town. That's why I brought it up."

Sighing, I leaned back until I could meet his gaze again. "Well, you're the only one who gets lap dances from me now."

His hands moved to my ass and squeezed. "And when will I get one from the famous Emilia Mendoza?"

"Hmm. Maybe if the kids go to sleep early enough

and you can imagine the music in your head so we won't wake them, you'll get lucky tonight."

He nipped my bottom lip. "Well, let's go finish that fucking game of Monopoly so we can start the bedtime routine, then."

"You're going to lose on purpose, maybe even cheat to do it."

He raised his eyebrows. "Do you want to play until two in the morning?"

"Fair point."

He chuckled, released me, and headed for the door. "Come on. Let's get it over with. I'm sure they've hidden my money under the board by now too."

I laughed as we headed back inside. "Well, if it makes the game end sooner, I'm all for it."

He lightly slapped my ass. "I see how it's going to be —the three of you against me, always."

"Maybe not always."

As we smiled at each other and then focused on finishing the game of Monopoly, my head buzzed with everything I still wanted to say to my brother. He had texted me, so at least I could contact Rafe that way.

But soon we got the kids ready for bed, made up a bedtime story—about a unicorn and frog, to tie in with their birthday decorations—and then I forgot about everything but giving my man a private lap dance. One that ended with me riding his cock and swallowing his groan with a kiss as he came inside me.

Chapter Forty-Six

Weston

Emmy: I still can't believe Katie started a brand-new soccer club in Starry Hills just for Wyatt.
Me: Neither can I. Now I have to be extra nice to her.
Emmy: It's not that hard. I think she's trying to grow up a little and change her image. She even had Nolan smiling at the birthday party.
Me: I noticed them talking too. Which was weird because Katie always said Nolan was the most boring Wolfe sibling.
Emmy: Hey! That's not very nice!
Me: It's the truth. Not that I think he's boring. But she said it all the time growing up.

Emmy: Well, Nolan's just shy, and maybe Katie finally figured that out.
Me: Maybe. At any rate, are the kids and I still invited for dinner tonight?
Emmy: Of course. You're going to be scouting the pastures today?
Me: Yeah. As soon as the lawsuit is over, I want to hit the ground running with the ranch.
Emmy: And you're going to nail it too. <heart emoji>

After trekking through yet another pasture, I finally wiped the sweat off my brow and headed back toward Emmy's house. I now had a better idea of which areas to use first, which were the perfect balance of good grazing areas and enough distance from the house.

In the two weeks since my kids' birthday party—which was still the talk of the kids of the town—I'd been dividing my time between helping out Beck and forming a business plan for the ranch.

Talking to Beck and turning down his offer to be a bigger part of the family business had been hard, but he understood my heart wasn't in it like his and Zach's. As long as I didn't run away, he didn't care what I did. Oh, and once he finally got his dream restaurant up and running someday, I'd have to give him a discount on prime cuts of beef.

Having my family's support and faith in me meant more than I thought it would.

Things with Emmy were also going good, so fucking good, and if only this bullshit custody case would end, then I could start creating the future I wanted with her.

I reached her house and went inside, straight to the bathroom. After cleaning up a little, I exited and heard, "West, come into the kitchen!"

Emmy's voice was a mixture of excitement and nervousness. As soon as I entered the room, she held out a letter to me. "This came for you at the Wolfe place. Your aunt signed for it. I think it's to do with the court case."

Frowning, I took the envelope. "I thought Leila would've let us know of any updates."

Leila Hassan was the lawyer I'd hired.

"Just open it and see what it says already!"

I did and scanned the letter. And then read it again.

Emmy stood at my side, trying to see what was in the letter. "Well?"

I finally found my voice. "The case has been dismissed."

After handing her the paper, I tried to process what I'd just read. The fight was finally over. Even if they tried again, the proof they'd lied and used false videos against me meant my kids and I should be safe.

Emmy gasped. "Leila proved the videos were deepfakes and that your relationship with me was aboveboard. Given everything, the case was thrown out." She looked up at me. "We won!"

She jumped into my arms, and I swung her around

and around. When I finally stopped, I pulled her close and kissed her.

Emmy kissed me back, and I put all my relief and love and gratitude into it. When we both finally caught our breath, I murmured, "We're now free to plan our life together, Emmy."

She smiled at me. "We were kind of doing that already. But yes, now we don't have to say *if* we can do something but rather when." She cupped my cheek. "After all these years, we both finally get to move forward and go after our dreams without anything holding us back."

"I love you so much, Emilia."

"And I love you, West." She kissed me and then stepped away. "And I have a surprise, one I was saving for this moment."

I was about to say she didn't need to do that, but she raced out of the room and soon returned, carrying a small rectangular box. "Here."

After opening it, I took out one of the business cards that read "Weston Wolfe, Starry West Ranch."

"I knew you didn't like the Starry Dreams Ranch name, and since my wedding business is tied to that name, I thought maybe you needed a new one. Do you like it? I can get them redone if you hate it."

"I fucking love it. Come here."

I pulled her against me and kissed her, long and deep. "With the case over and a new name for our ranch, I'm going to have to work hard to make everything happen sooner rather than later. It might mean I get sweaty and dirty and will need lots of showers."

Amusement danced in her eyes. "Oh, we can't have you going all the way to the Wolfe house to clean up, can we? I think you need to take them here. And I'll make sure to help you reach your back too."

"Will you, now?"

"Imagine my hands nice and slippery from the soap, running up your back, your shoulders, and even down to your tight ass. Up and down, over and over again, until I was extra sure you were clean."

My dick hardened at the image. "I think I need your help. Right now. Just to make sure you know what you're doing."

"Oh?"

I put the box of business cards down and then tossed Emmy over my shoulder. She squealed and laughed as I carted her up the stairs.

It didn't take long for us to be naked and under the hot water, each of us making sure the other was clean, until I couldn't resist and fucked her against the tile wall.

And on the bed. And in the chair.

We were finally free of any lingering doubts about the future. And I wanted to start this new path how I wished to go on—by cherishing my woman, making her scream my name, and ruining her for all other men. Because Emilia Mendoza was the future for me and my kids.

And soon she'd know just how much I wanted her there. Always.

Chapter Forty-Seven

Emilia

Abby: Your brother made Thanksgiving awkward.
Me: Be nice. Rafe was fine with everyone else. You just kept making snarky remarks.
Abby: You forgave him too easily. He put you through hell, Emmy. And he needs to grovel some more.
Me: What is with you and West wanting Rafe to grovel?
Abby: We're protective of you. You're my sister, and West, well, you're definitely not his sister. But you're still important to him.
Me: I appreciate you caring, but I'm a grown woman and can handle Rafe.

Abby: Of course you can. But the Wolfe family takes care of its own.
Me: I know. <heart emoji> Are you sure you don't want to visit the orchard with me and the twins to help decorate?
Abby: Nah. It was your idea to decorate it for Christmas, like we used to do when we were kids, as a surprise for Aunt Lori. I'll help later, but right now, I'm applying for some jobs.
Me: I want you to find your dream job but also I'm selfish and want to keep you.
Abby: I know. But Samantha Evans is working out well for you. You'll be fine.
Me: Good luck! And remember, we promised to make gingerbread house materials with Avery later.
Abby: Wouldn't miss it for the world. <heart emoji>

Two days after Thanksgiving, I walked beside Avery and Wyatt, carrying a big tub of weatherproof ornaments and doing my best not to freeze my ass off. "Maybe we should've used a horse and cart to get this stuff up here."

Avery readjusted her grip on the two big bags of stuff she carried. "Maybe next time. I sometimes wish it would snow, and then we could have a sleigh."

Wyatt grunted. "Then we'd have to shovel snow all the time and always be cold and wet. No thanks."

"But we could also have snowball fights and build snowmen and make snow angels."

"I prefer paintball guns."

I smiled. The twins, West, and I had all gone to a paintball place a couple weeks ago. It'd been my birthday present to them.

Avery and I had ended up winning against West and Wyatt. And no, I'd never let West live it down either.

The orchard came into view, and as soon as the twins had a lull in their bickering, I spoke up. "Are you sure your dad said he'd meet us there?"

Avery skipped a few steps. "Yep. He wanted to set some stuff up first before we came with the ornaments and bead garland things."

The leaves had all fallen, so the branches were bare and perfect for decorating.

I couldn't remember the last time the Wolfe family had put Christmas decorations up in the orchard. Probably not since their dad died all those years ago.

But Aunt Lori had gone on about it over Thanksgiving and her memories with her late husband, and I'd started a group text with just the Wolfe siblings. We all agreed we could re-create the Christmas orchard from her memories and give it to Aunt Lori as an early Christmas present.

We reached the sign that read "The Wishing Tree Orchard."

I asked, "Have either of you made a wish lately?"

Both of the kids nodded, but Avery spoke first. "Yep. And I think it might come true this time."

Wyatt grunted. "Me too."

I looked over and studied them, their we're-just-angels look made me suspicious. "Do I want to know?"

Avery merely grinned. "We'll all find out soon enough." She dashed ahead. "Come on, Emmy!"

Wyatt ran after her, and I had no choice but to pick up my pace. The tub was too damn heavy to run with, but soon I reached the center of the orchard and stopped in my tracks.

West stood with his kids, near the stone bench and arch. White lights hung in the trees, and one of the songs I'd played the night I danced at The Watering Hole before West took me home played softly in the background.

After setting down the tub, I asked, "What's going on?"

West came forward, took my hand, and lowered to one knee before taking out a ring.

My jaw dropped, and my heart raced.

Before I could say anything, West did. "The night I saw you dancing to this song, letting go, being temporarily free of your past, I started to fall in love with you, Emmy. I already knew you were kind to my kids and that my family adored you. But that night I wanted you for myself, to dance with you and shout to everyone else you were mine. That realization scared the shit out of me, given my past. And I did my best to ignore you, both because I thought it might be awkward but also because I didn't want to risk my heart again.

"But as soon as I kissed you, I knew I couldn't ignore my feelings and attraction any longer. Every day since, I've fallen a little more in love. From your laughter and hard work and teaching my kids to swim. Or how you help me make stories with my kids and then remind me I'm more than just a dad when we're alone. I love you for so many reasons. You're smart and kind and beautiful, of course, but you're also there for my kids, for me, and you've never let us down. You're our future, Emmy. And before I ask the all-important question..."

Avery and Wyatt stepped forward and lifted a sign they must've had in the big bags that read "Will you be our stepmom?"

I placed a hand over my mouth as my eyes filled with tears.

West then squeezed my hand. "Will you do me the greatest honor and become my wife?"

Not long ago, this future had seemed impossible. But now, oh, now, it was perfect. "Yes! Yes to both questions!"

West slipped the gold-and-amethyst ring—my favorite stone—on my finger and then stood to pull me close. He kissed me, and I wrapped my arms around his neck. His kids cheered, which stopped us from taking the kiss too far.

I stared into West's blue eyes. "I love you."

"And I love you."

Avery and Wyatt came over and hugged us. Avery squealed. "The orc got the fairy queen after all!"

Wyatt added, "And he didn't even have to bring her any kittens."

I laughed—I'd heard this story before—and then moved my arms so I could hug the twins as well. "And I love you two as well."

Avery grinned. "We love you too, Emmy. And maybe we can train one of the cats to be the ring bearer?"

West scowled. "Maybe not."

Wyatt spoke up. "Then maybe we need to get a puppy too. One of them would be easier to train."

West's scowl deepened. "Now you want cats and dogs?"

"They can be friends, Daddy. I see it all the time," Avery stated.

I tried my best not to laugh. "Well, seeing as we're going to have *four* cats in one house after the wedding, let's hold off on new pets for now."

Avery's eyes brightened. "Oh, that's right! Our kitties will get to be reunited with their mom and brother! Maybe Sabrina and Uncle Beck can bring their two over for playdates and have a cat family reunion."

West sighed. "Six cats in one house?"

"It'll only be temporary, Daddy," Avery replied.

I cleared my throat. "We'll talk about that later." I glanced up at West. "Does everyone else know?"

"Mostly. But I think we should make them wait a little longer before sharing the news so we can get on with the decorating."

Avery bobbed her head. "Yes! I still want to make my gingerbread house parts today with Aunt Abby, so we need to get busy."

Wyatt and Avery went to the tub and bags and started taking things out.

West murmured for my ears only. "Maybe Abby and

Aunt Lori will watch them for an hour or two while we celebrate in private."

I tried my best to keep my expression serious. "And neglect your kids?"

He covertly slapped my ass. "It's part of that two percent I get for myself. And I thought my fiancée would be thrilled. Especially since I was going to do that producer fantasy of hers."

"This must be the special occasion you were saving it for."

West grinned. "The very one. I've been planning this for weeks now."

I wrapped my arms around his neck. "I love you."

He held me close. "I love you too."

He kissed me gently. Once he broke it, we stared at each other, and happiness bubbled up inside me. This wonderful man was going to be mine. Forever.

And more than anything, I wanted some alone time to celebrate. "Well, if we want to try out that fantasy, then we need to get busy and start decorating for your aunt."

"Our news will make her happier, though. Especially since she might start harassing Beck and Sabrina, and I'm here for it."

"Be nice. Some people need more time." I paused and asked, "I hope you didn't think you had to propose so early, West. I know we talked of being together one day, but I could've juggled dating and your kids and my business for as long as needed."

"No, I don't regret proposing so early, Emmy. I can't imagine a day when I wouldn't want to wake up with you at my side, or to see you at dinner, or make corny comments while watching movies with the kids. You're it for me, Emilia Mendoza. I'm ready to start our forever."

"Me too. You've helped me heal, discover myself again, and who could resist your kids? No one, that's who. They're your secret weapon."

His lips twitched. "So I played no part in your decision to marry me?"

"Maybe a teeny, tiny part."

He growled. "You're going to pay for that later."

Laughing, I broke free and went over to Avery and Wyatt. "Okay, so let's get decorating!"

I looked over my shoulder, and West mouthed, "Coward."

And so I stuck my tongue out at him.

Soon the four of us were decorating, getting the ornaments up, and singing Christmas carols. When Abby and the others arrived later—the entire Wolfe family except Zane, plus Sabrina and Katie—there was a lot of hugging and congratulations and even a few tears.

But they were all from happiness.

And much, much later, West did finally play out that producer fantasy with me and was very, very thorough during his inspection between my thighs. I came three times.

When we finally went to bed, we snuggled close, and I dreamed of what our life would look like. And I couldn't wait to marry my single dad orc and get started.

Epilogue

Weston

February 2nd
(A Little over Two Months Later)

Beck: Yes, I have the ring.
Me: I didn't even ask.
Zach: But you were going to. You've done it ten times already.
Beck: It's rather insulting.
Abby: Oh, stop it. He's nervous. He was the first to get married and is also now the second.
Aunt Lori: Really, when are the rest of you going to get

married? I hope it's while I'm still alive. <pleading emoji>

Nolan: I have a fiancée, remember?

Aunt Lori: Do you? Because it all seems fishy to me. <monocle face emoji>

Zach: Be nice, Aunt Lori. Katie and Nolan seem to be in love to me.

Me: Can we talk about this later? I'm about to get married. Again.

Beck: Yes. I'll be up shortly to get you. Can't shirk my best man duties.

Me: For once.

Beck: <middle finger emoji>

Me: Back at you, brother.

Watching Emmy as she walked down the aisle toward me had been perfect. Unlike with my first marriage, we loved each other, had chosen to spend our lives together, and I wasn't doing it out of a sense of duty and a plan of running away.

We were surrounded by our friends and family during the ceremony but kept it on the small side. Abby and Sam Evans—Emmy's new second-in-command now that Abby had left—had taken Emmy's plans and made them a reality.

The ceremony I barely remembered, but now we sat together at the head table for the reception, holding hands under it, and watched as Avery and Wyatt danced on the small dance floor with Nolan and Katie.

Emmy squeezed my hand and whispered, "Do you think they're for real?"

Ever since Nolan had brought Katie as his date to Thanksgiving dinner last year, we'd all tried to guess if they were serious or not. "I know Nolan mentioned once at the bar that he'd thought of getting a fake fiancée to stop the rumors started by his ex, but I don't know. They seem to care about each other and make a lot of sexy eyes over the table."

"Well, I hope it works out. They complement each other, I think. And Nolan deserves someone who sees him as a man and not a movie star or some kind of conquest."

"I agree." I brought our clasped hands up and kissed the back of Emmy's. "But it's our wedding day, and I want to dance with my wife. Will you do the honor, Mrs. Wolfe-Mendoza?"

"I would be delighted, Mr. Wolfe."

We smiled at each other, and I helped Emmy out of her seat, which took some maneuvering. "Why the fuck do you need such a big skirt?"

"I like it. I'm kind of like a princess for a day."

"You mean fairy queen. You even have a crown thing."

"It's a little tiara. Avery helped me pick it out."

I glanced at my daughter, who had her own crown on. "I think she did it so she could be the fairy princess to your fairy queen."

Emmy threaded her arm through mine. "That makes

you a king and Wyatt a prince. I wonder what the cats would be. Messengers?"

"They can be cats. I'm just glad Avery finally let the ring bearer idea go."

As we moved toward the steps leading to the main floor, Emmy laughed. "She did train Anna to walk on a cat leash. So it would've been possible."

"No. Just no."

"And there's my orc king."

I grunted. Extra loud. On purpose. "You're married to him now."

She squeezed my arm in hers. "Good. Because now I can tell other women to keep their hands to themselves."

"Hey, that was only the one time. And to be fair, the woman was pretty drunk."

"Still. You're mine."

"If it wouldn't scandalize everyone, I'd take off my shirt and jacket to proudly display my latest tattoo. That way they'd all see I'm yours."

I'd gotten another grown wolf on my arm for Emmy, to better reflect my new life. I would add any other kids we might have in the future. Although we were both waiting a little while before that happened.

"I'll have to stare at your tat later. Maybe even trace it with my tongue."

With a growl, I twirled her out onto the dance floor and then pulled her close. A slower-paced song played, and I gently moved her around the space. "I hope you're not planning to spend much time outside our cabin on Lake Tahoe. Because I want our honeymoon to be spent mostly naked."

"Well, it's colder there, so I definitely need your heat to keep me warm."

I leaned down and gently kissed my wife. "Are you sure we can't leave now?"

"No, we still have to cut the cake."

I smiled as I remembered Amber's face when we'd shown her our design. "While being naked with you will always take the cake"—Emmy groaned—"I can't wait to see what everyone thinks."

The cake was four layers, each one designed by the four of us. Mine was winery related for my family, Emmy's was the normal flower-type stuff for weddings, Avery's was cats and unicorns, and Wyatt's was soccer and horses.

So, yes, definitely a unique wedding cake.

It also had candy inside one of the layers, as a surprise. Because Avery knew Aunt Lori loved those types of cakes, and without my aunt asking me to come back to Starry Hills, I never would've made Emmy my wife, so we'd wanted to honor her as well.

The music died down, and Abby announced it was time for the cake. I took Emmy's hand in mine, and we made it over to the cake-cutting area.

Together, we cut the bottom layer—the one with cats and unicorns—and bright-colored chocolate candy spilled out. Aunt Lori laughed as Avery explained it was for her.

Soon everyone finished eating, and we were able to hug the kids, tell them to behave for Aunt Lori and their Uncles Beck and Zach, and escaped to my waiting car.

And as we drove to Tahoe for our honeymoon, we blared Disney songs and sang the entire way.

One day we'd also do this kind of trip with our kids. But for now, my wife and I started our new life with laughter and song, our future brighter than we had ever hoped for.

Bonus Epilogue

Emilia

Ten Years Later

Abby: Remind me again why we thought getting a family photo during our camping trip at Lake Sonoma was a good idea.
Me: Because it's a chance for all of us to make a memory.
Aunt Lori: It's going to be fun! <dancing emoji>
West: Says the woman who only has to share a tent with her husband.
Aunt Lori: Yes, he'll be my blanket. <face surrounded by hearts emoji>
Zach: She didn't use the overheated face, so that's a plus.
Beck: Don't encourage her.

Sabrina: You secretly love her emojis, Beck. <tongue out emoji>
Rafe: I'm with Abby. There are like 30 or 40 kids between the Wolfe family, your cousins, and their kids.
Amber: Don't worry. Mariah, Katie, and I have activities planned for the kids!
Katie: That's right. I'm a boss when it comes to keeping kids busy. This will be fun.
Nolan: I have faith in you, baby.
Katie: <heart emoji> <blowing a kiss emoji> and later <overheated emoji>
West, Beck, Abby, Zach, and Zane: <puking emoji>
Me: Eight a.m., everyone. Make sure all your families are ready for the photographer.
Mariah: I've never had a big family photo before. This should be fun.
Zane: Then you can be in charge of the kids to get the full experience.
Mariah: Oh no you don't. You're helping.
Aunt Lori: Stop whining, everyone, and just get your asses there in time.
Everyone: Yes, Aunt Lori.

As soon as the photographer said she was done, all the kids raced off to the nearby area with snacks, save for the babies who couldn't walk. Which included baby Mia on my hip, West and my fifth child.

Our surprise baby that we hadn't planned, but we loved her all the same.

West placed a hand on my lower back. "Do you want me to take her?"

Mia put her thumb in her mouth and snuggled more against me.

"No, she's in an I-only-want-Mommy mood right now. But if you can ensure Ben and Elena aren't trying to sneak off to the lake, that would help."

"Wyatt and Avery said they'd watch after their siblings."

I raised an eyebrow. "Normally, yes, I'd believe them. But Asher Fraser-Williams is also with them, and you know Avery has a thing for him, and she'll try to impress and get distracted."

West sighed. "I miss the days of her wanting a unicorn-and-frog birthday cake."

"Hey, she's become a kind and funny young woman. Be proud of that."

Even if Avery still struggled with what she wanted to do with her life, her optimism and abundant imagination always made our days brighter. She always struggled with staying on task, but her brother usually helped her out.

Well, except in the case of her wanting to hook up with Wyatt's best friend, who also had become his step-cousin once Zane married Mariah.

Beck and Sabrina's oldest, Charlotte, raced up to us, out of breath. "Ben and Elena took my inflatable raft thing and ran off! Mommy and Daddy said we can't use it on the lake by ourselves. I'm worried."

I shared a glance with West, and he crouched to Charlotte's level. "Which way did they go?"

Once she pointed to the more secluded beach area, West raced off.

After taking Charlotte's hand, I headed in the direction of Amber and Zach. "Luna was looking for you earlier. So while your Uncle West gets your raft back, maybe you could talk with her?"

"Okay. Although if they break my raft, I'll be mad."

"And rightly so."

Charlotte nodded solemnly, as if the raft theft was the gravest offense of all time.

Sometimes she reminded me of Beck as a teen far too much, even if Charlotte was only seven.

Amber smiled at me and then noticed Charlotte's stern face. "What's wrong, honey?"

"They stole my raft!"

I quickly explained what happened, and Amber put out a hand. "Come on, Charlotte. We're going to eat some scones I brought for a snack. They'll make you feel better."

"I suppose."

Amber nodded. "Want to join us, Emmy?"

"No, I should see what my children are up to."

"Welcome to my world."

Amber didn't need to say more—usually it was her daughter Luna who got into the most trouble.

Mia had fallen asleep, and so I walked carefully, readjusting her weight as I headed toward the lake shore. Once I reached it, I saw that Ben, Elena, and West were all wet.

And West's scowl was at full strength.

I heard Ben's voice as I drew close enough. "We both know how to swim, Dad! It's safe."

West shook his head. "Your sister struggled, and if I hadn't shown up, then what?"

I saw that Elena was crying. As soon as she spotted me, she ran up and hugged me, wet clothes and all.

After wrapping my arm around her shoulders, I asked, "Are you okay, sweetie?"

"I...tried to...swim. I did!" Sniff. "But, Mommy, it was too deep!"

While inside my heart thudded at the possibility that she might have drowned, I kept my face strong and empathetic. "That's why you're not supposed to go to the lake without me, Daddy, Avery, or Wyatt."

"They were busy. And you were busy. I wanted to go."

"Sometimes we have to wait to do what we want, Elena. Mommy and Daddy only want you safe, so you need to listen. Okay?"

She sniffled. "Okay. Can I have some hot chocolate to make me feel better?"

I rubbed her shoulder. "Let's get everyone changed first."

West walked up to us, his hand on Ben's shoulder.

Ben said, "I'm sorry. I shouldn't have gone out without an adult."

"And?" West prompted.

"I shouldn't have stolen the raft. Or broken it."

"That's why you're going to do chores to earn money to buy Charlotte a new one. But not until we get back from vacation. Let's get changed, as it's too damn cold to stand around in these clothes."

It was still funny hearing West trying to tame his language. While it didn't always work, at least it kept the kids from parroting his "fucking hells" from a few months ago.

As we walked back toward our tent, West and I hand in hand with the two older kids running in front of us, I smiled up at my husband. "Please tell me that now you've finally fulfilled your camping trip promise to Avery and Wyatt, we don't have to do a massive camping trip like this again anytime soon."

It'd taken years to put one together with all the family. But West always kept his promises to his family, no matter how long it took.

"I think I'd rather rent a cabin on Tahoe and relax a little more. These old bones can't take sleeping in the rough anymore."

"Pshaw, old bones my ass. You were plenty active enough just a week ago."

It'd been our ten-year wedding anniversary, and we spent it naked and sweaty inside a hotel room in Hawaii. One of the benefits from my business still going strong and Starry West beef being the envy of the West Coast was that we could travel sometimes. Although not going to Disneyland for once had been nice.

After kissing my cheek, he whispered, "That was on a soft mattress. I can't wait to get you on your back again. And on your knees. And straddling me."

"West."

He kissed me. "I love you."

"And I love you too. But right now, stop teasing me with sexy talk and go get the kids changed."

"Well, I do have a knack with cattle, so this should be easy."

Which, of course, it wasn't. Elena wanted to wear my clothes, which then swallowed her. And Ben had wanted to wear only his swimming trunks, which were too cold.

As I watched them and kept Mia occupied with some toys on my lap, I couldn't help but smile. It was hard to believe that at one time, I didn't think I'd ever have a family. And now I was living my own happy ending with five kids and a husband who was still the sexiest man alive to me.

Turn the page for a bonus scene with West, Emmy, Avery, and Wyatt.

Bonus Scene

Weston

A Week after Avery and Wyatt's 11th Birthday Party

Emmy: I'm excited! I've never been paintballing before!
Me: It can get intense. If it weren't your first time, I'd make it interesting. But I'll be nice.
Emmy: Don't even. What are the stakes?
Me: You're going to lose, love.
Emmy: What do I get if I win?
Me: What do you want?
Emmy: Hmm. For you to build me a picnic table near the creek.
Me: Okay. And if I win, I want the best fucking BJ ever.
Emmy: <eye roll emoji> You act as if you never get those.

Me: Hey, I always want more.
Emmy: Fine. I look forward to my new picnic table.
Me: Keep dreaming. You'll be on your knees tonight.

Wyatt and I were down to our last few paintballs and currently took cover behind a plywood wall hidden underneath some trees. What should've been a walk in the park had turned into the most intense paintball game of my life.

Apparently, my girlfriend had secretly been a Green Beret in another life. No matter what we tried, she was always one step ahead.

Wyatt whispered, "We can't hide forever, Dad. What do we do?"

"We know Emmy and your sister are hiding behind those rocks up the hill. Somehow, we need to go around the hill, through the bushes, and sneak up from behind."

"Can we do that, though? It's not like those pictures of the jungle, where there are so many plants you really can't see anyone. The bushes are kind of sad."

I glanced over and tried not to grimace. They were rather short. "We'll have to get on our stomachs and slither likes snakes."

Wyatt gave me a skeptical look. "I don't want to. I'm hungry and just want to eat lunch."

"We're nearly done, Wyatt. Let's just try this one last thing, and if we fail, I'll surrender to Emmy and your sister."

"Okay. Although if we do get behind them, I want to get Avery."

"Deal. Now, follow my lead."

As we slithered on our stomachs, looking like really awkward soldiers in boot camp, the rustling noise was excruciating. But foot by foot we progressed until we were nearly to the back of the hill.

Then Wyatt sneezed. And again.

Fuck. There was nothing to do but see if the girls had heard us.

Something hit me on the back, and then Wyatt yelped. Standing a few feet away, on the hill, were Emmy and Avery with shit-eating grins. "Got you!"

Sighing, I stood and helped my son up too. "Are you sure you've never done this before, Emmy?"

"Nope. I did play some laser tag with Abby growing up, though, whenever we visited her cousins as teens. Did I forget to mention that?"

I scowled. "Yes."

Avery chimed in. "Don't be a sore loser, Daddy. Now we get to have my favorite pizza of pepperoni and green peppers."

Wyatt scrunched his nose. "Green peppers are gross."

"Too bad! You lost, so you can pick them off."

As we headed toward the main entrance to return our gear and change, Emmy slipped her hand into mine. "I can't wait to see this fabulous bench you're going to build. Just think, next summer we can picnic near the creek." She leaned over and whispered into my ear. "And if you do a really good job, I'll give you that best-ever blow job too."

"I have to wait that long? You're mean."

She laughed. "We'll see. I just don't want to have to wait years for the bench."

The fact she thought of us together for years soothed my ego a little. I could suffer losing a paintball game if it meant I had Emmy in my life forever.

Because more and more I wanted that future.

After we changed and piled into the car, Avery spoke up. "Emmy told us about you singing in the car, Daddy. Let's all sing. There's one song the three of us like, and maybe Emmy will like it too?"

"What is it?" Emmy asked.

Wyatt replied, "'We Don't Talk about Bruno' from *Encanto*. Do you know it?"

"Oh yes. That song gets stuck in my head so easily. And now it's there, so let's sing it. I'll load it from my phone."

Once the song blared, we all sang together, as loud as possible, and were laughing by the time we grabbed a pizza and went home.

As I ate dinner with my kids and girlfriend, we decided to watch Encanto and sing along with all the songs. The twins later said it was an awesome day, one of the best ever.

But if I had anything to say about it, the rest of our lives would be like this—full of laughter and love with Emmy.

Author's Note

I hope you enjoyed West and Emmy's story! It's both fun and difficult to write a single parent romance. The kids are adorable, but it also takes more work to get the main couple alone for sexy times! But that pesky one bed struck again... ;)

The next story I'm really looking forward to. I know lots and lots of readers love a grumpy, alpha hero with confidence and swagger (hey, I do too!) but there's something about a hero who's a little shy that just steals my heart. Being shy doesn't mean Nolan is weak, far from it. But it's going to take someone with as much personality as Katie Evans to bring him out of himself. He's also the true middle child, and he just wants to find his person and a place to belong. Katie seems bold and brash, but she secretly wants someone to see the real her as well. Not only is all of that a good tease, we get a bit of a "Cinderella/Pretty Woman makeover" for Katie! Some of the story will take place in Starry Hills (with the Wolfe family), but some of it will take place in Los Angeles too. She's about to rock the red carpet like no other. :D

While I'm still learning how to write swoony contemporary romance (it's so hard sometimes!), I want to thank Ashley and Illiana — two great beta readers who help me find typos and minor inconsistencies. Thank you!

And to all of you who've read this far, thank you from the bottom of my heart. Being an author is both the best and hardest job in the world, and it's only possible because of you all. I hope to see you in Starry Hills again, and if you want to make sure you never miss a release, then please join my newsletter at:

KaylaChase.com/newsletter

Until next time, happy reading!
~Kayla~

Marry Me Forever

Starry Hills #3

He's a shy movie star who wants to stop the rumors started by his ex. She's the wild child of Starry Hills who dreams of seeing the world. They strike a bargain—a fake engagement for six months and she'll get the trip of her dreams. But all too soon things heat up and the lines begin to blur...

This will be Katie Evans and Nolan Wolfe's story. More detailed synopsis to come.

Marry Me Forever will be available in paperback in March 2024.

About the Author

Kayla Chase writes sexy, feel-good romance full of laughter, friendships, and family. Her stories usually include crazy get togethers, fun festivals or events, and communities you want to be a part of. She also writes happy endings because real life and adulting can be way too hard.

She lives near Seattle but also grew up in California, which gives her lots of beautiful places to include in her stories (such as Sonoma wine country). While she's also lived in Japan and England, she has yet to figure a way to get her characters to those places. (But she does travel on a shoestring when she gets the chance!)

When not writing, she loves to read, jog on her treadmill, fit in some yoga, or try new recipes in the kitchen. More often than not, her cats derail her plans and make things, er, interesting.

Printed in Great Britain
by Amazon